THE JESUS GENE

ANNE KELLEHER

Copyright © 2015 Anne Kelleher
All rights reserved.

ISBN: 1518607810
ISBN 13: 9781518607813

Prologue - Jessie

The snap and hiss of the machines keeping my father alive are the only counterpoint to the sluice of rain down the big square windows behind my chair. In the corridor, just outside the wide hospital-room door, I see an occasional nurse in a multicolored scrub blur back and forth. Every lunch hour of the last week has seen me sitting beside his bed, but there's been no real change in his condition. Nothing they're trying seems to work.

I don't even understand what happened, really. Rosie, his assistant and his significant other - his whore, as my mother would've called her – doesn't seem to understand it, either. He was healthy, she insists, over and over, to anyone who'll listen. He was in great shape, his heart was sound. He'd just passed his physical with flying colors. The doctors just look at her and shake their heads. *Not any more*, I can hear them think.

I pat my father's hand and watch his chest rise and fall. This whole week has been like a dream, a really bad dream. The one I had last night was the worst, though.

In it I was driving what seemed to be a cab. My father was in the back seat. We pulled up to University Hospital's emergency room, and he handed me a twenty. "Keep the change, Jack," I remember I heard him say. I didn't understand why he was calling me Jack, or why I asked, "Shall I wait?"

But I heard his answer clearly, and so loud it woke me up. "Don't bother. There won't be any bringing me back."

There won't be any bringing me back. The words spool through my head, replaying themselves against the memory of seven days ago, just about now, I was shelving books, thinking about lunch, about band practice, about a joint. Then the office phone rang, and even before the head librarian waved me into her office, I knew it was something bad.

Today his skin looks grayer, his lips bluer, and his hand in mine is clammy and cold. I've spent all of 13 days in his presence that I remember, seven of them here. *Johnny, I hardly knew ye.* Before I can control myself, a bar or two slips out. Then I bite my tongue.

That's a line from one of the songs my mother liked me to sing, and I don't want to think about my mother, now. I don't want to think about the songs she liked to hear. She let me think my father was dead. It was only months and months after she died I found out the truth – that not only was he alive, he was, in fact, living less than thirty miles from my own front door.

I clutch his hand. Miraculously, it tightens back. "Dad?" I whisper.

His eyes are open. "Hey, Jessie," he mouths. "Jessie." His voice is barely more than a huff. "Jessie – so much…to tell you…so much…"

"Do-don't try to talk, Dad," I sniff. "J-just rest, okay?"

He grips my hand with a strength that surprises me. "No!" he rasps. "There're things…things I need to tell you…things you need to know…it's good, you know, your mother changed your name, but you should change your birthday, Jessie – she wouldn't let me…you should…soon as you can."

Change my birthday? What the fuck did he mean by that? The drugs must be making him hallucinate. "When you're stronger, Dad – don't – don't try to talk now, okay?"

He shuts his eyes, makes a face, then struggles on. "You don't understand, Jessie…" He nods, squeezes my hand. "Jessie… there's a lot of things…" The machines beep and the rain pounds against the windows with renewed insistence.

I hold my breath. I'm afraid anything I say will only encourage him to talk and I don't like the way the one machine is beginning to beep just a little more ferociously, the way his forehead is starting to shine. But if he wants to tell me he loves me, that he's sorry for whatever lame-ass shit kept him away from me for twenty-three years, I guess that's why I've been sitting here, hoping. Waiting. I squeeze his hand back, and my eyes start to water.

But his words make me wonder if I'm hearing him correctly, if I've fallen into someone else's bedside. "Tell…Martha Sinclair…Ro knows… where to find her. Tell her she was right all along…she has to know…she was right." He struggles to breathe and I stare at him, so startled I'm not yet horrified. Is my father really confessing to some kind of crime? "There're just rocks in the baby's grave." This last he mouths. He struggles to breathe, then says, "I'm the one…who put them there."

He shudders and sighs and slumps back into sleep. The machine resumes a steadier beep.

I sink back into the hard chair's rigid embrace. What the fuck is he talking about? He looks so limp and gray against the pillow I think he must be dead, but the machines reassure me he's not. Maybe it's the drugs they're giving him – maybe he's just hallucinating.

Your father had all these crazy ideas, I can hear my mother say. Ideas that got him kicked out of Princeton and Penn. Ideas, and people, that are clearly more important to him than I ever was. For a moment, I hate both my parents equally.

"Jessie?" Rosie's standing in the doorway. "D-did he say something – just now?"

I look at her. Her dark brown hair is shot through with gray, the overhead light from the corridor cuts cruel shadows across her face. "Yeah, but… it… it didn't make much sense."

In a few quick steps, she's on the other side of the bed, searching his face. "David," she whispers. "David?" She looks back at me. "Wh-what did he say?"

I know what she wants me to say. They had an argument, apparently, just before he collapsed, but I can't bring myself to be kind. This is the woman who according to my mother stole my father from us both and got him run out of the Ivy League. "It was something about changing my birthday… and someone named Martha Sinclair?"

v

"Ms. Coulter?" The doctor standing in the doorway is a new one I don't recognize. "We have some new test results — if I may?"

He's holding a file, and he beckons to us both, but Rosie is so frozen, I wonder if she heard either of us.

"Rosie?" I say. I don't understand the foreboding that's rising in my chest, I don't understand why I feel that I'm back in the dream. "He said something about telling someone named Martha Sinclair there's rocks in a baby's grave? D-does that make any sense to you? Any sense at all?"

"Yeah," she says. Her face is white and rigid and she's looking down at my father with such fury on her face I'm afraid she must be wishing him dead. "Yeah, it does. I wish it didn't, but it does."

Part One - Jack

Chapter 1

The waiter smiles down at me as he removes what remains of my prime rib, the reward I've given myself before the Springsteen concert starts. I've come straight from the office. I'm wearing work clothes: a suit, white blouse, pearls and heels. The waiter's very tall, his skin is very black and his teeth are as white as the linen towel over the arm of his dinner jacket. With a nod at an arched and curtained opening, he says, "Mr. Springsteen and the band are in there if you want to say hello."

I look up.

The waiter's lips are the color of the meat on my plate. "I told them you were out here, having dinner, waiting for the show. Go on. He'd like to meet you."

I push my chair back, feeling disheveled and flustered. I look down at my legs encased in shiny tight pantyhose. My ankles are swollen and they look like Polish sausages. I hate pantyhose and heels on women and I don't understand why I'm wearing them. I want to dab a little lipstick on, run a brush through my hair, but I know there isn't time, there can't be time. The concert starts in less than two hours. I'm supposed to meet my boyfriend, the one who gave me the letter that gives us both promotional tickets to the show, front row seats. It's my job to pick them up, and I haven't yet. This is what I was telling the waiter.

But an opportunity to say hello to Bruce Springsteen doesn't come along every day. So I stumble out of my seat, the pointed shoes pinching my toes. I go through the arch, and I notice the shiny red silk drapes looped back like an entrance into some Garden of Earthly Delight. There's a door, partly open, and I can hear voices, the tinkle of glass and silverware and the rumbled bass of the Big Man's laugh.

I reach for the shiny gold knob and the waiter calls, "Miss? You forgot your raincoat." I turn in time to see him smile and hold it out. This is a dream, I realize - one I've had before. I take the rain coat and put it, and step through the curtain. Suddenly I'm standing on a stage, center stage and the concert is already started.

Bruce walks up to me, guitar in one hand and a glass of water in the other. Before I can say anything, even hello, he throws the water on my head, and the whole crowd cheers. "Are you ready," the Boss roars, and the crowd screams. "Are you ready?" the Boss roars again.

And this time, he looks at me.

Ready for what, I want to ask, but the only noise that comes out of my mouth is the blare of the alarm clock.

"Jack?" Lila's voice cuts through the clock. "Jack, you up?"

I open my eyes into the red glare of the alarm clock numbers: 5:55 and a leaden dusk. I roll on my back, struggling out of the depths of the dream. Another girl-dream. I lie flat, staring at the webbed cracks in the plaster ceiling above me. From earliest childhood, every once in a while, I've had dreams in which I'm a girl. I didn't know other boys didn't have them, so it didn't bother me until my Uncle Joey beat me for asking him if he'd ever had a girl-dream. I learned quick that Real Men don't have girl-dreams, at least not that kind of girl-dream, and if I expected to be a Real Man, I better stop having them, too. Mostly they did stop, except for this one, which is beginning to pop up with disturbing frequency like a bright penny in a dish of dirty change. It's always something about Springsteen, a lot of people, water, and in it, I'm always a girl.

The bedroom door swings open and my wife, Lila, rides into the gloomy room on a wave of perfume so thick I sneeze. "Jack? Shortman called - they want you to come in early. I made you coffee. And supper." She reaches down and tickles my toes under the covers. "Come on, the rent's due next week. We can use the extra cash."

We can always use the extra cash. We got married right after I finished my B.A. Last semester, I finished my MFA in poetry, and now I augment my lowly adjunct instructor's income by driving a cab six nights out of seven. Lila's a paralegal at a law firm downtown. Her salary keeps us in the apartment close to school. My driving keeps us fed.

"Yeah," I say as I swing my legs up and away from her pointed fingernails. "I'm awake. I'll be right there."

My foot rolls over a pencil in the gloom. I stumble and knock over the books and notes I so carefully laid out before I allowed myself the luxury of three consecutive hours of sleep. *The Allegory of William Blake* tumbles over *Milton's Mythology* and *Paradise Lost,* and lands splayed over open pages of *Yeats: Prophet, Poet, Politician,* displacing dozens of painstakingly placed notes for my final lectures. Hours of lead-headed work lie scattered on the dusty wood. Pages drift around my feet. "Shit." I pick up my jeans, step over the mess and head for the john.

"Jack, you up?"

"Lila, I'm coming." It's been a while since I said that with any enthusiasm. I flush.

In the kitchen, she's got my coffee already poured, a couple saccharine packets purloined from her company's cafeteria on the table. She plops an English muffin and a fried egg in front of me. She's all dressed up, her work blouse changed to something black and sequined. She's wearing lipstick and her shoes are high and pointy, just like mine in the dream. She clatters around the tiny kitchen, handing me salt and pepper and ketchup. I look at her. "Are we that behind, or you just want me out of here so your boyfriend can come over?"

"I make you supper and that's what you say?" Her stare slices into me, and the ketchup hovers just beyond my grasp.

"Sorry." I get up awkwardly; peel the ketchup bottle out of her unwilling hand. "I'm sorry - I thought I was being funny. I guess I'm tired. This semester's been a bitch, Lila."

She nods at the plate. "Yeah, I know." She looks at me, our eyes meet. "I'm sorry, too. You're not eating."

"I need a knife and fork." She's standing in front of the silverware drawer, and I notice how the curve of her hip, sleek in a tight black skirt, is accentuated by the hard straight line of the counter. There's a sheen on her that I haven't seen in a long time and reminds me that since I started working the last shift to accommodate my class schedule, we hardly ever see each other. We're not even home at the same time, let alone awake, most days or nights, and absence doesn't seem to be making our hearts grow fonder. Tonight is the only night of the week we have two hours together and not only has she given our time to the taxi-man, but she's dressed to have a great time. Without me. I want to throw the egg at her.

Fortunately she can't hear what I'm thinking. She hands me the knife and fork. "Sorry."

"You're not eating?"

She slips into the little chair opposite me, perches on the edge, steeples her burgundy nails. "It's Jodi Sobieski's birthday from work. I'm going over her house, then eating with the girls."

"You got all dressed up for that? Isn't she the one always complaining about the sty she lives in?" I glance around the closet-sized kitchen. I can only imagine what Lila tells her friends about our place.

"We're taking her out." She leans back and lights a cigarette. "Maybe we'll call you to pick us up and drive us around. How's that sound?"

I bite my tongue and grip my silverware so hard the cheap handle of the fork begins to bend. We do need the extra cash. "How well do you plan on tipping?"

"You'd take it out in trade, wouldn't you? Tara the hot blonde is going."

"Who's Tara?" She wants to fight with me, I can tell, but I'm too tired to take the bait.

"The one with the tits that you wouldn't stop looking at at the Christmas party last year."

The memory of dark blue velvet stretched across creamy hills rolling as the fields of Kansas flashes through my mind and I blink to clear it away. "You can't blame me for that - those things are the size of beach-balls. Everyone was looking, even the women. Besides, don't we need cash?"

"We always need cash."

"So how is it you're going out? I thought we need the cash."

Lila's expression doesn't change but her lips get very thin. "Are you kidding? After all you've done, you resent me having a little fun with my friends?"

I look down at my egg. My student loans aren't the only reason we're always strapped. Starting in high school, and through most of college, I tried everything and anything you can smoke, sniff or swallow - much of it financed by cash advances from the credit cards the banks were all too happy to send me almost weekly at one point. The semblance of order I have in my life now I owe to Lila. I am determined not to disappoint her, even though I sense her patience is wearing thin.

She crosses her arms, and turns her head so that the overhead light slices her face into two sides, one light and one dark. "After all you've put me through?" She stalks into the bathroom. I hear the door slam, the lock click, then unclick. The door opens. "I told Shortman you'd be there 6:30."

"Six-thirty? Jesus, Lila, it's 6:10 now - I can't -"

"So go." She slams the door again, this time with even more force.

I slurp down the egg and muffin, then grab the notebook I always carry in the hopes the Muse starts singing to me while I drive. Something stops me as I cross the threshold, one of those weird shivery feelings I get from time to time. I see a shimmer of blurred color, hear the echo-y screech of brakes, and despite how late, tired and annoyed I am, I say over my shoulder, "Be careful tonight."

"You'll be late, Jack," comes her muffled answer.

"I love you, too," I call back, and head out into the Brooklyn streets.

On the bus, I think about Lila when the dream doesn't intrude. I don't see much of her softer side any more. I don't see much of her at all. I wonder if the dream could be about her. Maybe there's a poem in it. I was in a blue and black checked suit with black shoes; the waiter was wearing a red vest and a black bow tie. I scribble furiously as I swing and sway with the bus into the broad bulk of the wool-coated woman beside me but fortunately she's so lost in her own thoughts, she doesn't react, or seem to notice that I whisper a line or two to myself now and then.

If I could get a poem out of the dream, that would be good. I could use a good poem right now. There's a poetry festival in upstate New York at the end of August, and another in late September, both of which publish small – very small – but prestigious journals and inclusion in either one might force the English Department gods to smile favorably on the renewal of my teaching contract. But since the beginning of the semester, and the cold wet spring, all the words feel forced, all the lines labored and nothing flows, not even the kind of stuff I used to write completely stoned.

The bus lurches to a stop and the woman next to me gets up. She staggers a little and her hand lands on my shoulder. At once I see a pale face, the flash of a gold tooth and a long dark car. *Your daughter's dating a drug dealer,* I almost blurt, but the woman pulls away in time and the vision vanishes like a puff of exhaust.

Sometimes these feelings, these images come to me. Once in a while, I used to hear voices, too. It's why I used to drink. But I can't bring myself to admit that to anyone, even Lila. As the bus roars into traffic, a flash of color catches my eye on the floor under my foot and for some reason I don't understand, I bend over and pick it up.

It's the joker from a pack a playing cards, the stylized harlequin grinning gleefully at me behind the grime. *If the fool would persist in his folly, he would become wise.* The line from Blake's "Marriage of Heaven and Hell" flashes through my mind. I'm thinking a lot of Blake recently, since I've started teaching my seminar in Milton, Blake and Yeats. The fool's face grins under rings of grit. I jot that down.

I'll take any kind of inspiration I can get.

It's pouring as I get off the bus. I shove my notebook under my sweatshirt and tuck the hood around my face. By the time I reach the garage, I'm mostly soaked. The fumes in the garage are choking, the windows and doors and bays all sealed against the night and the damp. I gaze up at Shortman as he hands me the keys to the dingy sedan that's quite possibly the worst car in the fleet. Taxiing is every bit as mean as the person Lila's turning into. Maybe there's a poem in that, too.

I shake my head. "Hey, Shorty, what's this? I'm doing you a favor coming in early and you wanna stick me with that?"

"Dutch showed up before you." Shortman gazes down at me from behind the chicken wire cage. He's tall and lanky and his clothes hang on him like a scarecrow, but the irony of his own last name prevents me from coming up with any other nickname. "His asthma's acting up and Rasta Ray had that car all day. You know smoke bothers him."

"Like it won't bother me?"

"Never did before." Our eyes meet and I feel the sting of his contempt. Shortman knows why I ended up at this garage, why I got fired from just about every other job I've ever tried to hold, and in his eyes, I'm just another loser cabbie washing through on his way down. He shrugs. "You don't want the hours, suits me. We're only one cabbie down, thought maybe you and Lila could use the cash." He glances at the clock, shrugs again. "I'll see you in what - two hours?"

I think about the books lying in a sprawled useless heap beside the bed, about the poems and the papers and the exams I'm not getting to. I think about Lila, out having fun. I think about my wet shoes, the sodden hems of my jeans flopping around my ankles. I think about the class I'm going to sleep through again tomorrow morning because I can feel the exhaustion in my bones.

I think about the grilling I'll get if she smells weed on my clothes, then about the bills piled up in the basket beside the front door. Lila will just have to believe me. I hold my hand out. "I'll take the car - for now. But I'm bringing it back. You're not sticking me with that thing all night. That's just wrong. I show up by the time my shift starts, I want a better car than that. Come on, you know the shit Lila'll give me if she thinks I've smoked."

For a second, I think he's going to shrug, but instead he nods. "Bring it in by ten - I'll see something's here by eleven, latest. All right?"

And miss the theater crowd. "Fine," I say.

I don't see the girl get into the cab as I pull away from the curb opposite Battery Park. All I remember is that suddenly, she's there in my back seat, a ghoulish drenched waif wearing what looks like a bloodied hospital gown with what looks like a rubber tube running out of her neck. I slam on my brake and do a double-take. For a split second, I think I must be seeing things, because the back seat is empty, and then I see her, a pale waiver of white this time wrapped in layers of shiny black leather. Her hair looks maroon in the neon glare. It *is* maroon, I realize, as I turn around. "Whoa, miss, I didn't see you get in back there. Where is it you want to go?"

She slumps against the back seat for a few seconds, eyes closed and for a second I'm seized by the fear that tonight I'm going to be called upon to do something I am absolutely in no way prepared for, like deliver a baby. Where I thought I saw the tube attached are two puffy bruises.

"You okay, miss?" I stop as her eyes meet mine. She looks about twelve years old. *Runaway.* The song whispers in my mind. *Runaway…run, run, run, little runaway.* "Can I take you home?"

The word seems to shudder through her fine-boned frame. "Okay," she nods. "Yeah. You can take me home."

Behind us another taxi honks, a bus blares and I'm forced to move. I pull out into traffic, glancing up and into my rearview mirror. The neon lights play red and blue across her face, making it impossible to see if she's really as soaked as she first appeared. At least I can still see her. I ease into the sea of traffic, and for a minute I'm too busy navigating to pay attention to her answer. "I'm sorry," I say when I can. "Where'd you say you wanted to go?"

She blinks. She has strange eyes, eyes that seem to swallow light, not reflect them. A shiver goes up my spine as the thought occurs to me that she has no eyes at all. Get a grip, Jack, I tell myself. The second hand smoke in the upholstery must be having some effect. I take a great gulp of wet night air and lean back against the partition to catch her answer. "What was that again?"

She stops in the middle of biting her nail, and I swear she looks no more than twelve. "1667 Park Place. It's in Brooklyn, off Ralph Avenue. You know where that is?"

I'm silent, thinking hard against the thump and swipe of the windshield wipers. Rain always washes the city in a surrealistic glare, and makes it feel like somewhere else altogether. But this is twice now, that I feel that chime of recognition. The address she's given me is on the street I grew up. "Yeah, I know where that is - you sure you want to go there?"

"Yeah." She gives me a quick glance out of the corner of her eye, and for a moment she looks hunted and haunted and hard all at once. "You got a problem with going there, cabbie?"

"N..No, of course," I say, caught off-guard. "Be glad to take you anywhere you want to go. But this time of day it might take a while."

"No rush," she replies. She's looking out the window now, her face turned away, and for a second I could swear I see her merge and blur and disappear into the shadows as we weave in and out of the streetlights' glow.

As we approach the bridge, I see there's an accident on the bridge itself, a problem that has both directions of traffic tied up. I stifle a curse, and turn to look at her. "Hey, we can turn around, and -"

"No, it's okay. Just stay here." But she rubs her chin and frowns over her shoulder and I, too, have a strong sense we should go back. "We have time." She shakes her head a little, looks a little disoriented. "Lots of time."

A bus slides past us, the kind with glazed commuters staring out over a glaring celebrity smile. The ad on the back of the bus as it lurches in front of me catches my eye. It's a snake wrapped around a sword, forming a stylized "S." *Since 1621* reads the ornate script above the bold block letters: **Savageux Holdings International Associates...First & Wall Street...First on Wall Street.**

The snake's eye glitters in the bluish glare of my headlights and I see it's crowned with laurel, like a Greek champion, its black forked tongue wrapped around the pommel of the sword. There's something in the image that makes the hair go up on the back of my neck and I wish the bus would move ahead, disappear, so I wouldn't have to stare at the flat-eyed snake.

I don't think we're going anywhere as I tap my fingers on the wheel. Sirens are screaming in from all directions. My passenger looks as if she could bolt out of the cab at any minute.

"Looking forward to getting home?" I ask. It sounds lame as I say it, but it's the first thing I can think of.

"I guess." She clasps and unclasps her fingers and bites her lip. She looks like a hunted animal and suddenly I'm worried about her.

"Are you in some kind of trouble?" I can't believe I'm hearing the words come out of my mouth. This is New York and everyone's worried they're in some kind of trouble.

Over the crest of the bridge, I hear shouts and the clash and scrape of metal. Then silence, and I wonder how long we might be stuck here. The rain is coming down in sheets, sluicing across the windshield. I wonder if Lila and her friends are getting wet. I wonder how bad the accident is.

"It's bad," she says. "But no one's going to die."

"How can you know that," I begin as I turn to look at her, but the words never quite make it out of my throat. She's leaning forward, her face pressed against the opening in the plastic partition. Her eyes are enormous in her pale white face and she's staring straight ahead at the back of the bus in front of us. "Turn around. We have to go back."

"Now?" The traffic up ahead is beginning to inch forward, the barriers must've been lifted.

"Yes, now," she says. "Hurry, before the cars start."

"You want to go back toward mid-town?" I'm sputtering now, the car in gear, my foot dancing gently on the accelerator.

"Yes - no. The East Village." She leans forward, tapping me on the shoulder, and I feel a jolt of something that puts me into motion. "Come on, go. Now."

This is really nuts, I think, before I press on the accelerator. I give the steering wheel a hard twist to the left, and we swerve in a tight hairpin, racing back to Manhattan like shadows on the crest of the floodtide of headlights.

Chapter 2

The place she tells me to take her is even worse than a backstreet neighborhood in Bed-Stuy. It's a converted church, and the crowd milling in the street out front surpasses some of the strangest of the strange sights I've ever seen. I'm forced to slow to a near crawl while still half a block away. "Are you sure this is it?" I ask, more to give her the chance to back out than because I really think I have the address wrong.

"Yes," she replies, in a voice so calm, so firm, I jerk around to look at her.

In the short time it's taken to find this place since we skidded off the bridge - she's morphed into something so different and unexpected I'm not even sure how to characterize her. If before she looked like a lost little runaway, now she's a Goth waif. Her maroon hair is spiked in different directions. She's got silver chains wrapped around both wrists, and her throat is long and white. Her cheekbones seem higher, her brows more arched, and her lips… I know Lila would want not just the name of the color but the brand. Whatever my passenger has applied has made her lips look as succulent as dark red cherries. I clamp my hands around my sweat-slick steering wheel and fasten my eyes on the street straight ahead. At least, for the first time in a long time, I know I'm not dead.

But most of the pedestrians peering into the cab appear to be. "What is this," I mutter. "First Church of Dracula?" We're surrounded by a sea of black leather, in which white faces float and swirl like flotsam and silver chains flash like foam. "What the hell -?" I breathe. Who knew on a Tuesday night so many vampires would be out to play? I glance at my passenger. "Full moon, huh?"

"Yes," she says, and I see her eyes glitter.

"I thought that brought out werewolves, not vampires."

"Just drive," she says, and she won't look at me.

My trepidation mounts as we approach the entrance of the church. I slow the car to a near crawl. The crashing cacophony that periodically blasts from the partially open doors sounds exactly the way I'd imagine music from Hell, and the doorman is a seven-foot giant, wearing a black leather loincloth and lace up boots. The rain's let up, at least, but the puddles look like pools of blood in the reflection of the lights laced around the structure. The bouncer is arguing audibly with a short blonde woman in a black leather jacket and jeans, who looks completely out of place. She's flashing what appear to be press credentials, and she's yelling, so loudly her high-pitched voice punctuates the noise. *This is all pretty damn strange.* I wonder exactly what Rasta Ray might've been smoking in the car all day and if it could be having any effect on my perception.

I glance up at my passenger. I can see her in the mirror so I know she can't be a real vampire. She looks intent and focused, her lips pressed hard and tight, her eyes hooded. For a split second, I'm afraid of her. "Are you sure -"

Shrill curses erupt from the blonde at the top of the stairs. As I glance at the leather-clad giant, now been flanked by two others, a vampire leading a woman wearing a white lace dress on a leash darts in front of me, forcing me to slam on the brakes. I hear the car door open, and just as I think I'm about to get stiffed, my passenger leans forward, presses a crinkled bill in my hand. "I think that covers everything," she says, and then she's gone, slamming the door, dissolving into the press of the crowd.

Stunned, I look down at the money and my jaw drops. I'm holding a hundred and a fifty. Both are sopping wet. And here I was afraid the kid would stiff me.

The back door opens, and the blonde woman slides in, her flat white press credentials swinging around her neck from a lanyard that advertises

Traveler's Insurance. "God, that was stupid - I can't believe I did that - that was so god-damn dumb." Her voice is pure Bronx and I have this sense of falling back into ordinary reality, ordinary time. She leans back in the seat, curls flooding across the top of the cracked imitation leather. "Drive, will you? Just drive - I can't believe I was so fucking dumb."

"Where to?"

"Oh, I don't know - just drive." She waves me vaguely back toward uptown, but as I make the turn onto the avenue, she digs her nails into my shoulder through the gap in the glass partition. "No- no, not *away* - just pull around the corner - yeah, that corner, too. Careful, that's a cop - no, just keep going... no, no, don't stop while he's looking at us - oh, don't worry. I know a lot of the cops - hah, that's Luis Hernandez. At least, I think it was Luis. It looked like Luis. Don't worry, we'll be fine. Just drive, okay?"

I concentrate on coming to a complete stop at the sign. "Lady, I haven't done anything wrong."

"But smoke a lil j, maybe?" She sniffs.

"Not me." I shake my head. Damn Shortman. I roll down the window a few inches and the rain stings my cheek.

My passenger is flipping through a notebook, still swearing under her breath. She sees me glance at her and her lips quirk. "Sorry - I didn't mean to snap at you. I'm just - it's just - I'm not usually so stupid. I guess that's what I get for listening to a dream."

That makes me look at her again. "You listened to a dream?"

"Pull over here a few minutes - this is far enough."

I glance around. It's an empty lot, with what looks like a cardboard shanty precariously wedged against the burned foundation of whatever had once stood in the center. I don't like the feeling I get when I look at it, and I shift around to look at her. "I got to tell you the meter's running."

"I know the meter's running. I don't give a shit, okay? Just let me sit here and think. Then I'll tell you. Christ, I might as well tell someone."

"Think of me as a rolling confessional."

A police cruiser pulls around a corner, sees us, and stops. In this neighborhood, anything and everything is suspicious simply for being here when there are so many better places to be. He stares at me. I raise my head, meet his eyes, motion as if I'm counting change. *No trouble here,* I think. *Lady's a little looped, but no trouble.*

As if he's heard me, he drives on, slowly. I breathe a little easier.

"A what?"

"A confessional…. It's a Catholic thing… never mind."

"Well, thank God – Catholic, Jewish, or whatever flavor you want, you were there." She says it like she means it. "Fuckers wouldn't let me in - I even have an invitation. See?" She holds out something that looks like a thick piece of white cardboard.

I take it. It's roughly the size and shape of the announcements Lila sent out to tell everyone we eloped, but its folded like an invitation, and it has the silhouette of a half-naked woman with her hands tied behind her back, bending bare-bottomed with her mouth open over an apple. "Maybe they didn't want the press?" I nod at her lanyard.

She snorts, waves dismissively. "If they didn't want the press, why'd they send the invitation to the paper? No, they wouldn't let me in 'cause I'm not the one they sent it to." She blinks hard as her eyes well up with tears and stares out the window. "There's a cop over there watching us."

"There's no law against being upset in New York. If he comes over, we'll tell him you're working on a story, right? Because that is what you're doing, right?" The tears are rolling down her cheeks now, and she's fumbling in her purse, pulling out a crumpled wad of disintegrating tissue. She either has a bad cold, or she's been crying a lot lately. That thought makes me soften my voice. "What paper you write for? I ever read anything you wrote?"

She sniffs and nods at the invitation. "It's in there."

I flip it open as she blows her nose. "Winnie Chen? *The Sun* - we shine it where it don't shine? Or something like that? You write for them?" I'm always curious about other people who manage to make a living writing. Up to this point, all my writing's bought me is a few cups of coffee and a lot of scholarships, but no true prospect of something secure as a salary. I scan the inside of the invitation that promises among other things, tarot readers, dungeon masters and mistresses, prophets and seers and other "moonlit mayhem." The hair goes up on the back of my neck. The last thing I told my class this morning was how Blake regarded himself and Milton as poet-prophets. Apparently vampires do, too.

"I'm not Winnie." She stuffs the tissue in her purse, reads the name on my license and holds out her hand. "I write under Casey McGuire. They usually send me after celebrities. I'm pushy, you know." She flips her blonde curls. "Much good it did me tonight. My real name's Shirley Shulman." She looks at me for a long moment, then starts to sob.

The expression in her eyes reminds me of the one in the eyes of the dog who died in my arms when I was twelve. It hurts to watch her, but even if I look away, I feel as if I'm drowning in waves of this woman's pain. "So why didn't Winnie go?" I try peering through the rain-blurred window to see if the cop is still watching and I roll down the window next to me a little further, hoping to replace the marijuana miasma with the cold damp. The rain floods down my collar. Damn Rasta Ray to hell and back.

Shirley wipes her eyes again, presses her lips together and shakes her head. "Winnie's missing - it's been – six, no - seven weeks."

"And you think someone in there knows where she's gone?"

"I think someone in there did something to her. I keep having these dreams about her…she… she tells me to do stuff… check stuff…" She breaks off, wraps her arms around herself and stares out into the night. "The dreams…at least the stuff I can remember…it's turned out to be right." She looks directly at me. "You think I sound nuts, don't you?"

"Wow," I say, because I don't know what else. "Like what?"

"Stuff about the other bodies… the Jane Does –"

"What Jane Does?"

"What planet do you live on, buddy? You haven't heard about all the bodies they're finding? There's been around a dozen, all young women, all unidentified, at least most of them are. I'm so afraid Winnie'll be next, if they don't find her in time." She pulls a pack of cigarettes out of her purse and lights one. "You don't mind, right? It'll get the pot smell out of here if the cops do come over." She peers around.

"Look, maybe we better drive. I can cruise up and down - same meter, you know, but less chance anyone will bother us."

"All right. Just make a big circle around the church. I'm not ready to give up yet."

"But if it's a private party, they don't have to let you in."

"I'm not saying they have to let me in. But Winnie was working with people who go to these shindigs, getting to know them - maybe I'll see one I recognize. Some of them let her take a slew of pictures - all in costume and makeup of course, so there's like zero chance you'd know them on the street. Or in a line-up."

She lapses into silence. The hackles at the back of my neck go up and I glance around the empty, eerie streets. "So what was she talking to them about? How to be a vampire?"

"She was doing a series for the paper about this real-life vampire game these people play." She sees my expression in the mirror and she suddenly gets very serious. "Don't roll your eyes. It's all over, in all the big cities, and spreading out. You've no idea how pervasive it is. They pretend to be vampires, all kinds of vampires. They have families and territories and power struggles. For most of the people in there, it's a game and they know it's a game." She waves her cigarette in a circle. As the smoke billows around our heads, I think a joint would be good right now. "But I think Winnie… I think Winnie got involved in something that's not a game…" She sniffs and her voice breaks. "Something that's gotten her in terrible trouble."

"Maybe she found out there really are vampires." Our eyes meet in the mirror and hers are flat calm. I remember the mottled face of the homeless woman who choked on her vomit by the dumpster at the end of the alley, broken yellow teeth bared in a death-grin. I have to blink hard more than once and stare into the street lamps to erase the memory. I mean to be funny but it doesn't come out that way.

She shifts forward on the seat, face serious and when she speaks, her voice is calmer and more thoughtful than before. "Listen, those people in there do all kinds of things, including drink real blood from willing donors – keyword there is willing. But I think at least one of them knows where she is and what happened to her, and I think the rest of them are protecting him all in the name of the game."

"You think one of them's a murderer, if not a real vampire?"

"Or worse." Shirley meets my eyes with disgust. "I guess you haven't heard about the mutilations? About the drugs? Someone used fangs on these girls –" She clamps her hand over her mouth. "Shit, I shouldn't have said that. No one's supposed to know about that."

For a long moment I stare at her. I don't have time to read the papers. TV puts me to sleep. The only news I hear is snatched from the radio in between traffic reports when I drive. I rack my brain and try to remember. "Uh…" What have I heard? I wrack my memory and come up with snippets: grisly discoveries, young women, all drained of blood; missing organs…they had a name for a while, too.

"The Jack-the-Drac murders?" I wondered what tabloid wit coined that one. Now I understand what it means.

"There you go… you have heard, haven't you? That's what the *Post* was calling them till the police asked them not to… they didn't want public panic." She leans forward. Clouds of nicotine envelop my head on her exhale. "You want to know who I think it is?"

"Sure."

"The one who threw this little shindig – he's 'Magister Nicholas the Blood-lord' down here." She makes a noise between a snort and a sigh and contempt ripples across her face.

"So why haven't you gone to the police?"

"You think I haven't?" She stabs out her cigarette and lights another. "The thing is - this guy's not just another fruit loop with fangs. This guy's like American royalty, like the Kennedys – hell, you'd know him if you saw him – to the rest of the world, he's Nicholas Savageux."

I rack my brain. Could it be possible Lila's mentioned him? "Nick the Savage?" I say in the same moment she does.

"You got it." She waves her cigarette in the direction of the church. "He lives in Connecticut with his wife and three blond kids they adopted from Eastern Europe. He's rich – his family's like professional philanthropists, they have so much money. But he likes to play vampire – him and his wife both, and so a couple years ago, they got involved with the vampire game. It caused a stink, actually, in certain circles of the game... some of the established players complained that ole Nick bought his way in... he used his real world clout to create a game world advantage he shouldn't have had. But he throws great parties and everyone... I mean everyone... wants to come."

"Everyone, including naïve young kids?" Like the one with the maroon-spiked hair. I wonder, just for a second, how it happened she had all that money on her, how she got so soaked and if she really meant to give so much to me as I pass the invitation back to Shirley.

"Especially naïve young kids. If Savageux's not the guilty one himself, I think he's connected. I think the person or people come to these parties he throws."

"He hosts a lot of these?"

"Every full moon. See...Some of these people here pretend they're vampires...and some of them... they're not. Unless you're really in on the game, you don't know who's who or who's what. It's like a living soap opera, only with monsters for characters. He's alienated a lot of society people with his shenanigans, and I've met his mother....very nice woman, very blonde and very Greenwich, if you know what I mean? She's mortified. But I think Old Nick thinks he can get away with it because his wife likes it, too. It's the consenting adult thing - they're married, so who can say it's wrong? And Fitzgerald was right - the rich are different. Right?"

She meets my eyes in the mirror and I realize she's younger than I thought she was, maybe late twenties, instead of late thirties. The dark circles, the drawn worry lines on her face and the extra weight make her look older. But she's not stupid, I realize. She's scared. This isn't about some story, I realize. It's the girl herself. "The girl who disappeared is a friend of yours?"

"Yeah." Shirley blinks, looks down and shrugs. "She's a friend. She's my best friend. She's my lover, my life partner. We met in college, we – well, we both...we came out together... it was a big deal for both of us, you know? *Her* parents disowned her – mine, well... Jesus, why I am telling you all this?" Her face crumples. "I'm so scared I'll never see her again."

I feel the air leak out of my lungs in a low sigh as we roll to a stop at a red light. Angry as Lila is with me, I know she wants me to come home every night. I try to imagine how she'd react if I turned up missing, and I can't quite get beyond an inferno of fury. "Wow. No wonder you lost it."

She's weeping now, softly. "Winnie's not like me. She writes under her own name - she's not ashamed she writes for a tabloid - my family would die if they saw my real name in a paper like *The Sun*. But not Winnie. Winnie's got guts and..." She breaks off, closes her eyes, and folds her lips together. "And I'm so afraid they got her killed. Or worse." She bites her lip but not before I see it quiver.

There's a knock on my window. I roll down the window and a cop looks past me into the back seat. "Casey, that you? Yeah, I thought that was you."

"Sergeant Hernandez? That you?"

"You're fine, driver," he says, as he sees me start to fumble for my wallet. "I think you might want to come with me, Casey."

"Where?" Her face lights up. "You found -"

"We got another Jane Doe just pulled out of the East River."

Shirley, or Casey, tips me generously, too. I finger the three twenties she hands me on top of the fare, along with the soggy bills my last passenger gave me. *We got another Jane Doe pulled out of the river.* The cop's voice echoes through my mind, over and over as I finger the bill. The light changes and I enter the flow of traffic. I'm just going to cruise a while, I think, up and down. I've done okay tonight already - I can take a little break. After all, I think, it's only - twelve-thirty? I blink.

Twelve-thirty in the fucking morning? I wonder what the chances are of Shortman saving me another car for more than the time it takes for someone else to ask for it. It's not worth going back now, I think. The bars are starting to close. But where the hell did the time go, I wonder. I picked up the girl around - eight, eight-thirty, right by Battery Park. *We got another Jane Doe pulled out of the river.*

The kid I'd picked up hadn't looked capable of killing a fly, let alone a person and dumping the body into the river. She hadn't looked capable of picking up so much as a heavy suitcase. But she was all wet...at least until she got to the church.

I finger the wet money, wondering again if maybe the kid made a mistake. Maybe they wouldn't let Shirley in, I think. But they might let a taxi driver in - especially one who said he was already paid to show up. *Just doing my job, man.* I envision myself saying this to the Jolly Leather Giant. *Just doing my job.*

I finesse the car through the burgeoning crowd. One A.M. is early in the vampire world, I suppose. I get as close to the curb as I can and put Old Bessie into park. *That's your name*, I tell the car, invoking my old childhood game that the things I named, even inanimate things like doors and windows were therefore somehow imbued with the magical power to protect me. *That's your name. You be good.*

I grip the money, hope it's my ticket in, and wonder what I'll say if I do find her. She gave me far more than twice the fare, so that's what I'll say. *I figured you wanted me to wait.* "I figured she wanted me to wait." My voice is even, strong. At the very last minute, something tells me to grab my taxi license with my picture off the visor. Then I get out.

I weave my way in and out of the crowd, my eyes meeting those of assorted vampires and victims. I'm struck once more by a strong sense of deja-vu as I mount the steps but I'm sure I've never been here before.

The crowd is bigger now, and the music is screaming from the gutters. The theater must be underground, and for some reason I remember the name of the place is called the Village of the Damned. Or is it Theater of the Dead? At the top of the steps, the big guy in black leather blocks my way.

"I got a fare waiting," I say. I flash my hundred-dollar bill and he lifts it out of my fingers, quick as that.

"Show me your license." He flashes fangs. I fumble for my wallet but he shakes his head. "Taxi license."

For a second our eyes meet and I feel a jolt of something, a push, in my head, my throat and my gut. Then I remember I have it. "Sure thing."

He stares at it for a long time, looks at me, looks at the license and I have the awful feeling he's memorizing it.

"My fare," I say.

"Sure thing." He grins, hands the license back so carelessly it nearly drops, then pushes open the big red door. "Go right in, Mr. Chance."

Inside, I look down into a face so gaunt it appears to be nothing more than a layer of skin covering a skull. The air is thick with noise and sweat and perfume, and the smell of something else - something I don't quite recognize, and can't quite place. There's a gritty, metallic undertone to it, sweat and sawdust, maybe. My sneakers are crunching on fine grit. I remember stepping over the dead junkie in the hallway of the fourth floor walkup we lived in till I was thirteen, and I wonder if any of these people have ever spent a minute being really afraid of anything in their lives.

"Good evening, Mr. Chance." A woman materializes around the skull. She's dressed from head to toe in black lace so she blends into the gloom, and she's standing so close to the door, she must've heard the bouncer.

"I'm here for a girl with purplish-reddish hair," I say. "Spiked, about your height, black leather?" I glance around and see fangs, black in every possible fabric, piercings of every possible description and I wonder how many would-be monsters ever hid between the stove and the wall when strangers tried to break through the front door. Things got bad for Mom and me when Dad went to prison and the neighborhood turned into a ghetto around us.

But the atmosphere is intoxicating and disorienting, like a bad trip or a mix of too much tequila and anything else. There's an odor in the air that's getting to me, something that's making my head spin. The light wavers, and everywhere I look I see the flash of flesh. The woman's face is very white and her mouth is very black. "Red-head? Leather? This high?" I hope I sound as normal as I did in the cab.

Her fangs flash silver when she smiles up at me. It doesn't matter how many dead junkies you've stepped over, or how many knives or guns you've stared down – a woman with fangs is intimidating, especially when she presses her breasts into the fleshy part of your arm, and you feel her nails stab through three layers of fabric. "Feel free to look around, Mr. Chance. Don't let it get to you if everyone looks back."

She laughs and turns on her heel, and she's so easily swallowed up by the writhing mass of bodies it makes me dizzy. There's some kind of mist in the air, too, some kind of fog, that causes the light to refract into colored ribbons that appear to rise and swirl around everyone in the place.

I start to ease my way around the periphery of the cavernous room. The floor is vibrating under my feet which only adds to my disorientation. People point and stare and whisper. *I'm the normal one,* I tell myself, even though the glitter in their eyes makes me feel uncomfortably like prey. The back of my neck tingles. *I shouldn't be here,* I think. *I should leave now.*

LEAVE. NOW.

The voice is so clear, I turn around, expecting to see a woman standing next to, or at least near me. Instead, I see a young man with long black hair dressed in a flowing white lace blouse leering at me. He moves toward me, his face intent and I know he's going to speak to me. But in that moment, there's a surge in the power, because all around us the lights flicker and the ribbons of color all wheel and twine in one direction.

Even I have to look.

The man standing just inside the doorway inside a pool of light gives the impression he's taller than the bouncer at the door.

By the pricking of my thumbs, something wicked this way comes. I feel a throb in my palms. Everyone is looking at him. *They call him Nick the Savage on Wall Street.* I feel dizzy, almost high and I wonder why I heard that last sentence in Lila's voice.

The hair goes up on the back of my neck as he scans the crowd, searching, probing. The weight of his gaze falls on me, glances away, comes back. *He sees me,* I think and a ripple like an electric current runs down my back as a surge of energy seems to snake out from him. He's not like these others, I think. *He's not pretending. He's the real thing.* Then I see her, the girl from the cab. She's standing just to his left, a pace or so behind. She's looking back at me. I know she sees me.

"Get out now, cabbie." The guy I noticed whispers in my ear, before I can raise my arm or draw attention to myself. He makes a fast motion with his hand, and I see the flash of a badge. "N.Y.P.D. You don't want to be here, pal." He slips past me and I sense more movement in the crowd.

Leave, Jack. Leave now.

I hear that warning again, and this time I go, stumbling out the door, scrambling down the steps as fast as I can. And can't quite believe it when I see another woman sitting in the back seat of my cab.

Chapter 3

This time it's a girl who looks not much older than the first kid. She's wearing a shiny white raincoat over what seems like not much else, and her fists are jammed deep into the pockets. She looks up at me as I peer inside the cab, and her voice sounds young, way too young to be out so late at night as I open the door and slide behind the wheel. "Please," she whispers. "Please could you just take me home?"

From inside the church, I hear angry shouts and startled screams, and from just a few blocks over, I hear the blare of sirens. "Uh, yeah, sure, miss. Where's home?"

She looks at me blankly for a moment, as if she expects me to know. "Bethel," she answers finally.

"Bethel? That's a street?"

"Bethel, Connecticut. It's a town." She turns her head and stares outside.

"I – uh- I can't take you all the way to Bethel, hon," I say. "How about the train station? Penn Station? Grand Central?"

"Grand Central," she says, through a deep sigh. For a split second, in the volley of flashing lights that pierce the darkness, I think she's disappeared. The hair goes up on the back of my neck and a chill goes down my back.

The church is almost surrounded now by police cars flashing blue and red, but I put the car in gear, and manage to ease through the crowd like a sharp knife cutting through butter. We turn onto the silent avenue, the engine rattling in the eerie stillness. The sirens fade in the distance. The sky above is milky gray, the cavernous buildings dotted with rectangles of light. The male model on the side of the kiosk looks a lot like Savageux.

We slide past the Empire State Building and the bum sleeping beneath the street lamp opens his eyes and lifts a bottle as we pass. The lights turn green as if by magic as we approach each intersection, and I feel as if I've slipped into some sideways space where the more things look the same, the more you know them to be different.

I glance at my passenger in the mirror. She's watching the avenues slide by, sitting still as a statue in her ghostly white raincoat. Her hands aren't balled up in fists anymore. They're sitting flat on her lap, so that I can see the flash of long red nails against the white of her raincoat. She looks younger than she did before, way too young to be taking a train anywhere in the middle of the night. "Ah, miss? You know if you can get a train this time of night?"

She looks at me with a flat expression. "I just want to go home."

I am both surprised and not surprised to see that we've pulled up next to the station. Grand Central looks deserted but for the pigeons roosting around the ledges. I hear them cooing as I brake. I look to my left and see a woman standing on the sidewalk, as if she's waiting for a cab and I feel awful, because I'm going to have to tell her my shift is long over.

As she bends down and opens the back door, I see she's wearing a long dark cloak.

"Uh, ma'am," I begin. "I'm not –"

"Quite all right," she says with a burr of brogue. "I'm here for this young lady. I don't need a cab." She beckons to my passenger. "Let's get you inside."

She holds out her hand and I hear the squeak of the vinyl raincoat across the vinyl seat. The fall of her long, flowing red hair blocks my view, and there's something so surreal about the scene that it verges on the dreamlike. Toto, I think, we're not in Kansas anymore.

The girl in the backseat hesitates. She looks even younger than she did a few minutes ago, and the rain coat looks bigger, bunchier, around her suddenly curveless frame. "I want to go home."

"Let's get you there, then." The red-head offers her hand again and my passenger scrambles out.

"Hey, now!" I say, pushing open my door. Surrealism gives way to the numbers flashing on the meter. "Hey – come on – don't stiff me."

The girl in the white rain coat looks at me, and I do a double take. She's a kid, with braids and big blue eyes.

"That'll be ten bucks," I stutter. "P-Please."

She can't be more than nine or ten, I think, as I watch her feel around her in her suddenly oversize pockets. "Look at this," she cries. She holds out a wad of cash.

"Give it to him, honey," the woman says. "I've got your ticket here."

"Okay," the little girl agrees. She pushes the money into my hand and I see that her nails, once so long and bloody red, are now short and stubby and pink.

As she takes the red-haired woman's hand, my eyes meet the woman's. "Thanks for bringing her," she says. "And, Jack, stay away from Savageux."

At least that's what I think I hear her say. I can't be sure, because her face is ringing bells in my head. In the most rational corner of my mind, I know I've never seen this woman before in my life, except maybe in a museum, hanging on a wall, staring blindly back at me across time. She's got one of those Renaissance faces, big eyes, broad forehead, generous mouth, creamy skin stained peach on the cheeks. Surely that's the only place I might've seen her.

But I know her, I know I know her. I know I've seen her before. I know I've walked with her, talked with her, sat with her through long, sun-drenched afternoons. I stare at her and smell something earthy, spicy and warm. I just can't imagine where.

"Stay away from Savageux," she says, before they both disappear.

What the fuck -? I think. There's no one on the street, on the sidewalk. I don't even hear footsteps echoing. I wonder how it is that the street's so deserted. I look both directions, but there's no one - not even a street person huddled near a bench, not even another cab at the stand. I look down at the money in my hand. I'm holding three hundred dollar bills – two dry and crisp, the third, soggy and limp as the bill the first girl gave me.

It's nearly three by the time I get back to the garage. Shortman tallies up, but I don't have much on the meter. He collects my money with a grunt. "Make sure the car's clean," he says, just before he turns off the light, and I realize I'm the last one to cash out that night. It's the last thing Shortman always says and mostly everyone ignores him.

But something tells me to take another look under the back seat. The white edge of a piece of cardboard beckons from underneath the front seat, and I realize what it is. It's Shirley Schulman's invitation - the one that didn't get her into the party. It's stuck to its own envelope and I read the address, finger the thick stock. It's vellum. I remember Lila explaining the nuances of fine papers to me. *Ms. Winnie Chen, The Sun, 1231 Avenue of the Americas, New York, New York.*

They call him Nick the Savage on Wall Street.

I run my finger over the raised type. On impulse I put it in my pocket. The bus home is equipped with a police radio and several times, just as I'm starting to drowse, the name Savageux blares through the static, echoing eerily in the almost empty bus. It stays in my head all the way home.

Lila stirs and mutters as I fumble my way into the bedroom. "Jack? That you?" Her voice is thick and hoarse and I can smell beer on her clothing, in her sweat. She's going to have one bitch of a hangover and I feel sorry for her, because I'd rather die than do what she does every day.

I strip off my clothes and slide into bed beside her. My entire body collapses into the mattress.

"You're late," she mumbles.

"Busy night. Go back to sleep, babe. It's almost time to wake up." She'll be pleased when she sees the tips. But tired as I am, I can't sleep. My mind ping-pongs between the woman who disappeared into a weirdly deserted Grand Central and the man she warned me against. *They call him Nick the Savage on Wall Street.* Lila's voice echoes over and over in my overtired mind, and I wonder if maybe its just my memory, if she did tell me she met him and I've forgotten. That's entirely possible. But I know as I lie awake with the feathered ends of her hair spread across my pillow, that she hasn't.

Stay away from Savageux. I watch Lila sleep and tell myself there are no such things as vampires, that I must've misunderstood the red-haired woman. Lila's hand slips across my chest, and I glance down in the gloom. Her nails are dark against the white sheet, and for a split second, the image of my passenger's fingernails as she handed me the fare flashes through my mind.

I shake the image out of my mind and turn my head to see Lila looking at me. The alarm clock on the other side of the bed reads 5:55. In the alley outside I hear brakes, the clatter of trashcans and at least three angry male voices start to curse. "You okay?" she asks.

She looks younger and softer than I've seen her in a long time. I remember when we thought our differences made us a good team. "Just tired," I say.

"Me, too."

"Have fun?"

She shrugs. "We didn't go out. We each just brought a six-pack to Jodi's."

I roll over to look at her. "What happened to girls' night on the town?"

"We didn't go. No one really has the money. I'm sorry I was so mean last night, Jack. I just get so fucking sick and tired -"

"Shh," I say. I slide over and pull her into my arms. She's warm and squishy in all the right places, and round and firm in all the rest. "You were mean but you weren't wrong. We do need cash."

"Things have been so crazy at work, Jack. Fucking Sussman's driving everyone up the wall with his neurotic obsessive shit. And a big case for the firm doesn't mean more money for me, you know? Just more work."

I cradle her close. It is the way I think it is, I tell myself. We've just hit a rough spot - everyone does. We're both cranky and overtired. "There's bonus time, though, and raise time. C'mon, Lila, you know they love you. I'll get my contract renewed, you'll see. Show a little faith, baby." Whatever there was last night, I seem to have connected to it.

Her breasts are pressed into my chest, I can feel the hard nubs of her nipples against my side. "I'd rather you looked outside the city, though, Jack. I want to find a nice place to raise kids, and you can teach..."

I lift her chin with one finger and stop the flow of words with a kiss, a real kiss. I have a flash of an image of an enormous cage constructed of a white picket fence and containing a house with four bedrooms, a two car garage and two point three children waving from the windows, settling over me. Lila's arms and legs twine around me, her belly round against mine. Our bodies fit together like a foot in a well-worn shoe. I slide myself into her, and forget everything for a while. The sex is good, in a way it hasn't been in awhile, and I drift off thinking that it's going to be okay, after all.

When the alarm goes off at 6:15, I am just easing into the deepest, most restful sleep I can remember. Lila sits up with a sigh, shakes my shoulder. "You want me to reset this?"

"Yeah, for seven." That's pushing it, but I can't even think about opening my eyes.

"You got any cash you want me to deposit?" That's Lila's delicate way of asking if I had a good night in tips.

I smile, knowing she's going to be even happier than she is now. "Yeah, some. Leave me a twenty, and take the rest."

"Leave you a twenty and take the rest? Listen to you, Mr. High Roller. How much's the rest?"

"Check for yourself and see." I roll over and snuggle down. As I drift off, I hear the rustle of the sheet, the clink of my belt as she searches through my pocket. I hear a squeal of pleasure, the whisper of cash. But instead of the kiss, or the hug, or the sexy whisper in my ear I'm expecting, I get a swat on my head.

"I can see you had a busy night." Lila slams the bathroom door closed. "Maybe at some point you can tell me what exactly you did to earn all that."

Then I remember the picture on the invitation. "Lila, I can explain –" I start to shout, but the roar of the shower cuts me off. I roll upright with a groan. She's quite capable of ripping it to shreds. With a sigh, I reach for my jeans, almost knock over the lamp and manage to turn the radio on as I fumble for the lamp switch.

"ANOTHER JANE DOE WAS FOUND NEAR BATTERY PARK LAST NIGHT–" I hit the on/off switch and then immediately hit it again.

But the brief report is over — they're on to traffic woes in New Jersey — by the time I find the station once more. I let the radio babble, hoping to hear more, trying to remember where exactly, I had picked up the first weird passenger. Battery Park. *We got another Jane Doe pulled out of the East River.* I slump onto the sagging mattress, and remember the three strange women from last night.

I reach for the money on the dresser, spread it out, and examine it carefully under the lamp. It looks like normal enough money to me, but I notice that it's crisp, the way money gets when it's been soaked.

"I don't care how you got the money." Wrapped in towel, Lila stands in the door of the bathroom, water dripping down her arms and legs. She opens her mouth and her lips work, but no intelligible words come out. She spins on her heel and slams the door.

"Lila, listen - this isn't what you think — somebody dropped this in my cab - I stuffed it in a pocket cleaning out the cab and forgot about it." I jiggle the knob. "Come on, babe, this is silly - you really think someone gave me that for sex?" I rattle the knob again in frustration and nearly fall inside the bathroom as she pulls the door open abruptly.

"Jack, are you on something?"

"What?"

"Just answer me. Have you tried anything new?"

"You mean a new drug?"

She nods. Half her face is done, her eyes big and dark, the circles beneath expertly concealed, but her lips are colorless and pale. "Don't bullshit me, okay? Tell me the truth."

"Christ, Lila, you know how hard I'm working, how much I want this to work —" I glance at myself in the mirror. I sound the way I used to sound, strung out on coke and tequila and whatever else I could afford. I hate that person. I shut up, straighten, take a deep breath and look her in the eye. "Why?"

She shrugs, turns back to her mirror and make-up. "You're being a little weird, Jack."

"I'm tired."

Our eyes meet in the mirror. "You know our deal?"

"I know our deal." I lean on the doorframe and a piece of paint chips off onto my shoulder. "And you know I don't pay attention to the news." *Except maybe just now.*

"Last night, all the girls were talking about the women they're finding. Some of the papers are calling them the Jack-the-Drac murders cause they're so gross. All the victims got some strange drug in their bloodstreams, something so new no one's quite sure what it is. They don't even know what it does to you."

"You really think I took some new drug last night, and serviced a bunch of women?" I hold her eyes with mine, then lean in and kiss her cheek. "Come on, I thought I was the one who writes fiction."

She makes a little sound, half way between a sob and a curse, and pushes past me. Then she turns and presses a hard kiss on my mouth. "I'll stick with you through anything. "But you have to keep your part of the deal."

"I know." I lean forward and our mouths lock briefly. She drops the towel in front of me, which is a good sign, and I watch her pull on pink lace panties, lock on her bra. "I did have a weird night last night," I say. "I ran into someone who's afraid one of the victims is her partner. She's the one who left the invitation in the car." Tentatively, I hand the invitation to Lila, a peace offering of a sort.

She takes it, runs the edge of her thumb over the picture on the front. "This is engraved," she says. "And wow, will you look at this vellum?" She flips it open and her eyes bug wide. "Oh, my God, you drove Winnie Chen around last night? Is she the one who gave you the tip? If you take this back to her, do you think she'd give you her autograph?"

"You read *The Sun*? Since when?"

"Not me - Rosalind our receptionist - she's really hooked on this series that this woman Winnie Chen was writing. She did two installments, and then I guess there's been nothing, but if you were driving her around last night - oh, my God, were you at vampire party? Wait until I tell Rosie - can I take this and show her?" Her eyes gleam as she smiles, and then widen. "Oh, my God, no – I had a better idea." She presses the invitation against my chest. "Here. You take this. Take it back. And be nice. Maybe –"

"I can't ask for a tip."

"No, idiot, a job. Ask her about a *job*. You're a writer – aren't you?"

"I guess I didn't think–"

"Well, it's time you did think. Wouldn't you rather make money writing than driving that cab?"

For a long moment I stare at her. This is something completely new and unexpected and my mind feels too shocked, too numb to process what she's suggesting. "I-I was going to send it back…"

"Jesus, Jack, think. This is fate giving you an opportunity – all you have to do is reach for it." Her eyes are shining, her cheeks are pink. That's my Lila, my cheerleader, always urging me on to bigger and better. But I don't think I can do this – I don't think I should do this.

I don't want to see Shirley again. Looking into her eyes was like looking into pain so deep I was afraid I might lose my way out. I don't want to feel that again. Even the invitation resonates with it.

But Lila is looking at me with those enormous dark eyes of hers. I have to say something. "Something sort of weird did happen last night." I sink down on the bed beside her while she pulls up her hose.

I don't mention Savageux. Instead, I tell her about all the strange women. I tell her about the one I picked up at the spot where a body was later discovered, who morphed from sopping wet runaway to vampire Goth in the space of a taxi ride. I tell her about the woman who met the girl at Grand Central, as if she were expecting us.

Lila listens while she pulls on her skirt, buttons up a blouse, fluffs her hair and chooses her jewelry. She turns around and faces me as I hold up my finger. "But the weirdest one, Lila, was the one who seemed to get younger and younger. I saw her hands… I looked right at her fingers and the first couple times, she had these long red nails, and then, when she got out, I saw her hands, clear as day, and she didn't." I sit back as Lila slips into her pumps and suddenly she's looming over me, her hand splayed out before me. "How do you think she did that?"

"Like this, Jack," says Lila. She peels the fingernail off the end of her pinkie, and I see the real nail, short and round, underneath. She shakes her head as she presses something thin and hard and plastic as a communion wafer into my palm. "You have such an imagination. Haven't you ever heard of these things called fake nails?"

Chapter 4

Lila prods me into the bathroom, urges me to call *The Sun* and find out when Shirley's there. I let the water wash over me and listen to her leave. In the silence that descends, I am tempted to crawl back to bed. But I don't. In the kitchen I find a fresh pot of coffee and the invitation propped up on my favorite mug. I pick up the invitation and I feel a tingle in my fingers, then a flash of Shirley peering into a computer screen. I know she's in her office. I know I could take the invitation back to her right now. It would kill two birds with one stone. Even Lila would find it an acceptable reason to cut the mandatory weekly department meeting I know I'd only sleep through. I can nap on the bus.

But I don't want to go.

Shirley's pain hurts too much to even think about. I don't understand why.

I sink down with my coffee. There's a pulse in the space between my eyes and it's throbbing. I hold my coffee against the spot and the pain flares into my right eye. A kaleidoscope of images from last night explodes in my mind, and it takes me a moment to understand I am seeing things that I wasn't there to see – cops running in, ambulances pulling up. I see a prone figure, a glimpse of a white raincoat, the flash of limp hands that end in long red nails, then a sheeted corpse being carried out.

I slam the mug down, spilling hot coffee all over my hand and the images fade. This must be some kind of weird flashback, I think as I mop up the mess, change my clothes, swallow aspirin. My hands are shaking. No wonder Lila thinks I'm on something. Maybe Rasta Ray was smoking something stronger than weed in Old Bessie yesterday.

At least, I'm sure I'll sleep on the bus.

But on the way to Manhattan, I can't stop thinking about the three strange women last night. Even if I try to think about something else, my attention is snagged by a headline, a snatch of news blasted from a car window, or a picture flashing on the screens of TV's in appliance store windows. Other than the new Jane Doe story, the arrest of Nicholas Savageux in a drug raid appears to be the only other thing that happened in all five boroughs last night. But there's no mention of a murder and I decide I must have hallucinated due to lack of sleep. Get a grip, Jack, I tell myself as the bus rolls toward Manhattan. Get a fucking grip.

There's a drug... in all the Jane Does... so new they don't even know what it does... Lila's words echo over and over in my head as I stare out the window. The press, and not just the tabloids, is having a field day with Nicholas Savageux and his arrest, and the story is splashed everywhere. Even *The New York Times* shrieks: *Demon Playboy of Wall Street Arrested.* I look for a copy of *The Sun,* but it seems to have sold out.

In the lobby of Winnie's office building, the security guard eyes me suspiciously but agrees to call upstairs when I show him the invitation. Before he even hangs up, he's pointing me to the second row of elevators. "She really wants that invitation back. Fifteenth floor. Turn left off the elevator. She says she'll meet you there."

As I wait for the elevator, I look up into a bank of television screens, all playing the same clip of Savageux being shepherded into the precinct office that's been playing over and over on every station in the city. He looks directly into the camera. In a heartbeat, I'm back to last night, when our eyes did meet, and I feel a weird sense that we're somehow linked, somehow connected. *He sees me.* I stamp my feet and look away and tell myself I have such a fucking imagination I must be going crazy. The door in front of me slides open and I step inside, feeling sweat trickle down my sides.

You have such an imagination. The memory of Lila's voice is like a tether that anchors me to this side of reality. I see again the exasperation in her face, her spindly fingers as she peels off her fake nail. She can be hard on me, but she keeps me here.

Shirley is standing in front of the elevator. She grabs my hand and drags me out. "This was so nice of you." She holds the invitation close for a second, then slips it into her pocket. "Come on," she smiles. "Let me show you around. Didn't you say you taught writing? What kind of writing do you teach?"

I wonder when I told her that. There are huge stretches of time I don't remember last night, and it worries me. But I thought I remembered all my conversation with Shirley.

She wants me to stay. I don't understand why. Our hands brush as she hands me the Styrofoam cup of burnt coffee. Suddenly I know that the body from the East River wasn't her partner. That's what she wants to tell me. She holds open the double doors, beckons me through, and I slam into a wall of noise and chaos that makes my eyes water and my head ache. On one level, I know that the environment is no worse than any other office - people are milling around desks and copy machines and faxes, phones ring, keyboards click. But on another level, nothing rational explains the way I feel.

She's talking, gesturing, and I hope I'm managing to look like I'm paying attention. Sweat is beading on my forehead, my pulse is drumming in my skull. Finally she settles behind an old desk that looks like it's been here since they filmed King Kong – the original version. It's in a nook by itself, tucked into a corner near a window, and on the crowded floor, it's the closest thing to private a cubicle could be. There's a different kind of feeling in the space, too, that I don't expect – calmer, greener. Spreading spiders and lush palms surround the window. I sink down into a battered wooden chair and tell myself to breathe.

I look down and realize I'm holding a doughnut and a cup of coffee and I have no idea how they got there. "This is Winnie's desk," Shirley is saying. "No one's said anything. I don't think they dare." She laughs abruptly then. "They know how it was – how it is – with us."

Her pain is sweeping me up and into its spiral. I clutch my doughnut and my coffee and wonder how fast I can safely consume both. "It's – uh – good you feel closer to her here."

"Yeah," she says, looking at me gratefully. "So it wasn't her, you know. Last night. Maybe you saw it on the news. They don't know yet who it was. Just like all the others. I wish I'd been around to see the drug bust – I got all my info off the police radio."

"I was there," I say before I can stop myself. I have to blink away the memory of Savageux's eyes.

"What do you mean – there?" Her tired eyes turn fierce. This isn't about a story; it's about Winnie. She wants to know what I saw. But I don't want to talk about Savageux. I should've listened to myself, I think. I should've just sent the invitation. Coming here is turning out to be the bad idea I was afraid it was going to be. The phone rings, and she waves a finger at me.

"Newsroom," she says. She covers the receiver with her hand. "Don't go anywhere," she mouths.

Our eyes meet and hold and I suddenly know that wherever the person on the other end of the line is, it's surrounded by a lot of trees. I can hear them, whispering in the background, raindrops pattering off their boughs. Then the lined face of a gray-haired woman wearing a pink sweater speaking into the handset of a black telephone bursts into my mind with such intensity I gasp. My hand jerks, and I spill drops of coffee all over the desk. It's so real, I feel like I have a live video feed in my head. I can't hear her, but I see her lips move when Shirley stops talking.

"Listen, Mrs. Sinclair – Martha –" Shirley stuffs tissues into my hands. I mop and dab and try to get the image out of my head but it won't go – if anything, it's becoming clearer and clearer, as if the signal's getting stronger and stronger. "Listen, no, this isn't Winnie - no, we don't know where she is…. Yes, that's right, she's missing. Uh, what?" She pauses, looks at me, and frowns. "What? Look, Mrs. Sinclair, I know you lost a baby and it's painful but you're not my story - no, I haven't replaced Winnie. I'll have her call you when she gets back to work."

"Casey, can I have a word with you?"

The new voice scares us both, but fortunately I've put my coffee down. I turn to see a skinny guy with ears like Alfred E. Neumann peering around a filing cabinet. Shirley hangs up and the image in my head goes dark, like a light bulb blowing out. It leaves me feeling like I've been punched. I look up at Alfred E, and see that on top of his rumpled corduroy jacket, he's got something that looks like a thick black scarf or a rope around his neck. The ends of the rope wave like snakes. A sick feeling spreads out from my solar plexus, and I feel all the coffee I've had this morning gurgle up the back of my throat. *I'm having a flashback.* That's the only explanation that makes sense, I decide. I break out into a cold sweat as my mouth fills saliva. I grab the edge of the desk and pull myself out of the chair, praying I don't hurl all over Shirley.

"Who the fuck are you?" Alfred stares down at me, as I clamp my jaws against the nausea.

"You got a men's room?" I manage.

Shirley nods, points, right, then left. I get to the men's room just in time to throw up into the porcelain bowl. I heave and heave until finally I am a spent quivering mess. I'm coming down with something, I tell myself. I must be getting sick from exhaustion. But as the seconds tick by, I feel better and better, as if I've purged something more than breakfast out of my system. By the time I stand up to splash water on myself, I'm feeling better than I have in quite a while. When I wipe my face in the mirror, I see *her* – the red-haired woman who met the other girl in front of Grand Central last night, almost like she was waiting for her – behind me. She meets my eyes with reproach in hers.

"Stay away from Savageux, Jack. You're not ready."

"What the fuck -?" I whip around. "Who the fuck are you?" My voice echoes in the empty room.

When I open the door, a bespectacled man gives me a cold look. "Who the fuck are you?" he sneers, as he shoves past me into the men's room.

I pause, gather myself, collect my thoughts. Something must be triggering flashbacks, I think. Maybe it's food poisoning. White Castle burgers sometimes don't agree with me, but I know I didn't stop for any last night.

Shirley and Alfred are standing in front of an open office doorway, yelling so loudly I can hear the argument floating across the tops of the cubicle maze. "I did clear it with you - I faxed it so you wouldn't even have to get your flabby ass out of bed."

"I approved the headline," he screams back. "Not this over-the-top rant -"

"We're a tabloid, Harry, we're supposed to go over the top. You want a retraction? You want me to say I'm sorry? Is that what you fucking want, Harry? Every word I wrote is fucking true. But for the suits upstairs, you want me to lay my head on the fucking block?"

"I'll write the retraction. You get your ass on the three o'clock train to New Jersey."

The entire newsroom falls silent. I decide that now would be a good time to leave. I start to edge around the room, Shirley's voice echoing off the flat-tiled ceiling, so it seems to come from everywhere at once. "What the fuck's in New Jersey?"

"Remember that aliens-stole-my-baby story Winnie was working on? It's yours now. I just had a call from the local Sheriff. They're digging up the baby and I want you there."

"Jesus Christ, that woman..." Shirley's jaw drops. "I don't want to go to New Jersey."

"Then you should've thought of that before you let your poison pen rip, Ms. Femme Nikita. You either put your ass on that train or clean out your desk." He lopes into an office and slams the door.

I glance around. The other workers are frozen in place. Shirley sees everyone looking, raises her chin, and stalks into Winnie's cubicle. I slink along the edge of the room, toward the elevators, doubly sure I shouldn't have come.

But just as I raise my hand to hit the down button, I hear Shirley cry, "Hey!" She looks as tired as I feel, but her eyes are kind, not scared or angry. "I always knew the coffee was poison. You okay?"

"Yeah – I must've had some bad food someplace. Thanks for the tour, though."

"I'm sorry you had to see that. Harry's just a shmuck." She pushes back her tumbled hair. "I still want to talk to you about what you saw." She presses a notebook and pen into my hands. "Give me a way to reach you and I'll call you, okay? I shouldn't be down in Jersey more than a couple of days – God, at least I hope it's not more than a couple of days. You ever been to the Jersey Pine Barrens, Jack?"

"No," I say. I don't think I can tell her much, but if it makes her feel better to have my number, I don't mind. As I start to write, I get another flash of the woman in the pink sweater and dizziness overwhelms me. I have to get away from this woman or I'm going to be sick again. I don't know why, but I am. *Get a grip, Jack.* "I've never been south of Hoboken."

"Brooklyn born and bred, huh?"

"I don't really know where I'm from. I'm adopted."

"No shit," she says. "So no idea at all from where?"

My father, who, according to my mother, just showed up with me one night, said I was left on the step of some church. But my mother didn't believe him. Like the other men he ran with, he had a woman on the side. My mother loved and hated me for the same reason – because she figured I was his by his girlfriend. "No," I say.

The elevator doors slide open. "Go, Jack." She pushes me toward the opening. "I'll call you –"

The elevator doors slide closed and once more I am eye to eye with the red-haired woman. "Who the hell are you?" I shout. She doesn't flinch. Her eyes remain sad, her face composed. "*What* the hell are you?"

"I'm trying to protect you, Jack," she says, just as the doors open behind me.

I glance over my shoulder to see a uniformed deliveryman eyeing me suspiciously. He steps in and moves to the furthest corner. I turn to face the doors. There's just the two of us, and no sign of the red-haired woman at all.

Chapter 5

stumble out of the elevator dizzy and disoriented. Lila works just a few blocks away. The thought of Lila steadies me, strengthens me. I decide to surprise her. I buy a bunch of flowers at the corner stall. As I pass newsstands, I look for a copy of *The Sun* because despite all that's happening, part of me is curious about what Shirley wrote that got her into so much trouble. I should've asked to read it, I think, because every single copy appears to have sold out at every newsstand I check. It's on the early side for lunch by the time I get to Lila's office, but I hope she can sneak away.

A feeling of being caged closes around me as I walk toward the somber banks of elevators. Other buildings bustle, but this one's always silent as a tomb. Lila says the lobby was designed to absorb the sound, supposedly with the intention of allowing the occupants to enjoy a deep quiet after the hustle of the busy streets. I think it's like walking into a mausoleum.

The elevator woman pretends not to recognize me. I hope Lila's happy when I tell her Shirley wants to talk to me again. I don't have to tell her why.

She is happy to see me, which surprises me. She gives me a kiss, takes the flowers, guides me back into the elevator and down to the coffee shop on the corner faster than I can say "Hi-honey."

"I'm so glad to see you," she says. She picks up my hand and holds it between both of hers. Her eyes are dancing and her cheeks are pink. "Just wait till I tell you."

"You got a raise?"

"No." She twitches her lips. "Even better."

"A promotion?"

"No," she shakes her head and her earrings dance. "You'll never guess. You know how we were talking just this morning about you getting a job writing, Jack? They announced a new position today – and look, it's a writing job, Jack. I've been trying to get you on the phone all morning. Look, I started typing a resume and everything –" From the pocket of her jacket, she pulls out a folded piece of paper and I am reminded of the letter in my dream.

"A position?" I repeat slowly as I unfold the paper. It's a resume – my resume, with a lot of blanks. "What is this? What kind of a position?"

"A position – a real job. Here, with the firm - as a copywriter. I know it's not exactly what you want to do, but Jack, the salary –" she glances over her shoulder. "I hear it's forty grand to start."

Forties are what we like to drink, I want to say, but I don't think she'd be amused. I scan the resume as a constriction spreads across my chest. I remember the thing I saw around Shirley's editor's neck.

"Forty, at least. Maybe more." Her cheeks are flushed rosy red. If I know Lila, she's already calculated not only the amount of my take-home pay, but how much we'll save from every paycheck. "Come on, Jack, don't you see? We don't have to keep doing this to ourselves – we can live another way. You realize that, don't you? It doesn't have to be this hard."

I finger the resume as I look up into the television monitor above the lunch counter, directly into the eyes of Nicholas Savageux. I want to throw the pages at the screen, because they're still playing the same fucking clip. How can nothing else have happened anywhere in the entire fucking world? I glance away and feel a shiver run down my spine. *I'm trying to protect you, Jack.*

Maybe I'm sick, really sick – like with a brain tumor. The idea of wearing a tie around my neck every day makes something howl like a wounded puppy deep inside. "But…but, Lila, I…I can't work forty hours and teach, and write, too, Lila. You know I can't."

"And I can't work sixty and keep us fed," she snaps. Her fingernail clicks on the table beside the paper, and I'm momentarily mesmerized by the contrast of the red crescent beside the stark white emptiness of my resume. "*And* keep us housed *and* clothed while I pay off all the goddamn bills you ran up."

"I thought we were doing fine," I mumble.

"No, Jack." There's a grim finality in her tone that makes my head snap up. "*You're* doing fine. *We're* not doing fine – not at all."

"But…but Lila, I'm sure they're going to offer me something full-time… I just have to get another semester or two of teaching under my belt, and a few more poems published… it's not going to take much longer-"

"How long do you expect me to wait?" She glances over her shoulder. "I'm tired, Jack. I'm twenty-six years old and I feel like I'm eighty-six. I can't keep doing this – the bills are starting to be more than I can bear. If you don't start to bring in some decent money soon, we're not just not going to get what we've worked for; we're going to lose everything we got. So here, you take that resume, what there is of it. You fill in the blanks, best you can. What you can't, I'll help you make up."

The wolf-child howls again in the pit of my soul and I feel sick, abandoned, as if I'm suddenly alone in this crowded sea of sound and smells. My stomach roils and I wish I'd stayed home and taken that nap. I fold the paper and put it in my pocket. "Look, you know I'll get more driving hours in the summer- can't we talk about this later, after I've had some sleep? I came to eat with you – not fight."

We eat in silence and when the waitress brings our tab, I reach to pick it up.

Lila stops my hand. "You'll blow your whole week's allowance," she says. "It's on me."

"Lila, I can take you out to lunch –"

"No." She looks at me sadly as she slaps a twenty-dollar bill down on the table. "You can't. Now, isn't that a lousy way to live?"

She's got me there. The whole way home the idea gnaws at me – *like a worm in the bud* – every time I feel the edge of the resume pushing into the thin flannel of my shirt. That's a line from Shakespeare but I can't remember the play. I stare into the bleak faces of the people around me. The bus reeks of old clothes and exhaust, and it pummels us in our seats as it lurches through traffic. *This is what she does every day,* I think. *I don't want to do this.*

"Of course you don't, Jack." I hear her voice behind me.

I jerk my head around to look, and the red-haired woman smiles back in the very second that the driver slams on the brakes. Everyone almost falls into the aisles and when I look back, she's gone. I glance down into the flat black eyes of Nicholas Savageux, on the front page of *The Sun.*

Another lurch conceals my gasp. It's just the front and back pages – someone has taken the rest. Gingerly, as if it could be diseased, I pick it up. Most of the photograph is grainy, and a little blurred, but Savageux's face isn't. That's what makes it so startling. There's just a couple lines of text under the picture – teasers, leading into the meat of the main article that's buried deep in the pages I don't have. But it's the last couple words on the page that catch my eye, the opening fragment of the next sentence: *According to a statement issued immediately by Savageux's attorneys, Armstrong… cont'd page 5.*

Suddenly, I am desperate to read the rest of the sentence. Armstrong, Henderson, McPherson & Sinclair is the name of the firm Lila works for. There is no page five, so I can't see the full name. The constriction in my chest starts to feel less like a rope and more like a tentacle.

Get a grip, Jack. A woman's backside pushes into my face as she gets off, but I hardly notice. How do I explain, let alone understand, the rising sense of panic that I feel? There's got to be at least a dozen other law firms in New York that begin with Armstrong. It's a common name – the odds that Lila's firm could represent Savageux in any capacity at all are surely too high to be possible.

But if it is… could it be possible she's met him?

The bus rumbles into a steady pulse that lulls my head against the rain-streaked glass. I feel myself drift into that drowsy gray twilight I perfected in the long hours when I was alone while my mother worked, too afraid to really sleep. I open my eyes and see a billboard of flame red roses splayed out before my eyes.

Nothing says I love you like roses, says the billboard.

Unless there's a worm in the bud...In the center, I see a splotch of angry graffiti that looks, as we slide past, exactly like a fat black worm. I decide I need a nap.

The guy at the newsstand nearest my apartment tells me *The Sun* never got delivered that day. "Whole day was a mess," he says. "We got the fucking Jersey papers this morning. Can you imagine? Like we give a shit what happens in Newark. Guy pulls up, starts pulling papers off the truck – thank God I had the sense to check what he was flinging at me. Asshole acted like he didn't believe me – I says to him, can't you fucking read?"

Stay away from Savageux. The sunlight glints off passing cars and makes my eyes water. I spend an extra fifteen minutes prowling the neighborhood for *The Sun* and not one store or stand has a copy. I grind my teeth together and try to think how to find out. I could call Shirley, I think. Or wait for her to call me. *Or just ask Lila*.

At home, I slide back into my girl-dream the minute my head hits the pillow. This time I remember my raincoat, and I make it into the room where Bruce and the band are waiting. They invite me to sit down, have coffee, and soon we are joking and talking like old friends. But I still need the tickets, because all I have is this letter.

Bruce offers me tickets – of course he offers me tickets – but I demur, saying I have a letter. I reach into my pocket and pull the letter out, smooth it on the table for the Boss to read. He looks at me, shakes his head. "Honey," he says, "this thing isn't getting you into anywhere."

I look down and to my horror see it's my resume.

I wake up in a cold sweat with Lila standing over me. "Have a nice nap?" A white paper flutters from her fingers, lands on my chest and floats to the floor as I groan and struggle out of the dream. My life and my girl-dreams have finally intersected, I think.

"Hi," I say.

"Must be nice," she says. She strips off her clothes in three long angry swipes, pulls on sweats then yanks the overflowing hamper from the closet.

"All hell broke out at work this afternoon – I come home late and here you are napping. Must be *real* nice."

"Lila, I'm sorry –" The laundry is supposed to be my responsibility.

She holds up her hand. With the other, she lugs the hamper out the door she's propped open with one foot. "Don't bother, Jack. Just don't bother."

The coffee from the morning is burned and bitter, but I heat up a cup anyway and gulp it down lukewarm to try and clear my head. It's after eight-thirty. It bugs her when I don't get the chores done.

I start to follow her down to the laundry room, when a letter on the heap beside her purse and raincoat catches my eye. It's from the Chairman of the English Department, Matthew Proulx. I've never been his favorite. A finger of foreboding traces down my spine. I'm afraid to pick up the letter, afraid to touch it, even and I don't understand why. The smooth white envelope feels greasy. I don't like the thin film I feel it leave on my fingertips. Lila comes back to find me sniffing it.

She stares at me, shuts the door, stands in the tiny foyer with her arms crossed. "You going to open that or snack on it?"

"Just a little scared to open it," I say, trying to lighten my tone. "Maybe they want to revoke my contract."

She actually looks hopeful and I hate her for that.

Savagely, I rip open the letter. What I read staggers me, makes me collapse on to the chair. This can't be happening, I think. Either I'm going crazy, or I really am being hunted.

"What's it say?" Lila asks. There's an edgy note of triumph in her voice, on her face and I realize with a sickening pang that she wants me to be kicked out of teaching so I'm forced to take the job she wants me to take.

Where's my Lila gone who believed in me? "They're offering me a contract for the summer," I say. "On Cape Cod. They want me to work with a group of inner city youth. It... uh... it sounds great." Too great, in fact.

She reaches for the letter, reads it and looks up. "So what's wrong? You look like you seen a ghost."

"There's nothing wrong," I stutter, jamming my hands in my pockets. I don't even want to take it back. Nothing wrong but the name of the foundation that's funding the program: the Margaret Savageux Sinclair Charitable Trust.

The phone rings and Lila picks it up. "Hello? Oh, sure, I do. How are you, Dr. Proulx?"

I glance up at the clock as she hands me the receiver. It's the chairman of the department. "Dr. Proulx?"

"Jack? Hello, Jack." The voice oozes into my ear, smooth and rich as butterscotch caramel. "We missed you at the meeting today, Jack."

"I threw up today, Professor." It pleases me to be able to say that. "I thought it was better to stay home and keep my bugs to myself."

There's a pause for a couple of beats and I know I've needled him. "Well, absolutely, Jack...but when you're better I want you to come in and see me. You did receive our letter, didn't you?"

"Just now."

"So you read about the grant? This is quite an opportunity and we feel there's no one more deserving."

I'm drowning, I think, and I don't know why. My palms are starting to sweat and I'm getting sick to my stomach again. But oddly, all I want to do is run into the street, into the fresh night air. I want to go somewhere, anywhere, I can breathe. "Dr. Proulx, I gotta go – I'm not feeling too well -" I slump down on the couch, and hang up with a click.

She puts the letter down on the table. "Did you just hang up on the department chair?"

I wipe the sweat off my hands. "Look, Lila, I did throw up today, okay? I think I've got a bug. I'm not trying to give you or anyone else a hard time. I just feel like shit."

She looks at me, eyes narrowed, and I can tell she doesn't believe me. Someone or something put it in her head I'm using. Acting anything less than reasonable isn't going to convince her otherwise. I pull myself up. "Can we talk about this later? I don't want to be late. We still need the cash, right?"

She stares at me steadily. I feel cold all over. "Okay, Jack. Sure. We'll talk when you get home."

Chapter 6

I leave the apartment feeling hopeless and disoriented, like I've stepped inside a life that isn't mine anymore. I hope whosever life it belongs to shows up soon. I can't think of anyone to talk to about how I feel. The therapists at the health center – all of whom know me on a first name basis - will recommend anxiety medication, or tell me I'm afraid of success, because after all, most people in my position should be jumping at the chance for either of one. A job at Armstrong Henderson or a summer on the Cape hardly sounds like part of some masterwork of evil.

Maybe Lila would take me seriously if I offered to take a drug test, though there probably isn't a test yet for a drug so new its effects aren't known.

On the way to work I try without success to find a copy of *The Sun*. I wish I'd remember to ask Lila if her employer is the same Armstrong mentioned in Shirley's article. Every time I think about it, I feel a roil of nausea. It's the only thing that keeps me from sticking my hands into trash cans.

For once, I get the best car in the fleet. There's a theatre festival the next few nights. I head toward Broadway and thankfully, I'm busy, hustling back and forth between theatres and restaurants and hotels. For a while it all seems so normal, I relax. I was just overtired, I tell myself. Now that I had that sleep, I'll be able to talk to Lila rationally.

Maybe a job writing ad copy wouldn't be so bad. And who couldn't use a summer on the Cape? I look carefully at the faces of my fares, all sleek and unlined. The back seat traps clouds of their scent, and they glow as if they possess some secret inner knowing that eludes me.

At some point, I'm not sure when, I realize I'm tracing and retracing the same route, over and over again. So I start to pay attention.

It has to be a series of random coincidences, I tell myself. It's just that the theatres are all in the same general direction, the hotels in another. Then I realize there seems to be a pattern to my destinations. Theatre, restaurant, theatre, hotel. Theatre, restaurant, theatre, hotel. Every third fare, however, it switches, and becomes restaurant, hotel. I realize I'm describing a spiral, circling in then out. The third time it's due to turn into restaurant-hotel, I decide to see if I'm right, if there really is a pattern.

In front of Tavern-on –the-Green, a tourist couple spills into the back seat. As we pull away from the curb, an image of the Pierre Hotel on 62nd and Fifth flashes in front of me. I glance up, meet the man's eyes, and instantly know that he's hiding something from his wife, something she already suspects. "Did you say the Pierre, sir?"

"You didn't say yet - honey, how did he know where we want to go?" The woman's nasal twang bites through my haze. She's wearing as much makeup as any of the vampires last night, but at least she's made up to look alive. All the suspicion she already feels for her husband turns itself on me and she looks back at me as if I had two heads.

"Seems to be a popular place tonight, ma'am," I say. We weave in and out of traffic and that's when I start to notice the numbers on license plates, on street signs, on awnings and buses. 438 – my mother was born in April of 1938. 14911 – my father's cell block number. 87 – the number of the public school down the street. 603 – my wedding anniversary. 8066 – the last four digits of my first telephone number. Every number I glance at has some meaning for me. A pattern, a pattern… I'm seeing a pattern but I can't figure out what it is or what it means.

My scalp begins to crawl, my palms begin to sweat. Get a grip, Jack, I tell myself over and over. Everyone has associations with numbers. I lean back and close my eyes at the next red light.

The man leans forward, taps on the glass. "Driver? Driver, isn't this –"

I look up and see I'm about to drive past the hotel. "Sorry, sir." I slam on the brake, and the woman gives me another look. *Is he on something?* I can hear her think it as clearly as if she'd spoken the words aloud. I flush. "Sorry, ma'am. It's eight-fifty, sir."

A uniformed doorman leans down to open the door, the man turns to put bills in my hand. A light rain is starting to fall, the people on the sidewalks are putting up umbrellas. The drops sparkle on the doorman's gold epaulets. I glance up and across the street, a couple comes out of Central Park. I blink and take a closer look. Heading in my direction, is Nicholas Savageux himself.

There's no doubt in my mind it's him. He's moving with the same effortless glide as last night, his eyes reflect the red and yellow light. At first I think he's dressed in a cape of some kind, but then I realize it's just the way the shadows gather and swirl around him. He's not dressed like a vampire this time, just wearing a dark blazer, a lighter turtleneck, and he could be anyone – but he's not. He's holding the hand of a woman who is easily the most striking platinum blonde I've ever seen.

She points right at me. His head swivels around, our eyes meet and I feel a jolt of some kind, right down the back of my spine. The first girl from the other night - the first of the Three Weird Sisters, as I'm starting to think of that strange trio - the one with the spiked maroon hair, steps out from behind the couple. She sees me, too, because she smiles and points at me, too. The bills in my hand drift to the seat. Out of the corner of my eye, I see that the doorman has noticed the three of them as well, and is waving them to my cab. I can feel myself getting nauseous. "It can't be him," I mutter. "That's just not possible."

"Of course it's possible, Jack." The mysterious woman with the long red hair – the third Weird Sister – is sitting beside me in the front seat. The next minute, I see her standing outside the cab. She kicks the tire so hard the whole car rocks under the impact. There's a loud pop, and the hood sags as the tire deflates. "What the fuck-?" My mouth drops open.

The doorman's fawning smile fades into a snarl. "Get that thing outta here." He slams the door so hard the car shudders again.

"How the fuck do you want me to do that?" I start, but he's already opening the door of the cab pulled up behind me, gesturing to the couple and the girl who's trailing after them like a stray puppy. I almost expect to see her on a leash. Savageux turns his head, and glances directly into my eyes as he passes. Again our eyes meet, and I feel a sense that is more than connection.

I know you.

Recognition burns between us and in that instant I feel a fleeting shock of power. *I* have what *he* needs. I feel wanted in a way that's so potent it's sexual. His eyes sear all the way through mine with something that feels like a promise. I feel them burning into me long after he disappears into the night. As ridiculous as it sounds, I feel like I've been *chosen*. I have what *he* needs. It's one thing to be wanted, I think. It's another to be *needed*. My knees feel weak, I can feel myself tremble with a kind of power so unfamiliar I'm not even sure that's what to call it.

"You have to get away from Savageux, Jack." The woman's there again, sitting in the back of my cab, and then she's gone.

Another doorman opens the front door, an older man whose lined face is only marginally more sympathetic. "You gotta move this boat, buddy – I got some boys coming up from the basement. They'll help you push it around the corner – you gotta spare, I assume?"

But of course there's no spare. Shortman is less than happy to hear from me. I settle down behind the wheel for a good long wait. I'd hoped tonight was going to be as good for tips, if not better, than last night, but I can see I'm going to be wrong.

It's still early – shows are still letting out, clubs are getting busy. Happy laughing couples dodge the puddles gleaming in the street lights, groups of tourists weave around each other against the backdrop of old bricks. All of them, it seems, are smiling. All of them, it seems, want a cab. A dime for everyone who points then looks at me in disappointment would make up for all the tips I'm losing. I think of all the money I'm not making, of how unhappy Lila is going to be. Maybe writing ad copy wouldn't be bad. Wouldn't be bad, I tell myself. What am I thinking? Wouldn't it be fun? Another salary would sure make things easier.

Maybe I really am wasting my life writing poetry.

A sudden downpour sends a group congregating beneath the mostly-bare branches of the trees along the park wall. Despite the rain, they're all laughing and joking, happy as an I-love-New-York commercial. They gleam in the light and I think about the shiny people I've been ferrying around tonight.

Lila and I could be like them. I imagine us making out in the backseat of a taxi between Tavern on-the-Green and the Pierre. Let's not go home tonight, I can hear myself whisper into the perfumed valley behind her ear. Her eyes glitter and the image dissolves as a car splashes past me.

I realize that every place I've pulled up to tonight has been a place we've never even considered crossing the threshold of. I wonder what it would be like to have money to spare when the bills are paid. As far back as I can remember, there was never enough. I think about wearing a shirt and tie every day, how ties always make me feel like there's a rope around my neck. Sometimes I swear they tighten on their own. But maybe it wouldn't be so bad once I got used to it.

I can see myself leaning back in a black leather chair, throwing a lime-green tennis ball against a white ceiling, cute little ad jingles running through my mind. My collar's open, my tie loosely knotted, my legs are propped up on a wide, glass-topped desk. I have a rolodex, of course, and a phone… a big computer monitor so I don't get eyestrain. And plants, I think, a lot of plants because… well, because I'd like a lot of plants. There's a nice woman just outside my door who fields my calls and schedules my lunches and hair cuts.

I've got the walls painted a soothing shade of cream and the rug flecked with touches of blue when it occurs to me that law firms – at least law firms like Armstrong Henderson - don't advertise. Why would they need someone to write ad copy? I must've misunderstood what Lila said the job was, I think. She has to have it wrong. I feel the fantasy go pop. There's no way they need a writer like me with no legal background at all. I feel around for my notebook, and then I remember I was in such a hurry I left without it, so I can't even use this time to write. I feel useless and stupid and frustrated. What am I doing, I ask myself. Maybe I'm not right for a law firm, but there must be a thousand writing jobs in New York. Lila's right. We don't have to live like this. There is a better way. I slam my hand on the steering wheel. A steady job writing anything would have to be better than this. After all, does the world really need another wanna-be poet?

"What makes you so sure it doesn't, Jack?"

I jump so high, I bang my head on the roof of the cab. "Jesus fucking Christ," I blurt, as I turn around to see the woman with the long red hair sitting in the back seat of the cab. "You don't need a cab to get around, do you?" In the shadows her eyes are dark and I can't quite see the color but her teeth flash white as she chuckles softly. "Come on, lady, level with me. What the hell are you? A flashback? A ghost? I know you're not real – and how the fuck do you know my name?"

"I know your name because I can read it on your license. Mine's Dougless Woodwright and I'm trying to protect you."

"From Nicholas Savageux?"

"Yes."

I tap my fingers on the steering wheel and let out a long breath as I try to think about what to ask next. Dougless is a name I haven't heard outside obscure English poetry, and while she's told me her name she hasn't answered my question. But whatever it is she might be, I can't take her seriously because I really can't believe that someone like Nicholas Savageux would give a rats' tail hair about anyone like me. I twist around in the seat and I grip the door handle in case she lunges at me with her shiny white teeth. "I'm just a speck of fly shit on a camel's ass to someone like Savageux. Why would he even care I exist?"

"Because he does, Jack." She leans forward, her eyes big and wide, the color of oak leaves in autumn. "You know he cares - you felt for yourself how much, just now. I know you did. I could feel it, too. Everyone on the street did. You have to believe me – Savageux's a demon, and he *is* after you."

I'm not admitting anything to a hallucination, but for a split second, I'm back in that moment when my eyes connected with Savageux's, and I feel that shudder of desire, that thrill of being chosen. He wanted *me*, I think. "I'm not buying a word you say until you tell me what you are."

"Think of me as your guardian angel, Jack."

And then I remember. I remember where I've seen her before. It was a long time ago, I was a kid, maybe five, six. Coming home from school one day, I found a dead junkie sprawled across the landing. I had to step over the body to get to my door. The red-haired woman was bending over the body. She looked up at me, and I remember looking into those eyes, those very same eyes.

I feel the blood drain from my face. "I remember you," I say. All the references to bodies, to death that I've heard all day tumble through my mind triggered by the memory of that terrible day – *gruesome discovery….Jane Doe… pooling vomit.* "Oh my God, I *do* remember you." I grip the handle with all my strength because I really do think I'm going to puke.

The bang on my trunk sends me into the roof again. "Yo, buddy? Sorry we took so long – bad night, you know?"

I glance to one side into the dark brown eyes of the tow-truck driver, then back at my companion. She's gone. Of course.

▲

I have an imaginary friend *named Dougless. She says I should run away because a demon who pretends to be a vampire is out to get me.* Imagining the look on Lila's face if I tell her what happened tonight makes me snigger maniacally as I try to stifle the laugh. In the two AM stillness, the bus driver and I are alone. He raises his eyes and looks at my reflection in the mirror. "You okay, buddy?"

"Oh, yeah," I say. "Something funny happened at work tonight - not the kind of thing I can tell my wife, though. Just thinking of the look on her face if I told her." Again, it makes me snicker.

"Hah," the driver says. "Well, tell me."

For a second I'm stunned. Tell him? I can't possibly tell him. But he's looking at me, expectantly, as the seconds crawl by and the light stays red. 2:22 read the red numbers on the bank across the street. "I-I think it was one of those things where you had to be there," I say.

"Aw, try me," he says. "Believe me, I can use a laugh." The light turns green, he takes his gaze off me and onto the road. I see his entire body behind the steering wheel reflected in the huge windshield. His expression is empty, hard. The shadows of the streetlights shift and I look into the reflection of his eyes, two pinpoint holes of light that broaden into a tunnel. The vision widens and becomes a sagging double bed covered in pink chenille, rumpled on only one side, then tilts to a pair of worn women's loafers covered in dust, woven together by cobwebs. I blink, but not before I feel every hour of his loss as if it were mine.

It slams into my body with a palpable weight that makes me gasp and open my mouth. To my own amazement, I hear a story pour out that bears no resemblance to anything that happened to me tonight. Instead it's a lurid combination of every taxi story I can remember telling Lila. I sprinkle it with snippets of pure fantasy, weaving it all together into some Technicolor hodgepodge that somehow makes the driver laugh so hard tears seep down his cheeks. "Naw, man, you're right," he says, as we mercifully roll to my stop. "You're right - don't ever tell your old lady that one. But, man – hah, you made my night with that."

The doors belch open and I stumble out. He waves as he pulls away and I can see he's still chuckling. Well, good for him. At least that's one of us.

"Not many see what you see, Jack," says a soft voice at my elbow.

"Why can I only see you when other people aren't around?" My elbow slams into the bus kiosk, sending a lightning bolt of pain up my arm.

"Because only you can see me, Jack."

"Lila already thinks I'm on some fucking drug." For the first time, I see her – Dougless – full length, and I peer at her in the neon-shrouded light. She's covered in a dark shawl or cloak, but underneath, I see the ruffle of a calf-length skirt, and a pair of shoes that look like low moccasins of some kind. There's something odd about them that I can't immediately recognize and don't have time to consider, because her words stop me cold.

"She's right, Jack. That's why you need to get away."

I glance up and down the avenue in both directions. Not a single soul's in sight, and I remember the other night at Grand Central, where I first saw her right before a murder. I back away. "Look, lady – you can just leave me alone. I'm not on any drug, I haven't done anything wrong, and I'm not leaving town. So just –"

"Jack, please –" She takes a single step toward me, arm outstretched.

"Stay away from me," I yell as I sprint down the street.

Chapter 7

At school there's a message in my in-box that Casey McGuire of *The Sun* called for me and will try me later at home. I'm walking down the hall fingering the message when the department secretary, Mary Ferlinghetti-no-relation, calls after me from the doorway of Dr. Proulx's office.

"Jack! Hey, Jack, is that you?" She beckons furiously, then scurries a few paces to intercept me. "Dr. Proulx wants to talk to you." She nods at the message in my hand. "He's a little concerned, Jack. Just so you know."

"A little concerned? Or flipped-out furious?" I can't believe anyone would care, but he's only hated me since I mispronounced his name my entire first semester. I had no idea how to pronounce it, so I mangled it into "prole-licks." Once I realized it annoyed him, I have to admit, I continued to do it until Mary took me aside and warned me I was in danger of having my contract for the following semester cancelled.

"That's a tabloid, Jack. You do realize that, don't you?" She looks at me over her bifocals as if I were a slow five year old. "I think he wants to know why they want to talk to you."

I follow her down the hall, letting her lead me into the lion's lair. She precedes me in, hands fluttering, lips pursed like a nervous little bird. "Here he is, Dr. Proulx."

She pats my arm as she passes, as if to reassure me, but the look on the Great Man's face is anything but reassuring, as he peruses the red-marked paper before him. He places the cap on the pen, then the pen on the paper with deep deliberation, before he sits back with a sigh. "How're you feeling today, Jack?" The eyes behind the steepled fingertips appraise me when he finally deigns to raise them. "You do look a bit peaked. Perhaps you caught the bug that's going around?"

"Yeah," I say. "Maybe." I don't feel all that bad. I had a solid five hours of sleep after I got home last night and I feel better than I've felt in days. "I feel a lot better though now. Mary said you wanted to talk to me?"

The Great Man looks at me so hard I wonder if he's trying to burn a hole in my forehead. The paper in my pocket feels like it's burning a hole in my jeans and I wonder what Shirley wants. He takes a breath, hesitates, and tries again. No one finds it easy to ask about something that's none of someone's business, I guess.

"You know, Jack, we here in the department – we long ago recognized your talent. But..." He pauses and raises his eyes to the ceiling. It's the same gesture I've seen a thousand times at the obligatory weekly meetings. The implication seems to be that he's got a direct link to some kind of Higher Power. "I happened to overhear Mary talking to someone who identified herself as a reporter for that tabloid – I believe they call themselves *The Sun*, Jack? Would you mind telling me what that's about?"

I want to ask him why he cares so much that a vein is pulsating on his forehead. It looks remarkably like a purple worm – *a worm in the bud* – clinging to his temple. I've never seen that before.

Don't tell him. The voice sounds like Dougless's, but it's inside my head. There's an ugly reddish light around his head that's murky, shot through with darker threads, like a tangled cobweb. I blink and it fades out, then comes back momentarily stronger, then blinks out completely. "I-I guess I won't know until I talk to her."

His look is as sour as the feeling churning in my gut. "You know, Jack, we're aware of the challenges you've overcome in your short life – and they've been significant, not one of us doubts that. We're all proud of you that you've been able to wrestle such enormous demons... and succeed. We all believe in you, Jack. We're all rooting for you." *So don't fuck it up.*

His gray eyes are hooded, but I can feel his predatory stare. *What big eyes you have, Grandmother. What a long nose.* I think about telling him the truth and decide that in this case, the truth is not only unlikely to set me free, but may well get me locked up for overnight observation. So I spread my hands, and give him the innocent look I perfected a long time ago. "Uh…look, Dr. Proulx. I'm sure it's nothing. You know I drive a cab? I picked this lady up the other night. I have no idea why she wants to talk to me." I don't quite understand why the vein continues to palpitate visibly, but I'm watching it throb in time to my words. "I really doubt it's about the college."

His face relaxes infinitesimally, but I wonder if that's all it is. There's an edgy urgency to the way he's still looking at me. I wonder what the connection is between the department, the Margaret Savageux Foundation, and the Great Man.

"Dr. Proulx, I have the Bursar on line one." Mary's voice cackles over the phone's intercom.

"I'll call him back, Mary." The vein bulges and the skin around it flushes an ugly red.

"He has a lot of questions about the preliminary budget you submitted."

"We submitted a final, didn't we, Mary?"

"Dr. Proulx, all I can tell you is the Bursar says he needs to talk to you."

I jump up, blessing the Bursar from the bottom of my soul, afraid the Great Man's vein might pop. "Please don't be worried, Dr Proulx. I'd never say anything bad about a place that's given me so many chances. I'll come back later – we'll talk more." I don't wait to see whether or not he believes me.

I forget how petulant Proulx is when he perceives his dignity has suffered some affront. He refuses to see me for the rest of the day, even though I hang conspicuously around between both sections of Freshman Comp. When I finish my last class, my upper-level course in Milton, Blake and Yeats, I do my best to charm Mary, but while she's friendly, it's all for naught. The Great Man's door remains closed.

Consequently I don't get home till after five, to find Lila sitting at the kitchen table in a scrupulously cleaned up apartment. She's obviously been home for hours. The first words out of her mouth are, "Where the fuck've you been?"

"At school." I'm bewildered by her hostility. She shouldn't even be home. "Something wrong? I'm really glad to see you, too, honey."

"I took half a sick day."

"You did what?" Lila doesn't even take sick days when she's sick. She is of the school that dictates one goes to Work no matter how deadly the disease. Personally, I think it's because she believes that the more coworkers she infects, the more opportunities for an astute and diligent employee to get ahead. It's germ warfare, on a micro scale. "Are you okay?" Maybe she's sick and that's why she has this idea in her head I've taken some kind of drug. She has a brain tumor and she's going to die.

*She doesn't have a brain tumor, but she **is** going to die.*

I'm watching her mouth move and her head bob but I don't hear anything above the burning throb in my solar plexus shuddering in my bones. *She is going to die and there isn't a thing I can do about it.* I slink into the chair, pick up her hand, press it between both mine. She feels warm and solid and I can't even imagine a world without Lila in it. Surely it would have to be a whole different world, a whole different time. "Say that again," I manage, as I pick up her hand and press a kiss into her palm.

Impatiently, she shakes me off. "Are you listening to me? Did you hear a word I said?" She bangs a fist on the table. "Sometimes, Jack, I don't think you're even on the same planet as the rest of us. Could you just pay attention?"

"Sure," I say. This must be really bad. I feel helpless as a broken rag doll slumped against the chair.

"Stop looking at me like you think I'm going to die, for Christ's sake. I'm not sick. Didn't you hear that part?"

I sit up, bewildered and confused by the impressions swirling around my head. "What's wrong, then?"

"I want to take you shopping."

"Shopping?"

"For a suit. An outfit, a couple outfits, really. My friend Dolly up in Trusts has a brother who owns a store in Queens – she said Louie could get you fixed up real nice – for less than a thousand bucks."

"You want to spend a thousand dollars on clothes? For me? Are you sure you're okay?"

"They're interviewing, Jack. For the job. Remember? The one I told you about?"

"Yeah…uh, Lila – what makes you think…I don't even have a resume and I –"

"Yeah, you do."

"I do?"

"You think you're the only one who learned how to write in high school, Mr. Brilliant? Maybe I can't spin shit together the way you can, but I can put sentences together into paragraphs. So, like, you know how you write me all those poems for our anniversaries and stuff? Well, I wrote you a resume."

"It's not our anniversary yet." My palms start to sweat. I wonder if this is the way mouse feels as the trap swings down on the back of his head and I tell myself this is all Dougless's fault. If she – whatever she is – hadn't put this idea in my head I had to get away, surely I wouldn't feel like this.

"If you get this job, Jack, by the time our anniversary does roll around, you'll have a paycheck – a real paycheck. And you know what, your first paycheck - it's yours. You take it, spend it any way you want. Buy your wife a real anniversary present – you know, the kind that comes in a real little box with a real big bow?" She smiles, and licks her lips. It reminds me of how Proulx looked at me. *What big teeth you have, Grandmother.*

"Lila, what makes you think I'm even going to get an interview, let alone get hired?"

"Cause you got an interview – day after tomorrow at four." As my mouth drops open, she continues, "See after I finished your resume, I walked it over to my friend Loretta in HR, and I explained how not only are you the cutest up-and-coming writer in all five boroughs, you really deserved a chance.

And since I've bailed her ass out so many times even I've lost count, she scheduled you in, no questions asked."

"With who?"

"I don't know who, exactly. One of the partners, I guess. And the HR guy – Gervais. He's nice. Just remember he'd stab you in the back before he's finished his first coffee if he had to, but he's nice."

"Sounds real nice."

She looks up at the clock. "The store closes at eight tonight. If we leave now, we can get there by six, six-thirty. I called ahead with your general size and shape, and they said they'd have a few things picked out. We can be home by nine."

"But I…What about work?"

"I already called Shortman, told him you were sick. He agreed." She rolls her eyes. "That's a joke, Jack. He gave you the night off. I told him you might be a getting real job. He said about time."

The thoughts are spiraling around in my head again. I try to figure out what question to ask first, since they all seem likely to spill out at once. "Lila- this job. You say it's writing – what kind of writing?"

"Copywriting."

"You keep saying that, but what kind of copywriting? What kind of stuff? Law firms don't advertise –"

"Big law firms publish stuff." She raises her chin. "They need stuff written all the time."

"Yeah, briefs and motions and shit like that. What do they want someone like *me* to write?"

"Articles and stuff, Jack. Our partners are multi-published. They don't have time to write the first drafts. Usually it's an associate, or maybe a paralegal like me. But that takes away from billable time, so I guess they've decided to hire someone like you to do the first drafts, and then a partner will do the edits, and…"

"Take the credit."

"What do you care who gets the credit? The firm doesn't get paid for most of the shit - it's like charity, you know, so they can contribute to law journals and such. That's how they get their names out there, Jack. It's marketing, but not selling. You get it?"

What I think I get makes me nervous and queasy. She's looking at me so eagerly, with such desire to please. But under the coral on her cheeks, under the brown shadow on her eyes, I see the glint of something hard. It's time, she's saying without saying it. She can't continue to carry the entire burden alone – the minimum payment we worked out with the credit agency is more than some people's rent. I owe Lila, I think. I should be thinking of some line from poetry, from literature or at least a song, but my mind is a gray blank. "Yeah," I say finally, because she's expecting an answer. "I think I do."

The phone rings just as I'm turning the key in the lock. Lila tugs on my arm. "Let the machine get it."

But I know it's Shirley, so I twist the key and push the door open. "Let me get it."

"Come *on*, Jack –"

I hold up one hand while I lift the receiver with the other. "Hello?"

"Jack? Finally. God, I think I made a pest of myself with your wife – I even told her I wasn't into boys, but listen – I think you gotta come to Devil's Door."

"What?" Lila is standing in the doorway, lips pursed, tapping her foot. She's not looking at me and I know she forgot to tell me deliberately. "Shirley, I can't –"

"What if I told you I found your long-lost mother?"

"What?"

"I'm not kidding, Jack. I think I know where you came from."

Leave, Jack. Leave now. "I can't leave now," I say over the echo in my head. "And – and Shirley, with all due respect, my father said I was found on the door of some church in Brooklyn – Sts. Anthony and Jude's, I think it was." I wink at Lila. That's a Catholic joke. "I don't think anyone came from New Jersey to leave me in Brooklyn, Shirley. I mean I appreciate you're thinking of me but, really –"

Lila's making gestures across her throat and tapping her watch.

"Really, Jack – you remember there was a woman who called while you were at my office yesterday? She described you, right down to the fact you got sick. She says you're her son, Jack. She was right about the baby, you know."

"What baby?"

Lila's eyes bug out of her head. "There's a baby?"

"No," I say to her, "no babies – it's the story Shirley's working on – it's about a baby that disappeared, right, Shirley?"

"Yeah, right. And the mother thinks you're the baby."

"The mother thinks I'm her baby." I say this to Lila with a straight face and she bursts out laughing. "Shirley, that sounds too crazy to be believed."

"She *knew* things about you – she described *you*, she knew you got sick, she knew you ate a doughnut. Would you at least call her? Talk to her? Please?"

"Are you coming, Jack?" Lila's arms are folded across her chest.

"Shirley, I gotta go."

"Bye, Jack." She hangs up and I feel like I've been slapped.

"You *are not* fucking responsible for every fruit cake that crumbles into your life, Jack Chance. Do you understand that?" Lila takes my arm, drags me down the hall. "You have to get out of this fantasy crap. That's what's wrong with you, I think. All this working nights and teaching days – it's too much. No wonder that woman writes for a tabloid – she's loony as a 'toon. If you don't stop this nonsense, you're going to end up crazy as her."

"Why didn't you tell me she called?" I ask as we reach the street.

Lila shrugs. "I knew she'd call back."

Shirley doesn't know what nerve she's struck. I guess every adopted kid wonders. It's natural, I guess. Who doesn't want to know who they look like, which side of the family has the blue eyes, the curly hair? In my family, I wasn't the only one who wondered.

I think it drove my mother crazy. She thought I was my father's kid, by some *gomar*. After he went to prison, she started dressing up and going out late at night, where the men and their girlfriends congregated at the local bars. Sometimes she came home drunk, but she never came home with a man. I know why. She wasn't looking for a man. She was looking for a woman who looked like me.

I don't know what she intended to do if she ever found such a person. The drinking destroyed her liver and she died when I was sixteen. I don't think she ever believed I was a genuine foundling, but I never felt connected to the man who called himself my father any more than I felt connected to her. I tried to explain this to her once, but all I got was a horrified stare and a stone-cold silence.

I watch myself in the mirror as the tailor extols the breadth of my shoulders, the thinness of my waist. Poverty does that to you, I want to say. Eat an egg and an English muffin for dinner every night and see how low your weight can go.

I can't stop seeing the face of the woman in the pink sweater in New Jersey. She looks out of the tailor's three-sided mirrors; she's in the faces of the older women browsing through the racks, the sales clerks on the floor. How could a series of random coincidences connect me to a mother I've never even thought to look for? At least she's replaced most thoughts of Dougless my imaginary friend.

Don't do this, Jack. Leave the city. Leave now. I bite my cheek till it bleeds. The sting brings me back to the dusty store that sells men's *furnishings*, as men's clothes are apparently called by finer shoppes like this one run by Louie. I like Louie. He's used to ignoring bossy women in a way that's genial enough so they don't feel insulted. He communicates with me in a series of grunts and gestures and winks.

Lila chatters on, oblivious, discussing the fine points of navy blue or black as the foundation color of my new wardrobe. She fingers the fabric, examines the drape of jackets and ties, bends the shoes. She makes me hold shirts against my chest while she and Dot the saleslady drape ties across my shoulders. For a few minutes, I get into it and play along. I sashay and turn, then strike a pose. I'm an actor, I think, strutting across the stage of my life, putting on my faces, playing the parts I'm expected to play.

"Oh, give me a break, Mr. Burlesque." Lila swats me across the ass. "We'll take the charcoal suit, the navy blazer, the pinstriped slacks and the khakis. And these four shirts – the white, the pink, the blue-striped and um…" She hesitates, her fingers skipping over the array of shirts.

"How 'bout the cranberry stripe?" suggests Louie with a wink at me.

I'm too shocked by Lila to respond to Louie. I figured we swing a suit, and maybe a couple of shirts. My jaw drops. "Lila?"

"Sure," she says. "And these three ties. Yeah, these two and this paisley to go with both striped shirts."

As they gather the items, I pull her aside behind the racks of overcoats, where I hope the thick fabric will muffle the fight we are about to have. "Lila, are you crazy? What the fuck are you doing? How do you expect to pay –"

"You need clothes to get a job, Jack. A suit for your first interview, a jacket and nice trousers at least for your second. And then once you get hired, you have to show up every day in something other than a t-shirt and jeans. Every day." She plucks at the sleeve of my denim jacket dismissively, then turns and fingers the sleeve of the nearest overcoat. "Oh, look at these – these are on sale. Maybe we should get you one – you'll need it for next winter. I wonder if they do layaway. Dot?" She raises her voice and peers over the rack.

"Lila, what makes you think -?" I stare at her, stunned. She has such a sense of fait accompli about this whole thing – like it's been ordained or something. She's not even entertaining the possibility that I could prefer to take the job on the Cape. It comes with a sizeable stipend. If I live on bread and peanut butter all summer, we could pay off a chunk of debt.

Her eyes glint red and yellow. They remind me of Savageux's as he passed me on the street. I gulp hard, and I tell myself it's just a trick of light from the harsh fluorescents on the ceiling. "You need these clothes, Jack. This is the month I get an extra check. Don't worry. I planned."

"What if I don't get the job?"

"Then you'll get the job on the Cape, and if you live on bread and peanut butter, we'll be able to pay off a chunk of debt by the end of the summer." That she so perfectly echoes my thoughts makes my blood run cold. "But I just have a feeling, Jack. I just have a feeling you're going to get this job."

"Why?" I say, stunned by her stubborn insistence.

She raises her head. Our eyes meet and I feel the words stab into me. "Women's intuition."

The face of the woman in New Jersey who thinks she's my mother flashes in front of my face.

Chapter 8

My hands are glowing pinkish gold and I know I'm back in the dream. It's the same dream as a few days ago, but now it's shifted because I'm backstage with the band, surrounded by workmen setting up for the show. The entire band has gathered around to stare at the glow that begins at my elbows and extends down my forearms, all the way to my fingertips.

"Would you look at that?" says Bruce.

"She's the one," says the Big Man. "She's the one we've been waiting for."

"Here, hon." The Professor who offers the guitar looks just like Proulx. He's wearing a bow tie and a clown nose and he grins evilly. "Try this."

Even in my dream as a girl, I recognize the instrument from my childhood. I back away, holding up my glowing hands. "I can't," I scream, as the alarm starts to blare. "I can't!" I sit up sweating, and think a girl-dream, even a bad girl-dream, is a small price to pay for a night without worrying about running into either my imaginary friend, or Nicholas Savageux. I wonder how the memory of that guitar got tangled up in the girl-dream.

I was six years old. I wanted to be Elvis. For some reason, my imagination had been captured by the movie, Jailhouse Rock, which was followed by a documentary on the life of the King. Although money was tight, my mother scrimped and saved and somehow managed to get me a guitar – a kid's guitar - for Christmas. Two weeks later, our apartment was burglarized. They took our TV, our stereo, all my mother's jewelry and my guitar.

Three weeks after that, I found it, smashed inside a garbage can in one of the alleys that ran between the old apartment buildings. A year or so later, I overheard my mother talking. Apparently, the thieves told Julie the reason they broke into the apartment in the first place was they heard me playing the guitar and decided it must be an expensive instrument. I don't remember holding it, let alone playing it. As I get out of bed, I remember the dead feeling in my gut as I stared at the ruins of my gift. I stagger into the bathroom and expect to see a haggard face staring back.

Surprisingly, I think I look better than I have in days. The sleep's done some good, after all, I think, as I manage to forget the dream. The sun's shining; Lila's left me a note. My clothes are being delivered to her office. I'm not to leave for work until she comes home and cuts my hair. I meet my own eyes in the mirror and I hear Dougless's voice whisper through my mind. *LEAVE. NOW.*

It's just not that easy, I think. I half expect to find her waiting for me in the kitchen, but she seems to have taken my request to stay away seriously. Obliging apparitions are certainly preferable to those less cooperative. I remember a short story about a man haunted by the ghost of a drowned woman who fell in love with him from the afterlife. Every time she manifested, which was every time he was home, she made her surroundings very wet. He was only able to live a mold and mildew free life by seducing her into a walk-in freezer.

As I settle down to grade papers, I see Dougless sitting opposite me at the kitchen table. I nearly spill my coffee all over the students' work, yelp and swear.

She only looks at me sadly. "Do you really think that just because you don't see something, it isn't there?" Then she's gone in a burst of reflected glare through the blind.

I can't work at home after that.

At school, Nathan Orlosky, one of my most earnest students, finds me trying to concentrate on a poem. He approaches me nervously. He has a bundle of papers in one hand. His glasses are held together by pieces of duct tape. He slinks into the chair beside my desk and I know why he's here. The amount of effort he's putting into his final paper is worthy of a dissertation, but he's only a sophomore. I can't imagine living with the kind of intensity I feel oozing out of his pores.

He peers at me owlishly as I scan his latest draft and I wonder if he can see the hair going up on the back of my neck. His topic is Blake's poem, *Milton,* one of the poet's most difficult and one that always made me vaguely uncomfortable. Most of the other students in the class found it so difficult, they dismissed it as an unavoidable but necessary link in the thematic lineage and were happy to go on to the much more accessible Yeats. But not Nate.

I read his conclusion, then look up at him. He's a good thinker, a driven and passionate student. But he didn't have the benefit of a Sister Frances in eighth grade, and a Mr. Rabinowitz in tenth, so his writing tends to be a bit murky, and in this case, as in prior first drafts, I'm not quite sure what he's getting at. He's waiting for me to say something. "Your analysis is…uh… certainly interesting, Nate. But if I understand you correctly… you're saying that Blake's visitations were… uh… real?"

He nods. "Do you see it, Mr. Chance?" He clutches and unclenches his fists, nodding like a bobble-head doll, his eyes huge behind his scratched lenses. "I was reading this book… Twilight of the Gods… and the guy who wrote it talks about alien visitations, and he quotes from the Book of Ezekiel… and I… well, I realized I recognized that language from *Milton,* and so –"

"But, Nate," I say gently. "Blake used that language intentionally. He mined the Bible… deliberately… remember, we talked about it in class?"

"But you also said in class that the poem is Blake's attempt to show recurring patterns throughout history, that he was writing about things that happened over and over again."

"So you're saying Blake's visions are the result of alien visitation?" I scratch my head.

"Aliens. Angels. I guess it depends how you read the texts, and how you want to interpret all the others. The pattern's there, if you want to see it."

Fools see things differently. The whole premise sounds crazy, but then, I'm seeing and talking to apparitions. So who am I to discourage the flight of an unfettered mind? I know Proulx would certainly think I should. As I'm trying to decide what to say, the phone on my desk rings. As my hand descends over the receiver, Shirley's face pops into my mind's eye.

"Jack?"

I'm right. "Hi, Shirley... yeah, it's me."

"My God, is that really you? You know there are some rock stars easier to get a hold of?"

"Hang on a second, will you?" I put the receiver on my shoulder. "Listen, Nate, I can't say I've ever seen anyone make that argument so if you want to try it, go for it. Just remember... quotes, other opinions... back yourself up, and I'll give it a fair read. Okay?"

He charges away, papers clasped to his chest like a Holy Grail, but Shirley hasn't stopped talking. "Jack, did you hear me? What's your birthday?"

"March 2."

"Really." There's a short pause. "Are you sure?"

"Are you seriously asking me if I know my own birthday?" The face of the woman in the pink sweater pops into my head. This time she's wearing the kind of old-fashioned apron I remember my aunt wearing to clean her house. She's looking up at someone, and I see her lips move, her tiny hands wave like fragile birds. She's explaining something, shaking her head.

"Uh...Jack," says Shirley at last. "Are you sure there's not some kind of correction on the certificate? On the date?"

That's when I go cold all over. I grip the receiver hard and remember the afternoon I overheard my mother and Aunt Maggie having a conversation about me. They were looking at something on the pullout table in the living room that I couldn't see, and I overheard my Aunt say, "Why do you suppose they'd change the date?" They left the paper on the table and later I sneaked a look. I was disappointed when I found it, because it was just a tattered copy of an official-looking document I couldn't understand. But I do recall, clear as the scratches on the scarred surface of my desk, that someone had changed my birthday from March 1 to March 2..

Shirley just keeps talking. " – year were you born?"

She has to ask me twice. "1971."

"Wow." There's another pause, I hear a door slam, and then Shirley speaks in lowered tone. "Listen, Jack, if Harry agrees and we pay the fare, would you come down here?"

"What?" I blurt, not sure I've heard. I can't concentrate because all of a sudden I SEE Shirley, plain as if she stood before me. Shirley wants me to go to New Jersey to meet someone she thinks – no, she's sure – is my mother. Between the guitar dream and this, I am even more freaked out than I am by my recurring hallucinations.

"Look, Jack, don't you want to find out? Don't you want to see if maybe, just maybe this zillion to one coincidence is real? Come on, Jack, think of the story – think of the publicity. You have anything you want to publish? Now's your chance if this works out to be true."

Visions of book deals and movies are jumping in and out of my head like Santa's reindeer on speed. "Look, Shirley, sure, I want to find out…look, I'd love to meet the lady. But I can't – I just can't leave – not right now. The semester's almost over, I have final papers to assign, an exam to make up, stuff of my own to get done. And I have a job interview tomorrow. At four."

"Come for the weekend, Jack, at least. You have your birth certificate, don't you? The one with the correction? Bring it. Look, if fucking Harry wants me down here on the south side of Bumblefuck, he can pay for you to come, too. Think of the story this could turn out to be – I can see you two on Oprah."

I can see me on Oprah, too. I wonder if the Great Man would approve of *her*.

"I'll call you back." Shirley assumes my silence implies consent. "Just sit tight." She hangs up and I think that's usually what the hero says to the girl before he disappears into the swamp.

The next time my phone rings, I know it's Lila. My class starts in ten minutes; I think I finally know what the poem I've been struggling with is about.

I consider ignoring the call, but the other three instructors with whom I share an office stare at me. "Hey, honey," I say.

"Jesus, Jack, I wish you wouldn't do that. How the fuck do you always know?"

"I guess you just have a special ring," I say. "So what's up? Did my suit get delivered?"

"No, that's not why I'm calling. Wait till you hear this, Jack. Wait till you hear this!" She sounds so happy and excited I can only imagine one thing.

"You got a raise?"

"No, silly – would you stop thinking about money all the time? You'll never guess so I'll tell you – we got an *invitation*, Jack. We got an *invitation*."

"To what?"

"To the annual clients' cocktail party, that's what. The one all the partners and their wives and their husbands get to go to – but even all the associates aren't asked, Jack. Jack, this is a big fucking deal. You have no idea – it means I've been noticed."

"Yeah," I say. "So, when is this?"

"Saturday…Saturday at the New York Athletic Club…six-thirty o'clock." The sound she makes is somewhere between a crow and a squeal. I've never heard her sound so happy about anything.

"Sounds great, babe," I say. "Listen, I might not be able to go."

"What?" Ice water poured into my ear would be less bone-chilling than the shock in Lila's voice.

"Well, you know that reporter, the one who keeps calling? She has a story she's working on." Out of the corner of my eye I see three heads cock. "She thinks it involves me, or it could and she wants me to-"

"You have no idea what this means, do you?" she hisses. "You have no fucking clue. Don't you get it?"

"Get what?"

"This isn't just about me, Jack. This is about *you*. Especially since your interview is tomorrow at four. Don't you get it? This isn't just a reward for me. This is so all the partners get to see *you*."

Mercifully the clock reaches five of three, and my fellow office mates gather books and notebooks and file out toward their classes, just as another platoon of adjuncts arrive to take their place. For the next twelve hours, my desk belongs to one Alison Perone, who's already shoving around the back of my chair.

Lila's so fucking sure I'm going to get offered this job, it spooks me. But what really bothers me is that *I'm* sure too, and I don't think I really want it. And I know I won't know how to explain *that* to Lila. "Look, Lila, we can talk about it tonight, okay? I'll be home right after class. I have to teach now." I hang up, my palms so wet I leave imprints on the receiver.

"They have stuff for that, Jack." Alison's lip is curled.

"Stuff for what," I ask, as I stumble around her. I pull my jacket out from under hers.

"That sweaty palm problem of yours." She reaches into her backpack and pulls out a can of Lysol and a wad of paper towels.

The phone's ringing as I jiggle the key out of the lock. I know it's Shirley before I pick it up. My ESP seems to be intensifying so that every time I hear a phone, I get an image in my head before I answer it. Since yesterday, I haven't been wrong once.

"They'll pay, Jack," she says as soon as I say hello. "Aren't you excited? Don't you want to come?"

I take a deep breath. "It's not I don't want to come, Shirley," I say. "It's just – this weekend's not good. How 'bout next weekend – I've waited my whole life, maybe she can wait another week?"

"No, Jack – she says you *have* to come. Please. She swears she *knows* it's you, Jack. Look, maybe it is crazy, but what if I told you there's a link back to Savageux? And possibly to Winnie? What if I told you I think I may be on to what happened to her? If I told you I think she's still alive?"

"Look, Shirley, I'd love to help you but what you're saying is so fucking unbelievable –"

"There *is* a mark on your birth certificate isn't there, though? Isn't there?"

Yeah and I can't deny I see Shirley plain as if she were sitting in front of me, on a faded flowered bedspread. But I don't think Armstrong Henderson is going to be any more eager to hire someone who just had his face splashed all over the cover of *The Sun* than Proulx would be to award his grant to the same someone. And Lila is going to be really angry if I ditch the party. "Shirley, I didn't say I'd never come – just not now. It's just not–"

"Jack, don't you get it? This is bigger than just you, Jack. Come on, Jack. Please, just a weekend. What would it kill you? Just twenty-four hours? Please, Jack, I'm begging here."

"There's this party at Lila's firm, Shirley. It's a big deal, she gets to show me off – you know how that stuff –"

"Look, Jack, you can probably even make a piece of your party. The only train I could get you on leaves Penn Station at nine. Nine at night. Then we'd take the early train on Monday AM, be back in New York by ten. Come on, Jack, please? Do you have any idea how hard a time I had convincing Harry to get this ticket? So think about it, but call me back, okay? Look, here's the number – 609-555-1123. I'm in room 5. Got it?"

I mumble something and hang up just as Lila walks in with a bulging suit bag hugged to her chest. "Don't tell me it was that squirrelly reporter? Could you please just tell her not to bother us any more?" She kicks the door closed, and heaves the bag down on the chair with a sigh. "I guess they thought they were doing me a favor – Louie's delivered everything – jacket, slacks, suit, shirts, the whole shebang - to the office. Can you believe I had to schlep all this stuff home on the bus?" She sinks down, rubbing her feet, then looks up at me. "What?"

I shrug. "It's nice to see you, too, honey."

"What did that woman want? It was her, right?"

There's no sense lying. "She wants me to go to New Jersey on Saturday – late Saturday. I could leave from the party – take a cab to Penn Station. I'd be back Monday morning."

"Are you kidding?" Lila looks at me as if I've suddenly spoken fluent Chinese.

"Well." I jam my fists in my pockets. "No."

"You're crazy, Jack. You're either crazy, or you're on something. You can't do this." She shakes her head. "You can't get involved with a tabloid of all things – Jack, don't you understand? This is a position that works closely with the partners, the big clients. It matters how you present yourself. You're not just interviewing to be the kid in the mailroom, Jack. This is the real thing." She stands up, hangs up the suit in the closet. "Don't you get it? This is like getting a try-out in Yankee Stadium. You wouldn't want to screw up in front of Joe, would you?"

The genial bulldog face of the Yankee's manager flashes in front of me. *Go get 'em, tiger*, I hear him say. But when I walk out onto the mound, I have to ask myself, what the fuck am I doing here? I blink. "No-no, I don't want to screw up, Lila." I don't know if I want the job, but I don't want to discuss that. "What if I asked Shirley to keep my name out of it? You know, there's some little old lady in New Jersey who thinks she's my mother. How can it hurt to make her happy?"

"How can it hurt to prove her wrong? You can't possibly – didn't you say your father found you on the steps of some church? No, wait, I remember… Sts Anthony and Jude?"

"Yeah… it was a joke, Lila. St. Anthony is the patron saint of lost things, and St. Jude is the patron of hopeless causes." I spread my hands. "Look, I'll talk to Shirley, ask her to keep my real name out of it – hell, maybe we can even make up a name - but I still want to go. I want to meet this woman, Lila. Even if she's not my real mother, I still want to meet her."

Lila stares at me, arms folded across her chest. "You're a grown man. I can't stop you from doing anything you want to do. But you know, Jack, I don't have to watch you throw away the biggest chance that's come down your street in a long time."

"I'm going to the party, Lila. It starts at what – six?"

"Six-thirty. We can't be there before seven."

"So we show up at seven, and I take a cab out of there by eight, eight-thirty. We stay an hour. How long did you plan on staying, anyway?"

"There's awards and speeches. It's a big deal, Jack."

"So we tell them I have a sick relative or something. We tell them I had other plans. Jesus, Lila, they just handed you this invitation today. Don't they think you might have a life?"

"None that counts."

That same sick feeling slams into the pit of my stomach. I don't understand how this is happening. Last week, Armstrong Henderson didn't know I existed, and this week, I not only have an interview with them, my presence is required at, of all things, the most important party of the year. That's ridiculous, I tell myself. Lila's exaggerating. She has to be. "Come on, Lila. I'm doing the interview, I'm going to the party – part of it, anyways. I promise I'll stay long enough to show them I don't spill food and fart in public."

The look on her face is contemptuous. "You don't need my permission, Jack." She spins on her heel, walks into the bathroom and slams the door.

"So I guess your blessing's out of the question, Little-Sister-of-St-Suck-up?"

"Fuck you, Jack."

She's right, though, I think, about three hours later when I'm stuck in the middle of the Long Island Expressway, going nowhere. There has to be a better way to live. My first fare of the night drags me out to Kennedy Airport; my second fare demands to be taken further out on the island.

He's a salesman, home for the first time in two weeks, and he didn't make his quota. His face is pale and sweaty, and I think of Willie Loman when the guy gets into my backseat, clutching his cheap square box of a suitcase. He gasps out the address, and I don't have the heart to tell him I don't have any idea where that is. But he sees my hesitation. "It's just a couple exits," he huffs and puffs. "I'll let you know where to turn off."

"You all right, buddy?"

There's an invisible weight that accompanies him into the cab. It pervades the entire interior, settles around my shoulders like a shroud. In the rearview mirror, his lips look purplish, the skin around his mouth grayish blue. "Heartburn, just heartburn - I got it bad."

I pull out into traffic and almost immediately we hit a snarl. The minutes tick by, the meter ticks on. He looks at me in the mirror and shrugs. "It is what it is."

I can't shake the feeling. It feels like some solid reality has invaded the cab, like an invisible granite block. I don't know any other way to describe it. It's just there. We inch along, yard by yard. "Love me tender, love me true," croons the radio, and a burst of Elvis fills the air. The connection to my dream makes me sweat and I put my hand on the dial, but the guy in the back speaks up.

"Don't touch that – I love the King." His face is so wet it shines against the imitation leather seat., and he mops his head weakly with one sleeve. "You got any Tums, buddy?"

"Sure," I say, and I hand him the bottle I keep under the seat.

"Mind if I keep it for the trip?"

"Not at all." The next song is Springsteen's *Promised Land*. I lean my head against the rest, and drag behind the endless line of traffic, thinking about what it's really like to drive straight into a storm. Tomorrow is the interview, then the party, and then New Jersey. I want to believe in a promised land, too, I think. At least I wish I could sound as sure about it as he does. The traffic loosens up, and I hit the accelerator.

A really bad smell and a gurgle make me look up, into the mirror, and I see my passenger slumped back, arms sprawled, a spreading stain in his lap, and his eyes open and fixed at the ceiling. I slam the brake and veer onto the shoulder. "Holy shit," I yelp, because I have no idea what to do. I bolt out of the front. As I yank open the back door, I notice my hand is glowing, not as brightly as the dream, but definitely emitting a radiant light that shines softly pink from the nails. I bend in to the backseat, and find myself face to face to Dougless.

"Just let me take him, Jack," she says gently. "It's time."

"Take him where? He's fucking dead," I scream.

"Not quite," she replies. She moves an inch or two, and I see a silvery shimmer coming up out of the body. It has a face that vaguely resembles my passenger, but a younger, thinner, happier version, which smiles at me as they both vanish.

I'm left to figure out how to deal with the disgusting reality of a poor shlub who had the misfortune to die in the middle of the L.I.E. I remember Alison and her Lysol and wish I was half as well prepared. The last thing I do that night is explain to Shortman why the backseat stinks like shit and piss. And Tums.

Part Two - Jessie

Chapter 9

There's two weeks 'til finals, but already the air on Nerd Level reeks of desperation. The click of keyboard keys isn't quite enough, however, to drown out the squeaky wheels of my book cart, and predictably, a wave of heads rise and turn at my approach. The expressions on those heads are anything but pleasant. These are people who don't understand the need for books, let alone libraries, and regard librarians as nothing more than antiquated —though mobile - search engines. Even a cute redhead like me isn't appreciated.

I tuck my best Sweetheart-of-Sigma-Chi smile around my mouth, and tip-toe as quickly as I can between the rows of stacks and carrels. I don't give a shit about their hostile looks. It's the smell. Between the damp, the sweat, and geek grooming habits, the whole floor stinks like cheesy feet. Unfortunately, the short cut to the elevator leads straight through engineering and computer science.

"Hey, Jessie. You playing down on Front Street tonight?" A tall pale kid in black from jacket to boots slides beside the cart just as I round the last corner.

A slimy, slithery feeling rolls up my left arm, almost as if I've gotten too close to something reptilian. I know this kid. I've seen him lurking in the library, standing under the exit signs on the periphery of the Goth clubs my band plays in. He insinuated himself under my nose a few weeks ago, and like a bad penny, he won't stop showing up. I think he calls himself Wraith.

I don't understand my reaction to him, though. I feel repulsed, nauseated. It's the smell, I tell myself. Just the smell and the blatant animosity from the geeks. There couldn't possibly be anything truly unsettling or dangerous about this skinny weed in shiny black leather and too much hair gel.

"Nah," I say. "Practice tonight." I pause; make eye contact with the same cool stare I use behind the mike. "We open for Mayhem at the Khyber Pass tomorrow."

I punch the elevator button and pray it gets here soon.

"You could do better than that piss-ant place."

It's not the insult that makes me pause. It's the certainty with which he says it, as if he knows anything at all about music, about the band, about me. He looks all of 19 – he sounds a lot older. He puts his arm up on the wall, above the elevator buttons, and I see the long line of piercings snake under his skin, lead-gray against dead-white skin. "You know you could, too. Maybe not the other girls… but you… you have that voice…" His voice trails off and a feeling not unlike an itchy sweater settles around me.

I'm used to this kind of thing. "Thanks," I say, wondering where the fuck the elevator is.

"You really have something, don't you?" His eyes are pale, pale blue, and faintly bloodshot. I wonder if he's on something, decide he has to be.

The elevator door slides open and I thank whatever God is watching. I'm starting to get that pressure in my chest that I feel when I'm about to see or hear something no one else can. I don't usually feel that way in the library – the weight of all the books, all the people, all the thoughts seem to buffer me somehow. There's something off about this kid, but I don't want to have to figure out what it is.

I push the cart over the hump, smile as I navigate it awkwardly around. He's watching me as if he wants to eat me with those big pale eyes of his. I punch the circulation desk level out of habit, and wave as the doors start to close. "See you somewhere," I start to say.

He's standing next to me.

"How'd you do that?" The elevator doors close with a whisper that sounds vaguely like a hiss. We start to sink right along with my stomach.

"Nothing you can't learn to do, too, Jessie." He leans down closer, and I smell wintergreen on his breath. His canine teeth are silver fangs. "Nothing you can't probably already do."

I feel myself relax. He's just another weirdo who may well want to suck my blood, but he wants to fuck me first, and I know how to deal with that. "You get those things put in over at HUP?"

The pointblank question doesn't take him down quite as far as I thought it would, but he blinks, steps back. "Around the corner, actually. Place on 33rd Street – not much more than a guy and his chair. You interested?" He smiles more broadly.

I let our eyes connect and hold the look for just a second. "No."

That doesn't faze him either. "Too bad," he says. "The way you sing about vampires... you'd make a good one...maybe too good?" The elevator jolts just a little.

If it gets stuck, I'll scream.

But we keep moving and he keeps talking. "There're people who'd really appreciate you, Jessie...really open up your talent to a whole new level. I know you think I'm just another jerk-off fan. But I'm not." His eyes bore into mine, making it tough to remember that I'm the one with the power.

I can feel my pulse picking up; feel prickling at the base of my skull, in the place where my neck connects. He's the real thing, I think. But that just can't be.

The elevator doors slide open. He steps out first. "If you ever want to find out, I can make it happen. See you somewhere." Then he literally seems to melt into the crowd milling in front of the doors.

I feel like I've been touched by a slug. I don't quite understand what's happened, I feel dazed and out of it, like my head's been too close to the amp. He's just another weirdo geek, I tell myself. It's the rain, the rain and the smell. The light is gray on the lobby level, but at least its natural light.

I stumble up to the circulation desk behind the cart, and Julie, one of the other assistant librarians, catches my eye. "Hey, Jessie, head's up. Miz Diz has her cranky-pants on."

Desiree Bainbridge – Miz Diz to her underlings – doesn't like me. Or maybe it's not that she doesn't like me, it's more that she doesn't approve of me. I'm a faculty brat – or I was – and now that my faculty member has died, Miz Diz seems to think her personal role in my life is to show me how unfit I am for the job of assistant librarian.

And maybe I am unfit for it, but so far, there haven't been any others I've been any more successful at, and rock star keeps eluding me. It's the music, I know that – it's edgy and metallic and black. We're the Goth version of opera – you either love us or you don't get it. But as long as the band and I are together, I'm not going to stop putting it out there. I don't think I can.

As I trundle over to the pile of books waiting reshelving, I see her stare at me through the window of her inner sanctum. *I'm watching you*, I can almost hear her say. *I'm watching you.* I smile and wave and decide not to blow her a kiss. I know what bothers her about me. It's the same thing that bothered my mother. I know what it is, but I can't seem to figure out what to do about it.

I have no ambition beyond the band, beyond the music. I don't really care if we make it big – I just want to keep playing the music. I can sing in the shower. We can play in basements. I know my attitude is different even from my band-mates, and sometimes, it causes conflict with them.

I don't know why I feel this way. I just can't explain it.

All my life, I feel as if I've been waiting for something to happen, someone to come along. I don't know who or what I'm waiting for. I don't know what's supposed to happen, or who's supposed to show up. I don't why I feel this way. But this library is a good place to hang out, as I've found, and so Miz Diz and I exist in a state of mutual détente as long as I avoid being caught at the kinds of things I know she expects me to do.

"Is there any reason for the cranky-pants?" I ask, as I load books onto my cart, taking care to avoid any having to do with any kind of science. There's no way I'm going back to Nerd Level today. "It's Friday? It's raining? Her date had to be euthanized?"

"You're funny, Jessie. She's going to hear you some day. No, I think what pissed Diz off was some woman from some tabloid." Julie pauses in scanning the returned books. "She was looking for you."

"Me?"

"Miz Diz sent her packing, but… yeah. Maybe you'll be on the cover of the National Enquirer, Jessie… you know…enquiring minds want to know, and all that?"

"Me?" I blink. "What for?"

"What for? For your band – what else?" Julie's looking at me closely. "Jessie, are you okay? You look a little dazed. You didn't get stoned on your break, did you?"

"Jesus, Julie, keep your voice down, will you? I haven't done that since they talked about random drug tests. Shh!" I can see Diz watching us. I'm sure she has the circulation desk bugged. Video, too, probably. *I'm watching you.*

I glance up, to the round walls of the rotunda above us, and see, or think I see, the kid from the elevator smiling down at me. I jump, just a tad.

"Jessie, are you okay?" Julie comes to stand beside me. "Were you out playing last night?"

"Not late," I say. The whole band thing is a problem, I know. Vampire-heavy metal-Goth-biker chick doesn't fit the Ivy League image Penn likes to foster. It doesn't matter how many J Crew sweaters and pearls I wear on the job. "I-I haven't been sleeping too well. Bad dreams, stuff like that. Ever since my dad died…" I let my voice trail off. It's true, too. All my life weird shit's happened to me, but ever since I reconnected with my father, it's been an evolving spiral of things I just don't know how to explain. Like that kid, just now.

Julie adores her father. She thinks my mother was a horrible bitch to let me think mine was dead. Now that he's really gone, I think she feels more keenly than I do the loss of all those years. "Oh, honey," she says. "I'm sorry." She pats my shoulder. "Look, I didn't mean to imply there's anything wrong with it, Jessie – just, you know how they feel. Some tabloid writes some story about librarian by day, biker by night – look at the circus they raised when Playboy did that spread. I'm sure that's the deal."

She goes back to scanning books. I push the cart toward the rear elevator. "Come see us tomorrow," I say, as if Julie would ever venture out of the safety of her Main Line neighborhood on a Saturday night. "We're opening for Mayhem. At the Khyber Pass."

"Jessie, you're incorrigible." Julie shakes her head as a few passing students hoot.

The elevator doors slide open. I push my cart inside and the blonde woman standing beside the buttons hits the top floor. "I'm looking for David Woodwright's daughter."

"That sounds like fiction," I say automatically, as the doors slide shut, before her words really register. "Try the next floor."

"She's a person," the blonde woman says. "Her name's Jessie." Her nasal New York voice bores into my skull, even as her eyes flick down to the nameplate pinned above my left nipple. "Like yours."

"My name's Jessie," I say slowly, as I realize she's looking for me. "Woodwright's not the name I use." I use my mother's maiden name. She changed my last name legally from Woodwright to Carpentieri when I was 16, apparently with my father's blessing. I never got around to asking him why.

"But you *are* his daughter? David Woodwright?" As the doors slide shut, she says, "You are, aren't you? Attila the librarian said you weren't employed here."

"What?"

"I guess if you don't use that name here she didn't know who I meant."

"No," I say. "She knew who you meant." More than a few of my father's old colleagues stopped by to offer their condolences. I had no idea he'd been so fondly remembered. But that's not the only thing about my father that's surprised me. The baby-napping thing pretty much blew my mind. Rosie's never really sufficiently explained it, though she did give me an awful lot of shit to read, as well as a selected list of books to look up.

The woman pushes a square white laminated card into my hand. "That's not my real name, either." It says PRESS in very large letters across the top. Casey McGuire, the name reads, but her accent is anything but Irish.

"What's your real name?"

"Shirley Shulman. I write for *The Sun*."

I have to bite back my grin. I can just imagine Miz Diz's reaction. "You know, if you have questions for the band, you should really talk to Ging-"

The elevator doors begin to open, but Shirley pushes the button that keeps them closed. "Honey, this isn't about your band. This is about your father – your father and why he died."

"Why he died? He... he had a heart attack...a blood clot...he...it was just a freak thing."

"No, it wasn't." Shirley looks at me. "Did you know his girlfriend was brought in for questioning? By the police?"

"What?" I stare. "Why? About what?"

"About the possibility your father didn't just drop dead, honey. There's a question he was poisoned... but no one's made a stink and there's not much to go on. But I have a friend...Winnie Chen... who's been working on this story about a clinic over in Jersey, asking questions, digging around and..."

I haven't had much contact with Rosie since Dad died but this is the first time I've heard this. "Ex-excuse me, you're telling me that the police questioned Rosie? Rosie Coulter? Dad's assistant?" All the weight I felt before, all the bad feelings I had in the elevator with the kid who wants to be a vampire come crashing back with the force of a freight train. I push the cart against the doors and they slide open of their own volition. "You're telling me someone thinks my father was *murdered*?"

"That's exactly what I'm telling you." Shirley takes a deep breath as I push the cart out into the hall. "Please, maybe you can't tell me anything. But ...if you'll just give me half an hour, there's things I'd like to ask."

Chapter 10

I stash the book cart on the loading dock, where no one will think to look until Monday at 8 AM, and follow Shirley down the street and around the corner to a quiet little bar I thought only locals know about.

It surprises me that she does.

I slide in opposite her in a back booth as the bartender puts two beers down on the table. "I have to tell you...I ... I don't want you making up shit about my father just to sell news-"

"I'm not making anything up." She whips out a cigarette and lights up. "Look, I don't give a shit about that stupid paper. This isn't about some article. This is about..." Her eyes fill up, and she bites her lip. "I know you lost your dad. I've lost someone, too. The girl who was working on the story in the first place -"

"What story?" My head's spinning.

"I'm sorry." Shirley takes a deep drag on her cigarette, and then a long drink of her beer. "Let me start at the beginning. My friend, Winnie – my colleague and partner and friend - Yeah." Shirley lights another cigarette. "We were close." From the way her mouth is twisted, I know it was very close. "We both work for The Sun, both went to Bard..." Again she makes a little face, takes a deep breath, and starts again. "Winnie was working on a story. Originally it was about this game – this real-life role playing game called 'The Mask.' People get together, have parties, pretend to be real vampires, real victims."

I nod. "Yeah... I know about that. We get invited to play sometimes... there's a whole Goth side to that that really likes our music." A chill goes down my spine and I shake it off. It's just the icy glass, the bitter frosty beer.

"In the process of writing that story, she started to concentrate on one of the top people involved in the game in New York – a big time Wall Street guy named Nicholas Savageux, and his wife."

"But what does that have to do with my father?"

"In the course of the story, Winnie discovered a link between Savageux, his wife's family – whose name happens to be Sinclair, just by coincidence - and a little maternity clinic over in Jersey that the Feds shut down years ago. I have no idea why Winnie thought it was important enough to pursue. She didn't even tell me what it was. She packed up and came down here to Philly." Shirley grinds out her cigarette, and lights another in a motion so smooth it reminds me of the way my mother used to smoke. I'm alarmed. No one should smoke that much.

"I still don't understand where my father fits in."

"She met him the afternoon he collapsed. I'm not sure, actually, if they ever got together or not, any notes of their meeting, disappeared with her."

"Disappeared?"

"Winnie's missing. She never came home. No one knows what happened to her. No body, no evidence. Just poof." Shirley snaps her fingers and stubs out her cigarette.

My head's spinning. Before she can light another, I turn to the bartender. I need something more fortifying than beer. A lot more. "Shot of Jamieson's." Then I look at Shirley. "What did she want with my dad?"

"I don't know for sure. But from the notes Winnie did leave behind, I think it was about a woman named Martha Sinclair." Shirley is watching me closely. "You know who that is?"

Tell Martha there's rocks in the grave. Till the day I die I won't forget that rasping whisper, that cold, chilling charge. How could I forget that? I thought I was going to hear an "I love you;' instead I got some weird deathbed confession. "I've never met her," I say. It creeps me out to think my father had something to do with a kidnapping or worse.

"But you've heard of her?" She's not backing off. "You know that name?"

The bartender puts the whiskey in front of me. I swallow it and enjoy the slow dark burn all the way down the back of my throat. It's getting late, I have practice. Dad's dead and I'm pretty sure Rosie didn't poison him. I'm sorry for Shirley's loss but there's nothing I can do about that either.

She's looking at me as if she thinks maybe I know where the body is – where all the bodies are. Momentarily I'm afraid – more afraid of her than I am of the kid in the elevator. I knew what he wanted. I'm not so sure about Shirley. I don't understand why she reeks of the same kind of desperation as the air on geek level, but I know that desperate people do dangerous things. I've seen kids threaten suicide over a bad grade. I've seen kids mean it. "My father mentioned her name in the hospital. He said he'd put rocks in the baby's grave…something like that. He was dying, all doped up. Rosie was the one who said it made sense – why not go ask her?"

"She won't talk to me."

I can see how if Rosie had been questioned on suspicion of murder she might not want to talk to a tabloid. I glance at the clock on the wall.

"He didn't say what happened to the baby? Or why he did what he did?"

"No – I got the impression he wanted this lady's mind put at ease. I guess she thinks her baby's dead."

"He didn't tell you how to contact her?"

"Rosie knew the name. I-I assumed Rosie told the lady – she said she understood."

"So that's how Martha got her order," Shirley says, more to herself than to me.

"What order?" Apparently there's no denying my father was involved.

"The exhumation order. They're digging up the baby tomorrow. Want to come?"

"No." I don't even hesitate. I can't think of anything more horrifying. "I still don't understand … my father wasn't… wasn't a criminal. This doesn't make any sense at all."

Shirley smiles as she shakes her head. "No, no, it really doesn't, does it? Especially now it's clear to me that just about everyone associated with that clinic is dead. That's why, when I was updating and filling in Winnie's notes, and I noticed your dad's name and the fact he was dead... and then there'd been just that passing question of possible foul play...Do you know of anyone who might've wanted your father dead?"

"Other than my mother?" That makes Shirley laugh. "No. He struck me as fairly mild mannered – I didn't exactly know him all that well, though. I-I don't even know how long ago this happened."

"1971."

"That's the year I was born."

"What a coincidence, huh?"

"Too much of a coincidence to mean anything – I mean, how could something that happened twenty five years ago have anything to do with my father dying a few weeks ago?"

"How could it have anything to do with Winnie disappearing? With a vampire game that's going on now?" Shirley shrugs, smiles. She clicks her fingernails on the table. "Look, Jessie, there're a lot more people dead than just your dad, and maybe Winnie, and I really think there's a lot more people who're going to die. So if you could just tell me anything, anything at all, that you know about your father, anything...I'd be grateful."

I don't know what else to say. If I stay another minute I'm going to need another drink, and I can't. I have to drive home, get to practice. I can't be late – that pisses off everyone, not just Ginger. "I hardly knew my dad. My mother let me think he was dead. I didn't know he was alive until after she died, and I didn't find him until a few months ago. I'd only seen him like... six times before he collapsed. I spent more time in the hospital with him than out. Martha Sinclair... he mentioned her to me when he was dying." I look around. The bar's getting crowded and noisy, and outside, rush hour traffic has clogged the narrow avenues. I have to leave soon if I'm to have any prayer of getting to Ginger's on time. "Thanks for the drinks, Shirley. But I really have to get home. I have dogs to take care of before practice."

"Well. Thanks for talking to me. If you... if you happen to speak to Rosie Coulter, would you please tell her I don't bite? I don't think she killed her lover? That's not what I'm going to write. Please?" She pushes a card toward me. "That's my cell-phone number underneath the office number. You can reach me there pretty much any time. If you think of anything, that is." She pulls a pen out of her pocket. "I'll be in Redemption all day tomorrow, I think. Can I have your number? Just in case?"

I've given my number to far less reputable people. "609-555-1845. I have an answering machine. It doesn't always work." I'm not sure why. Electrical equipment seems to short out around me a lot.

"Thanks, Jessie. I really appreciate your time."

I feel bad as I say good bye and I don't know why. I leave her sitting alone in a sea of suits. I remember I left my jacket at work. When I get back, Miz Diz is waiting for me. She beckons me into her office, hands me a white envelope. "I hope you'll consider what's inside very seriously, Jessie." She raises one eyebrow, purses her mouth. "And your books have come in. The special order you made last week? Who shall I notify?"

"Oh, thanks, Ms. Bainbridge. Those are for me." I stuff the envelope in my jacket. "I'll pick them up tomorrow, okay? On my way to the gig." That was stupid, Jessie, I think to myself. But I can't stop the words that come rolling out of my mouth. "We're opening for Mayhem at the Khyber Pass. Come check us out." I spin on my heel before she can answer.

I crumple the envelope in my pocket as I run for the bus. I don't have to read it. I know what it says. I've violated some rule, forgotten some regulation, or ignored some crucial, critical detail. I wonder, just briefly, if the same thing got my father in some kind of trouble.

I'm twenty minutes late for practice. Ginger won't even look at me when I walk into the room. "What?" I say. I take off my jacket and open my water bottle. Heather tightens her strings. Kimie fiddles with her drums.

"Nice of you to join us," Ginger says at last.

"Hey, I got out of work late. The dogs had to pee. I'm sorry if I'm the one who works in Philly. And besides, you have to tune up. All I have to do is turn on the mike."

Ginger's fingers dance through a riff. "Are you ready?" She looks pointedly at me. "Cause I am." She launches into her very own *Necrophilia Now or Never* with all amps blazing.

I feel almost ambushed by the music. The other girls are ready, obviously, 'cause they don't miss a beat. And neither do I. I throw back my head and grab the mike and the words pour out of my throat, loud and rough and raw.

I don't know where the sound comes from, how the music seems to form somewhere deep inside my chest and high inside my head, then comes pouring out my mouth. I don't understand the place I go when I sing, a place where sound has color, texture and form. I see and feel and smell and taste the notes as much as hear them. I don't think the others experience music quite this way.

I close my eyes and let the song take me wherever it does.

A silence rising around me makes me open my eyes. I'm still singing, but the other girls are staring at me, instruments slack.

"What the fuck are you doing, Jessie?" asks Ginger.

I look at each girl in turn. "Singing?"

"Yeah, but what the fuck were you singing?"

"You're singing *Sweet Low, Sweet Chariot*, Jessie." Heather is staring at me.

Kimie leans over her drums. "You know no one here gives a shit if you like your weed, Jessie. We all like to take the edge off. But… what kind of weird shit are you doing?"

"You think I'm on some drug?"

They exchange glances that say everything.

"Are you kidding? With all the random tests at work? I…I…" I don't know what to say. I turn off the mike and back away. "I lost my focus, okay? I'm sorry. I got a slip at work today… weird shit happened…"

"Jessie, weird shit is happening to you all the time now," says Kimie. She does a little ratatat-tat her drums. "All the freaking time." She underscores each word with a beat.

Heather looks at Ginger, bites her lip, then back at me. "Honey, can't you see we're worried about you?"

Ginger puts down her guitar. "We listen to that stuff you tell us, that stuff you seem to forget about. The knocks on the doors at night, the phone calls, the singing… Jessie…now you're even getting written up at work. Are you sure there's nothing going on?"

They've been my friends since grade school. We've been a band since junior high. They know all the sorry little secrets of my soul, mostly because they witnessed a lot of them. "You really think I'm on something?"

"Or maybe you need to be." Kimie shrugs. "Prozac helped my brother."

I sink down on one of the amps. "The reason I was late was because a tabloid reporter showed up late this afternoon and started asking questions about my father, and how he died. She thinks maybe he was poisoned." I look at all of them in turn. "Yeah, I know it sounds crazy. I got into an elevator today with a big fan who thinks he's a vampire. A real vampire. And you know what the really crazy part is? I thought so, too."

"Maybe you should go talk to someone, Jessie." Heather puts her bass down. "Maybe there really is a demon after you."

"Would you shut the fuck up?" says Ginger. "The last thing she needs is to be encouraged. That's what's so freaking crazy - she thinks it's all real, and you're as bad as she is." She makes a little noise of disgust. "Just not as freaking weird."

"I *was* hearing knocks. The dogs heard them too. But they've stopped. I thought I told you. Rosie gave me some ideas what to do – they worked."

Ginger shakes her head. "I don't know, Jessie. I don't know what's going on with you, but you really have to get a grip."

"Try to stay focused," says Heather, as she slings her bass back over her shoulder. "Come on, let's try our new song. I think we sounded a little rough in the middle still."

Ginger adjusts her amp. "All right," she says. The look she gives me reminds me uncomfortably of Miz Diz. *I'm watching you.* And she does.

Heather bums a ride home. She puts her hand on my arm before she gets out. My throat is raw and I don't feel like saying much. The rest of the practice went amazingly well. No one could've asked for more from any of us. If we're half as good tomorrow night, we'll blow Mayhem right into the river. "You know, Jessie, Ginger can't see any of the stuff you can."

I just look at her.

She squeezes my arm. "You know what I mean."

I know exactly what she means. I remember driving home through a snowstorm, my mother, white-knuckled over the steering wheel, me uncomfortable in my snow suit, one late January afternoon, when I was five or six. As we slid to an uneasy stop at the corner beside the playground, I asked my mother who all the children were who were playing outside without coats. At first too distracted by the weather, my mother became quite angry when I insisted I saw children running with gleeful abandon all over the equipment.

Then her face got white, her lips turned gray. Her eyes got very big. I thought she was going to say something, maybe even hit me, but she snapped her mouth shut. We skidded through the intersection and when I looked back, I could still see the children, racing merrily in the snow.

It wasn't until I was eight or nine that someone – I think it might even have been Heather - told me how a school bus full of school kids had lost control of its brakes and crashed into the playground one sunny afternoon in June of 1959.

"Yeah," I say. "I know what you mean. But this isn't… this isn't the same, Heather. Really. It isn't."

Her eyes remind me of a doe's, big and dark and liquid in the porch light. "I'm always here when you need to talk, Jessie."

"I know."

"But-but you have to start talking, you know?"

"I know." I don't know what else to say. I'm waiting for something more inevitable than death. But how do I explain that?

She leans over, gives me an awkward hug. "Call me. Okay?"

But we both know I won't. I watch Heather turn the key in the lock, see the door open, the light flare. I put the car in gear and back out.

I wave to the ghost of the hitchhiker who got killed in a hit and run accident a few years ago as I turn the corner onto the road that leads to my street.

Part Three - Jack

Chapter 11

I look good in my suit. Louie and his tailor did a great job. The collar clings to the back of my shirt like it's sewn in place, the shoulders ease over mine. Even the sleeves hit my wrist at exactly the right spot, so that the requisite inch of shirt peeks out. Lila intercepts me in the lobby. She drags me into a telephone nook, then brushes my lapel, straightens my tie, smoothes back my hair. Then she stands on tiptoe and presses a kiss on my cheek. "That's for luck. You look great." She steps back. "You have your resume? You remember what it says?"

"Yeah." Lila is clearly more creative than I ever gave her credit for being. "And samples – I got writing samples." I hope they want to discuss those and not my years thinking up color names for Revlon and Max Factor.

"Good." She gives my sleeve one last tug. "Let's go get 'em, tiger." Head high, she marches toward the elevators. She's so sure I'm getting the job, it makes my heart hurt.

The problem is, so am I. The fact that Lila and I are both so squarely on the same page alarms me. We're not usually so in tune with each other, but in the last twenty-four hours, I've heard her complete my sentences, answer questions before I've asked them aloud, and insist I'm going to get offered this job. I wish I knew whether I wanted the job. I also feel this terrible sense that what I want doesn't matter. At all.

A weight has descended around my innards, a weight as real and heavy as the presence I felt last night. Every minute that guy was in the cab I've replayed in my head, over and over. Was there something I could've done? Should've done? Who – or what - the fuck is Dougless? Over and over I hear her soft voice: *Just let me take him. It's his time.* Over and over, I see that unmistakable smile on the face of the gray shimmer. Again and again, I watch myself stare at the corpse, unable to move despite the traffic skidding by inches from my backside.

Is that what Dougless my imaginary friend is? The fucking Angel of Death? So what exactly does that mean? Am I going to die? I could really use a drink. Or maybe a joint. Anything to take the edge off this raw fear that threatens to swallow me whole.

The customary sharp clicks of Lila's heels are so dulled by the acoustics they sound vaguely like the thud of a muffled bell. My vision splits and in one half of my mind I'm following my wife down toward a bank of elevators in a skyscraper in New York City, and in the other, I'm following a wheeled cart up a muddy hill. I'm wearing a sack, I have a chain around my neck, my beard is long and scraggly, I'm carrying a Bible in one hand, and a fiddle in the other.

Yea, though I walk through the valley of the shadow of Death…

I see Dougless standing behind us in the polished steel doors of the elevator. She's standing in a shaft of sunlight, her hair a blaze of red. I look down at her feet and I see what's wrong with her shoes. There's no differentiation between right or left foot. I gasp and start to spin around, but the elevator doors open, Lila takes my hand, and pulls me inside.

I will fear no evil. I think I hear Dougless chanting the psalm. This is crazy, I think. I close my eyes hard and whisper words that are rapidly becoming my mantra: I believe in a promised land. Lila clings to my hand as if she's afraid I'll bolt.

I fully expect to die in the elevator.

The doors open and we step out. Lila points to the right. "That way. Right around the corner." She blows me a kiss. I look in the direction she points, right into a picture that seems to depict the very scene I saw in my head downstairs. I walk directly toward the picture, stunned, squinting, wondering how it is that I can possibly see what I think I'm seeing. "Jack!" Lila cries sharply. "Not into the wall."

"I'm looking at the picture, Lila."

"Oh," she waves her hand. "Those paintings. One of the senior partners has a kid or a grandkid who's autistic or something. She paints these things as therapy and we have to look at them. Thank God they only hang them in the hallways."

Why the hell do they hang them at all? I wonder. It's a massive painting, framed in heavy dark wood that's ornately carved into leafy vines, done in brilliant, disturbed oils that appear to shift and become something else entirely. One minute I think I'm looking at this crudely executed rendering of my own vision, the next I think I'm seeing an explosion of confetti out of a cannon.

"They're creepy but you get used to them. Yeah, they change depending on your angle." She walks up beside me, bursting into my bubble where the only things that exist are this painting and me. "Hey there. Earth to Jack, earth to Jack." She pokes me in the side. "You remember why you're here?"

"Yeah," I say, "Sure." I stamp my feet, look away, swallow hard, bite my tongue till I taste blood.

"You didn't take anything, did you, Jack?"

"No," I reply, definite and firm.

She nods at the corridor leading to the right. "Your interview is with Gervais D'Eyncourt, remember? HR's that way. Ask for Mr. D'Eyncourt. You've met Loretta – remember that underwear party? The one we had to call you to come take us all home? She was the one who flashed the guy on the corner. Don't tell her you remember that, though, okay? She's a little ashamed."

The last time I met Loretta she was wearing bikini underwear and a black see-through bra and dancing on a coffee table. The good thing about this image is that it's earthy enough to ground me. I walk in to the reception area, which is smaller than I expected, and make eye contact with Loretta. She'd had a lot of tequila that night. Sobered up, she's a lot prettier. "Hello, Jack."

I pretend I don't remember ever seeing her before in my life. "Lila says we met, but I really can't recall." I put out my hand. "Jack Chance."

The expression that floods her eyes as she briefly touches my fingers is a mixture of gratitude and relief. "Mr. D'Eyncourt's on the phone, but I'll buzz Mr. McPherson and let him know you're here. Just have a seat."

There's another strange painting on the wall opposite, and I notice Loretta's desk is angled so that she never sees it, no matter which way she turns. A chill goes down my spine and I get out of my chair to peer at it. This one looks like watercolors over a light pencil sketch. It appears to be not quite finished. A girl in a sailor hat stands on one side of a window, a boy with his hands clasped to his chest, in apparent supplication, is on the other. There's a full moon in the sky above the boy's head. Above the girl's hat, something that could be a disembodied head appears to be emerging out of the wallpaper. One eye stares directly at me, the other, foggier and vague, appears to look directly at the girl. The only thing fully realized are the red lips that curve in a sensuous arc to reveal gleaming white teeth. *I'm going to eat her up*, the eye seems to say.

"Jack?" Barbie's Ken, enlarged and brought to life, stands beside me, hair as gold and glossy as an eagle's wings. He has the perfect preppie's eager grin, hearty handshake, and gleaming white teeth. "Let's go talk in my office. Tell Ger when he deigns to get off the phone." He says this to Loretta with a smirk and a wink, then claps an arm around my shoulder. "I'm Phineas McPherson V. Forgive the dubious alliteration; I come from a long line of dubious poets. Call me Phinney."

Dubious poets, perhaps, but great lawyers obviously. He steps aside and lets me precede him into the biggest room I've ever entered in my life outside a museum. The entire apartment I share with Lila could fit in it. His desk is bigger than our bed. This room belongs in the Smithsonian behind a velvet rope with a brass sign: Rich Person's Room, Circa Twentieth Century. I am bedazzled by the sheer weight of age and opulence that seems to gild every object in the room with a platinum sheen. The very air feels thicker and richer, as if over the years it's absorbed so many particles of the treasures with which the room is furnished, it's achieved a kind of patina all its own.

I know there are people who live better than I ever have. I aspire to be one someday.

I didn't know there are people who have rooms in which Medici princes would feel at home.

"Yeah, it's awesome, isn't it?" Phinney spreads his hands, sinks down into the leather throne behind the desk, motions me to an equally impressive wingchair in front of it. "This was my great-great grandfather's office. I'm the fifth of the name to occupy this space. They can't kick me out, so I guess being stuck with a goofy name like mine isn't too big a price to pay, huh?" He slaps the desk. "Call me Phinney. What a hoot, huh?"

Phinney and I hit it right off, which is even more of a hoot. It turns out he was an English major in college, and a member of his prep school's version of Dead Poet's Society. We start trading lines of poetry, and next thing you know, we're reciting sections of *The Wasteland* at each other. I can't bring myself to tell him how much I hate T.S. Elliot, nor how impressed I am with myself I seem to remember so much.

Then out of nowhere, he makes some reference to *Under Milkwood*, and in an instant, I hear a sonorous voice reciting the rolling lines in my head. I remember that the poet, Dylan Thomas, died not far from here after collapsing in an alcohol-induced stupor. Phinney gives me a quizzical look. I shut my mouth with a snap. Was the voice coming from *my* throat?

Then the door behind me opens, and Mr. Gervais D'Eyncourt the HR guy walks in. The temperature drops forty degrees. "Hey, Phin. I thought you were conferenced in with Boston."

"I have an associate for that." Phinney winks at me. I've already understood that he likes to be considered the young, artsy one among the partnership. This whole position was apparently his idea and he has allowed his imagination lurid reign. "Let's hire this one, Ger. He knows more poetry than I do."

"Great." Gervais finally deigns to look at me. The hand he extends is as cold and dead as my poor passenger's when it brushed against mine as the paramedics got him out of the cab. A fifty-dollar bill had fallen from the stiffening fingers.

Keep the change, buddy.

I hear the whisper of his voice.

A shiver goes through me and Phinney snickers. "Yeah, it is cold in here, isn't it? Hey, let's ask Nancy for some coffee, okay?" He pats Gervais on the back. "I'll go hunt her down. You guys talk money and benefits."

Gervais clears his throat and gives me a look sour as curdled cream. He grimaces and I wonder if he's in some kind of pain. Then I realize his expression is meant to be a smile. "Would it were that easy."

But it is that easy, because Phinney, with his pedigree that goes back to God, has decided I'm perfect for the job. It's Gervais's job to be a hardass and so he is, just like Lila thinks it's hers to be a bitch. When Phineas returns with coffee, I decide to play hard to get. I tell them about the grant on the Cape and watch Phineas turn green. "I have a better idea," he says, with a wink. "You come do my job – I'll take the summer on the Cape."

"He's not an attorney, Phinney," says Ger. There's *A Separate Peace* quality about this whole conversation, mostly because of the eerie similarity in names, but it has a meaner edge.

At six the intercom buzzes and the secretary announces that Phineas's wife is on hold. "Dinner with the outlaws." He gets to his feet with a groan. "It's just been great talking to you, Jack. You're a real breath of fresh air around this morgue." He shakes my hand, slaps my back, then points at Gervais. "Hire him."

He picks up his blazer and strides out with a jaunty swing, leaving me feeling as if a light has gone out. Something collapses inside me, and I feel hollow, exhausted. "Would it were that easy." I stand up, then extend my hand to Gervais. Suddenly I really need to get out of this place. "I've taken enough of your time. Maybe I'll see you tomorrow night?"

"No." Gervais looks like he's simultaneously swallowed lighter fluid and a rod's been shoved up his ass. I remember that Lila said being invited was a big deal. "You won't. But based on your conversation with Mr. McPherson, I'm sure we'll speak next week."

In the elevator on the way down, Lila gives me a sidelong look. "Hey, Jack," she whispers. "You wanna fool around?"

I can just about breathe. "I don't feel so good," I say. The lower we go, the deeper I'm sinking.

"You do look kinda green," she says. "How'd the interview go? You were in there more than two hours with Mr. McPherson and Gervais."

"Phinney," I say. "Phinney and Ger. Ger and Phinney." She looks at me as if I've taken leave of my senses. "I guess you had to be there."

"Well, how'd it go? You didn't puke or anything, did you?"

"No, I didn't puke." I feel like it now, though. I don't think I can stand to spend my days playing what's-my-line with Phinney. "I guess it went well. Phinney kept saying, 'Hire him.' Ger...every time Phinney said that, Ger looked like he was going to- puke, that is."

"McPherson said that? McPherson said to hire you?" Lila claps her hands in front of her mouth, and her eyes fill with tears. "Oh, my God, Jack, you did it. Now you just don't fuck it up tomorrow night, and honey, I think you're in like Flynn."

Flynn, I think, as in Errol Flynn, who was tried for statutory rape. Not exactly the kind of in I'm looking for. Beads of sweat break out on my forehead. The elevator bounces as we hit the lobby level. Lila looks at me with concern. "Honey, are you okay? Jack? You're not going to faint, are you?"

"No," I say. I grit my teeth and bite my tongue until I taste blood. "No." The tie around my neck feels like a noose, and I tug at it. "There a men's room on this level?"

"Oh, yeah, sure there is. Let me show you. Splash some water on your face, Jack. You look real pale." She tucks her arm in mine and guides me solicitously across the black marble floor.

In the men's room, I don't throw up, though I feel like it. Instead, I splash water on my face, on the back of my neck. When I look up, Dougless is standing behind me.

"Don't do this, Jack," she whispers. "Please. You don't understand yet. Please."

"Look, lady, you don't understand. I owe a hundred and eighty thousand dollars," I whisper back. "Not counting my student loans. According to Lila, if I don't get a better job soon, we're screwed."

"Jack, you don't understand. Please don't do this. You have a gift, but you're not ready. Please, Jack. Go."

"I can't fucking do that!" I scream. "I don't know what you are, or what you want, but I want you to leave me alone. Do you hear me? Leave me alone!"

I open the door and see Lila standing there, mouth open, hand raised to knock. I can tell she's heard me.

"Some kook's in there," I say. "We better tell security."

Lila wants me to take the night off, but I don't want to. I get the worst car again, Old Bessie, but I don't care. In fact, I'm sort of happy to see her. For the first time in a long time, I'm looking forward to driving up and down the silent avenues, watching the lights shift and refract off the windows and the walls. I've remembered why I liked taxiing in the first place, what drew me into driving at night. Inside the cab's my own little world.

I'm on Avenue D heading toward Houston Street, when I notice a woman in a trench coat signaling for a cab. I pull over to the curb. For a split second, I wonder if this is yet another strange passenger, but her whole demeanor is so refreshingly down to earth I breathe a sigh of relief. "Grand Central, please."

"Train to catch?"

"Yeah, but not for a couple hours yet. You can take your time."

I glance up in the rearview mirror. The woman's face is broad, without a hint of makeup. Her hair is straight and cut in a bob. Her clothes are simple, utilitarian. I look back at the building she was waiting in front of. "NYPD" reads the sign. "Don't worry, Officer," I say. "I've never gotten a ticket." And I haven't, which, given my predilections, has been pretty damn miraculous.

"How'd you know I was a cop?" She looks amused, intrigued.

"Lucky guess. You were standing near the station. But you're not from around here, either."

"That a lucky guess, too?" She leans forward and looks at my license. "You're pretty good, Mr. Chance. You're right. I'm from a little town in Connecticut. Bethel. Ever hear of it?"

We glide up to a red light. "Can't say as I have." Bethel does ring a bell though...it's a Biblical name... Jesus performed a miracle there... it must be something the nuns beat into me, I decide, along with all the other crap. "What brought you down here?"

"Local girl died not far from here last Tuesday."

A chill goes down my back. I glance up at my passenger.

She's looking out the window, at the hookers on the corner. As I tap the accelerator, she says, "I came to talk to the police...her parents are pretty devastated. It's a small town, and they don't understand." She shrugs. "I was just trying to get some answers so I can explain to these people what happened to their daughter."

"That's nice of you," I say.

"We're neighbors. Today's my day off."

"That's really nice of you," I say.

We pull up beside Grand Central. "My name's Sergeant Fescue, Eileen Fescue - like the grass. You ever come to Bethel, Connecticut, stop in and say hello." She pushes money into my hand.

As she gets out of the car, something makes me pause. I feel a moment of déjà vu, and I remember the girl in the white raincoat, after the party. I remember asking her where she lived. I remember her answer in that little-girl lisp. *Bethel...Bethel, Connecticut.*

I watch Sergeant Fescue make her way into the gaping doors of Grand Central and be swallowed by the crowds.

My next fare raps on the window. "Driver? Can you take me to Queens?"

I drive off, but the reminder of the girl, of the ride, of the policewoman – Sergeant Fescue, like the grass – haunts me most of the night.

Around one, 1:11, to be exact, I decide to take a break before heading back to the garage for the night when I find myself in the Bronx near Co-op

City. I buy six White Castles and devour four in a few gulps. It's the first time I've been hungry all day. I slump back in the squishy seat, and let my head fall back. My eyes are gritty and sore, but the way the light-spotted towers of Co-op City rise all around me, the sky is lit an eerie iron gray, the color of Blake's dark, satanic mills.

I think about the hundreds of thousands of people who live in these square fortresses. I wonder if it's ever dark enough here to see the stars. I wonder if any one who lives here ever looks up to check.

Suddenly I'm aware I am conspicuously alone. The restaurant parking lot is deserted, even the restaurant itself is empty but for the sleepy staff I can see yawning through the windows. Trash drifts across the tarmac like tumbleweeds and from far away, a siren screams mournfully then fades. A flicker of movement by the dumpster catches my eye. Shadows with long tails scamper and flit around and over mountains of garbage.

The magic rats are alive and well in Jungle-land tonight, I think as I reach into the glove box for my notebook. It falls open, to a poem I worked on a while ago, and never could finish. It's about my father in prison.

Maybe I don't have to go to New Jersey after all, I think. Maybe I could ask him, and he'd tell me the truth. Far across an ocean of time, I hear my mother's immediate scoff. Sure you can ask him. Getting him to tell you the truth – that's another story. But why not ask him? What's he got to lose now? Mom's dead... if I'm his kid by another woman – I go cold all over. Even if Martha Sinclair isn't my mother, I have a mother out there somewhere. So why not just ask the one person who might have the answer?

I'd have to go talk to him. This isn't the sort of thing I can just call him up and ask, and I don't even know if prisoners can get phone calls. I could go out to the prison on Saturday. It's an hour or so outside the city. I wonder if he'll tell me the truth, but why not? What's he have to lose now? I try to imagine sitting down opposite the convicted killer who is my father for the first time since my mother dragged me out to see him when I was ten. What do I say to him, I wonder... *Hey, Dad, how you been? Now that the old lady's kicked, can you tell me who my real mother is?*

Hard as it is trying to imagine sitting down with him at all, a trip to White Plains is a whole lot easier than one to Jersey, and it would seem logical to start there. It seems less ridiculous than bolting off on the whims of a senile old woman, and a desperate reporter. I look around, half expecting Dougless to show up and add her two cents.

Instead, I see a kid huddled at the lone outdoor table, scribbling in a notebook. He's wearing a ragged windbreaker and a wool hat, and he looks young, far too young to be out so late and so alone. The light from the streetlamp streams down over him, and it seems he might be crying, because every so often, he stops and wipes his face with his sleeve.

He shakes his pen, tries to write, shakes it again. I put the car in drive, and ease up beside him. "Hey. Your pen crap out?"

He looks at me with all the immediate wariness bred by a life on the streets, then sniffs. His eyes are watery, and huge. "What?"

"I said, did your pen crap out?"

"Yeah." He shrugs, his glance slides away.

"Here, have mine." I hold it out through the window.

His body tenses, prepares for flight. In his oversize jacket and rounded head, he looks like a big baby bird.

"You hungry?" I hold up my White Castle bag. "I got some burgers I can't eat." He reaches for the bag with a wary hand and snatches it away. His hand is ice cold as his fingertips brush mine. "You want to sit in here a few minutes – eat and get warm?"

He hesitates.

Trust no one. I learned that lesson young myself. I hold up my notebook. "I write a lot myself. I know what it is when your pen craps out. Sucks."

"Yeah," he says, still wary. "You a cop?"

"I'm a cabbie." I point to the roof. "See my sign?"

He's fourteen, he's cold and he's hungry. He gets in the backseat, wary and tense. He keeps one hand on the door while he wolfs down two White Castles, then two more in what looks like a blink. When I see him reach into the bag and pull out what looks like another, I turn around. "There's more than two in there?" Was it possible the counter-girl gave me more than six?

"Looks like there's at least three more," he says. "And fries at the bottom. You want one?"

"Help yourself." My stomach rumbles and I wish I had my Tums. The little burgers are starting to repeat on me and they don't taste quite so good the second and third time around. I take the straw out of my soda and offer it to him over my shoulder. "Thirsty?"

"Thanks." He munches away, concentrating on the food.

Something inside me is alive and tingling, roused by the boy's pain. Images flash in front of me, sensations explode on my skin, across my back, memories of beatings and losses and disappointments that aren't mine. "You always stay out this late?" I ask.

"When I feel like it."

What I feel is similar to what I felt when I talked to the bus driver the other night, but this pain is more acute. The bus driver's loss was relatively old, relatively healed, compared to this. This is fresh pain, raw as a new wound. *The first cut is the deepest* sings Sheryl Crow in my head. His eyes are hollow, his mouth is slack. I nod at the notebook on his lap. "You write when you feel like it, too?"

"I write all the time." He shrugs. "I won't be writing much any more though."

A deep foreboding fills my bones, and I know exactly what this ragged, starving, beaten kid is thinking. I take a deeper, harder look, but he won't meet my eyes. "Why not?" I ask.

"I'm out of paper." He flips open the book, shows me how every square inch is covered with tiny writing. There are kids for whom a notebook is a luxury beyond imagining. I know, because I was one of them.

"Here," I say. From some more rational corner of my mind, I watch myself open the glove box. I pull out a notebook. Attached to it is a pen. It's just a simple ballpoint, nothing fancy, but the notebook is a thick stenographer's notebook, just the size to be hidden inside a jacket. I have no idea how it got there, or how I knew it was there, though I suppose I must've left it there and forgot about it. The kid's eyes pop out, when I hand it to him. "You can have this one. Take the extra pen, too. If it writes, now you have two."

The kid looks at me really hard. "Are you shittin' me?"

I just shake my head. "Can I take you somewhere?" The look on his face changes, hardens and I hasten to add: "Like home?"

He flashes a glance in my direction. "I ain't got no home. Not since my mom died…" He looks the other direction, sniffs hard, then says, "They been trying to find my brother – he went into the service, they think. No one knows where he is."

I think about what my life might've been if my mother had not been there at all. Against the wider world, she protected me as well as she could. It made our difficult dance all the more difficult, but at least she was there.

I put the car in gear. "Where do you want me to take you, kid?"

"I don't have any money," he says. "My foster mom ain't going to give you any, either."

"Don't worry about it," I say. The address he gives me is a project blocks and blocks from Co-op City. He has to bang on the door, but it finally opens. The woman who lets him in is skinny, and wrapped in a shiny red silk robe. I can hear her screech at him from the pavement. When she sees me, she makes a motion for me to shoo, then drags him into the house and slams the door so hard the light fixture over the door frame sags to one side.

As I drive away, I see Dougless sitting in the back seat. "He'll be okay, Jack."

"W-why?" I slam on the brakes, nearly veer through a stop sign. "How the fuck can you know that?"

"Because you fed him, Jack… just what he needed to be fed." She leans forward, and hands me a piece of crumpled paper. She smells good, crisp and clean, like the thin air into which she vanishes.

I understand more than I ever want to understand about anyone as I read and realize my intuition about the kid's suicidal intentions was correct. I'm still not sure how the paper got out of the kid's notebook, though I guess if it were the last page in a well-worn notebook, it could slip out on its own. But crumpled? Had he done that deliberately? Just as a result of talking to me?

The kid's a good writer, I think, as I untangle his tiny tortured sentences. I'm glad I left that notebook in the glove box. I must've, because that's the only way I can think of that it got there.

On impulse I tear the paper into shreds. These are the kind of feelings you expunge, expel and expurgate, but you don't go back to visit very often. Those are the places where the demons dwell. And Dougless said he'd be okay. Whoever the fuck Dougless is.

Chapter 12

The first thing I do Saturday morning is pull my birth certificate out of the neat file where Lila keeps our important papers. To my surprise, there're actually two of them – one that looks like a copy of an official form that was filled out at the time of my birth and the other issued by the State of New York on July 23, 1987 – more than seventeen years after I was born. That certificate shows my birth date as March 2, 1971, and gives my parents as John Cianci and Irene Antonelli. I remember now that I needed it to apply to college, because the first one, the clearly older one, is just a photocopy - and a very bad photocopy at that.

I take it in the bathroom and sit on the closed seat of the john. I understand now what my mother and aunt were looking for as they stared so intently at it. It wasn't the correction in my birthday that mattered to them, though that was the only thing that made sense to me at the time so that's the only thing I noticed. Mother's name and father's name, city and state of birth weren't blank – they were all ruthlessly blacked out. I peer as closely as I can at the worn photocopy. My mother must've stared at this for hours. I stare at the space for state. Could it be that what she – and I – assumed to be NY for New York is really NJ? For New Jersey?

Why else would a woman in New Jersey think she's my mother?

There's only one person who might be able to tell me.

I call the prison near White Plains, find out that visiting hours are from noon to six today. I learn I'm on my father's "list."

When I tell Lila this, she is incredulous but reserved. I think she's decided to back off until after I get offered the job. I know if I refuse to take it, all hell is going to break loose. "You'll be back in time to get dressed for the party?" she says.

"I have to pack, too," I say.

She bites her lip, says nothing. There's a wall between us, ever since I pulled out my suitcase. I haven't told her about the kid last night, or the guy the night before. She'll just see them as two good reasons to get out of taxiing.

I load my backpack. It's a two-hour ride to the prison, and who knows how long a wait? Maybe he won't even want to see me. I am on his list, so maybe that means he's wanted – hoped – I'd come to see him some day. My mother never said one nice thing about him. Neither did anyone else. Loyalty to my mother on what was clearly a painful topic prevented me from asking her too many questions about him. After my mother died, Lila convinced me that the last thing someone fighting an addiction problem needs is a relationship with anyone so dysfunctional as to be in prison.

"Can I just ask you one question?" she asks, as I put on my denim jacket. "Why now? Don't you understand how important it is not to fuck this up?"

"I realize," I say. "But it's come up –"

"So it waited twenty-six years. It can't wait another week?"

In front of my mind's eye flashes the painting in the elevator lobby, the one with the figure approaching the gallows, holding what looks like a violin. I think about Dougless, who seems to have a knack for being in places people die. *Just let me take him.* Take him where? I wonder every time I think about it, which is uncomfortably too often. Maybe she's the Angel of Death the nuns were so crazy about, and I don't have long to wonder. I want to tell Lila that I'm afraid I might be dying soon, but that sounds crazy too. But all I say is, "No," because that's the only thing there is to say.

The first thing I see on the newsstands is that another Jane Doe has been found, this time in Central Park. Because of all the recent rain, it's hard to know exactly how long she's been dead, but speculation is that she'd been there since at least Wednesday night. I remember how I could've sworn I saw

Savageux and his companion materialize out of a wall that separates Central Park from Fifth Avenue. On Wednesday night.

On the way to the prison I stare out the window so I can't see if Dougless decided to come along. I know I'm not on drugs. I just don't understand why this is happening. There's no reason in the world to believe there's anything any more special about me than any other struggling writer-artist-musician-sculptor-dancer. A billboard catches my eye. LIVE PSYCHICS – CALL NOW AND CONNECT. 1-800-TUNE-U-IN.

I'm not one of those people, I tell myself. They're all crazy or lying and trying to make a buck off innocent people. I just know things. Sometimes. A lot of times, I amend myself as a rising chorus of memories remind me how far too often my hunches and guesses prove correct. Doesn't seem to work with the lottery, or the horses, or anything that might be useful.

It connects you to people.

I think I hear Dougless's voice and I jerk my head around to see if she's sitting behind me. The aged face of an Asian man stares back at me. He's wearing a shabby Yankee hat and I know he's going to see the son who is at once his greatest love and his worst disappointment. He gazes at me blankly behind the wall of his pain. I don't want to connect with that, I think, and I turn away, eyes lowered.

Maybe I should think about scheduling an appointment at the clinic, I think. I don't understand why it is I'm being bombarded by sensations I just can't explain. I get off at my final destination and confront the sprawling gray block of concrete before me. It's a huge pile of barbed wire, surveillance cameras at every angle, armed guards. But it's not dead, not by any means. Instead, the whole building pulsates with rampant energy so palpable I can almost see it. It makes the air hot and heavy, makes the guards sweaty and red-faced.

I join a long line of relatives and friends. The air stinks of sweat and desperation, anger and despair. Kids cry, metal chairs ring. I pull up my collar and tuck my chin down to chest and pretend to fall asleep.

At last, around two o'clock, I hear my name called. I'm led to a row of cubicles that look like library carols but instead are fronted by glass with two way phones. On the other side of the phone is the man who brought me home.

"Hi, Jack."

"Hi." I don't know what to call him. Dad doesn't seem appropriate. Father seems too formal for this steel-eyed, steel-haired, squared-jawed felon. Finally, I say. "Thanks for putting me on your list. It made getting in here easier."

He nods. There's a flatness to his expression, and his eyes slide over mine, smooth as marbles. Behind him, I think a shadowy flicker, the outline of a man in a suit standing just behind his shoulder. I glance up and the outline vanishes. The hair on the back of my neck goes up and I wonder if Dougless is anywhere around.

My father clears his throat. Whatever the intent of his years spent here, it hasn't punished him for anything he's done – it's honed him, so that now he's something truly dangerous, something that feeds on the incipient energy that I feel seeping into the cubicle from all directions. When I look at him directly, the shadow of the man standing behind the chair appears again. It vanishes when I glance at it.

My father shifts, and his muscles bulge beneath his blue prison-issue shirt; his cheeks are rough and pitted. His voice is a gritty growl. "They ain't gonna give us much time."

"I...uh... I wanted to come to see you – to ask you..."

"Ask whatever, kid. That's why I put you on the list."

Maybe it's a trick of the light, but I can't find his eyes. They're hollow, empty, as if he's staring out at me from the end of a long dark tunnel. I pull out the old photocopy. I plaster it to the partition as I cradle the receiver on my shoulder. "Can you tell me who any of these people are? Or where I came from?"

"No."

"No, you don't know, or no, you won't tell me?"

He shakes his head with a snort. "I tell you what I know, kid. We found you in a wreck. Paper was folded up wit' you."

"So...so how'd you come to adopt me?"

He shrugged. "I brought you home, priests greased the skids. No one asked questions – they knew your mother wanted a kid bad."

"Mom thought I was yours. So that's not true?"

He leans forward, his nose so close to the partition, his breath clouds the glass. He's in jail for murder, and I wonder who he killed, and why. The shadow flashes into form behind him, and for a moment I see him clearly, a man in a dark silk suit, wearing a white shirt and bright blue tie. There's a dark red hole where the breast pocket should be. He's smiling, and I realize he's delighting in his murderer's misery.

I wonder if Johnny Chance has any idea that the ghost of the man he murdered follows him around, enjoying every despicable moment of his existence. I blink and the ghost vanishes, leaving behind a sick knowing that clouds the air like a foul miasma.

He wants me to see him, I realize. *He wants me to know my father's guilty. He wants me to hate my father, so he can enjoy that, too.*

For the first time, my eyes connect with my father's, and I am jolted by the emptiness in them. I feel a pang of something I can't quite put a name to.

"I let her think that."

"Why?" I blurt. He has no idea of the penance my mother extracted from me for that single omission. "What difference did it make?"

"It was the times, I guess, kid. Where I come from, a man without a son ain't quite a man, somehow." He sits back, crosses his arms over his chest, then shrugs. "Me and the old lady – we been married awhile, no kids – meanwhile her sister's popping them out like doughnuts. Letting everybody think you could be mine made it not my fault. You know?"

I don't know what to say. "So...so you just found me, in a car wreck? By the side of the road?"

"Yeah. Me and your Uncle Joey – remember your Uncle Joey? No? He was in here for a while. Anyways, we was coming home from Jersey one night – happened by an accident on the turnpike. Bad one – we stopped, looked around. Cops weren't there yet, but we could hear the sirens – someone had called it in already.

"The worst of the fire was over – everybody in the car was dead. We was carrying some contraband ourselves, you know – we didn't want to hang around. But I heard something, and we looked around, and there you was, wrapped up in a blanket and screaming your head off. Somehow when the car crashed you landed in a bush. Kinda like Moses. Didn't they find him in a burning bush?" He laughs, pleased with himself.

"That was God," I say. "God spoke to Moses from a burning bush." A drink would be good right now, I think. A shot of tequila would help. A lot. I shove the thoughts of booze out of my head, and try to concentrate on what my so-called father's saying.

"Whatever. So I see you laying there, and the cops are coming, and we gotta leave, but I says to Joey, Irene wants a baby, right? Let's bring her this one." He shrugs. "So we did."

Somehow I think there's more to the story, because the idea he'd stop out of the blue on a dark road, at night, to help strangers – there's something about that story that just doesn't square with the person sitting on the other side of the partition. It's cloudy with fingerprints and smears that look like tears and worse. I finally understand why my mother didn't believe it. I cock my head. "Were you the reason the car crashed in the first place?"

"You should be a cop, kid. No, as a matter of fact – we did just happen to stop. Car had nothing to do with us."

"So you just stopped?"

"Well." He hesitates, looks over his shoulder. He looks me directly in the eye as he speaks, and I know he's telling me what he believes to be true. "I ain't ever told no one this, but I'll tell you cause I got this feeling you ain't coming back here again, not that I blame you. But I could've sworn, as we got closer – we could see the glow from the accident down the road, and we knew it was bad. But about five miles before it, I started seeing this naked woman walking down the side of the road, just in front of us. She had this long dark red hair, and this white ass that curved...mmmm." He makes a motion with his hands. "One minute, I'd think I'd see her, next she wasn't there." He breaks off, shakes his head. "Joey didn't see nothing. He thought I was nuts. But then we found you, and he agreed I should take you home."

A naked woman walking down the side of the Jersey Turnpike would certainly get anyone's attention at any time, day or night. But one with long red hair, who could only be seen by some – that sounds so much like Dougless, a chill runs down my spine. "Do you remember what state the plates were from?"

He hesitates. "Nah. Probably Jersey, cause I didn't notice." He looks at me through the glass a long moment. "I'm glad to see you made it, kid. Picking you up was maybe the one good thing I did my whole life. I'm glad it worked out." With that he hangs up and walks away. The ghost behind him flashes into view, and winks at me before he vanishes.

I slump, expel a deep breath I didn't realize I'd been holding. I feel empty and drained and horrified all at once. It's not just a ghost that haunts Johnny Chance. In a sad kind of way I'm sorry I'm not his son. Maybe things would've been better for him if I had been. In Johnny Chance's universe, a man who doesn't meet his definition of a man is somehow not quite human. That's what he believed, and that's what he became.

And he became what he beheld. Suddenly I understand that line from Milton in a far deeper way than ever before. I think about that the whole ride back.

I walk in the door on the dot of quarter to six to find Lila fuming. She's pacing back and forth like a caged lion, wearing what's probably the most beautiful dress I've ever seen. So dark a green it's almost black, the neckline is cut straight across her shoulders, the sleeves are long and simple. It ends just above her knees. From the front, it's almost too simple, too severe. But then she turns, and I see that the back plunges below her waist and ends in point just below the dimple in the small of her back. A simple satin bow rides right above her ass, drawing the eye inexorably to the point where creamy flesh and lustrous velvet meet.

"Where the fuck you been?" are the first words out of her mouth.

"Where the fuck you get that dress?" I respond. I am mesmerized by the vision before me. She doesn't even look like Lila. Her hair is brushed straight off her forehead and pulled into a glossy bun low on her neck. This reveals a tiny triangle of silky dark hair just at the top of her spine. The affect is amazingly sensual. She's wearing green velvet pumps, too, with tiny satin bows at the heels, just like the one on her ass. It is easily the best I've ever seen her look.

"For your information, a client was so happy with the work I did for her, that she gave me this – right out of her closet. It's couture – but it didn't fit her right." Lila preens a minute in the mirror, momentarily forgetting about me. Her lipstick makes her mouth look like a wet red slash across her face. She's dressed up for someone, I think. I remember my sense that Lila's met Savageux, and I wonder if it's possible that he's the client who gave her the dress. No, I think – Lila said *she* gave her the dress. Right out of *her* closet. But I look at Lila as I strip and duck into the shower.

"How could it?" The water is freezing, but I don't care. "It looks like it was made for you."

She looks so prim, almost puritan from the front, where the dress only suggests the outline of her curves. It's the contrast of the back and the front, the covered and the exposed that makes the dress so appealing. Not to mention the fact that Lila is the possessor of some of the most beautiful curves I've ever seen on a woman – and this dress takes advantage of every one.

I don't hear her reply. I find myself scrubbing and scrubbing, as if I'm trying to remove dirt embedded in my pores. For some reason, I feel inexplicably drawn to dump a box of Epsom salts over myself. Lila rips the shower curtain open as I do so. "What the fuck are you doing in here?" she asks savagely.

I remember the shower scene from *Psycho*. "Getting clean, babe." I yank the curtain closed. "Can a man get some privacy?"

"I have your clothes laid out," she says, as she slams the door.

She hustles me out the door so fast I nearly forget my suitcase. Only the ringing of the phone saves me, and although the look Lila gives me is enough to send me into rigor mortis, I pick it up anyway. "Hi, Shirley."

"Hey, Jack, how'd you know it was me?"

"Just a special ring, I guess. I'll be there on the midnight train, Shirley. Will you be there to meet me?"

"No," she says. "I'm stuck out here in Bumblefuck. I'm sending someone else – that's why I'm calling. Her name is Jessie Woodwright and she's actually very nice."

"Actually very nice? What's that mean?"

The words Lila's mouthing are unprintable. "Well, she's coming from a gig."

"A gig? You mean she'll be in costume?"

"Yeah – exactly. A costume. Don't worry – you'll see when you get here. You won't miss her. She'll meet you outside the station."

Lila takes the phone out of my hand and hangs up. "We need to go. Now."

Lila won't speak to me on the subway. I sidle close, and speak into her ear. "Why're you so mad at me? I'm here, we're going, you look great. You smell yummy, too." I take a deep breath, intent on inhaling her musky scent, but she moves and I get a lungful of subway fumes instead.

"You look like a fucking street person hauling that thing, Jack," she hisses back. "I can't believe you – we get an invitation to the fanciest party the firm puts on a year, and you have to show up at the New York Athletic Club looking like a fucking bag person. What the hell is wrong with you?" The look she gives me has daggers in it. I sit back and cradle my battered suitcase close, remember once again the guy who died in my cab and the way he held on to his, as if his life depended on it.

"I'm sorry, Lila," I say. "I guess I just don't know how to explain it to you. All my life I've wondered who my parents are. My mother was so sure I was my father's kid. But I'm not. See, Lila, that's why I went out and talked to him. He said I wasn't."

"And you believed him?"

I blink. "Why wouldn't I believe him?"

She throws back her head and laughs so loudly people at the end of the car turn to look at her. "Because he's a felon, Jack. He's a criminal, a murderer. An armed robber, a mobster. Jesus, what isn't he? A pedophile? I bet he told you he was innocent, too, right?" She shakes her head, holds up her hand. "Spare me, Jack. You don't have to say any more. I'm sure we can check your bag."

The coat-room attendant doesn't give me a second glance as she hauls my bag into the coat-room. She hands me two tickets – one for the bag, one for Lila's coat. Not once does she meet my eyes. Lila tugs me past long rows of glass cases full of gold and silver and bronze trophies and photographs of solemn white-sweatered men standing beside boats, in front of golf courses, beside racehorses. I feel I've stepped inside *The Great Gatsby*.

Phinney descends on us like a schooner in full rig, his phantom of a wife in tow. I notice Lila being noticed, I see eyes slide over her, to me, and then back to her. Without realizing it, I think, my dear wife has managed to entirely eclipse me. I imagine myself dressed in a gorilla suit, standing ignored next to Lila, and I burst out laughing just as Phinney reaches the punch line of his joke. My hearty laugh delights him and soon he has me under his wing, shepherding me around the room. He likes me, he really likes me, and so does the phantom wife, who appears to be on the verge of tears.

I don't understand the wringing of the hands, the sighs and anxious glances, until Phinney explains that Muriel's sort of hosting the event, along with a couple of the more senior wives. This is a test and she's flunking badly because she's failed to ensure the availability of the favorite libation of the most senior partner, one Mr. Alberoye Armstrong, Esquire - I don't catch his numeral.

Mr. Armstrong looks like the animated corpse of Winston Churchill, standing among a cluster of jacketed men, all with bulldog jowls, cigars in their mouths, hands conspicuously empty. None of the other partners are drinking either.

No one looks happy.

Phinney pats my shoulder, and finishes whatever he was saying with, "We won't go over there just yet. I still have hopes Muriel's going to pull it off – she can be amazing when she wants to be." I see a fine sheen of sweat on his forehead, though.

About half an hour into it, I meet Lila coming out of the ladies' room. "So what'd'ya think," she asks, sidling up to me. She winks, squeezes my bicep through my cashmere-blend blazer. Drinking makes Lila friendly. "Pretty fancy for a couple kids from Brooklyn, huh?"

"Pretty fancy," I agree. Poor Muriel is in deep shit. I've overheard her discussed in sepulcher tones and even Phinney looks worried visibly. "But I don't get why everyone's acting like Poor Muriel's committed a mortal sin or something."

"Poor Muriel fucked up," Lila says. She pats her hair. "Big time." Across the room, I hear someone call her name, and Lila's head jerks around. "Christine? Is that you?"

She heads into a gaggle of overdressed women, and I edge around the room, hoping to find a potted palm or something to hide behind until it's time for my taxi. My head is ringing, my ears are burning, my gut has gone rigid as a rock. I'm starting to feel sick again, and I head for the bar. Maybe a soda will settle my stomach. I arrive there to find Poor Muriel pleading with the head waiter or usher or whatever he's called to just check one more time to see if by any chance the Middleton's has arrived.

He is less than accommodating- rude, even. He has a job to do, and scurrying back and forth between floors isn't it. The staff are well trained; if a delivery for the party - especially a delivery as important as a case of Mr. Armstrong's whiskey - had arrived, they'd know what to do.

"Did you look in the coat room?" I blurt. I can see the carton, somehow, in my mind's eye, my suitcase stacked on top of it, beneath a row of coats. They both ignore me, but the image is so strong, I have to say it again. "Did you look in the coat room?"

"The staff in the coat room would notify us immediately," Mr. Buttoned-Up says. He looks at me and somehow assesses at once that I am Not Important.

"Why don't you come with me?" I say to Poor Muriel. "I really do think I saw it there."

If I had suddenly announced an ability to make the blind see and the lame walk, I don't think the look Poor Muriel gives me could be more ecstatic. In the elevator she starts to weep. This is her first involvement with this kind of thing. It's a rite of passage for all the partners' wives. She's terrible at organizing – details aren't her thing. Darling Phinney doesn't deserve this. She hopes it won't have a negative affect on the way he's treated by the firm.

No, I think. I have a sense of foreboding that's similar but different from the one I felt with the kid last night. This fuck-up isn't going to affect how Darling Phinney's treated – it's Poor Muriel who's in for it. If she can't fix this, they'll be divorced within the year and the rest of the spiral that unfolds in fleeting glimpses isn't pretty. I really hope I'm right about the whiskey.

The woman guarding the coats goes to look but says it isn't there, just a couple cartons of bottled water.

But I can see it, I know I can, sitting directly under my suitcase. "Please," I say. "Take another look. Here's my ticket. I'm positive it's there."

"Sir, I saw your suitcase. It's on the floor – there's no case of whiskey under it. There's nothing under it. Just the floor. Those cartons you see are full of water bottles – not whiskey."

The palms of my hands are burning and I can see the six carefully wrapped bottles as clearly – more clearly, in fact - as I can see Poor Muriel, who's standing like a forlorn ghost in the shadows, looking as if she wishes she could disappear. The elevator doors open. Lila strides out, her color high, the impact of her dress as stunning as when I saw her in it the first time. "Can I look?" I say.

The attendant's first impulse is to say no. Poor Muriel sniffs. The woman's face hardens.

"Please?" I say.

She rolls her eyes, then shrugs. "Be my guest."

She steps aside and lets me in, and I grope under the coats, reaching for my suitcase, under it, where I *know* the crate of whiskey is. Time seems to stretch, to slow, the air itself takes on weight and form. The skin of my palms feels like it's on fire. I feel a curious jolt and a tingle pass through my skin. And then my fingertips touch it – smooth cardboard, tissue, and six bottle tops, *Muriel McPherson* scrawled in black felt tip across the side.

Triumphant, I pull out the carton, and hold it up. "Is this it?"

The attendant's jaw drops, her face flushes, then goes pale. "*Madre de Dios.*" She crosses herself. "I got down on my knees to look." She stares at me as if I've pulled a rabbit out of my ass. "There was nothing back there."

Poor Muriel steps forward, eyes shining. I feel as if I might collapse. As if from very far away, I hear Lila say, in very slow motion: "Get your suitcase, Jack – the cab's here."

My head feels as if I've stuck it inside a ringing bell, my heart is hammering against my breastbone. I have to tell myself to breathe. Poor Muriel kisses me, hugs me tight, the attendant watches my every move. Lila drags me across the lobby, out the door. We intercept a couple who've obviously just gotten out of the cab that's waiting by the curb.

The lights illuminate their faces. It's Nicholas Savageux and the woman I recognize from the other night. Trailing after them, is the girl from the other night, the one in the black leather and the maroon spiked hair. I think it's really strange they'd bring this odd little waif along, but then I blink, and the girl isn't there.

Savageux and his wife head directly for us, and the smiles that wreathe their faces make my blood run cold. Because Lila is smiling back, opening her arms and squealing "Clarissa!" as the woman steps forward to embrace her, enfolding her for a long moment in a tangled web of silvery lace.

Savageux looks at me, and once again I feel that stab of recognition. Then his gaze slides off me, cold as an ice cub. Tonight, I'm not the chosen One. I feel a tiny sting of disappointment. His flesh glows incandescent, and his teeth are very white as he smiles at my wife. "Lila, right?" His voice has an overtone as seductive as the brush of sand-washed silk across a polished floor.

Lila raises her face to his. Their eyes meet, she blushes, he smiles, she's enchanted.

I look at the wife. Her back is to me, and I am effectively shut out of the dazzling little triangle. She's the one who gave Lila the dress, I think, and in that moment I know that not only did she give the Lila dress, she had it made for Lila. On purpose. I remember what Dougless said about Savageux, that he could follow me to Brooklyn. *He's found a way in.*

I look at Lila. Her expression is beatific, her face is gleaming too, as if she somehow shares in their reflected glow. "Oh, my God, Lila," I begin. I tug on her arm. "You have to come with me…"

Instead she turns to me and pushes me away – not hard but firmly enough that I know I am dismissed, cast off, unnecessary. Savageux meets my eyes just as the doorman pulls me toward the cab, pushes me inside and slams the door almost on my hand.

Lila blows me a kiss as the cab pulls away. Savageux looks at Lila like a piece of candy on a tray he intends to savor. The last thing I see as the cab goes around the corner is Savageux's hand on my wife's back, on her skin, just above the bow, and the smile on the face of the girl with the maroon-spiked hair, who waves before she skips inside, tagging after everyone else.

Chapter 13

I almost don't get on the train. The idea that Lila's in Savageux's clutches, whatever that means, awakens something primal in me that it makes me want to tell the driver to stop the car so I can get out and run the ten blocks or so back. I lean forward, about to tap him on the shoulder, when Dougless stops my hand. I turn to see her sitting beside me. "Leave. Please."

The cabbie is listening to the Yankee game that's going on right now at the stadium. There's a new player this year, someone from Atlanta, I think, because as he comes to bat for the first time they play *The Devil Went Down to Georgia* in the background. The fiddle screeches through the speakers, sizzling through my mind. For a split second, I'm trudging up that hillside, wearing that shroud.

"You all right back there, buddy?"

This time Dougless stays visible – I guess the cabby can't see her. "Yeah," I say.

"I'd be pissed too if it was my wife looked like that and some guy put his hand on her ass." The cabbie sounds completely sympathetic. "Hell, just thinking about my wife looking like that gets me pissed." He nods at the road. "You want me to turn around?"

And miss the train. The ticket's non-transferable, I can't use it for a later train. It's this one, or another trip all together – another trip I know isn't likely to be willingly financed by Lila. I know this is my chance to put to rest a lot of questions. Dougless is watching me intently.

I take a deep breath, make my choice. "Nah," I say. "She's a grown-up."

"You must really trust her," he says, just as the newcomer from Atlanta hits a home run out of the park. The crowd goes wild, the high squeal of the fiddle uncurls in a long wild reel, and Dougless disappears.

We pull into Philadelphia near midnight. The minute my foot touches the platform, I start looking for a pay phone. It rings six times before the machine picks up. "Hey, babe, it's me – wanted you to know I got here and you looked amazing tonight. I miss you and I love you. Call you later." She's not there. Or she's so sound asleep she can't hear the phone.

There's a sick feeling in the pit of my stomach. I have to call someone, anyone, to make them go check on her, but there's no one I can call at this hour. *And the vision that was planted in my brain still remains,* Simon and Garfunkel carol in my head. I remember my conversation with her the other night, that sick and certain feeling I had that Lila had a brain tumor and was going to die.

She **is** *going to die.*

This time the feeling's so strong I go directly to a ticket counter, but they're all shut down this time of night. Maybe I *am* crazy, I tell myself. I've risked everything I have to lurch out here to New Jersey on a whim and a prayer, just so I can turn around and go home.

I bang on the desk and fume and wish I could conjure a ticket agent as easily as I apparently conjured up the whiskey. What the hell was I thinking, listening to a tabloid reporter and an imaginary friend? If I'd stayed, whatever was happening to Lila wouldn't be happening.

A janitor, seeing my distress, explains they'll reopen at 4:00 AM. He points me in the direction of the nearest pay phone. My fingers are trembling as I push in the change, and I will the phone to ring and ring and ring. But the machine answers anyway, and I plead, "Lila, this is Jack. If you're there will you please pick up? Please? I want to know you got home okay, babe – I just have one of my really bad feelings, so babe, if you're there –"

There's a click, a rustle and then a throaty, "I'm asleep, Jack."

The line goes dead. I let the air out of my lungs and sag against the booth. I'm wrong, I tell myself. I'm wrong, I'm wrong, I'm wrong. I've never been so happy to be wrong in my life. So why do I still feel so bad?

Maybe because it's nearly one in the morning and I'm starting to feel dizzy with exhaustion. I'm finally in a state to notice my surroundings. Compared to Penn Station or Grand Central, this place looks almost homey. My footsteps echo across the cavernous space as I make my way to the entrance. I'm looking for someone I've never met. I have no idea what she looks like. All I know is her name - Jessie Woodwright.

My name is Dougless Woodwright.

That thought stops me cold. Woodwright isn't any more common a name than Dougless is. What kind of a coincidence is it that the person who's meeting me is also named Woodwright? I peer up and down the sidewalk. *Turning and turning the widening gyre... what rough beast slouches toward Bethlehem to be born?* I wish that line would stop repeating itself in my head. I sink down on a bench and a cab driver approaches, speaks to me in an accent I find at first unintelligible. I realize that not only do I not know who I'm meeting, I don't know where she's taking me either. I fumble in my breast pocket, wondering if I had the foresight to remember to bring the telephone number of Shirley's motel. But of course I haven't.

I slump back, shut my eyes. The air is as warm and soft against my cheek as the brick is hard and rough against the back of my head. I stretch and try to get comfortable.

A black van pulls up to the curve. The driver's door swings open, and a figure gets out, one so startling I slam my head up against the wall. At first I'm blinded by the flash of pain in my head. I blink, trying to clear my vision and then I realize that the woman standing in front of me really *is* wearing a spiked black leather collar around her long slender throat, under which, on one side of her throat is a packed wad of white bandages soaked in bright red blood, some of which has seeped down her skin and onto her ragged white t-shirt, which peeks out under her fringed leather jacket. She steps into the light and I see her hair is spiked and black, her ears pierced with safety pins.

"Mr. Chance?"

I blink. I guess this is what Shirley meant when she said my ride would be in costume. I struggle to my feet, still dazed. "Uh, yeah…

"I'm Jessie Woodwright." As easily as I might fling a shirt across a room, she picks up my suitcase and heaves it into the open passenger side door. She has to move stuff to make it fit. This does not please her or any of the other occupants, because I hear a lot of muffled cursing, a couple thumps and a muffled "Fucking shit," from Jessie.

"Get in." She jerks a thumb toward the van, then sticks it in her mouth, and I realize she hurt herself somehow flinging in my bag. I feel badly as she climbs back in the driver side and slams the door, not to mention about as welcome as a bedbug. Maybe this really was the terrible idea Lila said it was.

The side door of the van is emblazoned with a silver guitar over which the words "BITCH FEAST" appear to drip blood. I open the door and peer inside. Most of the space is taken up by equipment, and the space that isn't is taken up by three other women. They're all dressed like Jessie, more or less – black leather pants and boots, ripped and bloodied t-shirts, tattoos and piercings all over. I fit myself into a space between two amps and a girl with slave bracelets around her wrists adorned with short lengths of broken chains. "Sorry we're late," she says.

Jessie glances at me sideways. "We had a gig tonight." Our eyes meet. In the shadowy light, her eyes appear to be the same color as Dougless's.

"What kind of music you play?" The tension in the car is palpable – the face of the woman beside me is streaked with tears.

There's a long, strange silence, that's broken by a snort from one of the two women behind me. "Ask Jessie."

Jessie pulls out onto the highway, eyes fixed on the road ahead. It's pretty clear to me she's angry – they're all angry - about something. I hope it's not me. The van feels like a tight metal box full of soft leather flesh and hard black cases. If they all lean in just an inch or so more, I feel like I might drown. I close my eyes and try to relax. Moist air rushes in through an open window. April may well be the cruelest month, but here the air that washes over my face is tender compared to Brooklyn's acrid streets.

We barrel over a suspension bridge. Its graceful arches gleam in the opalescent mist rising off the river. *Running water,* I think, wondering how many bodies of running water I crossed tonight. A lot, I imagine. I have to be safe now – whatever that means. But what about Lila?

Bless me, Father, for I have sinned. As we reach the crest of the bridge, my vision splits in half the way it did before my interview. On one side of my head, I'm here, squished uncomfortably; on the other, I'm a kid, in a confessional, sweaty palms pressed tight together, words tumbling out of order in my head. I don't know who's listening on the other side of the wooden screen, but I can sense a presence there, a presence and a light. I can remember a thousand thoughtless sins. But there's only one thing that has me terrified. *Don't let anything happen to Lila. Please, not while I'm so far away. That's just not fair.*

Incredibly, I feel agreement from whoever or whatever it is on the other side of that screen. In that same moment, a palpable weight lifts off me and the tension I didn't realize I was carrying dissolves between my shoulders. I've been given a reprieve.

I know this in the same moment my vision comes back together. Below us, the river shines flat and silver in the moonlight, dotted here and there with black rectangles of barges and tugs. Just off the bridge, we turn off the highway, onto a long curving road that leads eventually to a condominium development. In the lamplight, the houses are all cream-colored, with traces of antebellum embellishments – balconies, wrought iron curlicues, tiny cupolas and columns. It isn't the kind of place I expect a band that calls itself Bitch Fest – or Feast – to have a lair. Silently, we turn onto a quiet cul-de-sac.

As we pass a corner playground, I see a group of children running up and down, swinging, sliding, popping up and down on the see-saws. There's a strange kind of glow around each kid. "What the fuck –" I begin. Jessie glances up at me in the mirror but says nothing. As we pull around the corner, I get another look at the playground. This time it's deserted.

Jessie turns into a short driveway. She stops, opens her door. One of the women in the back seat reaches around me and a guitar case hits me in the head as she throws the side door open. "Don't bother," she snarls at Jessie.

"We'll talk," Jessie says. The first woman to get out doesn't answer – just stalks into the house and slams the door. "Won't we?" she says, to a second woman, whose now pulling out a huge amp, which is snagged on the corner of my suitcase. I lean over to help, but her look freezes me in mid-motion.

The second woman pauses as she's clambering out of the van. "Jessie – this shit you do? It's ruining everything." She slams the door with enough force to sever fingers, and tired as I am, I wonder exactly what it is Jessie's been ruining.

"Uh-where're we going now?" I ask, as we drive by the now silent playground.

"We have to take Heather home," Jessie replies. "And then…" She looks up in the rearview mirror, "we're going to my place." When I look surprised, she said, "Didn't Shirley mention that?"

"Uh…no," I say. No wonder she looks so thrilled. Pick up a stranger in the middle of the night, and take him home. Shirley wasn't kidding when she said she was pushy.

"Devil's Door's only about an hour and a half from here as the crow flies, but the roads aren't well-marked. We'll go first thing tomorrow." She tightens her hands on the steering wheel and stares straight ahead.

Heather snores softly beside a stack of drums. We pass a church, and I hear music, faint and sweet, echo on the wind as we drive by. I see Jessie's knuckles go white, as I lean out to get a closer look. We pull out onto a highway, and I see a young girl walking down the road. She's wearing a white dress, a shawl clutched around her. When she hears us, she turns, sticks out her thumb. "Stop," I say. "We should –"

Jessie drives past, stony-faced, and won't look at me, even in the mirror.

I turn around, but the girl's gone.

On a street corner, a child darts across the street, and Jessie drives right through him. "Jesus Christ," I say. The whole place seems alive with ghosts and phantoms who flit past the corner of my eye. I decide it's exhaustion. I lean my face against an amp and fall into a dream.

At first I think it's a girl-dream, but I'm not a girl. My hands are glowing gold again, and this time I'm holding a fiddle. I have a chain around my neck and my chest is bare. I'm standing on a rock, on the side of a mountain. A woman is standing next to me. I turn to look at her, and realize that behind me is an audience, of what looks like thousands of people watching us. In the center of the stage, Bruce and the band are tuning their instruments. I put my hand on her shoulder, intent on asking her who she is when she turns to me with a hiss and a flash of fangs. She leaps for my throat and I tumble, backwards off the rock, into the oblivion below. I wake myself up with another thump on the side of my head.

Jessie says, "We're here."

We've pulled up in front of a brick bungalow that reminds me of the one in Far Rockaway my aunt and uncle used to rent. Heather is no longer snoring behind me, and I wonder if it's possible she wasn't there at all. Then I remember Jessie mentioned taking her home, and I feel a little reassured.

She hits a button on the dash, and the garage door slides up. "Careful getting out – there's a lot of shit along the walls." She gives me a quick glance, as if assessing whether or not I understand what she's said. "Some of it's sharp." She pulls my suitcase from where she's wedged it, gets out and slams the car door.

In the light of the open car door, I see planes and lathes, hammers and chisels arranged in orderly rows all over the walls. The back wall is lined with shelves filled with cans. "Your husband a cabinet-maker?" I ask as I clamber after her.

"I don't have a husband. The tools are mine. I refinish furniture in my spare time."

But she does have a dog – two of them, in fact, enormous animals that appear to be half St Bernard and half Great Dane as they come loping through the cluttered breezeway between the garage and the rest of the house. They attack her joyfully, then leap on me with the same exuberant abandon. "Wow," I say. "What big friendly dogs. They love everybody, huh?"

"No," she answers. She's looking at me as if maybe I've stashed a steak under each arm. "They usually don't like anyone." She flicks on a light and I stumble into the kitchen. My first impression is that I've stumbled onto the set of I Love Lucy. Crockery spills all over the shelves, plants riot around the window. The cabinets are painted the color of butter, with a blue checkerboard border. Where the tile counters aren't covered in dishes or pots and pans, there's books.

It's warm and homey, right down to the stack of dirty dishes piled in the sink. "Sorry." She sees me glance at them. "Not much time for housework." Jessie punches another switch, and continues through the kitchen. "Angus, Lucy... here – go find a treat." She distracts the dogs with a quick toss of biscuits from some invisible stash. "Here's the living room. You can sleep on the couch."

The room on the other side of the half wall is a tumbled hodge-podge of book-laden shelves, sagging furniture and liquor store cartons, all brimming with books. Maps and charts are pinned to the walls. A battered coffee table holds a profusion of books – some with spines splayed open, others with papers stuck in them. The entire house looks like my side of the bedroom in our tiny apartment.

"There's a quilt and some pillows." Jessie waves an airy hand in the vague direction of the couch. "Come on, puppies, come help mamma. Please don't disturb the books." That sentence is addressed to me. She reaches up to her hairline, and gives a jerk. The spiked black hair comes off and sweat-soaked curls fall all over her face, but not in time to hide her sour expression. The one thing that is absolutely clear to me about Jessie Woodwright is that she is not at all happy about my presence. I also have the feeling the rest of her life is as messy as her house.

I can't help staring at the piles of books. "Are these all yours?"

"They are now." She pauses under an arch that I presumes leads to her bedroom. "Bathroom's down the hall to your left. If you want tea-"

"Have you read them all?" The depth and breadth of subject matter is bewildering – it seems to encompass anything and everything, from quantum physics to Chinese history, from paleontology to music theory.

"-it's on the shelf above the stove. Mugs are above the sink." The last thing I see her do before she closes the door is reach around to unhook her leather collar. The entire assemblage comes away in one piece, and I see that the whole get-up is, indeed, just a costume, because the glimpse I get of her neck is that it's long and unsullied as a swan's.

I feel gritty, dirty, and completely worn out. I sink down onto the lumpy couch that's covered in stained red velvet, worn thin as a confessional kneeler, which feels as if it will be as comfortable to sleep on as Old Bessie's seat. Out of curiosity, I pick up the top book on the table. It's a copy of Milton's *Paradise Lost*. I open it, and it falls open, as if by force of habit to a page toward the beginning. The highlighted lines leap out at me: *Who overcomes by force hath overcome but half his foe.*

I remember the way Savageux looked at me as Lila looked at him, that brief second when I'd read dismissal in his eyes. I think about how the wife looked on, and how sure I am she had that dress made for Lila deliberately. But why Lila? Lila, for all her bad-girl bluster, is as conventional as any good Catholic girl in bed. And how hard up for kinks could they be? It's one thing to throw a costume party – it's another to have a dress made for someone. Get a grip, I tell myself. The idea that anyone would go to so much trouble is ludicrous. But if Savageux really is connected to all the Jane Does, as Shirley believes, then Lila really could in trouble.

He's found a way in. Dougless's voice echoes in my mind. It's not Lila Savageux wants, I remember. It's me. And that just makes no sense at all. At least I know she's home from the party. I can't call her again until the morning.

More to distract myself, than out of real curiosity, I browse a few of the other books piled high on the table. Ms. Woodwright's interests are as catholic as they are eclectic. *Wealth of Nations* sits on top of *The Human Genome Project Report*. Stephen Hawking rubs elbows with William Blake, *Dark Matter and the Nature of Quantum Reality* sits under *Irish Myths and Yeats*. Books on Chinese pictograms, the Mayan calendar, and astrophysics are piled under Sun Tzu's *Art of War*, Gibbons' *Rise and Fall of the Roman Empire*, and something that seems completely unrelated, *Milton: Poet as Prophet*.. Another pile appears devoted solely to the stock market, all things. The top title is *Plotting the Elliot Wave*. Inside, the book appears to consist mostly of complex graphs I have no clue how to decipher.

On the wall above the couch, a graph of overlapping red and blue and green lines charts the rise and fall of the stock market since the turn of the century, while another uses the same colors to track the spread of something I can't discern across the globe from the end of World War II. A map of Europe in the fourteenth or fifteenth century hangs beside it, red and green and blue pins fanning out from a point in southern France. I'm used to people who study obscure subjects with intensity, but I've never seen anything like this. I wonder what she does when she's not a vampire rock chick. It's interesting that her taste in poetry seems confined to Milton, Blake and Yeats.

Jessie comes out of the arch, flanked by the dogs. She's washed her face, changed out of her costume. Unlike the other women, she doesn't have permanent visible piercings. She's wearing a white robe, and her hair is pulled back in a loose braid. In this light it looks darker than Dougless's. There's something else besides her eyes that's so familiar about her, I find it hard to look away, and she's so pretty I can't help but smile. Jessie isn't smiling back. "You read all these?"

"Bathroom's free," she says. She's holding a box of salt – kosher salt - in one hand and a black-feathered fan in the other. She stops and stares at me pointedly. "You can use it now." She looks annoyed, and I wonder why she agreed to meet my train, let alone let me stay here, if it were such an imposition.

"Look, I can call a cab and go somewhere else. I don't mean to put you out." I don't need anyone else's complications. I have enough to worry about. I also have twenty dollars in cash. I don't know where I'll go if she puts me out.

She glances away and looks faintly embarrassed. "Look, I'm sorry if I seem less than… gracious. It's just that… it's late…" There's a droop in her shoulders and a line between her brows. She's worried about something that has nothing to do with me. "I have to go outside now. Go stay in there till I come back inside, okay?"

"Why?"

"Because otherwise you might think I'm crazy. Come on, Angus, come, Lucy." Jessie snaps her fingers. The dogs perk their ears, turn their heads and whine in her direction. She looks at me with steel in her eyes, as the dogs circle and sniff my suitcase, then sit down opposite the coffee table, eyes bright, tongues hanging out. They look like they're ready to chat.

"Your dogs are real nice," I offer. She steps aside to let me pass, and I brush against her robe. For a split second, our eyes meet, and I feel something nearly identical to the feeling I had when I first saw Savageux up close on the street. *I know you.*

It isn't just that she resembles Dougless. There's something about Jessie Woodwright herself that makes me feel as if I've always known her. In the way she holds her body I can tell my presence is upsetting her. Maybe it's just that I'm a stranger, it's late at night, we're alone and her dogs, that she obviously relies on to protect her, are treating me like a prodigal member of the pack.

The bathroom tile and all the fixtures are bubble-gum pink. As I close the door, I hear a screen door slam. Outside the window I hear rustling and smell something burning that's sharper and crisper than weed. The smoke wafts over the shrubbery and I hear Jessie cough. I even think I hear her swear under her breath, and then I hear an unmistakable: "Shit!"

I peek through the gingham curtains. In the foggy moonlight, she's walking backwards, muttering, scattering the salt and waving the fan, in a circle around the house. I can't tell if she's praying or swearing, because it sounds like she's doing a bit of both. I lean forward to get a better look at what she's doing, and that's when it occurs to me that it's not so much Dougless she resembles; it's me, in my girl-dreams.

Part Four – Jessie

Chapter 14

Jack's sitting on the couch, leafing through a book when I come in, which instantly pisses the shit out of me. He's changed out of his preppy clothes. I have to admit I'm surprised to see how ragged he looks. His sweatpants are faded and bleach-spotted, and his moccasins are so worn, his little toes peek out the sides. But it's his sweatshirt that makes me pause, because it's patched and neatly mended in about a dozen places. Who does that, I wonder. Who bothers to mend a sweatshirt? "I thought I told you to stay in the bathroom." I put the feather fan and the salt on the counter, and glance automatically at the clock. It's 1:11 in the fucking morning of the worst day of my life so far, my thumb is still throbbing where I jammed it into his suitcase, and I just can't bring myself to be nice. "*And* not to touch the books?"

He shuts it with a snap and places it carefully in the exact spot it was. I wonder if he's being a smartass. "What were you doing?"

If I really wanted to get rid of this guy, I could just tell him the truth. "It's like this," I imagine myself saying. "Ever hear of things that go bump in the night? I have things that knock on the doors. The salt and the smoke keep away them away." I don't like to even think about things like this, however, because it makes me afraid I might be as crazy as my mother said my father was.

He doesn't seem like a bad sort, though, and he's cute, in a scruffy kind of way, not to mention that I've never seen Angus and Lucy take to anyone like they've taken to Jack. I don't want to run him off screaming - not yet, any way. So instead, I say, "It's just... uh... just something I do. It's like, uh... religious."

"Oh." For a split second he looks even more intrigued. Then he glances around. "Look, I'm really sorry. This is clearly an imposition. Shirley sprang this on me last minute. I have to guess she did it to you, too."

He sounds so genuinely nice I start to feel sorry for him. I remember how I felt the night before meeting my father for the first time after more than twenty years. Jack must be feeling as nervous as I was, but if the night I spent before I met my long-lost parent was sleepless, at least I spent it in my own bed, not under the roof of an angry stranger. I soften my tone and my stance. "She's not used to taking no for an answer, I guess."

"This isn't the kind of story she usually works on," he says. "Celebrities are her usual thing."

"I can see why. I've seen sharks go after chum with less determination." Tired and stressed out as I am, I realize I don't want to go to bed yet. I want to talk to Jack. "You want some tea?"

He brightens. "Okay."

I move around the kitchen, acutely aware that he's there, on my mother's old red sofa where I lost my virginity a thousand years ago to Danny Goodman one hot summer afternoon when my mother was teaching a graduate summer seminar and I was supposed to be dusting.

I'm not sure if he's really that interesting, or if it's just easier to think about Jack than the gig. All the girls are furious, and I guess I can't blame them. It's my fault the show went to shit. But there's definitely something about Jack that makes the bungalow feel smaller and a lot more crowded than usual, almost as if he takes up more space than he should.

I bring us both mugs of chamomile tea. I'd really like a joint, but my stash is in my bedroom and I don't know Jack well enough to risk asking him if he'd like to smoke. The dogs are completely besotted with him to a degree I find bizarre – when I come back into the living room, I see they've snuggled up with him, one on either side, on the couch. I put the tray down, gesture to the honey bear. "There's milk if you want that, too."

"No, this is fine," he says. He twirls the honey wand between delicate fingers. Jeremy, my last boyfriend, was a medical student. He had long fingers, too, that he proudly referred to at every opportunity as surgeon's hands. I hated when he said that, because I always saw a scalpel slicing into rubbery flesh. But Jack's fingers look gentle, as if they'd be good at massaging toes or braiding hair. He looks up at me and cocks his head. "So're you an old friend of Shirley's, or something? Is that how you got stuck with me?"

He's looking at me with an intensity the question doesn't seem to deserve but I don't mind. I'm used to intense looks from men. "No," I say after a quick sip. "I guess Shirley didn't explain…anything?" I sit back, just a little nervous suddenly. I don't know anything about Jack Chance, and Shirley didn't seem to know much more. "Would you mind telling me how Shirley tracked you down?"

"Tracked me down…Is that what she told you?" He sounds perplexed. "She didn't track me down. I-I guess you could say it was just a really weird coincidence."

A really weird coincidence. Those words have meaning for me Jack can't know. I found my father because a book happened to fall off a shelf in the library and hit me on the back of the head. I remember I picked up the book and noticed that the author's name was the same as my father's. Then I opened it up and saw it was inscribed "To Helen, Love David." My mother's name was Helen.

That's what got my search for my father started. It didn't take me long after meeting him to discover that my father had a lot of strange ideas. I try to remember if Shirley told me anything beyond enough to reassure me Jack wasn't an ax murderer. "I guess I assumed that's what happened. What do you mean… you just showed up?"

He spreads his hands apart. "You probably won't believe me. I just came to Shirley's office to bring her something that she left in my cab. She wanted to show me around – I'm getting a degree in writing. We were just talking when the phone rang and it was this woman in New Jersey."

The rest of the story he tells me is so improbable I think only my father would've believed it. "So in other words… the only reason you're here is-?"

"Because I happened to be sitting in Shirley's office. But when Shirley came down here, and met with Martha, Martha described me down to my clothes, and said I was her kid." He shrugs, spreads his hands. "I know it sounds pretty strange." He breaks off, stares off somewhere beyond my shoulder. "But she knew things... she knew...things...about me."

I sit forward, chin on my hands. As much as it makes me feel better that strange things happen to someone else too, I'm starting to wonder what anyone's told him about Martha Sinclair. From the little contact I've had with Martha, I'm amazed she knew anything at all. "Like what?"

"I-I have this paper." He fumbles for his battered black suitcase. It's one of those old hard-sided Samsonite monsters my mother used to haul around from conference to conference. From it, he retrieves a manila folder. "See? It's not a birth certificate – it's a copy of the form you fill out when a kid is born, you know? But in this one... all the information was blacked out, but for my date of birth – which had a correction on it. Someone changed my birthday. It was originally filled in as March 1. Someone changed it. To March 2. See?" As I scan the blurry photocopy, the first thought that goes through my head is that we were both born in the same month, in the same year. The second is that there was some official confusion about my birthday, too. In fact, according to my mother, my father went so far as to do the same thing on my birth certificate application. Only her interception got it changed back. When the certificate arrived with my correct date of birth, they had the first of the fights that eventually drove them apart. But Jack's continuing. "She knew what I looked like, she knew I got sick in Shirley's office."

Okay, that's weird but hardly means anything, just like the odd coincidences of our birthdates being altered. I give him a long hard look. "Have you spoken to Martha Sinclair?"

"Not yet. Shirley – well, you know I'm supposed to meet her tomorrow. Have you met her? Do you know her?"

"No." I bite my lip, wondering what to say. I've never met her but I can imagine her. Parts of the Jersey Pine Barrens resemble Appalachia. People who come from places like Redemption and Devil's Door, New Jersey don't stay in them long if they've got anything at all on the ball. But I don't feel it's my place to tell that to Jack. "Didn't your adoptive parents tell you where they got you?"

"They never said much, beyond that the priests helped them find me. That was my mother's standard answer for just about anything she didn't want to talk about. But I... well, just today I...I went and asked... the guy who brought me home - he told me he found me in a car wreck on some highway in North Jersey. So I guess it fits. In a strange kind of way."

Suddenly it occurs to me that while Martha was thrilled to hear what I had to tell her, Jack might not be so happy. After all, my father not only helped fake Jack's death, he abetted a group of baby-nappers who were apparently taking a newborn infant away from a mother who was told he was dead. The dogs are asleep with their heads on his lap and I hope if Jack lunges at me, they wake up in time to bite him. "So, I guess it is possible, then."

"Yeah. Amazing coincidence... but... I guess stuff happens, huh?" He leans forward, elbows on knees. "So who're you, Jessie Woodwright? And how *do* you fit in?"

I take a deep breath, but I still have a hard time meeting his eyes. "Um... my father was the one who...who told me that there were rocks in the baby's grave."

"Why?"

"He... uh... I guess he wanted Martha to know she was right that her baby -"

"Yeah but why then? Didn't you think it was strange it was on his mind?"

Well, yeah, I had, I remember all too vividly. I twist my thumbs together and try not to sink too deeply into the details of that horrible day. "Yeah," I say finally. "I did, but he was dying – I...I guess he wanted to clear his conscience before he died."

"And he never, ever mentioned anything about this? Never once before?"

I realize Jack doesn't know any more about me than I know about him. "I didn't know he was alive growing up. My mom left him before I was two, and let me think he was dead. It wasn't until after she died, I found out he wasn't."

Jack grunts. "Believe me, if my mother thought she could've gotten away with telling me my old man was dead, she would've. So how'd you find him?"

"Through a friend of my mother's, a woman I've always called Aunt Edith. She helped me find him."

I want to tell him the story, because that was really the beginning of all the weird shit that's happened. I want to tell him how I was shelving books one day, deep in the stacks, last December during exams. I want to tell him about how the book flew off a shelf by itself and hit me in the head. I want to tell him how the author turned out to be my father. But Jack came here to find his family, not to hear about mine. "We met last New Year's Eve."

"So you didn't have that long together."

"No. And you know what? I always had the feeling there was something he wanted me to know – something he wanted, or needed to tell me. He just… I guess there wasn't time." I take another sip and a very deep breath to control all the emotions I feel right now. "Tomorrow – when I drop you off at Martha's, I'm going to go see my father's research assistant." That's as good a title as any for Rosie Coulter and a lot nicer than the one my mother would've labeled her. "I'm hoping she can explain how it all fits." I gesture once more around the room. "I think what he wanted to tell me somehow includes all this –these books? They were all his. But damned if I can understand what it is I'm supposed to see."

"What is all this?"

"I guess you could call it his life's work. He started off as a physicist at Princeton, but his ideas got a little too wild, according to my mother. He got denied tenure, and that's when my mother left, and he couldn't find another job teaching. I guess he started drinking and things got out of control for a while. But he never stopped working, even though he ended up working alone. I just…" I want to apologize for some reason I don't understand. It amazes me how much I care about Jack's feelings. "I can't imagine why he did what he did. But in the short time I came to know him, I know he would've only done it if he believed it was right, somehow."

There's a long silence. I brace myself. But Jack surprises me. "It's nice of you to let me stay here. I really appreciate it."

He sounds so sincere and his expression is so kind, I like him, I really like him. We should go to bed, I think. I bite my lip. I can't say *that*. That's the kind of thing I used to say, back in the days of my wild romp through sex, drugs and rock n'roll.

"We should go to bed," he says, as if I'd spoken aloud, but without any hint of invitation. "It'll be easier to figure it all out in the morning."

I get up, take the mugs and the tray and the honey back to the kitchen. The dogs flop on the floor beside him and refuse to budge. I guess I don't have to worry about him answering the door even if the knocks do come at 3 AM. Angus and Lucy wouldn't even let me out of the bedroom. I doubt they'd let Jack off the couch.

I crawl into bed, and listen to the familiar noises of the house settling. I don't know what to do. I should be over at Ginger's first thing – with hazelnut coffee and chocolate doughnuts, looking for a way to talk this through, like all the other stuff that's come up over the years. I know there has to be a way to deal with this just like we've dealt with everything else.

I don't know where the songs come from, or why I can be singing one song, and then, without warning, I start singing another – something sometimes totally unrelated to even the kind of music we're playing. Kimie plays some random riff, the beat inside my head changes, words rise up my throat, and wham – I'm gone – into this golden glowing place where the sounds and the words and the lights and all the people are all joined into this pulsing sphere of radiant colors that flash and mix and twine.

When it's worked – like the time Kimie's *Tribute to Master Alister* morphed into Ozzy Osbourne's *Mr. Crowley* - we've done some of our best stuff. When it hasn't - like tonight - the whole show goes to shit.

But I can't go make nice with my friends. I have to put them and that weird shit on the backburner because of all the other weird shit – which is all the weird shit my mother tried to protect me from. I guess I can't blame her if it all caught up with me after she was dead. I did go looking for it, after all.

At least Jack seems okay. He's cute enough to make me think more than once about jumping his bones, but I swore on my mother's coffin those days are all behind me. No more passing out at frat parties next to someone whose name I can't remember. No more waking up with some guy I brought home on a bet. No more stripping for extra cash. If I was wild once, I'm not any more. I'm the girl my mother wanted me to be – a nice girl, who's so nice and so nuts she's about to get kicked out of the band which is about the only thing that keeps her sane.

I'm getting too upset thinking about the girls. I wonder what Jack would do if I opened the door and offered him half the bed. Trouble is, I think he'd be appalled.

He was nice about my father. He didn't flinch at our get-ups and I swear he saw every freaking ghost between here and the bridge. I thought I was going to pee my pants when he asked me to pick up the hitchhiker and I know he saw those kids who died when the school bus plowed into the playground near Ginger's place.

I can't imagine what Mom would say. She didn't believe in ghosts, she didn't believe in bringing home strange men, and she ranked tabloid newspapers below used car ads in her estimation of worthless reading material.

Here she's gone, just over a year, and I'm up to my neck in all three. It's what she deserves for letting me think my father was dead all those years. *Rest easy, Mom,* I think, as I curl on my side. *At least the strange man is sleeping on the couch.*

And then I wonder, in that random kind of way I sometimes do as I'm drifting off to sleep, why my father wanted to change the day I was born.

Chapter 15

I wake up sweating from a messy tangle of dreams.

In one, I'm being hunted by something I can't quite see. I'm not sure whether it's a vampire or a zombie or a werewolf or maybe something else all together, even – all I know is that it's after me and I don't know why. The worst part of the dream, however, is that I've lost the only fiddle that will slay the monster forever, and no other fiddle will do. A red-haired woman is sitting in the back seat and she's directing me down narrow alleys and one-way streets, through underground tunnels and over impossibly high bridges that arch across skyscrapers, all in a frantic search for this all-important fiddle.

In the other dream, I'm wrapped around Jack Chance under the backyard willow tree like the ivy around its trunk. We're both naked. Just as the red-haired woman leans forward to warn me about a wall that's suddenly appeared up ahead in the one dream, my belly convulses around his cock in the other. I open my mouth to scream in one dream at the same moment I come in the other.

I bolt up out of my pillow, quivering from head to toe and covered with sweat. I punch the alarm clock before I notice the time - 5:55. I can't let all this get to me, I tell myself as I sink back down onto my pillow. I slip my hand between my thighs and rub myself gently, staring at the stains on the old wallpaper, and willing myself to relax.

So I did just have the mother of all wet dreams. I guess Jack made more of an impression on me last night than I realized. Or maybe my break-up with Jeremy is affecting me more than I thought. Maybe everything – work, the band, losing my parents - is affecting me more than I thought. Maybe I just need to let myself go a bit, give myself a break. I close my eyes and sink back into the memory of the dream that rises up to meet me on the crest of the sensations building between my legs.

As my body starts to calm, I tell myself I can handle anything, just not all at once. I have to take things one step at a time, not necessarily in the order I want to. Like the band - maybe I can make it to afternoon practice at Ginger's. There's nothing I can do about the write-up I got from work, so there's no sense worrying about that right now. Both my parents are dead, they're not coming back and I want to assume they want me to be happy. That brings me back to Jack and the dream under the willow.

I can't let myself think about the dream again. I should think about why my father might have gotten involved in kidnapping, and why poor Martha Sinclair's baby was deliberately taken from her at birth. I know my father would only have done something like that if he believed it was the right thing to do. Even my mother never said he was cruel or criminal.

On the other hand, maybe the best thing would be to drop Jack Chance off with Shirley, haul all this shit straight to Rosie's and go back to the life I used to have. I could stop this, I think. I don't really have to get any more involved in this than I already am. So what my father was involved in some weird shit nearly thirty years ago? What's that have to do with me? But it does have something to do with me, I know it does. There's something here he wants me to see, to understand. I have the feeling I'm not getting it as quickly as he hoped I would. Or maybe I'm not getting it as fast as he thought I would.

I have to talk to Rosie, I think. She has to help me understand. Otherwise, I think I'm going to have to walk away from it all. Lack of sex, lack of sleep, it's all getting to me. I can't go on like this. When the dogs start to whimper and paw at the door, I don't even pretend I'm going back to sleep.

I can't help but notice the woodie rising under Jack's quilt as I tiptoe into the kitchen to let Angus and Lucy out. The dogs bound joyfully out into the dawn. They sniff and roll and caper in the tentative sunlight. They obviously have no issues at all with Mr. Chance, even while I feel myself quivering like a guitar too tightly strung. I try to forget him lying on the lumpy couch, one arm bent behind his head, the other resting on his chest. I wonder if he could be dreaming what I was just dreaming, and dismiss it as impossible. People don't share dreams, and if they do, surely it has to be after they've known each other for a long time and made some deep, intimate connection. Picking a guy up at a train station and sharing a cup of chamomile tea at one in the morning doesn't seem quite enough.

The thought of spending the better part of the day in Jack's company titillates me. It's been awhile since Jeremy – a good six weeks or more. I guess I miss the sex more than I thought. I'm as bad as my dogs, which are sniffing out their territories in the special area my mother designated as their poop patch.

It's pretty out here, in the watery April dawn. My mother had a green thumb and devoted herself to this tiny garden with all the intensity she gave to her work. At the base of the drooping willow that figured so prominently in my dream, the red heads of the tulips are bursting in phallic glory. Even the sharp spike of the yellow forsythia reminds me of the dream. The long wet grass licks my ankles as I inspect the new tips of my mother's irises pushing their way up through the muddy earth and the buds on the ancient lilac. My mother bought the house for this lilac. I take a deep breath and I think I catch a ghostly whiff of lilac in bloom, even though its nowhere near time for the heavy flowers to open. I breathe again, and the air smells earthy and slightly sweet. The dogs are rolling on their backs in the dew, and on the edge of the fence, a pair of robins are fighting over a worm.

I miss my mother so much I forget about Jack. I remember all the mornings I'd found her out here, working in the still of a summer dawn, humming so off-key any melody was unrecognizable. "Amazing grace," I whisper. That was the one she liked the best. A shaft of sunlight breaks through the clouds and I feel the rest of the song rise, naturally as the breath in my lungs. But I can't do this, I think. I can't let it happen – I have to learn to control it or they won't let me stay in the band. So I don't let the song out. I clamp down so hard I bite my tongue and taste blood. "Come on, puppies." I clap softly.

"Want coffee?"

I practically jump out of my skin. Jack Chance is leaning on the door frame, wearing jeans and a t-shirt under an open flannel shirt. "Good morning. I didn't mean to scare you." He holds out a mug — my mother's favorite mug, in fact, and smiles. I'm back in the dream so fast my knees nearly buckle. Moisture seeps into my underwear.

To make matters worse, in the morning light it's clear he's the kind of rumpled gorgeous most often found in the pages of men's style magazines. His jeans reveal the slimness of his hips, the t-shirt hugs his flat belly, the shirt billows off broad, if bony shoulders. A glaze of beard darkens a chin with a perfect cleft, his nose and cheekbones could've been chiseled out of stone. I think he does resemble Martha Sinclair, especially around the full, soft mouth, and the way his eyebrows arch over his gentle eyes.

"Yeah," I say, with a belligerent edge I don't mean. "You really scared me."

"I heard you singing. I didn't want to stop you so — " he jerks one thumb over his shoulder. "I broke into the coffee." The smile he gives me is as tentative as it is disarming. "You sounded so pretty — I hope you don't mind." He holds out a mug.

I was singing? I blink. No, I thought. I was deliberately not singing. He couldn't possibly have heard me. But even as I open my mouth to protest, the dogs notice him. Before I can take the cup from Jack's hand, they bound into his arms, sending the coffee flying, and poor Jack ass over teakettle onto the deck.

"Angus! Lucy!" The dogs are beside themselves. They lick his face, his shirt, his thighs… anything they can get their tongues on and the thought crosses my mind I'd like to be doing the same thing. I wish I understood what is it about him that's making me feel like I want to peel those wet clothes off him myself.

"You got a washing machine?" he asks as I pull the dogs off.

I'm feeling clumsy and awkward and horribly flustered because all I can visualize is Jack, naked, under the hard stream of my shower head, soap suds slipping around the curves of his limbs. He's cute, he's nice, he's married. The thin gold band gleams on his finger as I help him up. "I'm really sorry – they're wild and spoiled…I'm-"

"Nah, it's okay, I like dogs." But he's drenched in coffee. It's soaked both shirts, stained his thighs. "It's just – I didn't bring a lot of clothes. I got some clean underwear but other than my jacket and stuff from last night -"

"So why'd you bring that huge suitcase?"

"It's the only one I got."

"Oh." For a long moment we stare at each other. For the first time I put together the big suitcase, the ragged clothes, and the worn moccasins. That's the real Jack, not the shiny preppy of last night that irked me so much. I realize the vision that just swept across my mind is about to come true. But it's the feeling of connection, of immediate recognition that makes my knees weak. *I know you.* The words resonate through my body like a single toll of a deep bell, even as a more rational corner of my brain protests I've never met Jack Chance before last night in my life. "Sure," I say. "Sure, come with me."

I push the screen door shut, leaving the dogs outside. With reproachful looks, they return to licking up the coffee on the deck. I hope Jack doesn't hear my heart thumping against my breastbone. The air that follows me inside is heady with lilac, lilac that isn't blooming yet. I don't understand this intense attraction that feels like someone's flicked a switch.

I swipe my hair off my face, and realize he's retreated half way across the kitchen. I wonder if he's picked up how I'm feeling. I can't bring myself to look at him, but I beckon, as I flee down the hall. "Uh, listen. I probably even have some clothes you can wear – they…uh…here, come with me."

I lead him into the second bedroom, the one across the hall from the tiny laundry room, the one that used to be mine. Now it's the storehouse for all the stuff Rosie insisted I take from my father's house and haven't had a chance to do more than glance through yet. In one of the cartons, I found clothes. I'd planned to take them back to Rosie today. I have no use for them and I'm sure she gave them to me by mistake.

Jack fingers the weathered flannel-lined khakis, the much-laundered chamois shirt with a little smile at the corner of his mouth. "They're soft." We are standing side by side beside my childhood bed and I am acutely aware of his scent, something green and earthy mixed with damp cotton and coffee.

"Then take them." I push the pile at him and our hands touch. A bolt of need goes through me. He gasps. I realize he felt something too. His hands have closed around mine, twining them together with the clothes, and his entire body is pulsating with a kind of radiant heat, strongly scented with coffee. We shouldn't do this, I think, as his face bends down to mine and our lips come together.

"Jessie?"

We're not kissing. I blink. Jack's just looking at me. What I just pictured didn't happen, any more than my dream under the willow tree, but my lips are puffy, and my whole body's tingling as if it did. I clear my throat, pull together the edges of my robe, acutely aware of the places my clothes touch my skin. "I'll...uh..I'm going to feed us to the dogs for breakfast... I mean I'm going to fix the dogs their breakfast and then feel something for us to feed..." I shut my mouth with an audible snap, then push past him, too flustered to look him in the eye. Maybe it's him. Maybe Jack Chance emits some pheromone that first the dogs responded to, and now it's finally hit me. Or maybe he *is* just the hottest guy I've ever met.

I drop dog food, spill water, break an egg on the floor. What the hell is wrong with me, I wonder, as I hear Jack moving around in the bathroom. I can't get the image of him standing under the shower out of my head. I can feel it in the softening of my pores, in the heat that rises from the marrow of my bones. I want him with a need I can taste.

I splash water on my face and hope I can behave halfway normally when he gets out. I have to start the wash. The minute the water goes off I tap on the door. "Um...hey, Jack?" My voice sounds high and shrill, the way it did when I was a giggly thirteen. "I-uh, I gotta start the wash...I need you to give me your stuff... I mean, your clothes..." I feel my cheeks start to burn.

The door opens, he's standing wrapped in a towel. Dark hair is sprinkled across his chest, gathers in a long dark line that draws my gaze inevitably down below his navel. *This was a mistake,* I think, as I sag against the door. "I need your stuff," I say weakly. Steam billows out around him, as he hands me the pile of coffee-stained clothing, and I am hot and cold and wet all at once. *I do, oh, how I do really need your stuff.*

Our hands touch in passing, and his is damp and warm compared to mine. I feel a wave of heat roll across the surface of my skin and sink into my bones. When I can breathe, I realize he's looking at me in the same way.

"Who the hell are you, Jessie Woodwright?" His voice is hoarse, his skin moist, his muscles taut. That he wants me as much as I want him is obvious through the towel. "And what the hell is all this about?"

Chapter 16

The telephone rings and shatters the moment. Outside the deck door, the dogs are yelping at the squirrels. I pull away from Jack, throw his clothes into the washing machine. "I'm coming," I yell, before I can stop myself.

The dogs are flinging themselves again the door, Angus's hackles are raised in a long ridge down his back. Lucy has the deeper bark however, and sounds even more ferocious. I pick up the receiver, even as an image explodes in my head. "Hi, Jeremy."

"Wow – you can still tell it's me, huh?"

"Yeah, you still have that special ring." I shut the door of my bedroom. I don't want to think about Jack getting dressed, pulling on clothes that belonged to my father. I don't want to think about how obvious it is he wants me just as much as I want him. I'm almost happy to hear from Jeremy, strange as a phone call at this hour is. "How come you're calling me at seven in the morning?"

"I'm sorry. I know this is early. I didn't wake you, did I?"

Sometimes I can't remember what I ever saw in Jeremy until I remember he was the sort my mother liked. As I got to know him better, I found he has a competitive edge that medical school is honing into something harder and colder than a scalpel. I decided I didn't like what it was doing to him. "You know the dogs get me up early. So…um… what's up?"

"I heard your name mentioned last night. I thought it sounded like something you ought to know."

"What?" I sink down onto my bed.

"You know those work-study kids under you?"

"Yeah – so? I never have any problems with my kids – they all like me." Some like me so much I've been known to take them on long tours of the Rare Collections Room, where the library's most prized manuscripts bask beneath glass in climate-controlled comfort and there's a wide couch, suitable for other pursuits, on which to peruse them. "Is someone complaining about them?"

"No. Someone's been asking them questions about *you*, about the books you've been requesting, and who you're requesting them for."

"Why?"

"I don't know, Jessie. Why are you ordering books?"

Say nothing. The voice that echoes in my mind is clear, firm and very sure. I decide to listen for once. "Um… Jeremy, I don't know how to break this to you… but that's my job. I get books for people, track down sources, help them with research. It's what I do."

"You're just a librarian – you're not supposed to be doing research."

"What?" I sputter. I can't quite believe this conversation. It's demeaning that I'm defending myself to Jeremy, of all people. I did just get written up at work, but this is none of Jeremy's business. "I'm not doing research – I'm fulfilling requests." That *"you're just a librarian"* stings like a whip.

"Look, Jessie, I'm sorry to be the one to tell you this. But I figured forewarned was forearmed. I don't want to see you get – you know – professionally murdered."

"Professionally murdered? What the hell kind of thing is that to say? Are you on something, Jeremy?"

There's a long silence. "Okay," he says. "That didn't come out quite right. I was up late and I guess I'm tired."

"So why don't you go to sleep?"

"I was asleep – that's why I'm calling, that's what woke me up."

"What woke you? Jeremy, you're starting to sound like you're drugged."

"I'm not drugged – I had a dream. A dream about you, Jessie, and it wasn't a very nice one."

"What the hell does that mean?"

"You start off dead. I have to do your autopsy."

"Oh, my God."

"Yeah," he says at once. "I think you should stop whatever you're doing. I mean, maybe I *am* way of line here – I know it's early and all - but I really don't want to see you end up dead. Not literally, not figuratively." He hangs up with the same kind of righteous indignation that broke us up. I just don't know what to make of it. Who calls an old girlfriend at seven AM and warns her because of a dream? A dream *and* a conversation, I remind myself. I decide to track the kids down myself. Maybe I should know what's being said about me. Great, I think, something else to worry about.

When I come out of the bedroom, Jack's petting the dogs. "Everything okay?"

"Just a phone call that was... weird. From an old boyfriend. Not what I was expecting."

Jack looks at me across the room. "Are you okay?"

I hope he assumes I'm flushed because of the phone call. "I got a slip at work the other day - I guess I've managed to offend the Powers-That-Be somehow. Jeremy called to tell me he overheard some of the work-study kids talking about me in the library last night." I shrug. There's nothing I can do about it now. One thing at a time, one step at a time. I can handle anything. I nod at the clock. "We should get ready to go."

"I hope he's not upset I stayed here?"

"I'm not sure what he's upset about." I feel uneasy, almost scared. "We broke up two months ago."

"And he called you just now?"

I'm glad I'm not the only one who thinks it's odd. "He said he had a dream, a bad dream. He assumed it means I'm going to get fired." It's hard to look at Jack without getting weak in the knees. I shrug, cross my arms under my breasts. They feel heavy and full under my t-shirt, the fabric is rough against my nipples. I have to keep my robe closed or he'll see how hard they are. "I-I don't know. It's... it's just... I don't know."

"Weird?"

I have to sink down onto the couch, onto the quilt that now smells just like Jack. The clock ticks audibly on the wall above my head as I ponder what to say. "I guess that's a good word for it."

"There's a lot about all this that's weird."

I clasp my hands over my knees, prim as any virgin. I keep my eyes down because I can't look at him. "This morning I...I had this dream." It's hard to talk because my tongue feels clumsy in my mouth. "About you and me."

He sinks down into the chair across the coffee table, looking visible embarrassed. He pulls an afghan into his lap and the first thought that crosses my mind is that he's chilly, and then I realize that in fact, he's really as hot as I am. "Were we outside, under the willow tree? And we were...?"

"Yeah." Our eyes meet and it's like two pieces of wire connecting, despite the uncomfortable silence that rises between us like a wall. It's one thing to dream about a stranger like that. It's quite another to sit across from him in this moist cold daylight and talk about it.

"You dream a lot?"

I shrug again. "Not like that."

"I dream a lot," he says, slowly, looking down at his lap. "Not like that." He pauses, twists uncomfortably under the afghan. "Sometimes I dream I'm a girl – well, a woman. A woman who looks like you." He says it flatly, without emotion. He raises his head and I can't look away.

I know you. I know you, I think, *I've always known you and you're the person I've been waiting for all my life.* They're the most clichéd words imaginable and in this moment, they are absolutely true. *I know you.* I do, I think. Beyond time or logic or any kind of reason, I not only *know* Jack Chance, I've been *waiting* for him.

"You ever dream you're a guy?" There's tension in his shoulders, in his hands. I can feel him hanging on my answer.

"I..uh... I don't know. Sometimes I have these driving dreams," I offer, mostly because he's so upset than because I'm really sure. "And...uh...I do think I'm a guy in them...sometimes."

"I... I didn't know what to make of it, ever, until I saw you last night, and I realized that I'm not dreaming I'm a girl – I'm dreaming of being *you*."

"Me? Maybe you just look like me – what makes you think it's me?"

He glances around, shrugs. "The dreams fit – they fit you, they fit with who you are. I dream about Springsteen – you live in New Jersey, you play in a rock band, you're kind of prim the way you dress for work...you're a librarian, right?"

Prim probably isn't quite the word, but these are dream images, I remind myself. Jack's continuing, looking more and more uncomfortable. "So... since last night, when I recognized you were the girl I am in my dreams, and then this morning, and I wake up and I can just about keep myself in this chair looking at you...I keep asking myself... why? What is this connection and... uh... why do I... why do we..." He looks at me helplessly as he twirls his wedding ring around his finger.

I simply don't know what to say. "I realize you're married."

He glances up at me, then away. "Yeah." He hangs his head between his shoulders and frowns.

"Look, I don't understand it, either, okay? I don't know I'd call myself prim, but that get-up last night was just a costume and I don't bring strange men home." Not anymore, anyway. "Just so you understand."

"I..." He shakes his head. "I wasn't thinking you did." He gets up, adjusts himself in his trousers as he turns away. "Let me... uh.. Let me get you some coffee?" He looks at the dogs. "And you two – you stay down."

I don't understand the effect he has on the dogs. They hang on his every word, follow him with their big brown dog eyes adoringly. The cup he hands me is just the way I like it. I taste it automatically, then realize he couldn't have known I like lots of cream and a tiny bit of sugar. "How'd you -?"

"Lucky guess. I get these feelings about things, sometimes." He settles down in the chair, careful to keep the table and a high stack of books between us, even as I realize I frequently get the same kinds of feelings. That this is something we share triggers another shock of familiarity that startles me, so that I nearly miss his question. "So what is it, Jessie Woodwright? What's this thing we feel? You have any idea at all? You think your father has an answer in all these books and boxes?"

I sip the coffee, and glance at the clock. We don't have all morning – as soon as the washing machine stops, I have to take a shower. I have to be naked under the same roof as Jack Chance. I imagine being in the shower with him, imagine the soapy water coursing over us both, imagine his hands cupping my breasts, those full lips pursing to suck the droplets off my nipples. I imagine cupping his naked ass and pushing my hips up to meet his. I have never wanted to give myself so completely to another human being in all my life. I want to bear his children, I want to be his wife. *I am my beloved's, and my beloved is mine.*

I remember running across a whole carton of stuff on the Beloved. I glanced through the notes, the half-filled journals, the underlined books. I don't think I saw it mentioned anywhere that simply gazing across the room at someone can be an orgasmic experience.

"I don't know," I say. I sip the coffee, cradle the mug close if only to feel something other than my own empty palm. "But I think, where we're going, I think…at least I hope… there's someone who can."

This can't be coincidence, I think. Someone has to know, someone has to understand. Someone other than my father has to have answers. We have to talk to Rosie, I think. Rosie knew him better than anyone. Some of the journals even contain questions and comments in her handwriting, and my father refers to her at times as RC. It confused me at first because he sometimes refers to the Roman Catholic Church as RC.

The washing machine commences its final spin. Jack's hands are shaking as he twists his ring. We both know his wife is the only reason we're not in bed right now.

The washing machine skids to a stop. I get up, tightening the sash on my robe. "I…uh…I'm going to jump in the shower – you can throw your stuff in the dryer. And then we…uh…we have to leave."

"Can I use your phone?" he asks. "I'll be glad to reimburse –"

"No," I say quickly, too quickly. The poor guy looks as confused as I feel. "Please – by all means. Use the phone. Call your wife."

He looks at me gratefully as I escape into the bathroom. I hook the latch and sink onto the toilet, wishing I could drain desire as easily as pee. When I hear him padding down the hall, I step under the roar of the shower, and let the hot water cascade down my back.

He's calling his wife…he's calling his wife… he's calling his wife. I murmur those words like a mantra, as I close my eyes, and soap my hair. I dig my fingernails into my scalp, churning up the suds, so that when I finally rinse, they explode down my body in waves of white bubbles. I reach for the bath gel, and feel fingers on the bottle.

I know if I open my eyes, I'll break the spell. I hold my breath as I feel him step behind me, naked as I am, but dry and firm and cool where I'm wet and warm and slick. He pulls me back against him, so that my face is tilted up to face the coursing water, then bends me over, so my legs splay over his cock. He pushes into me as easily as he did in my dream – in *our* dream - under the willow, and I let him fill me, over and over, again and again, until we are both utterly spent.

Chapter 17

When I get out of the shower, I see that I latched the door from the inside. Nothing really happened, and I'm glad in a way that it didn't. Jack doesn't want to cheat on his wife. I get dressed in the bathroom, and when I come out, he's sitting on the couch, flanked by the dogs, writing in a notebook.

I can't help but notice he looks troubled. "Everything okay?"

He shrugs. "Lila didn't answer the phone again. I guess she's still dead asleep." He looks up at me as I search through my purse for my keys. "I think we should make a list."

"What kind of a list?"

"A list of everything that's happened, everything that strikes us as weird - a Weird List we can call it."

"Yeah?"

"Maybe we have more than dreams in common, Jessie. You said there was a lot of weird shit going on."

I shoo the dogs outside, rinse out the coffee mugs. I guess we have to talk about something on the way to Devil's Door. I feel marginally better since my shower, but Jack's presence gives off this low-grade buzz that makes my teeth itch. The phone rings and I know it's Shirley Shulman. "Hi, Shirley."

"You and Jack, Jessie, I just can't believe the way you two do that. You are the only people who always know," she carols. "Is he there? Did he make it? On the midnight train to Jersey?"

She sounds manic, a little drunk. "Oh, yeah, he's here." I beckon to Jack. "Here. You want to talk to him?"

I hand the receiver over before she has a chance to answer. Shirley makes me nervous. When she's not asking questions, she's watching, waiting to pounce. But Jack seems to know the right note to strike. He's gentle, kind, and says absolutely nothing beyond that he's looking forward to meeting Martha and the rest of the family. Yes, he thinks it's a miracle, too and yes, he's excited. I wonder what my mother would think of Jack. I look at the way he fits into my father's clothes and decide she probably wouldn't like him just for that. When he hangs up, I say, "We have to go."

"You mind if I try home one more time?"

"Go ahead." I give him the receiver then fill up the dogs' bowls. I can't help hearing the hollow echo of the empty rings. They seem very loud for some reason, almost as if I'm somehow able to listen in on the line. From all the way across the room, I hear the click of the answering machine in Jack's ear. A frown creases his face, and then the machine's whine is interrupted.

"I'll fucking talk to you when I fucking wake up!"

I can hear the angry voice blast out of the phone all the way across the kitchen. Jack hangs up, his expression stunned. He looks like he was just hit in the head. "She okay?" I ask.

"Guess she had a late night, and a little too much to drink. She was at a big party last night, a big company party."

"Ah."

He picks up his suitcase and his notebook. I see he's folded the quilt, tidied the pillows. I bet he does windows and dishes. "I guess I'm ready."

The phone rings. His expression brightens. It has to be her, I think. Surely she realized how awful she sounded, and she's calling to say she's sorry. I nod at the phone. "Why don't you get it? It's probably her."

He looks dubiously at the phone, then me, but he picks it up. "Lila? Oh, no… you don't have a wrong number… I'm sorry. No, I'm just a guest… yeah, she's right here. Jessie's right here."

He hands the receiver over hastily.

"Jessie?" Static crackles on the line, and for a moment I don't recognize the voice. "Jessie, are you there? Are you all right? Who's that man? Jessie?"

It's Aunt Edith, my mother's dearest friend, who sort of adopted us both after my mother left my father. "Hey, Aunt Edith, yes, it's me, I'm here. That was Jack, Aunt Edith. He's a friend."

"Ah." There's another crackle of static, but I can imagine what she's thinking. Then she says something completely unexpected. "Are you free for dinner tonight?"

"Tonight?" That kills the idea of band practice. I glance at Jack. Once I hand him over to Shirley, I guess I won't have any reason to see him again. That thought makes me very sad. I guess I'd rather eat with Edith than fight with the band afterwards. "You want me to come there?"

"Well, actually, honey, I was thinking I could meet you there – at your place. I'd love to treat you to that Italian place in Cherry Hill."

"Are you sure, Aunt Edith? You haven't been this way since my mother's funeral…and I can't remember the last time before that."

"Now, honey, it's not been that long. You just tell me what time to meet you and I'll see you at the restaurant, how's that? I woke up with quite a yen for their Alfredo."

Then that's another thing to add to the Weird List, I think. Aunt Edith hasn't left her brownstone in ages. She doesn't even teach regular classes… only graduate seminars full of mostly hand-picked students. She even relies on them to bring her food and run her errands. I'm still not quite sure what the basis for her friendship was with my mother, but they seemed to have known each other forever. "Aunt Edith," I say slowly, "that Italian place has been Chinese for at least three years. How about I just come over to your house, say – oh, I don't know, around six?" I glance at the clock calculating. That gives me enough time to hand Jack over to Shirley, talk to Rosie, and feed the dogs. Of course it means I only have another two hours at most in Jack's company, and the disappointment that washes through me I feel in the marrow of my bones. "I can bring you great Alfredo, I promise." I hear a choking sound, heavy breathing, and I wonder if she's physically all right. "Aunt Edith, are you there? Are you all right?"

"I'm fine, dear... how about if I just meet you at your house? Say around five?"

"I-I'm not sure I'll be home by five," I say in disbelief.

"I have the key, honey. If I get there before you, I'll just let myself in. Okay?"

Let yourself in? Edith's sounding stranger by the second. "What about the dogs, Aunt Edith? Do you remember my mom's dogs, Angus and Lucy? Are you sure you can handle them?"

"Of course I do. Dogs don't scare me. After all, I helped her pick them out."

That was before you turned into a complete recluse, I think. "If you think so..."

"I'll see you when you I see then? About four-thirty, five?"

She really wants to get over here, I think. "Sure, Aunt Edith. Come whenever you want. I'll get home as fast I can." She hangs up and it's Jack's turn to look at me with concern.

"Are you okay?"

"Bring that notebook," I say, as I wave the dogs back in the house and grab my purse. "The Weird List is getting longer."

I realize I shouldn't have hesitated to tell Jack anything. By the time he's finished telling me about the job interview, the weird paintings, and the whiskey, my father sounds no worse than a poor man's version of *The Nutty Professor*. I recognize the name Savageux, too, which seems like a strange coincidence by itself, because I'm sure I've never heard of this Wall Street guy.

He jots things down while I drive my mother's battered Toyota and pepper him with questions, because some of it sounds so bizarre only my own experiences convince me that he can't be making it up. Then it's my turn. "Ask me questions," I say. It's hard for me to concentrate between figuring out where we're going and sitting next to Jack. "I don't know where to start."

"Okay," he says slowly. He taps his pencil on his list. "Well, let's take it in order. Why don't you start with why you were really salting your lawn last night?"

I wonder how it is that he happens to zero in on the single most supernatural thing that's happened. I take a deep breath, grip the wheel and check the mirrors. Then I say, "A few nights after my mother died, I started to hear this rapping on the front door." There, I said it. I stare straight ahead. We've turned off the parkway. Billboards rise up on every side, in between feed stores and gas stations and little strip malls.

"Did you answer the door?"

"I couldn't. The dogs wouldn't let me off the bed, let alone out of the bedroom. I managed to reach the phone, and I called the police. They came out – after four or five nights in a row of it, I was exhausted and they couldn't find a thing. One night, out of desperation, I sat up in bed and just yelled at whatever it was to stop and go away. And it did. Just like that." I pause and glance at him sideways. He's listening. "After my father died, it started up again, but worse, for some reason."

"Go on. How was it worse?"

"The dogs would start whining before it would begin. A few times, the knocks were strong enough to crack the glass. I called the police – especially after the glass got cracked – but still, there was nothing – not even a rock or a pebble under the windows. I'd tell it to go away, and it'd stop but it'd start up again. So maybe a week after my father died, I was talking to Rosie. She asked me if anything out of the ordinary had happened. When I told her what was happening, that's what she told me to do. So I did and it stopped."

"Okay." He writes that down. "But you don't know why?"

"She won't say much on the phone." I clear my throat, glance at Jack. "They were both- my father would only meet me in these anonymous public places. He wouldn't call me from his home phone. I was only at his house twice, and I could only come at a certain time of day and I had to leave by a certain time, too."

"Did he give you a reason? Didn't you think that was strange?"

I slap my hand on the steering wheel. "The house is pretty far out in the boonies – he said he was afraid I'd get lost. But me and my friends used to come down here and hang out – I have a pretty good sense of direction. I thought he didn't believe me. And he was my father, and – well, my mother said he was crazy. So I went along because —" I can't talk over the lump that suddenly rises in the back of my throat. If all this mattered so much, I don't understand why he left me alone all these years. I don't understand why my mother kept me from him.

"You wanted to get to know him." Jack sighs softly.

"Yeah."

We don't say anything for a few miles. We don't even look at each other.

Then Jack sighs again. "Sometimes I think I must be crazy. I've spent the last few days thinking I could be hunted by a vampire."

At once I remember the icy eyes of the kid in the elevator. *You'd make a good vampire. Maybe too good.* I glance at Jack out of the corner of my eye.

"I…I know that sounds crazy," he says.

"No, it doesn't," I reply. "Friday afternoon, in the library, there was this kid — I've seen him before…he's always creeped me out…but Friday, he followed me into the elevator. I guess I've never been so close to him before, and this time…this time he….well, he made me think the same thing." I glance at Jack. "I remember what I thought. 'He's the real thing.' And it was weird, because I've met a lot of kids like him, and I never once thought that about any of them. Ever."

"That's what I thought when I saw this guy," Jack says slowly. "Those very words. 'He's the real thing.'"

"And this guy… this is the Wall Street guy? Nicholas Savage — What'd you say his name was?"

"Savageux. Nicholas Savageux. I left my wife staring up at him like he was God Incarnate."

Savageux…Savageux. The name rolls around my head like a marble. We come to a stoplight. And then I remember. It's one of the four names on the big family tree Rosie sent over, that's now pinned over my mother's tasteful Impressionists. According to my father's painstaking research, the Savageux family emigrated from France to Scotland at the beginning of the fourteenth century, along with the Sinclairs. I'm sure of it.

The light changes green. "So what makes you think he's a vampire?"

"It's just something I felt."

There's a long silence while we both try to wrap our minds around the concept of vampires being real. Jack's next question comes out of nowhere. "You know, Jessie, I was wondering... if maybe... maybe the reason your father got involved with me was because he - he was in college, right? What if he just got this nice girl knocked—"

"Martha's old enough to have been my grandmother, Jack. She's very nice but she hasn't been a girl in at least forty years, and my father was married to my mother at the time – in fact, she was pregnant with me. Far as I know, Martha never said you were anyone but Jesse Sinclair's kid, just like all the others."

"You mean I have brothers and sisters?"

"You were like her ninth or tenth. A lot of them died real young, or were stillborn. I think there's only one or two who survived... you were... um... let me see... You would've been her seventh son." I glance at Jack again.

He's forgotten about his notebook, and is staring straight ahead. The air rushing through the vents has turned woodsy and sharp, the gravel along the roadside has turned to white-gold sand, visible beneath the patchy grass, clustered at the bases of the scrub pines. The landscape is shifting, from boggy farmland to brackish pine bogs. "I don't know what you know about this area, Jack, but the Pine Barrens – well, parts of them are as desolate as the Ozarks. In fact, where we're going.. Jack, I don't know what you're expecting, but Martha and her family – I'm sure they're nice people, but I'm also sure they don't have a lot. I know she has one son who lives with her. His name's Luther, I think – or maybe it's Lucas. And you should know, according to what Shirley said last night, I don't think he took the news all that well."

"Why? He's afraid I want a share of the family fortune? Look, that's not why I came here, you know that, right?"

He looks at me and I can feel my heart pound in time to the beat of the windshield wipers. Of course I know it. *I know it because I know you, Jack Chance*, I want to say. *I know you in a way your wife never will.* But I don't say that. I just look at the road that disappears over the horizon between a tunnel of charred, blasted trunks, and nod.

"What happened to the trees?" Jack asks. "They're all – they look skeletons – was there a fire?"

"All the time." I shrug. "If it's dry, like last summer, and there's a lightning strike, these trees go up like kindling. A certain amount of burning is good for them, I think, but what's bad is a lot of campers start forest fires, and the woods don't recover the way they should."

We turn onto a back road where the scrub pines give way to flat bogs that extend as far as the eye can see, broken in places where swampy inlets weave shallow streams. The road dips low enough I imagine it disappears in wet years and I wonder if I've taken a wrong turn.

"So tell me something about this place we're going then," says Jack, as we jounce along a rutted road. "What does Devil's Door have to do with the devil?"

"Ever hear of the Jersey Devil? Some people say Devil's Door is where he was born, and that's how the village got its name. It's the door the Devil got through."

"What's the Jersey Devil?"

"It's sort of like the Loch Ness monster or Bigfoot – one of those legends about something that lives in a wild place that every now and then someone sees. One of the things that makes the Jersey Devil different is that unlike other creatures – who mostly are assumed to have always inhabited a region – the Jersey Devil has a birth story, a family name – and more then one supposed homestead." I glance at him quickly. He's listening intently. "The name is always the same, too – Leeds. The woman who gives birth to the Jersey Devil is always called Mother Leeds. The other thing that most of the stories agree about is that he was her 13th child." I feel a pang of relief as we pass a landmark I recognize at last – an ancient two-pump gas station that was abandoned when according to the ghostly sign, Coca-Cola was still five cents.

"Go on," says Jack.

"When Mother Leeds realized she was expecting again, she cursed the child, and when he born, he had cloven hooves instead of feet, and bat wings and a tail – among other deformities, that tend to vary from story to story.

He flew out the window, after eating at least several of his brothers and sisters, though some stories say he wiped out the whole family. There continue to be reported sightings, even recently."

"How recently?"

"Last fall there were a few. I guess the creature, if there is a creature, gets more active in the autumn. A lot of animals do that."

"So you think it's some kind of animal?"

"*I* don't think it's anything. I mean, I think if it's something – if there's something around causing a disturbance, I think it's an animal. My father thought the story of the Jersey Devil was a – a metaphor, for something for which we don't have a name, but doesn't make any less real. Sort of like a vampire that doesn't suck blood."

His brow wrinkles, his eyes narrow, he spreads his hands and the notebook falls on the floor. "Jesus, Shirley wasn't kidding when she said she was in Bumblefuck. Is this even New Jersey?"

"We're almost there." I point to a green road sign as we pass that says: Devil's Door 5, Redemption 9, Atlantic City 25. "See? Civilization is right around the corner."

"That's pretty hard to believe. But back to the Jersey Devil… your father thought the Jersey Devil was real?"

"Yeah. He did." I say with a sigh. "He thinks some woman really did get pregnant with her 13th kid and didn't want it. He doesn't think it had bat wings and a tail, but he thinks it was unnatural in some way."

"You mean, deformed? Handicapped?"

"Yeah, something like that. Mutated, maybe."

"I see," Jack says slowly, though I think the only thing he's really seeing are the raindrops running down the window.

I grip the steering wheel as we jounce over ruts. The roads are getting worse and the rain is getting heavier. It's been sometime since we passed even a roadside farm-stand. Only the mile markers every tenth of a mile reassure me that we haven't crossed into another dimension ourselves. To make matters worse, it seems we're driving straight into a storm. There's a song about that, I think, but I can't remember the words or who it's by.

"How many kids did you say Martha Sinclair had?"

The abrupt subject switch startles me. "I don't know, exactly. A bunch. I know she'd already had a lot by the time she had you."

"Maybe I was the thirteenth and your father thought I was another Jersey Devil?"

Never once had that idea occurred to me. The people who live deep in the Pine Barrens cling to old ways, are clannish and don't seek outside help very often. The isolation of the pine woods fosters beliefs outsiders – like my mother - call superstitious. But Jack had been born in the maternity clinic in Redemption, precisely because Martha'd lost so many kids. She wasn't looking to get rid of Jack, even if he'd been number 13. "You don't exactly strike me as the Jersey Devil type, Jack. And, see, your mom had a lot of babies die, either at birth, or right after. She didn't want to lose you, Jack. She's insisted all along you were alive."

We come to a cross roads, and turn off the main road. I put my head lights on and slow down. "Why're we slowing down?" he asks, peering around.

"We're here."

"There's nothing here."

"Sure there is." We make a sharp left because I nearly miss the driveway of the Shady Brook Motel and Rest Stop, which is where we're meeting Shirley. I see a couple trucks, but nothing that looks like the blue Honda rental she described. I have no idea which unit is hers.

"Is this where Shirley's staying?" asks Jack.

"Yeah. Now you see why she couldn't come get you? She'd never have found her way back here in the dark." I turn off the ignition and glance around. There's no sign of Shirley. I roll down my window and gulp the cool wet air even if it is laced with diesel fumes. I wish I hadn't agreed to meet her here. All I can think about is being inside one of those squat little rooms, naked with Jack on one of those squishy flea-infested little beds. From the way he's pulled his notebook onto his lap and is avoiding my glance, I bet he's thinking the same. "I'm going to go ask the clerk," I say abruptly. I have to get out of the car or I won't be able to stop myself from dragging him into a room by his collar and throwing him down on the bed.

I stumble out of the car. The sandy gravel crunches under my feet and the wet air is strongly scented with diesel fumes and pine-tar. A red neon VACANCY sign buzzes and pulsates and I wonder if it ever gets turned off. I stagger into the tiny office. It has that funky, mold smell so many places get around here. The bored kid behind the desk with a piercing in his lip tells me that Shirley got a phone call about an hour ago from Martha Sinclair. When I ask for more information, he rolls his eyes in the direction of an open doorway leading down a dingy hall, then shouts, "Ma!"

A too-skinny woman in too-tight jeans minces out on too-high heels. "What now, Darrin? Didn't I just say I wanted to listen to the radio?"

"This lady's asking for that woman – whats'er name? Shirley?"

"Oh. My. God." The woman grabs my hand with both hers. "Are you Dave Woodwright's daughter? Shirley said you were coming here – but I just heard something on the police radio ... there's trouble at the Sinclair place." Her eyes get very wide, and she cranes her head over my shoulder. "And, oh-my-God, you have Martha's kid? Is that him? Martha's kid?"

"He's not a kid," I say, feeling as if a rope is going around my neck. I don't know why I'm afraid, but suddenly I have the feeling that something very bad has happened.

"You might want to prepare him." She puts her hand on my arm and behind the layers of make-up her eyes go soft. "What I just heard... it isn't... it's not good. At least, not if I got it right." She takes a deep breath. "Luke Sinclair's shot his mother."

Chapter 18

"**Luke shot Martha?**" I feel as if I've fallen into one of those soaps I got addicted to in high school, the ones that necessitated my rushing home from school and getting cozy on the couch, preferably with a guy.

"You want to drive over – you know how to get there?" asks the woman. "No? Get my purse, Darrin. You can follow me. I'll take you –"

"No, you won't, Ann-Marie. I don't think that's a good idea." A big man comes out of the back room, stuffing the back of his shirt tail into his jeans. "They got a real mess going over there - Luke's all lickered up and it sounds to me like he shot someone else, not his mother – who's that woman who's staying here?"

"Shirley?" I say with Ann-Marie as together we turn to the big man. "Shirley's been shot?"

"Martha's been having trouble with Luke over this. Weren't you telling me that, Ted?"

"Yeah, but this ain't like Luke," Ted answers. "To turn a gun on Martha, he's got to be out of his head."

"B-but Jack," I say, bewildered by this sudden turn of events. "He's come all this way- we have to let someone know he's here."

"I don't think you should over there either, ma'am." Ted's face is speckled, his bald dome is shaped like an egg, and his sandy eyebrows are puckered. "Police're all over the place – sounds like they got their hands full."

"B-but what about Jack – he's Martha's son...I know how much he wants to meet her -" I jerk my thumb over my shoulder.

Ted hesitates. "Get me your keys, Ann-Marie. You can follow me over there, but once we get over there, make sure you listen to the cops. I know Luke Sinclair. There's something gone wrong in his head, because the man I know wouldn't hurt a flea."

"Ted, I want to come with you."

"No, you don't, Ann-Marie. Don't get yourself involved."

I leave them bickering and return to the car, wondering how I'm supposed to explain this to Jack. I slide behind the steering wheel. A light rain is dotting the windshield. Ted comes outside, dangles his keys so I see them, then motions. "Follow me," he mouths. He disappears around the corner of the building.

I sigh.

"Something's wrong."

I notice that it's not a question. "Yeah." Jack just looks at me and waits. "They – uh – they have a police radio in there. And... uh... I guess Martha's son – Luke – they're saying he got all drunk and - there've been reports of gunshots and they think Shirley might've been-"

"It's not Shirley," he says.

"How can you be so sure?" I ask. I glance up at the rearview mirror, and to my amazement, I think I see a red-haired woman sitting in the back seat, her hands clasped in her lap. I blink, she disappears, and Ted pulls out from behind the office in a Buick the size of a boat. He honks, then peels out of the gravel parking lot. I follow him through a maze of winding roads hugged on all sides by identical looking stands of pine trees. I'm shaking, and suddenly it doesn't seem like a good idea to go there, after all. "What do you mean – it's not Shirley?" I glance over at Jack. "Look, you want me to take you right to Rosie's?"

"No, it's okay – we should- we should let the Sheriff know."

At least, that's what I think Jack says. I'm paying attention to Ted, who's suddenly slammed on his brakes. A tenth of a mile up the road, the road is blocked by police cars, all flashing red and blue. I see state and county police and a speckling of cars from neighboring townships and towns. "There it is," I say. I brake as Ted does a k-turn in the middle of the road. He slows down to talk to me before he drives past.

"That's the place up there. Go slow now – be careful. Tell Shirley – if you see her - that Ann-Marie'll mind her stuff."

Jack's pale, his face is beaded with sweat.

"Are you okay?" I don't know whether to go the short distance or take him to Rosie's – where we can call the Sheriff's office. But we're not related to Shirley and I'm not sure how much of Jack's story hospital staff might be willing to believe if anything's happened to Martha. Maybe this is really our best chance of finding out what's happening.

He nods.

"We can go back to Rosie's, you know. We can call the Sheriff's office. Want to do that?"

"I've waited so long to meet her," he says. "I've come this far, to turn around now – "

I know how he feels. I know how I felt when I saw my father walk up to me after twenty-some years on that gray December day outside the Liberty Bell. I remember how the glass enclosure stunk of the homeless people who congregate there at night, how my new mohair sweater, chosen so carefully for the occasion because it matched the greenish highlights in my eyes, itched like the fucking devil. I remember how I didn't care.

I put my foot on the accelerator and the car leaps forward. We don't go very far before a beardless cop waves us down, and starts to motion to us to turn around. I lean out the window. "This is Martha Sinclair's son, Officer – she's expecting him. Please – is there some way to let her know he's here?"

That changes everything. Before I know it, we're allowed into the outermost ring of cop cars clustered around the shambling house. I glance at Jack. I can't imagine what he thinks as he takes it all in – the peeling paint, the patched roof, the broken windows with boards, the tattered curtains, the pot of plastic geraniums on the porch. I don't know where he's from or how he was raised but he can't be feeling he missed out on much. A tall state cop wades toward us, motioning us to stop.

I put the car in park. As I get out, I see a movement in one of the second floor windows and I think I see a pasty white face peer out.

I'm not sure what happens next. Jack gets out as I do, and the two of us walk toward the cop, who removes his sunglasses and opens his mouth. What I hear is an explosion. The cop turns his head, and something sings in the air straight into me. When the bullet hits my chest, Jack's beside me.

In slow motion, I see the cop turn, feel Jack push me to the ground. He lands directly on top of me, and in some remote corner of my mind, I think a bullet in the chest seems an inordinately high price to pay just to feel him on top of me. Because that's what's happened, I can see it clearly as I float, partially in and partially out of my body, which seems to be lying motionless under Jack.

"Oh no," he breathes directly into my ear, with a hot rush of air that fills my skull with the scent of lilacs. "Oh, no, you mustn't leave me now."

At least I think that's what he says. The world begins to get dark, sirens start screaming and the earth under me shakes with the thud of running footsteps. I see my mother standing next to me. *Stay with Jack, Jessie.* She says it the way she used to tell me to brush my teeth.

He's holding me tight against him. I'm over him and under him all at once, somehow, and from every angle I can see the energy around his body glowing pink and gold. There's a silvery cord that twines between us in a figure eight pattern, intertwining with the double-helix of a pulsing light that appears to be wrapped around our spines. I can see a spiraling rainbow of colors ever more clearly as the searing sensations in my physical body start to fade.

Stay with Jack, honey – it's not your time. This time I see my father. He's standing next to my mother.

The next thing I know, I'm back in my body, and I can breathe, even though it hurts like a fucking mother. I can't breathe, though, because Jack's kissing me, breathing air so pure it burns in my lungs like a white hot flame, dissolving the bullet, pushing it out of my heart, out of my lungs, out of my body all together. With every beat of my healing heart, I feel each tiny cell obey, each miniscule structure open, then close, in perfect synchrony, that allows the bullet to tear through flesh and bone and skin, leaving me unharmed.

"Miss, miss, Jesus, miss – mister – are you two okay?"

I sit up. Jack's lying next to me on the ground, his eyes closed, his skin dead white. He looks deader than I felt.

"Take it easy, miss, you're bleeding."

"No, I'm not," I say. I'm fine – I really am fine. It's Jack who looks like he's been shot. But I'm the one with the red stains spreading across the left side of my chest and back.

"Miss," a medic says firmly. "All that blood came from somewhere - I've got to check you out."

"It's Jack's blood," I say. It has to be Jack's blood. I must be remembering things wrong. If I'm remembering right, then Jack just brought me back to life. Even Superman can't do that. He can stop bullets, not push them out of people all together.

People are starting to gather around us, and I know we should get away. There doesn't seem to be any explanation for the fact there's blood stains on the front and back of my jacket and a flattened bullet on the ground under me. "Here," I say, "must've been a nick." But the medic never answers, because just as he leans to take it from my fingers, more shots ring out, and someone screams, "No, Luke!"

We get away without being noticed because Luke turns the gun on himself after shooting at both Martha and Shirley. The women are taken to the hospital, Luke to the morgue, and in the ensuing confusion, Jack and I escape.

On the way to Rosie's, we drive in silence, mostly because Jack makes it clear he doesn't want to talk. But if what I think just happened really did happen, then that makes me alive despite all odds and Jack – what the fuck does it make Jack?

The drying blood is sticky on my clothes, on my skin, and both feel and smell remind me that I was dead, I was dying. Physically, for someone who's just died and been brought back to life, I feel pretty good – the way I used to feel as a kid when I'd come back to school from a long summer spent on the beach – in other words, better than I have in months. Emotionally, mentally, I feel like I've been crushed by a house. I don't even dare look at Jack – I'm afraid he might be glowing.

We reach a stoplight. I peek at Jack. His eyes are fixed, his expression grim. "Don't look so upset – I'm going to be insulted. After all, it weren't for you, I'd be dead."

"Don't say that, Jessie." He sounds almost angry, and the look he gives me is ferocious. "That's crazy- no one can -"

"You've been doing a lot of weird things lately. Pulling whiskey out of thin air, notebooks out of glove boxes, you knew exactly how I like my coffee, not to mention the way my dogs went gaga over you… did you read that list as you wrote it this morning, Jack? That bullet hit me, you know it did. I felt it go into me. I felt you push it out."

"I don't remember doing that."

"Do you remember kissing me?"

The light turns green. I take my foot off the brake at the same time he whispers, "Yes."

He looks stunned. There're so many questions I want to ask. How did it feel? What did he do? Did he really tell me not to leave *him*? Was that something he meant to say? What did he mean? I want to ask him all that and more. We were just part of a fucking miracle, after all.

I tighten my grip on the steering wheel and try not to look down at the gelatinous clots now forming on my skin and clothing. The coppery fresh-meat smell is starting to nauseate me. "I hope we don't get stopped by a cop," I say, trying to keep my tone light. "I don't know how we'd explain all the blood. Do you?"

"Jessie," he says, not looking at me. "I know you're as freaked as I am. But could you just – just be quiet?"

"Sure, Jack," I say meekly. What else can you say to the person who just saved you from a bullet? I bite my tongue from time to time and glance at him every now and then. Jack's looking out the window, and his eyes are a universe away. I notice he twirls his wedding ring around and around his finger.

Rosie is waiting for us on the porch as we drive up to the shambling hulk of a house she shared with my father. Apparently she has a friend in the county 911 office who phoned her to let her know we were on our way. She takes one look at me and narrows her eyes. "That's a lot of blood for a nick." Rosie is a woman of very few words. I can't tell what kind of impression she's making on Jack, because my eyes fill with tears and I want to throw myself into her arms. She ignores him, and draws me up the steps. "Elaine said you were nicked."

I don't know what to say. I can't lie to Rosie in my father's house. I feel his presence here acutely, almost as if he's standing over her shoulder. *It's okay, honey.* I can almost hear his voice. "Can I show you?"

She nods, leads us into the cavernous hallway, and gestures to one side of the foyer. "Mr. Chance? Why don't you wait for us in the parlor? Make yourself comfortable. We'll be right there."

In the dining room, I take off my jacket and pull my sticky sweater over my head. The blood peels off my skin in thick dark scabs, leaving a slimy film. I stand in front of Rosie in my bra. "When Luke went crazy, and started shooting... one of the bullets hit me, Rosie. It hit me right here." I touch a spot on my breastbone that still feels sore. "And the thing of it is, well, I think I'm supposed to be dead."

"Turn around," she says.

When I do, she runs a tentative fingertip over the skin of my back. "Ah." She touches a sore spot on my back, the narrow place between my shoulder blade and my spine. "That's where it went in. This is where it came out." She steps away from me, crosses her arms over her breasts. "You look pretty lively for a dead person, Jessie Woodwright. How do you feel?"

"Like I need a bath."

"Do you remember anything that happened?"

Other than floating in Jack's arms, pinned by his weight? Feeling myself at once dissolve and then collect around his kiss? I can't tell that to Rosie, but my cheeks get warm and I can't help glancing in the direction of the parlor.

"He had something to do with?"

I nod, close my eyes as a chill ripples through me. "I felt him throw himself on top of me. I could feel the bullet going in – I knew I was shot. It was like this 'oh shit" moment, you know? And then, almost before it started to hurt, I could see myself floating in the air, not quite out of my body, but not all the way in it, either. I heard my mother, and then my father say, 'Stay with Jack.'" I sniff. It's beginning to hit me what happened. I burst into tears. "Jack saved my life, Rosie... I know he did – I found the bullet *under* me, like it passed right through me without hurting me at all, and I know it was *Jack* who saved me. What the hell is going on, Rosie? Who is he? Why did Dad take him away?"

Rosie gathers me in her arms. She lets me weep a few minutes and then she pats my shoulder. "Okay, honey. It's okay. Remember how I explained that certain abilities run in families? And these can include things like ... well, like sensing things others don't... or seeing or hearing things that your other senses would tell you aren't there. Well, this would seem to be one of those things... I can't explain it any other way."

"You mean there's something special about Jack?"

"Or you." She pats my back then lets me go. "Or maybe it's both of you. Your father thought so."

"Wh-what do you mean?"

"I'll explain all I can after you get cleaned up. There's clean towels in the bathroom at the top of the steps and I'll find you something to wear. This stuff needs to be cleaned."

As she reaches for the bloody clothing, I hold up the sweater. "Is there a hole?"

But despite the crust of blood on both articles, there's no hole, in neither sweater nor jacket, any more than there is in me.

The bathroom takes my breath away. I've never been upstairs in my father's house. I assumed the fixtures would be as ancient and decrepit as the outside of the place. But they're not. In fact, the whole upstairs appears to be part of a different house all together, I notice, as I make my way up from the landing. The foyer and the stairs are positioned so that you can't see the upstairs from the downstairs at all, and when I turn the corner, the stairs are suddenly carpeted in a thick, soft berber, woodwork and brass fittings gleam. The long halls are lit by tall windows at either end, draped with filmy lace. The parquet floors are immaculate.

The paintings on the wall are of Tarot cards, enormous renderings in vivid oils that shine with a subtle burnish. The door immediately opposite the landing is partly open, and through it, I see white tiles and potted palms. I push the door open. The plants are clustered around a claw-foot tub, set on a pedestal beneath an octagon-shaped skylight, so that the tub itself beckons, half-hidden behind the lush green fronds.

"Your father got some of his best ideas in that tub," Rosie says behind me. She offers me a pile of towels, with a folded cotton sweater. "There's soap, shampoo – take whatever you need." She produces a tiny travel kit from a closet hidden within a wall recess, places it on a vanity that overlooks the front of the house, and shuts the door, leaving me gaping.

It's like being in a five-star hotel. I can't resist opening the glass doors of the enormous double-headed shower. Tub, shower? Shower, tub? I almost wish I had time for both.

In the end I settle for a shower. I pick up the little plastic travel kit. It's got a toothbrush, toothpaste, razor, brush, and sample size packages of deodorant, face and body cream. On impulse, as the shower warms up, I push open the door and am shocked to see a whole row of little kits, all stocked and waiting. Is Rosie running a bed and breakfast? I wonder. But... surely... wouldn't my father have mentioned that on at least one of my three visits? Could this be something she's doing since he died?

I step into the shower, and let the water sluice over my body like the rain is pouring down the glass skylight. I twist and turn and soap myself all over, mostly as excuse to use the creamy soap that smells of something spicy and green. The fragrance rises off my body in the clouds of steam. I shut my eyes and take in deep breaths of the warm vapor. I shut my eyes and let myself relax. I'm alive, I think. I'm alive because of a man named Jack Chance. What do you think of that, Mom?

I hear her voice as clearly as I heard it before: *Stay with Jack*.

Sure, I think, with a long sigh. I'd love to stay with Jack. I'm just not sure how well his wife would take it. *Look, honey,* I imagine him saying. *Look what I found in New Jersey. Can we keep her?*

Not bloody likely.

The last of the gobby clots swirls down the drain. To distract myself from thinking about that, I consider once more the likelihood that Rosie's opened the place to the general public, and conclude that's not much more likely.

This place is so far off the main roads, you have to know what you're looking for in order to find it. We'll have to leave before twilight, because otherwise the roads aren't lit well enough for me to feel confident that I can find my way back to the AC Expressway after dark.

I didn't notice a sign as we drove up, either. Nothing that said "Rooms" or "Bed & Breakfast," anyway. And the downstairs rooms – at least the ones I've seen - look like they belong in a different building from this sumptuously updated bath. I think about the water-stained wallpaper, the broken windows propped open with blocks of wood, the sagging curtains, the ancient heater that hisses through the radiators. My father was constantly apologizing and my impression was always they couldn't afford to fix the place up. The "powder room" I used before this was a toilet stuck behind the washing machine in the mudroom.

So who visits, and ends up staying unexpectedly so often that Rosie stocks travel kits? Add another item to the Weird List, I think, as I get out and dry myself off. The towels are plush white cotton, the lotions scented with lavender. I brush my hair, weave it into a loose braid, and pull on Rosie's sweater. My body feels replete, refreshed, and in a curious state of equilibrium. It was like a full-body orgasm, I think, as I fold the towels. I leave them stacked neatly on the vanity along with the rest of the toiletries. Then I stuff my bra into my purse.

As I turn to leave, I catch a glimpse of my reflection in the mirror across the room. It's a trick of the light, I think, or it has to be, because there can't possibly be another woman, standing behind me, her hair as curly and red as mine, dressed in the clothing of another century. I gasp and look over my shoulder, but no one's standing there, I'm alone in the room. When I look back at the mirror, the image is gone.

Part Five - Jack

Chapter 19

There's something odd about the house. At first glance it appears to be just another crumbling Victorian. Wallpaper's drooping off the impossibly high ceiling, the paint on the window frames is peeling off in sheets, exposing the bare wood beneath in places. The rugs are threadbare, the furniture is covered with patched slipcovers or draped with the kind of cloudy plastic lace to which my mother was partial. But there're no personal items in the room – no photographs, even the old ones you might expect, no books or magazines, no evidence of any hobbies or interests. The paintings are the bland landscapes you find in hotels. Even the plants are fake. I feel like I've stepped into a lobby. Or onto a stage set.

On impulse I lift up the slipcover. The sofa beneath the slipcover is covered in pristine pale green silk. I raise the cover higher and peer underneath, feeling the upholstery. It's taut and firm. Why, I think. Why would you take a lovely piece of furniture and cover it with something old and worn and falling to pieces?

"Looking for something, Jack?"

I hit my head on the edge of the end table as I come back up. My eyes meet Rosie's. There's something in her expression that reminds me of Dougless. "I thought I dropped some change." I stand up, feeling awkward. I can tell she knows I was snooping by the way she's looking at me. *This house does have secrets,* I think. "Is-is Jessie going to be okay?"

"I think so. She's gone upstairs to shower. Why don't you come back to the kitchen with me, Jack? You don't mind if I call you Jack, do you?"

I follow her through another shabby room, past a dining room table long enough to hold a coffin. The flowers on the table are plastic, and even the candles are covered in cellophane.

Then we step into the kitchen and another world.

"Are you hungry? Would you like a sandwich?"

She gently pushes me in the direction of a white tile-top table and she has to repeat herself, because I'm not listening to her. I'm too busy processing the stark difference between this part of the house and the front. I nod in answer, struck mute in amazement. Somehow I find myself sitting in one of the eight ladder-back chairs that line the table.

As Rosie bustles around, fixing my sandwich, I can only stare. It's the kind of blend of old and new kitchen magazines strive to achieve: old white shelves stacked with crockery that go all the way to the ceilings are juxtaposed by enormous stainless steel appliances, the bunches of herbs, strings of red peppers and copper-bottomed pans that hang from wrought iron racks are bright counterpoints to the black granite counters. As I gaze around the room, it occurs to me she's got an awful lot of dishes and pots and pans for two people.

She glances at me sideways as she places the sandwich and a glass of iced tea in front of me. She dries her hands on a white cotton dish-towel. Then she takes the chair opposite, clearing hesitating while I eat. When she finally speaks, it's slow, as if she's choosing each word with care. "I know you and Jessie came here hoping for some answers. But I have to tell you both – the more David and I pieced together, the more confused we got." She breaks off as her eyes flood with tears.

"So why'd he take me away from my mother?"

Instead of answering, Rosie looks up, past my shoulder, at the doorway. I turn and see Jessie standing there. Tiny tendrils of dark red curls spiral around her face. She's wearing jeans, a cotton sweater and no bra. "Jessie, are you okay?"

She doesn't look okay, I think. She looks like she's seen a ghost.

"Yeah," she says, as she slides into the chair across from mine. "Yeah, I'm okay." She wrinkles her nose at my sandwich.

"Are you hungry? Would you like something?" Rosie sees it, too.

"No," Jessie replies. "I heard what Jack just asked you though. I'd like to know myself."

Rosie looks from me to Jessie and back. "Okay. Let's start there, and then… well… we can move on to… to everything else. All right?"

"Okay," says Jessie.

"Okay," I say.

Rosie takes a deep breath and starts to talk. In my mind's eye, her words are a river of sound pouring out of her throat, carrying me away into another time, another place, and into another presence all together. The voice in my head falls a couple octaves, the cadence shifts and alters. The images that form across my mind's eye coalesce into an eerie solidity, and I realize what I'm seeing is somehow what Jessie's father remembered. I'm wearing his clothes, sitting in his house. In the shadowy light, it's almost like I'm listening to him.

Someone was retiring, I had no idea who. I'd only been there since the spring, and it wasn't even my department. Wasn't Helen's either- in fact, I have no memory of how we ended up there. For all I know, we were hungry, and hoping to snag enough hors d'oeurves to call it a meal. She was pregnant, then, with you, Jessie. She was always hungry, and we were always poor. So we're wandering around this faculty gathering, picking food, being sociable, when an old man, who looked as if he should've long ago retired himself, stuck out his hand over the punch bowl and whispered, "Did I hear you say your name was Woodwright?"

I shook his hand, leaned over the punch and whispered back, "Who wants to know?"

I was joking. He was scared. He startled back, eyes darting around in his head, and somehow the punch bowl upended over the watercress sandwiches. Your mother came scurrying over, of course, dragging me out of the way of most of the damage. The old man reappeared at my elbow about ten minutes later. His white shirt was now flecked pink. "Balthazar Allende. I'm a medievalist."

"Dave Woodwright. I'm really sorry about the punch."

He waved a hand in the air as if the confusion still massing at the refreshments table was a mere trifle. "I've tried to get in touch with you, Mr. Woodwright."

I can't imagine why. Our fields have nothing to do with each other.

"You see, I've been researching a family, a branch of which is named Woodwright. They go back quite far in history. I-I wonder if you'd be kind enough to let me ask you a few questions, some time? Regarding your family?"

I remember how the way he stared at me through his round glasses reminded me of a big owl. I remember looking around for Helen to come and rescue me, but it was as if the two of us suddenly stepped aside into another reality – one that functioned like a one-way mirror. No one seemed to notice us at all. "Sure," I said, because I couldn't think of any reason why not. "Call me at my office – or here, let me give you my home number."

"I'd be very grateful," he said.

Afterwards, Helen was upset. Allende's views were considered too outlandish to have any academic merit. In fact, even some of his friends were afraid he was in the early stages of dementia. He was the last person she wanted me to make friends with among the faculty. I told her a conversation about genealogy scarcely amounted to "making friends." We dropped the matter and for a long time it seemed that Allende had forgotten about me.

When the phone rang one wintry afternoon, I happened to be alone in the apartment. Helen had gone to a meeting of Resident Advisors which included dinner. I was tired of grading quizzes. Allende's invitation to join him for an early dinner at a diner a few towns south sounded sufficiently interesting to rouse my curiosity on a dull day. As we said good-bye, an operator's voice asked for another nickel. It occurred to me it was strange that he'd call me from a pay phone.

A storm was expected – I remember how prudent I felt as I laced up my hiking boots. I left a note for Helen. Allende met me at the curb outside the dorm in a beige Pontiac that was remarkable only for being easy to overlook. He had to honk the horn, twice, in fact, before I noticed he'd pulled up beside me.

"Are you hungry?" was the first thing he asked.

"No," I said, "not yet."

"Good," he answered, "Because our plans have changed. We have to make a stop – and I might need your help, David. I hope you don't mind."

"As long as I'm back before –"

"Of course," he said. "We'll do our best. Do you mind if we talk on the way?"

"Where're we going?" I see we're headed south – in the general direction of the town he'd mentioned before.

"It's not far from the diner in Glen's Neck. Place called Redemption – ever hear of it?"

"No." I was getting nervous. "Look – maybe we could do this another time. Why don't you just drop me off somewhere? I can walk home..."

"There's a baby in trouble, David. It might be too late even now."

"Too late to do what?"

"Save his life."

That shut me up. I didn't know what to say to that. Babies had a new reality for me, ever since Helen got pregnant. I think I said I needed to be home by six. Allende just nodded. On the drive, he started asking me his questions, so that by the time we turned off the dark, narrow road, he was quite certain I was a descendant of the family he'd been researching. But he turned off his lights as we swung into the parking lot of a low white building. A nun in a white habit was standing outside, holding a bundle. Beside the entrance, another car, a long, dark Lincoln, idled.

When Allende saw the nun, his face visibly paled. He turned off the car, then turned to me. "Sister may need some help, David. If you wouldn't mind." He took the keys out of the ignition and handed them to me before I could ask what kind of help Sister might need. "When you're finished here, take my car back to Princeton – just push the keys through the mail slot in my office door. I'll call you on Monday. I realize this is a lot to leave you with."

He opened the door just as I said, "Hey, Dr. Allende, wait!"

"I have to go, David. But here –" From under his seat he took out a thick notebook, bulging with papers, with paperclips and scraps. "Hold on to this, until I come for it. Don't give it to anyone else. And here." From his pocket, he pulled out a twenty dollar bill, an enormous amount of money in those days, enough to not only fill the gas tank, but feed us for a week as well. "Take your pretty wife to dinner instead."

"Where're you going?" He can't be doing this, I remember thinking. I can't drive his car back to Princeton – I don't even know where we are, let alone how to find Princeton.

"I have to take the baby, David." He smiled at me, nodded, and got out of the car. "Don't worry about the gas."

In shock, I watched him take the baby from the nun. They exchanged a few sentences. Then he got in the car, and it drove off. The nun knocked on my window. "Professor Wrightwood? Would you come with me?"

"That's not my name." I got out of the car.

"I have a hard time with names," she answered, her face absolutely deadpan, even though I was quite sure this woman never forgot a thing in her life.. "Please? Balthazar said you were here to help."

"Sure, Sister." Whatever else, I was raised a good Catholic boy. "Whatever I can do." And that's what I did.

"So that's how it happened," Rosie says. "David had no idea why he was doing what he did the night you were born, Jack."

"And Allende never came back?" I say.

"No. David was left with the notebook, so he read it."

"What happened then?"

Rosie looks at Jessie. "There was enough in Allende's notes to make it clear the Woodwrights were connected to these other three families. From what he could glean, there was a pattern of births in these families occurring on two dates, March 1 and March 31. So when you were born on the thirty-first of March, Jessie, with Jack having been born on the 1st, your father believed that maybe – maybe there was something about you, too... something someone else might want enough to kidnap you for. He was afraid that you could be in danger, too.

"You know that old saying?" Rosie asks. "March comes in like a lion and goes out like a lamb?"

"So what? That's just an old saying about the weather. What's that got to do with anything?"

"David came to that folk sayings are more than simply old wives' wisdom. He believed they contained information that alluded to other kinds of wisdom, esoteric wisdom, passed on down through the ages – things that made sense in one way and yet, made sense in another, if you were aware.

"He believed that this information could reveal some great, cosmic pattern that endlessly repeats, variation after variation. If you could understand the information, you could understand not just what was happening in the present, but also what would happen, because everything that's already happened is going to happen again."

Cosmic patterns... endless variations... repetition through time... I've heard myself say words like that recently. In front of my class, the one on Milton, Blake and Yeats. That's what Blake believed, among other things. I've said almost this very thing myself, I think, and I remember the kid who thought Blake was visited by aliens. Line after line of his poetry echoes in my head. It's a coincidence right there, I think, that I'm teaching a class in the very poet who believed that all other divinely inspired poets – like Milton – somehow got the vision wrong. *He didn't think they understood what they were really seeing...* But how does my own stuff fit into that?

"So what's that mean to us?" asks Jessie through very thin lips. She looks angry.

"Maybe the best thing to do is show you." Rosie gets up. "Come with me. Please."

She marches down the hall, then up the creaking steps to the second floor. That's when I notice the paintings. At first I think they're playing cards – elaborate playing cards, and then I realize there's titles scrolled across the top of each one. The Fool is the first – he resembles a joker about to step over a cliff. He's followed by the High Priestess and the Magician.

We round the landing, and that's when I notice the stark difference in the condition of the house. It's like they started renovating and simply stopped at the landing, then picked up in the kitchen. On the second floor, the woodwork gleams, the brass fittings shine. The wallpaper's crisp, the paint is fresh. The doors are open. We pass room after room of neatly made up beds, empty desks and chairs.

We round a corner and I am face to face with another painting, this one of a man dangling off a tree limb by one foot. *The Hanged Man* reads the caption. He doesn't look upset about his situation, though, I notice. He's just kind of dangling there, hanging out in space. I look closely at his face, at his expression, and in some weird way I can't explain, our gazes merge and I can see what he sees – a verdant forest rich and green – and he can see what I do.

"Jack?" Jessie's tugging at my sleeve and the vision vanishes. Rosie's waiting at the top of the steps, on a narrow landing next to a closed door. As we go up, Rosie fumbles in her pocket. I'm expecting a big iron ring, but it's just a single key on a plastic ring. I wonder who sleeps in all the rooms, who eats off all the plates, who enjoys the private gardens I can glimpse now from this height.

She fiddles with the lock, then pushes the door open, as she flicks on a bank of lights. "Go on in."

Around the walls are pinned at least a dozen enormous maps, Mercator projections of the world, similar to the ones now tacked on the living room walls of my bungalow. But these are bigger. In the center of the room, there's a long table covered in felt, on which are long brass cases that at first glance look like telescopes. But then I see that they're the sort of thing in which museums and libraries store old manuscripts.

"What is all this?" mutters Jessie.

Rosie touches another set of switches. Track lighting illuminates each map. "David had reached the Middle Ages by the time he died."

I take a quick stroll around the room, stopping now and then to peer at the canvas maps stuck with colored pins. Half way around, I pause and ram my fists deep in the pockets of Jessie's father's khakis. I wish I could've acquired his knowledge with his clothing, and then something clicks into place and I understand what I'm looking at. "This is some kind of huge family tree, isn't it?"

"Yes."

Out of nowhere, it seems, Jessie explodes. "Fuck you, Rosie. Fuck you. Will you stop with the cloak and dagger shit and just spill it? Is this *his* family? Is this my family? You're starting to sound like Alfred Hitchcock or that other creepy guy – the Night Gallery guy. For Christ's sake, spit it out."

"Jessie?" I ask.

"No, it's okay," Rosie says. "She's been through a lot. I'm not trying to hold back, Jessie. I'm just trying to explain what I do know so you'll believe me."

"Listen," I say. "I think I left *believing* behind about a week ago." I look closely at the tiny flags on the colored pins, and traces a set across the ocean. "I'm guessing this is my family… yours, too Jessie – look, here – the purple pins are Woodwright, right?" I look at Rosie for confirmation. She nods. Then I look at Jessie and our eyes meet, and I feel that extraordinary sense of recognition I felt before. *I know you.*

"What about Sinclair?" Jessie says, without taking her eyes off mine. The air between us feels heavy and charged, as if it's gathering weight, taking on substance and form beside me. A chill goes down my spine and gooseflesh rises on my arms. I know it's there. I think it's the blue pins.

"Sinclair is blue. So there's four colors – that means four families… McPherson. Savageux." I start to shake. I look at Rosie. "Are you telling me I'm *related* to Nicholas Savageux?"

"We're all one family." The voice who answers me isn't Rosie's. I jump about a foot because suddenly, Dougless is standing next to Jessie. Jessie turns and I know she can see her too.

"You have to be kidding."

"No, not at all, Jack. You, me, Jessie, Savageux – we're all part of one very large family."

Only Rosie doesn't appear to see or hear her. Jessie clearly does, because she's turned to Dougless, eyes wide, hands pressed to her mouth. But I can't quite wrap my mind around the idea I'm somehow related – connected by blood – to a vampire, a real vampire. He wants my blood, I think. He wants my blood because it's his blood.

A word on the map catches my eye – a word that means nothing to me – a word with a small star beside it that indicates it's a place of some kind. *Banff.* It's a town in Scotland, a market-town in Scotland, not a very big place. Before this moment, I never heard of it. But I know what it looks like, because suddenly I'm there. I've got a rope around my neck and a fiddle in my hand. I'm gazing out over the crowd, hoping to see the one face that isn't there. *Dougless.* The wood beneath my feet gives way and I fall, until the rope around my neck ends it all with a hard jerk and a snap.

Chapter 20

When I open my eyes, I'm clawing at my neck. It takes me a minute to realize I'm not squirming on the end of a rope, I'm not staring down into the faces of those who've come to watch me die. I'm staring up at paneled rafters lined with sleek chrome track lights. The vision that overwhelmed me is gone. I'm not holding a fiddle, and I'm not about to die. I touch my throat and feel nothing but skin.

"Jack?" Jessie's eyes are like huge pools of concern as she bends over me. "You okay?"

She's kneeling beside me, holding my hand. I turn to look at her and make my mouth and tongue move but nothing comes out. I try to sit up and start to cough.

The door opens and Rosie enters, carrying a stainless steel basin and a small white cloth. There's ice in the basin and the cloth is wet. She kneels beside me and dabs at my face. "Take it easy, Jack."

"I'm okay." I hold my head in my hands, more because I don't dare look at the map than that anything hurts. It was the map that made me faint, not the fact Jessie can see Dougless, or that both of us – or all of us, if we include Dougless – are related to Savageux. That thought makes me nauseous, not faint. I glance at the map without thinking and realize the name of a town's written in script so tiny I don't understand how I could even make sense of the letters. *Banff*

The name echoes in my mind and once more I feel grass and rough stones under my bare and bleeding feet. Rosie presses a glass of water into my hand and my head stops spinning. "Take your time, Jack."

"What made you faint?" Jessie sits back, hands primly folded in her lap. Our eyes meet and I know she wants to ask me about Dougless. I'm sure Dougless is the ghost Jessie saw, and that she both heard me speak to her and saw me react to her.

I feel as if I'm in two different places at once. "I'm-I'm not sure," I say. "Maybe- maybe we should go downstairs?" Another inadvertent glance at the maps, and this time I feel as I'm standing in front of that painting outside the HR department, the one that looked like two different things depending on the viewer's angle. I stagger a little as I get to my feet, and Jessie's there, her arm under mine, her surprisingly strong shoulder right where I need it to be. Our eyes are careful not to connect.

"I don't want you to fall down the steps," says Rosie. "Please take your time."

"I can make it," I say, certain that once I get away from the maps, I'll be just fine.

But it's not as easy to get to the door as it should be, and at the doorway, my knees buckle again, forcing me to hang on to the door jam as the room starts to spiral around me, and the stairs come rushing up to me. As if from a great distance, I hear Jessie and Rosie calling my name, but I'm looking at Dougless, whose somehow blocking my fall into oblivion. I hear Jessie shouting, "What the fuck is wrong with him?"

As Rosie pulls my head between my knees, I hear her say, "Breathe!"

I'm trying, but there's a rope around my neck, choking me, and I'm twisting, writhing, suffocating by my own weight.

"Jack, come back!"

For some reason, Jessie's voice cuts through the fog, rings clear as a bell and anchors me in the present. I roll to my side, lean my head against the wall, and say "What the fuck's going?" In the same moment, Jessie screams and points, "Oh, my God, Rosie, look at his neck."

I feel Rosie's breath on my neck, I hear her swift gasp. Reflexively, I touch my throat, and feel welts. "What the fuck…" I can't say any more because I start to choke.

Somehow we all get downstairs, at least as far as the bottom of the steps. Rosie runs for something to soothe my throat, and Jessie pounds on my back. I want to curl up in her arms and die, but each time I think that, I hear a voice bellow "No!"

Finally Rosie returns, waving a glass under my nose. A familiar burnt caramel smell wafts up my nostrils, sweeter than lilacs. "Drink this, Jack. It'll bring you back."

"I-I can't…" I protest.

But Jessie simply takes the glass and pours the liquid down my throat. I gulp, gasp, like an infant gasping for a nipple. The liquor shoots down the back of my throat like a fiery arrow, lands in my stomach and explodes into a warm velvety burn. *There is a balm in Gilead,* I think. I roll upright, my cheeks wet, my head steady. I wipe my face. I should not have swallowed that, I think. But it's too late now. "I'm okay."

"We've heard that before," says Jessie. I wish understood this connection I feel with her, that she's flesh of my flesh and bone of my bone in a way I've never felt Lila to be.

"You know, I just came here to meet my mother." I look at Rosie. I have the strongest feeling that there *is* an underlying pattern here – one so deeply woven and so intricate that to even begin to comprehend its existence is effort.

Before she can answer, the phone starts to ring. Rosie mouths an apology, then she turns and scampers away to answer it. "I don't know if I can take too many more surprises," mutters Jessie.

"Hey," I say. "How are *you?*"

In her eyes I see myself looking back at me. "I don't know," she says. "I feel… like me, but not like me. I don't know why. It's like I'm in two places at once – here, in this body, and then… somewhere else. God, I know that sounds nuts, but – ever since that bullet went through me -"

"It's okay," I say. I take her hand. "I feel that way too."

"You do?"

"Yeah.... Like I'm here and then I'm dangling off a rope. Something about looking at those maps... I just..." My throat feels sore and tender, though whether from the bruises which seem to be fading, or the whiskey I swallowed, I can't tell. I'm aware of myself in two bodies overlain as one: mine, and someone else's, that fits over mine like a badly tailored suit. "So where else are you?"

"I'm in this garden," she says slowly. "Standing on this rock. And there's a snake coiled around my feet." She looks at me. "So what do you think about that?"

I don't know what I think about that. It sounds like a dream image, or one of Blake's visions. Or maybe an image in one of these freaky paintings – maybe Jessie's having an experience similar to mine and the... The Hanged Man. "You saw the red-haired woman upstairs, didn't you?"

She turns to me with a startled expression and a nod. "I-I saw her in the bathroom, while I was getting dressed. She was in the mirror, and when I turned around she wasn't there."

"That's the first time you saw her?"

"That's the woman you've been seeing?"

We speak at the same time, and the fact that Dougless is now something else we share only accentuates the bond I feel with Jessie. I shut my eyes, which is another mistake, because immediately I'm back in the corridor in Manhattan, staring at that damn painting that seemed to have presaged this vision. When I open my eyes, Jessie is watching me closely. "This isn't the first time I felt this – this thing with the rope, like I'm choking – or had this vision, or whatever it is. I felt it once before – at a job interview – where my wife works."

The mention of Lila chills the temperature between us considerably. Jessie stands up just as Rosie walks back down the corridor. "That was Shirley Shulman on the phone, Jack, calling from the hospital. They're releasing her. She's on her way here." Rosie's lips quirk down momentarily and I can see she's not real happy about that. "How're you doing?"

"All I know is… I looked at that map… I read the name of a town… a town I never heard of before… and the next thing I know …I'm…" I touch my neck. "Hanging."

Rosie covers her mouth with both hands. "What was the name of the town?"

"Banff." The name rolls so easily off my tongue, and immediately my throat locks up. I start to choke. Jessie pounds my back, Rosie hands me a glass of what looks like water. When I can finally talk, I say, "I feel like I'm having some kind of flashback, but that whiskey you poured down my throat was the first drop of anything I've had in over two years."

"Well," Rosie says slowly, as if she's weighing every word, "I suppose David would say this is a genetic memory…from an event so traumatic, it's been seared into your DNA. Does that make sense?"

I notice she doesn't say what she thinks and I'm not sure what I think about what she has said. "I don't know what makes sense anymore." Before I can ask her for her version, the doorbell rings, and I sip the water cautiously while Rosie opens the door.

It's Shirley. The second she sees me, her face creases. "Oh, Jack," she wails. "Jack, I'm so sorry – I thought I was bringing good news but just as I was leaving they told me – she's gone, Jack. They did all they could to save her –but -"

"She's gone." I knew that somehow. What I don't know is how I feel about it. She's the whole reason I came here, I think, and she's gone. And in a way, it's my fault – she died over an argument about me. At least she died knowing I'm alive.

"How're you feeling, Shirley?" asks Jessie.

"Pretty good for someone who should be dead," Shirley answers. "Winnie's old bag saved me… How about you? They said you got nicked? And what about you, Jack? You look like you got dragged under a bus."

I get to my feet, give her an awkward hug and a peck on the cheek. "I'm fine, really. Glad you're okay."

"Well," says Rosie brightly, "shall we have some tea?"

The glance Jessie and I exchange as we follow Rosie and Shirley down the hall feels like a secret handshake. *March comes in like a lion and goes out like a lamb. I was born on March first, Jessie was born on March 31.* The thoughts tumble in my head like unruly kittens. Maybe if we're distantly related, though, it's not surprising I feel connected to Jessie. After all, I never felt like I belonged to my parents, or anyone else. Maybe this is what family feels like, I think, as I steal a peek at her while we settle around the table. What I feel is anything but brotherly.

Jessie blurts out the burning question. "So what the hell happened in there, Shirley? What happened with Lucas?"

"No one's quite sure," Shirley says. She doesn't even ask Rosie's permission to smoke. She just takes out a pack of Camels' and lights one. "Anyone else? No? You don't mind, do you?"

Rosie shakes her head, produces an ashtray and pushes it across the table at Shirley. "Go on."

"By the time I got there, he and Martha were ranting and raving and going at each other – I thought I had him calmed down, but... he'd just gone to find the gun." She shuts her eyes, and presses her lips together. "It meant so much to her, Jack, to know you were alive, that you were okay. She wanted to see you so badly."

I feel sorrier for Shirley than I do for myself at this point, because it's hard to feel the loss of something you never had to begin with. "Wasn't meant to be, I guess." I lean forward, shake her arm. "You helped poor Martha more than anyone, right?"

"Not me... I didn't even want to come. Winnie's the one who really listened to her." Shirley sniffs, and Rosie hands her a box of tissues. She weeps silently for a moment, then shakes her head. "I'm sorry... you know this isn't about a story, right? You know I want to find out what's happened to Winnie." She wipes her cheeks, blows her nose, crumples the tissue onto her saucer. "I had a dream about Winnie last night... she told me to look for the nuns... and at the hospital, just now, I met someone, a nurse, a nun, who worked relief at the clinic where you were born, Jack. She gave me the name of the nun who was there the night you were born."

"You did?" It's hard for me to keep up. I have to tell myself where I am, who I'm with. I'm not about to hang. But Shirley has no idea of what I've seen or experienced, and she's hot on the scent of the trail she's sure winds back to Winnie.

"And I think I found the link back to Savageux, the one Winnie was following. Not only was Savageux's wife's father the head OB, but the clinic was mostly funded by a private foundation, the Margaret Savageux Sinclair Charitable –

"Charitable Trust," I finish.

"You've heard of this group, Jack?" Shirley sounds astonished.

"Yeah," I nod slowly. "I just got offered a... a job... a teaching job. Out on the Cape, on Cape Cod." Maybe I really am being hunted, I think. "This same organization – the Margaret Savageux Sinclair Trust... whatever it is...they were funding it. It was one of their programs for underprivileged kids."

"What a coincidence," says Jessie.

Shirley keeps talking. "I'm hoping this nun can help me tie a lot of loose ends together – maybe explain exactly what was going on that got it shut down."

I lean forward. "I don't get it, Shirley. Are you saying that clinic was some kind of front? For what? Black market babies?"

"Something like that, Jack." She stubs out her cigarette. "That's what the Feds thought, cause that appears to be why they shut it down. But I don't think that's what was going on at all. I think it was some kind of breeding program."

Rosie stirs uncomfortably in her seat, as Jessie asks, "Breeding program? What kind of breeding program?"

"Well, that's what I'm hoping Sister Edith can tell me. I'm not sure she's a nun anymore. She lives in West Philly, teaches math at Drexel -"

Jessie gasps and makes a noise like a whimper. "Edith Chalfont?" she whispers. "Edith Chalfont who... teaches math at... at Drexel?"

"You know this woman?" If Jessie's head had suddenly spun 360 degrees on her shoulders, Shirley couldn't sound more incredulous.

"She was my mother's best friend." Jessie gets up and walks to the sink, stares out the window over the kitchen sink into the sodden, though pristine garden so different from what lies on other side of the wall. Someone goes to a lot of trouble to make this place look like something other than it is. "I'm supposed to have dinner with her this evening. She's the one who called, right before we left, Jack."

"Jessie, can I come with you? Would you mind? Please?" Shirley's eyes go big and wide.

I turn to Shirley. "What do you think this lady can tell you?"

"What was really going on at the clinic, of course. Because I think it's still going on now - somewhere else."

"But what makes you think that Savageux – this Savageux is involved? He's just a few years older than I am – in his early thirties, right? How could he possibly tie into all this?"

"His mother was a Sinclair. Until she married Nicholas's father –the one everyone called Old Nick - her name was Margaret Sinclair. Her brother was Edmond, Edmond Sinclair –and he's the guy who ran the clinic. The Sinclairs – his mother's branch of the family, at any rate, not yours – were the primary funders of the clinic through a special foundation that another Edmund – I think it was a great-great grandfather - set up. But what really ties it together, I think, is that Nicholas's wife, Clarissa – is also his cousin. Clarissa Savageux is Edmond Sinclair's daughter."

"Wow," says Jessie. "He's married to his first cousin?"

"You got it, sweets. That branch of the Sinclair family has been inter-marrying with the Savageuxs for at least three hundred years."

My head is starting to ache. I rub my temples and ask, "So what the fuck does this have to do with me?"

"Well, Jack, your mother – Martha Sinclair – was a Sinclair too, on both sides."

"So what?"

"That's what I don't understand, Jack." Shirley lets out a long white stream of smoke. "There's a lot of inbreeding in this part of the world. But in terms of the Sinclairs and the Savageuxs, it appears to be deliberate."

"Why?"

"That's what I don't know, Jack, and that's what I think Winnie did." Shirley leans forward, stubs out her cigarette and lights another in almost one motion. "Winnie figured it out – and I know…" She looks at me with desperation in her eyes. "I know that's what got her in trouble. I know Savageux's responsible. This clinic, the vampire game, the Jane Doe murders, they're all connected somehow and they all connect to him." She closes her eyes and sniffs. "And as God is my witness, I swear I'll see him hang," she says as she blows her nose and wipes her face.

"So you think maybe I'm a twin? A clone? Heir to the half the Savageux fortune?"

At that Shirley laughs, a sudden belly laugh that takes us all by surprise and makes us laugh right along with her. I don't see what's so funny. After all, what other kind of threat or danger could I possibly pose to Nicholas Savageux that he would hunt me as Dougless said?

"Okay, forget the family fortune," I say.

"I don't know what this woman can tell me, Jack," Shirley says when she can talk. "All I know is, I think this is what Winnie found out. I can't prove anything yet. But something was going on at that clinic – something someone doesn't want anyone else to know."

"Maybe they were doing abortions," says Jessie.

"Not with nuns involved," Shirley replies as Rosie lights a candle and places it on the table in the middle. As the gold light washes over our faces, Shirley's expression turns fierce. "Come on, Rosie. Tell me what you know. What was David – what are *you* - working on?"

Rosie glances at Jessie, then at me. She leans across the table, her mouth a thin line. "I don't intend to tell you anything, Shirley. I told you this before. Just because you got shot at doesn't mean I've changed my mind. There's no way I'm going to have my name and David's name splashed across some supermarket tabloid." She takes a deep breath. "No offense."

"Then let me make something clear to you, Professor Righteous. This isn't about the story. Fuck the story. I'm not here to write a goddamn story, okay? I'm here to find out what's happened to Winnie. She was down here,

I know she was – she talked to you, I have her notes. Why can't you just tell me what you told her?"

Rosie takes a deep breath. "I don't want any of this in your story."

"Come on, Shirley," I say. "You know you have to give your editor a story."

"Who said there wasn't going to be a story?" Shirley reaches into her capacious purse and pulls out a few sheets of folded legal paper. "Two can play the same game, Jack. Harry doesn't care what I write – as long as it sells newspapers. And just because I choose not to write the truth, doesn't mean I can't find out what's really going on."

I unfold the papers and stare at the penciled headline in disbelief. "Aliens Stole My Baby… then brought him home to me!" Attached is a black and white photo of an aproned farm woman holding what can only be a prize-winning cabbage.

Chapter 21

I think the cabbage picture convinces **Rosie** that Shirley really doesn't have any intention of writing anything even close to the truth. Her determination to find Winnie is what drives her, and until Shirley either finds her partner or uncovers the truth, she's not going to stop. I don't blame her. I'd feel the same way about Lila.

"So," says Shirley. "Now we understand each other, how did David meet Sister Edith again?"

"At a job interview," answers Rosie. "David met Edith Chalfont by chance on a job interview. She was head of the math department at a private girls' school near Philadelphia. Shortly after she hired David, she left and went to Drexel."

"But they stayed in touch." Shirley lights another cigarette.

"They did."

"Mom never knew that," Jessie says.

"No?" replies Rosie. "Don't be so sure, Jessie, about what your parents knew or didn't know about each other. Did you know they were still married to each other?" As Jessie's mouth drops open, Rosie nods and her face hardens. "It's why your father never married me." She shakes her head, looks as if she might say something else, then presses her lips together.

The two women stare at each other, and I can felt the tension building between them. I lean forward, more to diffuse the tension than I really need to ask the question. "So Jessie and I are related – distantly – to each other and to Nicholas Savageux – and his wife, and the guy who used to run this clinic where I was born, right?"

"Right," says Rosie.

"But if I understand that family tree up there correctly, we're all just branches of one big family, right? From Scotland?"

Rosie shrugs. "Scotland was where David traced the four branches – Savageux, Sinclair, McPherson and Woodwright. He was able to go as far back as 1307, when he discovered that one of the Sinclairs had fled from France with a member of the Savageux family. Legends say they – and their companions – were guardians of a treasure, of an ancient secret receptacle of alchemy or magic. Some think it was the Holy Grail."

"The Holy Grail? Another legend?" I say.

"David never believed that the Holy Grail was really the actual cup Jesus was said to have used at the Last Supper," Rosie says.

"Excuse me," says Shirley. "Would you mind filling this nice Jewish girl from Queens what you're talking about? I thought the Holy Grail was something out of King Arthur. What's it got to do with Jesus?"

"According to the stories," Rosie says, "the Holy Grail is the cup Jesus drank from at the Last Supper."

"Not just drank from," I say.

"He changed the wine into his blood," Jessie says with me.

We stop, look at each other. "Too many years in Catholic school," we say again.

"Okay, stop that," says Shirley. "That's weird. I get it. David didn't think this treasure was really a cup. What did he think it was?"

"We could never agree." Rosie folds her lips down, folds her hands, looks down.

"Would Savageux's ... interest in me have something to do with this treasure?" I ask.

"Yes," says Rosie. "At first, he believed it was something more ephemeral like knowledge. And then…" She paused, took a deep breath. "David believed that Edmund Sinclair was looking for ….for one specific genetic combination."

"You mean like some kind of Superman? Didn't the Nazis do that?"

Rosie shifts, sighs, plucks at the tablecloth. "Yes. But... he didn't think Edmund Sinclair was trying to breed a super-race... David believed he was trying to breed just one Super-Man."

"So David had access to the clinic records?"

"No," Rosie says quickly, maybe too quickly. "He... he learned all this from Edith Chalfont."

"But this hardly makes sense. What's so special about these people? Other than it seems that half of them are richer than God and the other half poor as dirt?"

Rosie takes a deep breath. "David wasn't sure. But everything points to a man who was born just over three hundred years ago in Scotland, in 1675, an illegitimate by-blow of a powerful Highland clan, and a woman who seems to have been a member of the people called the tinkers, or the travelers. His name was James McPherson, and in 1700, he was hanged. In a town called Banff." She looks at me.

"McPherson?" trills Jessie, even as a wave of chills washes over me and I feel myself start to shake. "Wait, I remember now. There's an old song about a guy named McPherson... he gets hanged because they push the clock ahead so the pardon didn't get there in time. But what's that got to do with the Sinclairs? With the Savageuxs?"

"Wh-what song?" I ask. I wrap my arms around myself and try to keep my teeth from chattering. Shirley looks at me with alarm.

"Jack, you okay?"

"If you look at the extended family tree that David was in the process of creating, James McPherson is related to every Sinclair and Savageux alive in that branch of the family at least four or five different times," says Rosie. "He's wound tight as a corkscrew through the family tree. But let me get Jack a blanket." She gets up as I keep shivering. "Jessie, pour him more tea."

There's something strange about this scene, something all together too weird. I've been here before, I think, in another time, in another place, huddled around a table, shivering under a blanket. But I was bigger then, and a lot dirtier, with lank hair hanging down my back and fleas biting my belly.

I think about Dougless. She's Scottish. Her name's Woodwright. On the scaffold I was looking for her. So who was she to me, then... and does that explain why she's settled on me now?

The women bustle and settle around me. I hear snatches of voices, ghostly music. I have to bite my cheek until it bleeds to concentrate on the conversation going on around me.

"The song was one of my mother's favorites," says Jessie. "She made me sing it all the time. It's about this guy who was a great fiddle player – so great he broke his fiddle before he died so that no one else could play it."

"How can you know that," I demand. "How can you possibly know that?" Coincidence is piling on top of coincidence like an improbable house of cards.

"My mother really liked Scottish folk music," Jessie answers. "I know... I know a lot of old songs."

"Wait," Shirley says. "What does this guy have to do with anything?"

"I think he has a lot to do with me, somehow," I say. "The... the genetic memories... these flashback things....is that what it is? Somehow... somehow I'm him? He was me?"

Rosie nods. "Yes... exactly. Somehow... whether by chance, or coincidence or design... David believed you must be an identical genetic twin to the man who was James McPherson –or as close a twin as it's possible for anyone to be."

"So?"

"And so is Nicholas Savageux."

"What?" That can't be possible, I think.

"I said nearly," Rosie says.

"That's possible," says Shirley. "Look at the Amish – look at Hasidic Jews. You see a lot of really close crosses – people end up looking like their second cousins once removed."

"I don't look like Savageux," I say. "No way –"

"Yeah, you do, Jack. You're thinner and scruffier, and your haircut's horrendous. You don't walk like you're lord of the manor, and you don't dress like a prep. But yeah... even Harry the shlub noticed. And he doesn't notice much." Shirley lights another cigarette. "I didn't think anything of it, till now."

"No one's ever mentioned it before," I say.

"I see it," says Jessie, her voice bright as a new penny in the gloom.

"People see what they want to see, Jack." Rosie pours more tea. "People see what they expect to see. And most people don't realize that appearance isn't just facial features. It's hair, as Shirley says, clothes and gestures... mannerisms, ways of moving and gesturing that most of us process in a subliminal kind of way. And even identical twins – those with the exact same DNA – even they appear different to the people who know them."

"So what's all this mean?" I ask. "Let's assume I *am* related – let's assume there's some missing piece that ties it all together – so what?"

"Whatever this missing piece is, Jack," Shirley replies, "people who come close to figuring it out seem to wind up dead." She stubs out her cigarette and holds up her hand. "Allow me. Every doctor, every nurse, every janitor, even, associated with that clinic is dead. The only ones who aren't are Edith Chalfont, and the nun I met this afternoon." She looks at Rosie. "That clinic operated for over ninety years, and it's like it's been erased. I can't find anyone who's ever been in it. I can't even find the road that led to it.

"Twenty-five years is a long time, but it's not that long ago. There should be people who were born there, mothers who remember giving birth. But there aren't." She turns to me. "See, Jack, the one conclusion I'm coming to is that the only reason you're alive is because everyone thought you were dead." She looks at Jessie. "Please... if you know Edith Chalfont... I really need to talk her."

When Jessie hesitates, Shirley reaches across the table for her hand, and I realize I've been holding it. "Jessie, don't you understand? Your father's death was no accident."

That's the point at which I have to take a break. I excuse myself, push through the back door and step into the most improbably beautiful garden I've ever seen in my life. In the rain it is lush and green and glistening. Statues peer from leafy nooks, spring flowers cluster and droop and preen. A flag-stone walkway leads into the center, where a fountain trickles from a water jar held by a bending nymph. A wisteria-laden trellis encloses a bench. I sink down, and notice that laid between the paving stones, patterned mosaics spin out in a wheel from the center. The one at my feet is the same Hanged Man. I swallow hard and feel my throat. He grins back at me, unperturbed. I take a deep breath of the damp, sweet air, and cover my face in my hands.

"You okay, Jack?" It's Rosie, which surprises me. I didn't think Rosie was happy about any of us being there, even Jessie. There's a thin brittleness around her, a shell that doesn't jive with the picture Jessie implied of her father and his long-time love. Rosie seems almost angry every time she says his name. Was it really love that held them together, here in this quasi-crumbling house?

"Yeah," I say. "I just needed a minute. This... this whole thing... this whole day... it's not what I expected, you know?"

"I know." She looks at the bench. "Mind if I sit?" She sinks down beside me. "I left Shirley and Jessie in there – I've heard as much as I can stand." She wraps her arms around herself and stares at the fountain.

"This is quite a garden you got here," I say. "You do all this?"

"This was David's work. I just kept the weeds down." She takes a deep breath and turns to me. "I didn't come out here to make small talk, Jack. I came out here to tell you ... to warn you... that Shirley... that Shirley could be right – right in a way she doesn't understand." She pauses, presses her lips together, and I see her eyes are wet. "It's hard for me to tell these things to Jessie, because I promised David I wouldn't talk to her until she'd read all his work. But I think you are in danger, you and Jessie both, from something David never even allowed himself to consider, let alone believe in." She adjusts her shawl around her shoulders. "So much... so many things you've said today, so many things that've happened... just convince me I was right and David... David, God bless him... well... he was so focused on every little branch, every little piece... he could never see the forest, let alone what else might be out there."

I look down at the smiling face of the Hanged Man. "What do you think is out there?"

She spreads her hands wide and shrugs. "Everything on that Weird List of yours. Everything and more. The stuff that knocks on Jessie's door at night – the ghost woman who's been warning you. The vampire you say is hunting you. See... David said I was crazy. But I think anything you can imagine is out there, potentially. I think that you and Jessie *are* obviously special in some way but it's got nothing to do with your health or your genius or anything like that. I don't think it's any accident that you remember being hanged. But whether you remember being hanged because it's a past life memory or a genetic memory, or something that hasn't happened yet..."

I stop her right there. "You really do think Jessie and I could be in some kind of danger?"

"Yes." She pauses. "And I don't think the threat's coming from anything in the physical world, though it may have physical world consequences."

"What? Are you saying we could be attacked by imaginary -?"

"Not imaginary. Mythical, maybe. Supernatural, definitely. Demonic, possibly."

I stare at her as a light rain begins to fall. "You think Savageux is some kind of unholy demon?"

"Don't you?" Her eyes are very clear and very blue, startling even, in her rosy-cheeked face. "Isn't that one of the items on the list? 'Vampire?' See, I think that sense you have – that's he's something evil, something unnatural - is correct. I think there's more to it all than David was ever willing to see."

She places one hand on my forearm. It's a gardener's hand, the fingernails filed square, the back tanned and freckled. I feel the heat of her belief radiate through her palm, through my sleeve. "You know the poet William Blake? You know what he believed – that poets are prophets, that visions are real? That's what I believe, too. Every generation produces a few people with the eyes and the ears and the ability to know and see and hear all the things no one else can. I don't know why – David used to laugh at me sometimes. He started to come around once he got deeper into quantum theory, but he never..." She hesitates. "He never quite got it."

"Maybe because he never saw things or heard things himself?"

"Maybe." She takes a deep breath, clasps her hands around her knees.

"But..." I stare down at the Hanged Man. "Let me ask you this... if I'm really the reincarnation or the exact genetic duplicate of this guy from eighteenth century Scotland -"

"Seventeenth."

"Whatever. If I was really him – why aren't I musical? I don't play the fiddle. I don't sing. I don't even hum."

Rosie stares back at me. "I can't tell you that, Jack. Maybe some talents are latent. Maybe you're not an exact copy after all. Maybe it got scared out of you – maybe your musical development was arrested or truncated in this incarnation. Or maybe you just haven't got around to discovering it. Ever try to write a song?"

I stare back at her. "I write poetry – never tried to put any of them to music, though."

"Well, maybe you should."

I glance down at my watch. "Look at that," I say. "Here's another coincidence – almost every time I look at the time, it's a number like this – see?" The face reads 2:22.

"Really?" Rosie looks at me intently. "You mean like 1:11, or 3:33? 11:11? 12:22?"

"Yeah. You think they mean anything?"

"Some people believe that those numbers are numbers of angelic vibration. When you see them, it means there're angels around."

"Angels?"

Rosie pats my knee. "Tell Jessie to keep reading."

"Why?"

"The books and all I gave her – I didn't just give her the stuff David was working on when he died. I gave her my things, too. If she puts them together, maybe she'll understand the truth."

"Can't you help her?"

"I'll help her." She takes a deep breath. "When I can. I think just reassuring you both you're not crazy has to be helpful. Winnie's questions sparked an argument between me and David. Our last conversation was a pretty brutal battle. Talking about it all… thinking about it all… having you here today…. It's just too painful. I can't handle it, not yet, not right now. Right now, I need to sit here and smell the roses David planted for me. I want to look at the mosaics he made me. I want to try and remember other times, better times. I don't want to have to think about any of this any more." Abruptly, she gets to her feet and walks into the house.

Chapter 22

As we're leaving, Jessie pushes me toward Shirley's car. "Go with her," she says, simply. "She can tell you about your mother."

My mother, I think. My poor, dead mother, the reason I was here in the first place. She died for my sake. I'm suddenly sad I didn't get within a hundred yards of her.

As we pull out of Rosie's drive, I notice it's only three PM. I feel I've spent six lifetimes in that house. There's a dull throb in the back of my skull. I expect Shirley to deluge me with questions as she follows Jessie onto the main road, but all she does is glance every now and then in my direction. We're almost to the highway before she asks, "You okay?"

"I think so," I say. Without Lila to keep me in the here and now, I feel I'm losing touch with some part of reality. We're following Jessie to her house. My clothes are still there. We left them spinning around in her dryer. "It's a lot to take in."

Shirley snorts. "Yeah, ain't that the truth. I can't wait to talk to Sister Edith."

"Aunt Edith," I say wanly. "What kind of a coincidence is that?"

"Oh, Jack." The look Shirley gives me is pitying. "I don't think it's any kind of coincidence at all. Sister Edith – wasn't so much a friend to Jessie's mother, as an overseer for Jessie. Question is – why?" A heavy rain spills down the windshield and she snaps on the wipers. She grips the wheel and peers straight ahead into the twin red lights on the back of Jessie's car. "What's so special about either one of you is the question."

She glances at me. I shrug. I remember what Rosie said about poets and prophets and things that go bump in the night. I think about Blake's Shadows and Emanations and Spectres. I think that she was trying to tell me there's a place where those things are real. But I have no idea how to explain that to Shirley, and she doesn't seem to expect me to have an answer. The thump and whoosh of the wipers lulls me back into another dream.

I'm not a girl in this one. Jessie is standing beside me. We're dressed alike, though, in leather pants and vests. She looks like a Goth princess. I feel like a fool. There's a rope around my neck. Bruce Springsteen and his band are milling around us, setting up equipment, checking microphones and sound, tuning instruments. At some point, Bruce looks at both of us. "She's the one," he says. "She's the one."

He hands Jessie a guitar and her arms from the elbows down are suffused in the same golden pink light I remember from the other dreams. I step forward, to follow her, because I want to tell them I can't sing the song – I don't know the words, when the Professor – who still looks like Proulx but is dressed in a clown suit – steps right in front of me. He's holding a bell pull or something similar and I know if he jerks on it, I'll be dragged into the air by my neck. He smiles at me. "Trust no one," he says.

Then he gives the bell pull a good yank, and I go up in the air, not by my neck, but upside down, by my foot, so that I dangle and spin over the stage, helpless and strangely mute, even as Jessie starts to play. I wave my arms, frantic, and knock my head against the car window.

Shirley is peering at me, shaking my shoulder. My neck is killing me, but at least I'm not hanging upside down anymore. "Jesus, Jack, you okay? That's some dream you're having, huh?"

I jerk upright, gulping for air. "Yeah." I glance outside, in the wet gray dusk. We're parked outside Jessie's bungalow, and the living room lights are already on. I rub my face with my hands, hope she's breaking out the coffee. "We're here, huh?"

"Yeah." Shirley unlocks her seat belt. "Are you sure you're okay? Maybe Jessie'll let you lie down."

"No," I say, for the thought of lying down on a bed that bears her imprint, her scent, would simply be too much. I feel like all my senses are stretched thin as wires, as if I've simply absorbed too much, too many memories.

Breathe, Jack. That's Dougless's voice, whispering in my mind. I whip around and Shirley gives me another strange look. She reaches over, touches my arm. "You sure you're okay?"

"Little woozy from the dream, I guess." I smile, try to shrug it off, but in reality I feel like shit. Not only do I feel like shit, but I have a real bad feeling about something that's about to happen. I just have no idea what it is. *I see a bad moon rising.*

I manage to open the door with Creedence screaming in my brain, then stumble to Jessie's door. The dogs are bouncing around the yard. I sink down on her couch like it's an old friend I am suddenly very glad to see.

"Jesus, Jack." Jessie frowns at me across the kitchen. "You look like death warmed over. Are you sure you're okay?"

"I think I just have to put my head down..." I say. I close my eyes against the back of the couch and a vision explodes into my head - I'm driving, over a bridge. I don't recognize the steering wheel or the scenery, and my hands are age-spotted and old. I'm terrified. I think someone's trying to kill me and I have to get to Jessie, have to warn her, tell her the truth.

Only I don't know what the truth is. The last thing I see as a light explodes in my head, is a sign at the base of the bridge, a sign I do recognize from just last night. It's a sign at the base of the Walt Whitman Bridge.

I jerk upright, holding my head.

"You should go lie down," say both women at once. The smell of fresh coffee hits my nostrils and it really does feel like I was somewhere else, witnessing something else, something much more immediate and real that Jamie McPherson's hanging in Banff.

"Maybe I just need a cup of coffee," I reply. Something, anything, to anchor me in the here and now, in this reality, in this body. The dogs whine at the back door, and Jessie looks at me dubiously.

"You mind if I let them in? They're dying to say hello."

"It's okay." The words aren't out of my mouth, and the door isn't half way open, when the dogs come barreling into the room. But they stop short, almost as if they're attention's been drawn to something else, something even I can't see or hear. They lick my hands, sniff my clothes, then circle and sniff some more.

"What's wrong with you guys?" Jessie asks. "Wow, they're acting weird."

"How so?" says Shirley, cocking her head.

"They're acting odd, that's all." Jessie grips the counter, and I can see the blood's drained from her face. Angus settles back on his haunches, throws his head back and begins to howl. \

Every vein in my body freezes, and the hair goes up on the back of my neck.

"Wow," says Shirley. "What *is* wrong?"

She crosses her arms over her chest and Lucy joins in mournful counterpoint.

"Jessie, are you okay?" I ask. Her eyes are brimming with tears.

"That's the sound they made…" she whispers. Her voice catches in her throat. "That's the sound they made the night my mother died."

Edith Chalfont never shows up. Around six o'clock, Jessie starts to worry. "Call and see if she left, even," says Shirley, who's practically worn a hole in the carpet with her pacing.

Jessie's hand is shaking too much to even punch the numbers. I get up, take the receiver out of her hand. "What's the number?"

She gives it to me in a shaking voice. Shirley wraps her arm around Jessie. I give them the thumbs up sign, and hope for the best. But I can't shake the feeling that's wrapped itself around my chest like the sensation of the noose around my neck, a granite certainty that the dream I envisioned was real.

The line rings and rings. Finally I hang up. "Now what?"

"Call the state police," says Shirley, briskly. "Both states. Explain you got a little old lady out driving around and you're terrified she's lost or something might've happened to her. You know what kind of car she drives?"

"An old black Buick," Jessie and I say together.

"How'd you know that?" she demands.

"Yeah," says Shirley. "How did you know that?"

I shrug. I wish I could shake off the grim foreboding that clings to me like the shroud.

"I feel sick," says Jessie. Beads of sweat are pearling across her forehead. Shirley pushes her into my arms, and I sag a little at her weight.

"I'll make the call," Shirley says.

It's easy to scoop Jessie off her feet and onto the couch. I hear Shirley talking into the phone, crisp and sure. She tones down her accent, but she knows all the buzz words, even, apparently, some of the Jersey cop codes. I hear her say something like, "A two-ten on the bridge?"

That's not good, I think.

I turn back to Jessie, and I meet her eyes. She's awake, alert, her eyes are clear. As if on cue, Shirley walks over, and by her expression, I can tell the news isn't good. "There *was* an accident on the bridge, right around the time Edith would've been on it. They're checking into it – they'll call us back."

"That's why Angus and Lucy were howling," Jessie says. Tears are spilling down her cheeks. "When they didn't make a fuss over you and started acting strange... I looked at the clock and I thought to myself, I bet Aunt Edith is just about at the bridge. And that's when they started to howl."

"Honey, maybe it's not so bad," puts in Shirley, looking distraught. "Maybe it's not even her."

Jessie shakes her head as the phone rings. Shirley fumbles for the phone, Jessie clings to my hand. "But it is, isn't it, Jack? You know, too, don't you?"

I realize I've been holding my breath. I let it out in a long slow hiss as Shirley says, "Are you sure?" She sinks on to a rickety chair that creaks audibly. "Oh my God, first Martha, now this. Yes, that's right... Martha Sinclair.... Right, I was at the hospital..." Before I know it, Shirley is off and running, sharing salient details with the person on the other end of the line. I don't understand her chattiness – Jessie's just lost someone close to her, and as for me, I've had as much death as I can deal with in one day.

Then I hear Shirley say, "Listen, I know you guys have better things to do, but I left a notebook with one of the nurses… Sister Mary Jonas? Yeah, you know her, too? What a doll… absolutely. So could I possibly impose on you to give her a message I'll be in touch?... Yeah? You will?... Aw, you are very kind… yes, I'm sure Miss Woodwright won't mind...she's had a bit of a shock at the moment….you'll call later? Okay… I'll let her know… no, I don't think she'll mind?" Shirley looks at Jessie, who nods vigorously. "Okay, yes, this is the number. Thanks, sergeant. You're a mensch."

When she hangs up, it's like a light bulb goes out behind her face. "I don't know what to say, Jessie. I-I guess it was your Aunt Edith."

"Do they know what happened?" I ask.

"Not yet. There's cameras on the bridge, on the toll booths. They want to see if anything got captured."

"Another coincidence," says Jessie. She looks at me, and in her eyes, I see shared lifetimes that stretch across centuries, and the feeling that resonates through me is not just I know you, but I found you. Suddenly I'm really worried about Lila.

Shirley makes coffee, orders a pizza. "Is there anyone I can call?" She exchanges a glance with me and I realize how greatly disappointed Shirley must be.

On the refrigerator, I notice a list of names followed by phone numbers. The top three names are the girls I remember from last night. Jessie glances at it, shrugs, and looks from me to Shirley and back again. "Please don't feel you have to stay for me. I'll be okay -If you leave now, you could be back in New York by eleven."

I don't know how I feel about that. I'm worried sick about Lila, but I don't want to leave Jessie. She seems so isolated, so vulnerable, so alone. But she can't be, I think to myself. Don't be silly. She's a grown woman, she has friends, a job. She's lived in this house a long time with her mother. She must know the neighbors. But I can't shake the feeling that the dogs, big as they are, are the only things between Jessie and the world.

Shirley pats her arm. "We're going to stay at least until the police call back.

Lucy whines and paws at my knee. "Let's go out, huh?" I get up. I don't want to leave Jessie at all, but I know I have to. Every time I think about Lila, a dull alarm sounds in my chest. I just can't stand the thought of leaving Jessie, so vulnerable and alone. "I'll take the dogs out. I want some air. This has really been one helluva day." But after today, I wonder, what's normal ever going to feel like again?

The evening air feels like cool mist on my face. I sit down on one of the deck chairs, and the dogs take up positions on either side of me. I pet their heads and they look at me, as if expecting me to do something. The moon is just a few night's passed the full and I can see it shining behind a veil of clouds. I look up. "Come on out," I say on a whim. "I want to talk to you."

The dogs turn and look up at the sky, as the clouds that cover the moon start to thin.

A shiver goes up and down my spine, then down through my legs to my feet. Suddenly, I feel as if a great current is flowing through my body, as if I've somehow plugged into something, something palpable and real. The moon is glowing bright. The face of the man in the moon is smiling directly at me.

"You got to watch out for her," I say, feeling a little silly, and yet, not really. "I have this bad feeling there are bad things out there... and I'm trusting you ... don't let anything get her." This is it, I think. The day's finally tripped my trigger over the edge of reason. I'm talking to the moon. The dogs, however, are gazing up at the glowing white sphere with shining eyes and hanging tongues. I blink and rub my eyes, because it seems like the moon's not only gotten clearer, it's gotten bigger and closer, so much bigger it looks like a complete circle. The man in the moon smiles broadly, his eyes twinkly and kind. "Keep her safe, okay?" I rub the dogs' heads.

"Jack?" It's Jessie. "Who're you out here talking to?"

"Angus, of course... Angus and Lucy. I'm giving them their orders – they're to keep you safe."

"Yeah?" She pushes through the screen, then leans against the railing, gazing up at the moon. "Wow, that's a bright moon. Finally came out from behind the clouds, huh?"

I look up. The moon's back to looking normal sized, or nearly, but it's still glowing bright. My scalp and the soles of my feet are tingling. I have no idea why I feel I've done something, but that's exactly how I feel, charged and depleted all at once.

"Hey, Jessie," Shirley comes to the door, peers out into the night. "The police, they'd like to talk to you – ask you some questions. Do you mind if they send someone tomorrow?"

"No," she says. "But I won't be home till six." She wraps her arms around herself. "I know this sounds crazy, but I think Edith was murdered."

"What do the cops think?"

"They don't know what happened. The cameras on the bridge – they don't show anything. There was a malfunction, about an hour or so before the accident. Wasn't until they checked the tapes that they realized the cameras were down. So they're going to ask for information, ask witnesses to come forward. I'm sure someone had to have seen something."

For a long moment we stare at each other. We're tired and confused, and I think we've all had enough, but neither Shirley nor I want to leave Jessie alone tonight. I glance at the refrigerator, and I know what to do. "Jessie, could I use the phone in your bedroom? I-I just want to call Lila." I feel like an interfering old biddy hen. I don't know why I'm going to call all the girls in her band. I don't know what I'm going to say. All I know is that this a wound Jessie can't bear right now and intervention is necessary.

She gives me an odd look but nods and steps aside. Shirley starts making sandwiches and cutting up fruit. Jessie sinks down at the table, buries her face in her hands. I feel the weight of her grief, of her losses, piling up in the room. Why so much, I wonder. It's not fair, I think. Why her? Why lose one more person, now?

Do you think you're the only one who's being hunted, Jack?

That thought both chills and galvanizes me. I start with Ginger. She answers on the second ring. I open my mouth. I feel my tongue move, I hear words echo around in my head. But I'm not consciously aware of a word I say – only that by the sense of it, by the responses, whatever I'm saying is exactly what she needs to hear. I hang up as she promises to pick up the other two on her way over here.

In the kitchen, Shirley's rubbing Jessie's shoulders. She looks at me in mute appeal and I know exactly what she's thinking. I sit down beside Jessie and pick up her hand. In Shirley's presence, I feel safe pecking the back of it, squeezing her cold fingers. "I called your friend, Ginger. She's on her way."

"Ginger's not my friend," Jessie wails. "They all hate me. The people who loved me are dead."

"That's not true," I say with another squeeze. My arms are literally aching with the effort not to pull her into them, my chest feels hollow and empty without her weight against it. "They're on their way."

She sniffs, looks at me. "They are? Why?"

"Here, honey," says Shirley. "Blow your nose."

"I called them," I say. "Well, I called Ginger. I explained what's happened. She said she'd be right over." I squeeze her hand a third time and this time, her fingers twine around mine. But the time isn't yet, I know, in the same way I know it's Sunday night and so I gently disengage her grip.

"What'd you say?" she asks, wide-eyed over pink tissue.

I shrug. I don't know what I said because I can't remember a word of it. I just opened my mouth and the words poured out. "The truth, I guess. Not about everything. Just… just that you'd had a bad day."

A quick rap on the front door saves me from further explanation. As the girls from the band sprawl into the room and over Jessie, Shirley steps back and nudges me. "So, Jack," says Shirley. "How fast you think we can be in New York?"

Chapter 23

We get back to Brooklyn by midnight. It's a surprisingly quick trip, straight up the turnpike. Shirley drops me off at my apartment building. I'm tired, glad to be home, and eager to see Lila. I feel like I've been away a thousand years and traveled a million miles as I turn the key in the lock.

I know as I push the door open that the apartment is empty.

The bedroom door is open. Lila never sleeps with the bedroom door open. I turn on the lights. The bed's not even been slept in since she last made it. Get a grip, Jack, I think, as I sink down on the mattress. You know she was here last night. Maybe she's at a friend's. Maybe she's at her mother's. *Maybe she's with Savageux.*

Please, I think, please don't let that be true.

Her overnight bag is missing from the closet. She didn't leave a note, but I guess she wasn't expecting me till tomorrow. I was supposed to be enjoying my reunion into the bosom of my family. So most likely she's gone to her mother's or to a friend's. I'll call her at the office in the morning. I roll over on my side, and fall instantly, dreamlessly asleep.

The ringing telephone wakes me. I open my eyes and see the time is 11:11. I'm too groggy to grab the phone in time to answer it before the machine picks up, but when I hear the message I want to weep, because it's Lila and she's saying: "Hey, Jack, it's me…didn't know if you tried to get me last night, but I was at my mother's. Wait'll you hear the good news. I'm at work. Call me when you get this."

Lila sounds so delighted, I know I must've gotten the job. I wonder what she'd say if she had any idea Savageux and I are related. She'd probably insist I make a claim for a share of the family fortune. I roll over on my back, and stare at the ceiling, webbed with the same spidery cracks as the ceiling over Jessie's couch. Before I can bring myself to call Lila, I fumble in my jeans for Jessie's number.

I don't expect her to answer, and I'm glad she doesn't. But I do tell her machine, "Just checking in... hope you're okay. Call me at school if you need anything." I can just imagine how thrilled Lila will be if Jessie starts calling the apartment.

I start coffee, shower, and dress before I can bring myself to call Lila. My body's exhausted, my mind is fried. I feel as if I've been dunked in a river and wrung out to dry. I'm not sure I'm ready to hear Lila's news. I punch the numbers in anyway, and catch her just as she's leaving for lunch.

"Hey, you, you're back. What time you get in?"

"Late last night, like around eleven. I figured you were at your mom's."

"Yeah, well, thanks for not calling me and waking me up. Hey, listen... guess who's got a new job starting next Monday?"

I clear my throat, feel the blood drain to my feet. "Um... aren't they supposed to offer it to me first?"

"You asshole, it's not official – I guess they're checking references and shit... oh, my God, Jack, you better not fuck this up."

"I'm sure I won't." I sink onto our sagging couch. "So... uh, when do you think they'll break the news to me?" Assuming I say yes, of course. Though, really, do I have a choice? Not if I want to stay married to Lila, I think. Jessie's face flashes unbidden across my mind. I can't think about Jessie, I tell myself.

"So how'd it go? You meet your mother?"

"Uh... no."

"You went all that way and she turned out not to be your mother? Oh, my God, Jack, I told you that trip was a waste –"

"No, she was my mother," I say. "She died. Before we could meet. It was really pretty strange the way it all happened. I'll- I'll tell you all about it later, okay?" There's no way I want to relive the gory details – or any details, in fact.

"Wow." She pauses, hesitates a beat or two. At least, as a Trusts & Estates paralegal, Lila respects death. "Oh. Wow, Jack, what a downer, huh? But look, at least you got the job, right?"

"Yeah," I say. "At least I got the job. So, when will you be home? You working late?"

"Aren't you taxiing?"

"Uh, yeah, I guess." But I don't want to give Shortman my notice. Something tells me not to do that tonight, no matter how satisfying the idea is. Because it's not really satisfying to think of it, not at all. I don't even know if I want this job. After all, I still have the grant offer on the Vineyard to consider. I've never felt so wanted in my life. I never imagined I'd feel this bad about it.

"I might be late getting in tonight…I have to meet a client after work."

"Oh? What client?"

"What difference does it make?"

There's a chill in Lila's tone. She doesn't want me to know who she's meeting. "No difference, I guess," I say. "Just be careful … if it gets late, call the garage, okay?" A tidal wave of anxiety sweeps over me and my tongue trips and stumbles over the words. "I'll come pick you up, wherever you are, okay? Just be careful."

"I'm always careful, Jack." She hesitates and I hear voices in the background. "Look, I got to go. Glad you're back, sorry about your mother. Love you."

Then she's gone, leaving me with the sickening feeling that I have spoken to Lila in the flesh for the last time.

At school there's messages from Shirley and Jessie. Mary doesn't look real happy to give me Shirley's. At least this time, Shirley didn't announce she was with *The Sun*. Mary just recognized the voice.

"The old man wasn't around to overhear, Jack," she says anxiously as she slips me the messages. "But, really, tell her not to call you here, okay?"

"Okay," I say.

"The grant committee is meeting tomorrow morning, Jack. Dr. Proulx wanted me to remind you." She glances towards Proulx's door. "And it's probably best... I know Dr. Proulx feels this way... don't get involved with a tabloid, Jack. You know no one's going to like that."

I wonder when they intend to run Shirley's Aliens Stole My Baby story, and how she feels about having to use Martha's sad story like that. "I think this'll be the last time I hear from her," I lie. "She was able to write her story with out using my name."

"Well, let's thank God for small favors." She rolls her eyes and shoos me out the door, leaving me to hunt for a vacant desk with a working phone because my desk-mate is firmly ensconced in my chair, Lysol can in view.

When I find a quiet corner at last, I dial Jessie first. I'm really surprised that she answers the phone. "Hey," I say. "Aren't you supposed to be at work?"

"I don't work there any more," she sniffs.

"What?"

"I don't know what happened – I was at work today and all of a sudden... they asked me to come upstairs and whammo... I was gone."

"Are you going to be okay?"

There's a long pause. "I think so."

"What's wrong?"

"Maybe I'm just being paranoid, but I thought I saw a car follow me home from work."

"What makes you think that?"

"Every time I looked around, in the rearview mirror, or to the side, I thought I saw the same car."

"Did it follow you all the way to the house?"

"N..no," she says with a slight stammer. "I seem to have lost him around the neighborhood."

"Well, that's good," I say. "Have you talked to the police?"

"About this? I hate to tell them things like that… it's like the looks they gave me after the knockings started up, you know, that 'lady, you're out of your mind' look?"

It's a look I know all too well. "I meant about… about the other…"

"Aunt Edith?" She sniffs again, and suddenly starts to cry.

"Maybe it's good you're getting some time off," I say as gently as I can. "You've had an awful lot to deal with."

"I talked to them this morning. They tracked me down at work. They don't know anything yet. They don't even have witnesses." She sniffs.

"Try to take it easy, Jessie." On the other end of the line, I feel the waves of grief rolling off her, over me, like a tidal wave of pain. *This is what it feels like.* The thought rolls unbidden across my mind, but I push it away. One problem at a time, I tell myself. "Just try to take things one step at a time."

"That's what my mom used to say."

"Don't look for another job just yet, Jessie, unless you have to, okay? You need a break." I need a break, I think. But I'm not about to get it. I feel as if I'm standing on the lip of some bottomless abyss and I don't know why.

"No, I'm not," she sighs. "I am going to go through all this stuff, though. Really take my time, try to make sense of it. Torture Rosie if I have to."

"Maybe you should haul it all back and make her help you." I think about the amazing tub, the potted palms, the garden with the tarot images embedded in the stones. That place seems a thousand miles away.

"She was adamant I take the stuff."

"Well, I guess she is just a phone call away, right?" Almost on cue, the line from Paul Simon's Mother-and-Child reunion song carol through my brain, this time with a chilling edge they never had before.

"Yeah." I hear a catch in her throat and she says, "Ginger told me how you called her, Jack. She told me what you said. That was really nice of you."

"I don't think neither of us felt okay leaving you alone."

"Well," she pauses, sniffs, "they all showed up." But she's hesitating, hanging on to something I don't quite understand. "I just … I just have to ask you, Jack… remember last night, when you were out on the deck, and… uh.. You were talking to the moon?"

"I wasn't exactly talking to the moon." I clear my throat. That makes me sound even crazier than I'm afraid I might be. "More like... whatever's up there and listening –"

"Yeah, well, apparently whatever it is, really listens to you, Jack. Cause... um... well, Ginger had a hard time finding my house... and then we ordered pizza, and the pizza man couldn't find it at all. We had to literally go stand outside on the curb to flag him down. Even Ginger, who practically grew up here, even she said if she hadn't known exactly where to look for the mailbox, she'd have missed it. She did miss it. She drove past the house three times. What the fuck is going on?"

"I...I don't know, Jessie." I twist the phone cord around my fingers while a golden kind of heat begins to tingle under the base of my skull, right at the top of my spine. "But...um... if someone really is following you, then I guess it's a good thing if they can't find your house, right?"

"Yeah," she says. "I guess that's true. So I guess as long as I stay in the house I'm safe?"

"And as long as you go back to it, right? Do you have trouble finding it?"

"No, of course not. I know my own house, for Christ's sake."

"Well, there you go, then." I look up, into the glowering face of one of my fellow adjuncts, the owner of the desk.

"I've got office hours now," he says pointedly.

"I have to go," I say into the receiver. "We'll talk again, okay?" I hang up a lot faster than I want to. "Sorry," I say.

The back of the receiver glistens with drying sweat.

"Jesus, man," the other instructor breathes. "See a doctor."

Chapter 24

I can't talk to Shirley at school. On the way home, on a whim, I stop at a payphone and dial Lila's office. After three rings, her voice mail picks up.

"You have reached the desk of Lila Chance and today is Monday, April 19th. Please leave a message, or if this is an emergency, dial zero so an operator may direct your call. Thank you and have a pleasant day."

I wonder what kind of emergencies crop up in the Trusts & Estates department of a big law firm. But I guess it's still possible she's at lunch. So I just say, "Hey, babe, it's me... I thought of something I wanted to tell you. Call me at home before five, okay?"

When I get home, the light on the machine is blinking, but it's Shirley, not Lila. I try Lila again, and get voice mail again. I look at the time. It's past two. Lila, good corporate camper that she is, never lunches past one-thirty. She thinks any later is obscene. I leave the same message.

I think about calling Shirley but I can't get Lila out of my mind. I have to warn her, I think. I pace around the living room. Maybe I should go to her office, just show up, tell her I'm going to follow her to her appointment. *Don't go out tonight...there's a bad moon on the rise.*

She'll be mortified.

I sink down on the couch and I don't know what to do. I want so desperately for her to be safe, but there's nothing I can do. I pick up the phone as it starts to ring. "Lila?"

"Oh, my God, he's wrong for once. Write the date down, someone."

"Hi, Shirley."

"Don't sound so happy to hear from me, Jack. You know, there's been a break-through."

"A what?"

"A break. In the case."

"What case?"

"Jack, are you okay?"

"Yeah, I mean, no, no, I'm worried about my wife. I thought you were her – I was hoping you were her."

"Oh. Why?"

"Just a bad feeling."

There's a long silence. "Why don't you try and call her? You can call me back… whenever, okay? Just do it. Call your wife." She hangs up.

I get Lila's voicemail. I leave another message. I pace. Half an hour crawls by, and I have decided to go to her office if she doesn't answer. I punch in her number with a shaking hand. One ring… two rings… three rings… a click. I think Thank God and a strange voice says, "Lila Chance's desk."

"Hi, this is Jack."

"Hi, Jack – oh, you're Lila's hubby, right? Didn't I meet you at the party? Wow, you're the guy who found Mr. Armstrong's whiskey, right? That was so amazing."

"Yeah, it really was. Um, listen, could I talk to Lila?"

"You know, I think Lila's gone for the day… her desk is all tidied and her coat's gone… but let me ask around, okay? Hang on." There's the clatter of a receiver being placed on a desk. I hear voices, faint and indistinct. I hear the rustle of clothing, the clink of an earring. "Yeah, she left… I guess she was meeting a client."

"I thought that was after work?"

"Oh, Jack, I don't know her schedule." The voice changes, goes smooth and impersonal. "How about I leave a note for her, in case she stops back in?"

"Sure, that'd be great. Um… you have any idea where she meeting the client?"

"I think she said she was grabbing a cab to the Pierre."

The Pierre. I saw Savageux outside the Pierre. So what, I tell myself. So fucking what? "Thanks... uh, Rita?"

"This is Christine, Jack."

I look at the clock. It's three-thirty, my shift doesn't start till five. Shortman will think I've gone over the edge if I show up early demanding a car. And what am I going to do? Drive to the Pierre and see if Lila's there? And if she is, do what? Barge into her meeting?

What kind of meeting is she having in a hotel?

I try calling Shirley but get her voice mail, too. I leave a message, and go to work.

At the garage, Shortman shrugs at Old Bessie sitting by herself in the furthest bay. "Roy just gave her a tune-up," he says. "She should be good for you tonight. How'd that interview go, anyways?"

"Pretty good," I say, and in that moment, even as sure as I am that I got the job, I somehow know I'll never work there.

"Have a good night," he says, for once like he means it.

"Thanks," I say. "You too." Old Bessie is in fine form, but a pall has settled over the city. The lights are dimmer, the sky is lower. The streets are dark and quiet and grim. Monday in Manhattan, and it's quiet as a grave.

I head straight for the Pierre. I turn off my on-duty sign, pull up by the side and put the car into park. "Don't let them tow you," I say to Bessie. Then I grab my cabby's license and head for the door. The bellman intercepts me.

"Can I help you, sir?"

"I'm here for a fare, a Lila Chance, a Mrs. Lila Chance?" Okay, so it's lame and she'll hate me but I have to try.

He narrows his eyes, looks suspicious. "I'll check."

I follow him inside even though the look he throws me says I'm as welcome as a horse turd. But she's here, I know she's here. I can smell her. A whiff of her perfume haunts the air, a thin thread of hope leading into the restaurant.

The bell captain's shaking his head.

"Mind if I check the bar?" I don't wait to let them say no. She isn't there, she isn't in the restaurant. She went up on the elevator, I think. I know she's still here. She's upstairs, I think, in one of those rooms. Sweat is rolling down my back, I feel like a light bulb is glowing from my spine. Lila, I think, where the fuck are you?

Find me. Help me. That's Lila's voice I hear, screaming through my mind, a voice I'd know anywhere.

"Can I help you, buddy?"

The bartender's looking at me strangely.

"Hi." I hold up my license. "I got a call… for a fare. Lady named Mrs. Chance? Lila Chance?"

"Buddy, I think you been had," he grins. "That doesn't even sound like a real name."

Help me, Jack. Something in me snaps. Lila's in trouble, and there's nothing I can fucking do. "She's my wife," I say before I can stop myself. Great, I think. Suddenly I've gone from a concerned employee to a crazed husband.

Help me, Jack. I see her, for one split second. She's lying crumpled on a high white bed, her face slack, her eyes glassy. She's naked from the waist down, and there's a tall form bending over her. I see the glint of a hypodermic needle, the spray of blood. Then the vision blinks out. I make a strangled sound. "She's upstairs."

I make a dash for the elevator, as the bellboys and the waiters and the receptionists make a dash for me, and the elevator woman slams the doors shut in my face. Of course I go crazy. Of course they call the police. Of course I'm arrested.

They let me call Shirley, because I just don't know who to call. I sit in the cell and wonder if I'm really going crazy after all. Shirley pulls a few strings, shows up an hour later. They let me go with her, and she takes me back to the car.

"What the fuck happened, Jack?" She doesn't ask until we pull up in front of old Bessie, who is, amazingly, just where I left her. She glances up at the Pierre.

"I know this sounds crazy, Shirley." I look at her with desperate eyes. "Lila was in there, somewhere. I could've found her if they'd've let me. She was drugged, I swear, I could see her. What the fuck am I going to do?"

"Oh, Jack." To Shirley's credit, she's not calling me a deranged fruit loop. "Look, I'll do what I can…okay?" She pats my knee. "You just sit tight – try to get some sleep. I'm sure… whatever she's done, whatever she was doing… I'm sure she's coming home."

I shake my head sadly. "No," I say. "I'm not."

"Jack." Shirley takes my hand, squeezes it. "Hang in there, okay? Nothing's happened yet."

"No," I agree. "Not yet."

She reaches into her purse, takes out a card, scribbles a number on the back. "Here," she says as she pushes it into my hand. "This is my home number. Don't be afraid to use it."

Chapter 25

Shortman stares at me when I turn the keys in. "Not one fare, Jack?" His baggy cheeks quiver like a hound's.

"I got sick," I say. I can't tell him I've been in jail. It's 2:30 in the morning... 2:22 to be exact, of the worst morning of my life. I don't feel the presence of any angels, no matter what Rosie might've told me. I feel sick and desperate and alone. "I had to pull over... I just about made it back here."

"Yeah," he says. "You don't look so good." He squints down at me, then shrugs. "I gotta charge you for the gas. But hey, seeing it's your last day, we'll say you was out sick, and I'll just charge you half. How's that?"

"My last day?" I blink.

"Look, Jack, you're a nice kid, but you're not cut out for this, you know? And besides, didn't you tell me you got a new job? Go on, Jack... you're as bad as a cabbie as I've ever had. You don't have to come back... we're even for the gas."

I've been fired and I'm so fried, so terrified for Lila, I don't give a damn. I put a hand on Old Bessie's cooling hood, and murmur thanks as I slouch out of the garage for the last time. I ride the bus home in a dark cloud of despair. At home, the apartment is dark, the bed empty. She's not home. She never came home.

Maybe she's at her mother's. I look in vain for a blinking red message light. I get back in bed and fall asleep for a fitful few hours. I wake up at 5:55. No Lila. She's not at her mother's. She's not here. She's not anywhere any more. I clutch her pillow and breathe in her scent. I grind my teeth and tell myself to get a grip. Maybe there's something Shirley can do.

So I do what she told me to do. I dig her card out of my jeans and I call her at home.

"Jesus, Jack." Her voice is gritty with sleep. "Don't tell me you're back in jail."

"Lila didn't come home."

"Shit." I hear the rustle of covers, the clink of something that sounds like a glass, a loud crash and another "Shit." Then she says, "Is there no where else she could be?"

"Only her mother's."

"Did you try there?"

"I'll call you back." I'd feel like an asshole if I weren't so sure Lila's not there. I dial her mother's number.

"Hello?" Mrs. Allegretto sounds completely asleep.

"Hi, Mom."

"Paulie, is that you?"

Paulie is her son who died at birth. "It's me, Jack."

"Jack who?"

"Lila's husband. Jack Chance – Mom, Mrs. Allegretto, is she there? Is Lila there?"

"Lila?" She sounds only marginally more awake. "Uh, I don't know, Jack, she was here night before last. Where are you? Why are you calling me at ten after six in the morning? Mother of God, Jack, is Lila all right?"

"She didn't come home last night. I was hoping she went to your place."

"What's going on with you two, Jack? Are you okay? Lila wouldn't tell me anything when she was here last night – oh, my God, she's not here. Oh, my God, now I'm going to worry myself to death. Jack, where is she? Where could she possibly be?"

"I...I don't know, Mrs. A– I mean, Mom. I'll... uh, I'll make some more calls. Don't worry, I'll find her."

"Call me back – have her call me back. Okay, Jack?" I hear her screaming "Holy Mother of God" as I hang up the phone.

I know I've made an empty promise.

Shirley's a peach. She gets on her friends at the NYPD, but they can't do a thing until Lila can officially be declared a missing person - 24 hours from the time she was last seen. At eight I call her office. I dial the main number, and explain who I am and what the matter is. The startled receptionist promises to have Lila call me the minute she walks into the office and promises to call me back if she doesn't.

She's not at work. She's not at her mother's. She was at the Pierre last night. And now she's gone. I sink onto the sagging sofa, feel the soft cushions part. I wish they could swallow me whole, swallow me alive. I don't want to go on, I think. I can't go on, not without Lila.

Come on, Lila, I think. Phone home. Please. For the love of God. Phone home.

But I can't connect, I can't sense anything. All I feel is a blank grey wall, implacable as granite, inevitable as the grave. She's gone, I think. She's gone and I couldn't save her, any more than I could save my mother. She died for my sake, too. Deaths come in threes, I can hear my Aunt Millie intone. Deaths come in threes.

Then I remember that Edith Chalfont died on Sunday night. Martha Sinclair, Edith Chalfont, my. wife Lila. Three women, three deaths, three days. No, please, I think. Please don't make me lose Lila. I can't handle that. I just can't. She's my rock, she's my anchor, she's my lifeline to all that's safe and sane. The idea that she could be gone forever brings tears to my eyes. I start to sniff, and my eyes cloud over. I can't fall apart, I tell myself. I can't. I can't. I have to keep a grip.

The ringing phone pierces the fog of my misery. I shoot up off the couch, grab the phone.

The woman on the other end says, "Jack?"

I say "Lila?" even though I know immediately it's not Lila.

"Jack, this is Mary Ferlinghetti. Are you okay? You don't sound so good."

"I'm not so good," I say. "What's up?"

"The committee's meeting, Jack. Did you forget? The grant committee? The Cape Cod grant?"

"Shit, Mary." I let out a long slow sigh. "Lila didn't come home last night."

"I beg your pardon?"

"My wife, Lila? She didn't come home last night. She's missing."

"Oh, my God, Jack. You mean you think something happened to her?"

I know it did, I want to say. But I can't. So instead I say, "Look, Mary, I'm sorry… I've just been waiting for her to call me… I guess I fell asleep."

"Have you called the police?"

"They won't do anything until she's a Missing Person."

"Oh, my, Jack. Oh, my. Well, let me tell Dr. Proulx – you won't mind if I explain to him and the other committee members, will you?"

"No, sure, that's okay… tell them… yeah, tell them," I say. I'm staring at the picture of Lila that was taken our wedding day. She's smiling but not directly into the camera - I was standing just to the right of the photographer. She's wearing jeans and a white lace camisole, with baby's breath in her hair. She looks happy and proud. I remember how terrified I was I'd let her down. "I want to make a few more phone calls, Mary."

"Keep us posted, okay? And… God bless, Jack. I-I really hope Lila's okay."

"I know you do, Mary. Thanks." I replace the receiver slowly, then dial Lila's office number. Her voice mail picks up after three rings.

"You have reached the desk of Lila Chance and today is Monday, April 19th. Please leave a message, or if this is an emergency, dial zero so an operator may direct your call. Thank you and have a pleasant day."

Today is not Monday, and I don't foresee too many pleasant days. "I love you, Lila Chance," I say. And then I grab her pillow and hold it tight against my face, allowing her scent to suffocate my sobs.

I can't go to class. I call or leave messages for everyone – outside of work – I can imagine Lila knows. I'm about to call Mrs. Li the Chinese drycleaner Lila sometimes uses, when I realize the sheer futility of my efforts. But I have to do something. I have to do anything. I feel caged and helpless, as if my skin might crawl off my body if I stop. This is my worst nightmare realized, the most terrifying possibility I ever envisioned as a kid hiding next to the oven, waiting for my mother to stagger home. *She's not coming back. She's not coming back.*

This time, she really isn't coming back.

I bury my face in my hands, and remember the slow warm slide of the whiskey down my throat at Rosie's. There is a balm in Gilead. There is… there is… there is.

I don't know what to do. I pace, I shake, I make phone calls. I want to call the Pierre, I want to pretend to be a private investigator. I wonder if the people at the front desk remember Remington Steele. But I won't be able to carry it off, I think. I'm too wired, too tense, too afraid, too…sorry.

Around one, my phone rings. 1:11, to be exact. "Jack?" The male voice is one I at first don't recognize. "Jack, is that you? What's this I hear about Lila not coming home last night?" It's Lila's brother, Vinnie. He sounds angry, but I know that's only because he's as scared as I am.

"I don't know what else to tell you, Vinnie. She just didn't come home."

"Whaddya mean, she didn't come home? Where the hell did she go?"

"She went to the Pierre."

"My sister stepping out on you, Jack?"

"No," I say, a little too fast, maybe. "She had a meeting with a client at the Pierre, and she never came home."

"Shit. And you haven't heard from her?" He swears softly under his breath. "Let me try talking to some people I know. I got friends from the neighborhood Lila grew up with. They'll remember her."

"What people are you talking about, Vinnie? Who do you think you are, the Godfather?"

"No, Jack," he says in perfect replication of Lila's disdain, only several octaves lower. "I meant a couple of the kids from the neighborhood are cops. Maybe we can get something happening here. Hang tight, Jack. I'll call you back."

He hangs up and I call Lila's office number again. The voicemail clicks on after only one ring, and this time, it's a message in a voice that isn't Lila's: "You have reached the desk of Lila Chance. Please leave a message and I'll return your call as soon as possible. Thank you and have a good day."

I have other plans, I think. "I love you, Lila Chance."

Then I hang up because I know Shirley's going to call. "Hi, Shirley," I say. I answer on the first ring.

"Radar's back on, I see." She clears her throat, lets out a long, slow sigh. "I-uh-I been talking to my contacts. They've agreed to start timing her disappearance from noon, yesterday, which is the last time you spoke to her."

"Yeah." I glance at the clock. 1:11. "Thanks, Shirley. I really appreciate it."

"I feel terrible about this, Jack."

"That's two of us."

"Try to hang in there, Jack. I won't let up. I promise."

Momentarily I feel better, but Shirley has her own problems. I make myself a pot of coffee and think about how good Rosie's whiskey tasted, how warm and sweet the after-burn. There's a liquor store right around the corner. There is a balm in Gilead… there is… there is… there is.

I sit and drink my coffee and think about all the promises I made to Lila. Every now and then, I wonder who changed her message and why.

On Thursday, Shirley knocks at my door. She brings a plains clothes detective with the improbable name of Melchior Gunn. By now the apartment is crowded with slips of paper and piles of mail. Vinnie's kept his word – I'm hearing from people I thought might be dead. But no one has seen Lila, and no one from Armstrong Henderson will return my calls. I haven't left a message on her voicemail since last night.

Melchior Gunn is an enormous black man with burnished skin and high cheekbones. His voice has the resonance of a Baptist preacher, and I wonder if he's missed his calling. He casts a dubious eye on the kitchen chairs, and sinks into the sofa instead. Shirley and I perch on the chairs. He starts off asking about Lila. I give him her photo, tell him everything I know, recount in excruciating detail all I can remember about our lives. Then we talk about the party Tuesday night. At some point, I ask about the body that the police found in the Church.

He leans forward, head cocked. Even Shirley looks stunned. "What body?"

"Someone died there, right? Wasn't there a body found?"

"How'd you know that, Jack?" He makes a note on his pad.

I glance at Shirley. I've said something wrong and I don't know what. She meets my eyes. "That information wasn't made public, Jack."

"That information wasn't given to the press, either." He looks at Shirley.

She flips her blonde curls. "Oh, so sue me. Look - it must be my fault. I must've told you, right, Jack? On our way back from New Jersey?"

I know why I thought there was a body. I "saw" it being carried out on a stretcher, red painted fingertips dangling limply from a shiny white sleeve. "Yeah," I nod. "Of course you must've told me."

"Any other way you'd know, Jack?"

"Oh, come on, Mel – everyone's not a suspect. Look at the guy – I bet he doesn't even know what day it is. He's the same kind of wreck I was right after Winnie... went missing." She blinks, swallows hard, glances away. "Cut the guy some slack will you?"

I shake my head and he backs off, but only momentarily. His own instincts, his own intuitions, have been aroused. I don't like cops as a rule, learned the hard way to avoid them. I'm sure he can tell, and it's making him curious. "Let's get back to Mrs. Chance. Have you talked to anyone at the law firm? Armstrong, Henderson... and who else.. God?"

I smile wanly. "No one will return my calls. I can only get as far as the receptionist. I think she's tired of hearing from me."

Shirley rolls her eyes to the ceiling. "Don't expect anyone to call you back, either."

"Why not?"

"Can you say the words... wrongful death?"

"Huh?" I look from Shirley to Mel and back. "What are you talking about?"

"That's what you could sue them for, son," answers Mel. "Big downtown law firm like that... sending a pretty young thing to meet a client at a hotel... whose already under suspicion of some kind of foul play... you could make the argument if the meeting really was work-related- and there's no reason to think it wasn't, after all- it's partially their fault if anything happens to her."

"So they're not going to talk to you, Jack. They're not going to say anything. Not until they're forced." She looks at Mel. "Right?"

The big man turns to me, and in his face I read a grim kind of sympathy. "I hope for all our sakes, this young lady shows up soon on her own." He gets to his feet. "Mr. Chance, I'll be in touch."

"How... how soon...?"

"How soon will we find her?" He hesitates, and I see he's struggling between the truth and a kind lie. "Mr. Chance, as I said, I hope I don't have to find her, because she comes home by herself. But I have to tell you if she's connected to the Savageux investigation, it's... going to take some time. It might take a long time. But we'll do our best."

"Hang in there, Jack." Shirley pecks my cheek, squeezes my arm as they leave. "I'm going to send you a pizza tonight. You don't look like you've eaten much in the last couple days."

I don't think I've eaten at all. I make myself some eggs after they leave, but the food tastes like greasy dead weight in my mouth. The yolk slimes all over my tongue. I manage to choke down a couple of bites, and then I throw the rest away. I'm taking the trash down when I realize our mailbox is stuffed to overflowing. I trek up to the apartment and retrieve the key, just as the phone starts to ring. I grab it and nearly drop the key into the toaster.

"Hello, Jack."

I've noticed that since Lila's been missing, I don't know who's calling any more, because I want it to be Lila so badly. I want it to be Lila so badly I don't even care where she'd call me from. A tropical island with a cute cabana boy would be great in my book, and I conjure up a vision of Lila in a red bikini stretched out on a lounge chair while a cabana boy who looks a lot like Johnny Depp rubs lotion into her back. She looks at me and winks, and I swear I hear her say: *You don't mind, do you, Jack? They said I could have my own idea of paradise for however long I wanted it.*

I hear her voice so clearly, I see her, smell the sand and feel the hot sun on my skin. I have that sense I'm in another place. I blink and the vision vanishes and Proulx repeats himself a third, fourth or maybe even tenth time. "Jack? Jack, are you there?"

"Yeah, Dr. Proulx, I'm here… sorry, I saw something on TV I thought might be about Lila. Did you hear about Lila, Dr. Proulx? She's missing."

There's a short uncomfortable silence. I wonder if he's staring at the ceiling, communing with his gods. "Mary mentioned it." He clears his throat and says, "Mary mentioned it at the meeting on Tuesday, Jack. The one you missed?"

"Yeah, I… I know I missed the meeting, Dr. Proulx, it's just that-"

"You don't have to apologize, Jack. We're all very worried about Lila, too. But I have to let you know, Jack… the grant? The committee decided it should go to someone else…especially now, given that… well, given the situation. I hope you understand?"

And the fact I didn't show up on Tuesday, I want to say. But I don't. I don't care. I don't care about the grant, I don't care about classes or exams or papers. I don't even care if my wife is fucking some grease ball stud-muffin in a hot air balloon around the world. I just want to hear she's alive. "I understand, Dr. Proulx." Then I hang up.

That night, I dream of Dougless. She's sitting in the back seat of Old Bessie, and directs me to an abandoned lot. As she gets out of the cab, she squeezes my shoulder, and says, "Don't worry – I'll help them find her."

Chapter 26

They find her body on Friday morning as the sun is coming up, at a place that looks exactly like the place in my dream. Mel and Shirley ring my bell around 11 and they don't have to tell me why they're there. I can read their faces more clearly than I've ever read minds. Shirley hugs me. We go downtown, where I have to look at Lila's body lying cold and flaccid on a metal gurney. They pulled her out of the river, too. At Mel's nod, the attendant slips her wedding ring off her finger and hands it to me. Memories come crashing back, of the exact moment I put this ring on Lila's finger, of the moment she tried it on in the pawn shop where we found it.

I push it deep into the pocket of my jacket. Outside the morgue, Shirley gives me a hug. "Is there someone you want me to call, Jack?" She peers at me as if I'm the one who's dead. "There're... there's things that have to be done... you know?"

"Yeah," I say. There are people to call and things to be done, but I know if I start with Mrs. A and Vinnie, the details of things will be mostly out of my hands, leaving me free to grieve. Which I intend to do, right after I talk to Lila's mother. Before I open the bottle of tequila. "You have any ideas yet what happened to her?" I look at Mel. He reminds me of the waiter from my dream.

"I wouldn't call it an idea yet." His voice echoes like James Earl Jones' in the tiled corridor. He glances over his shoulder, beckons to us both. As we step out into the watery sunshine, he says, "There're a lot similarities to the Jane Doe murders. But there are some differences... it's going to take some time to sort it all out. I'm not sure how soon the coroner will release her, Jack. You... you might want to plan a memorial service first."

"What do you mean, differences?" I plunge my hands into my jacket and encounter Lila's rings. They feel cold and empty as her body looked.

"For one thing, there's bruising on her arms, on her hands. Defensive injuries." He pauses, looks at me. "Unlike all the others, she fought back."

She fought back. The words burn themselves into my mind. Of course she fought back. My Lila was the scrappiest fighter of them all when we were kids - skinny, tough and mean. She never stopped fighting for me, either. I clutch the rings and try to swallow around the lump in my throat. I glance at Shirley. She smiles at me, blinks her watery eyes. "Yeah," I manage. "I believe that." Lila, I'm so sorry, I think.

"Let's get you home, Jack," says Shirley softly. She takes my arm like I'm an old person, or blind and guides me back to Mel's car.

They drive me back to Brooklyn. I tell them to stop at the corner. Shirley doesn't want me to get out, but I insist, promising to call her, promising to stay in touch. My first stop is the liquor store. I buy a bottle of tequila, then decide to buy two. As the guy behind the register is ringing me up, I retrieve a third. There is a balm in Gilead, there is, there is there is. And I'm about to plunge headlong back into it.

The bottles clink as I open the lobby door of my building. Inside the lobby, I am greeted by the mailman. He stares at me and then frowns. "Yo, aren't you 4-C?" He reaches inside his sack, and shoves a handful of white envelopes at me. "You want to empty your freaking box?"

I stare at the open line of mailboxes. Ours is overstuffed. I remember realizing that last night, and then I remember forgetting to empty it. "Sorry," I mumble. "If you just hand it over...I'll take it all now." I push today's stack into the bag and crush the rest to my chest. "Thanks. Sorry."

"Fucking alkie," he says under his breath as he turns back to sorting the mail.

Upstairs, I spill it all over the kitchen table, even as the enormity of my loss hits me like a truck again. This is the war Lila waged on my behalf, as I stare in horror at the snow white blizzard of envelopes spread across the table, two and three thick. These are the bills, I think, as I pick them up, one at a time, piling them into stacks. Not credit card offers, not junk mail – Lila found a way to stop that - not letters from distant friends. These are bills. I'm going to have to remember to pay them. I vaguely wonder how. I got fired from taxiing, I think. The contract for the summer's been rescinded. No one at Armstrong Henderson will return my calls about Lila…I seriously doubt they want me to work there any more.

I get a clean glass from the cupboard. I open the first bottle of tequila. And then I start to drink.

The first bottle is almost empty when I realize I'm not alone. There's a man dressed in rumpled tweeds sitting at the other end of the couch. He raises a shadowy glass as I lift the bottle to my lips. "Cheers," he says, so plainly I choke.

"Motherfuck," I say. "Who the hell are you, and where the fuck did you come from?"

"I think you remember me most recently as… Dylan Thomas," he says, with a furrowed brow and an air of being not quite sure. "I drank myself to death not far from here, you know."

"You come to keep me company?" The room's edges are nicely blunt and a gray fog is starting to settle over my limbs. If this is death, then let me die. Let me die and be with Lila.

"I've come to keep you alive."

"The fuck you say," I mumble, as I collapse into a black hole of dreamless sleep.

I wake up in a few hours, long enough to kick the phone off the hook, and start in on bottle number two. I'm deep in the midst of it, feeling that slow tequila burn, that hot tequila glow. I'm going to die, I think. I'm going to drink and drink and drink and then I'm not going to worry about it any more. I lift the bottle one more time, purse my lips, ready to drain it to its dregs.

A guitar riff sounds across the room.

This time, a guy with a curly beard and round wire rimmed glasses strumming a guitar shows up. He plays a few bars of *Friend of the Devil*, looks at me, and says, "I have to warn you T.S. Elliot's next."

"I fucking hate T.S. Elliot," I croak.

"Then don't drink any more," he advises, just as I start to puke my guts out.

At some point, Vinnie finds me passed out on the couch. I'm not even sure what day it is. He hauls me into the shower, makes me eat, makes me coffee. "You fucking shithead," he roars. "Lila didn't die so you can throw it all to shit."

I'm pushing my eggs around on the plate when the phone rings. It's Shirley, I know it is, and I grab the phone away from Vinnie. "Hi, Shirley."

"You okay?"

I shrug before I consider the futility of the gesture. "I'm trying, I guess... Lila's brother's here... making me eat."

"That's good," she says. "You looked like death warmed over at the morgue." Then she pauses and says, "There's been a break in the case. A big one. An even bigger one than before. I can't say exactly, but... well, a cabbie came forward with a capsule just like the one found on the girl in the church."

"No shit," I say. I look at Vinnie. "They think they might know who did it?"

"Well, I wouldn't go that far," says Shirley. "But they're getting closer."

The trouble is, I do know who did it. I know who did it and I can't do shit about it. I push the plate away. "I guess that's good news, Shirley."

"What're you doing about the arrangements?"

"Service on Friday... yeah, sure you can come. See you then." I hang up.

"Girlfriend already, Jack?"

"She's gay... lesbian, I mean. Her partner went missing six or seven weeks ago. They still haven't found her body yet." I get up, cross my arms. "Thanks for coming by, Vinnie. You don't have to stay."

He gets up, mutters, "I don't know what Lila ever saw in you," and leaves to inflict his rage on someone else.

Chapter 27

Somehow, much to my dismay, I stay alive till Friday. I stash the third bottle where I won't see it but can still think about it. That bottle is my insurance policy that I really am not alone. I make it through the memorial service, which is heavily attended by Lila's old friends and absolutely no one from her job. The firm sends flowers, an enormously showy arrangement but that's their only presence. Mrs. A sobs audibly, Lila's aunts moan and sigh. The male side of her family leers at Shirley where she's slipped into a back pew; the female side sneers at me.

Even at her memorial, my appearance, as far as Lila's family is concerned, is persona non grata.

Afterwards, however, a woman with a black lace veil like the old ladies wore and sunglasses approaches me. She's vaguely familiar. Her nose is red, her face is puffy. She looks as bad as I feel. "Jack?" She touches my arm and I feel something, like an electric shock through the fabric of my new suit. "It's Loretta – from Lila's office?"

Loretta from HR, Loretta from the underwear party. "Hey, Loretta. Thanks for coming."

She sniffs, dabs at her nose with a balled up tissue. "Yeah, well. This… isn't exactly an approved company outing, you know? But, um, Lila was always so good to me… she knew what a prick Gerry D'Eyncourt is, and she always helped me out. She was such a hard worker, such a good friend. I don't know what we'll do without her." She shakes her head, gazes blankly over my shoulder. "I don't know what I'll do without her." She hiccups softly. "I'm just so sorry that she's gone."

She turns away, and I stop her, with a hand on her forearm. "Maybe you should look for a better job." I have no idea what prompts me to say that, or why the next words come pouring out of my mouth. "You should find a place that appreciates you. You have a real knack for HR, Loretta. Have you looked in today's paper?" Inexplicably, a flash of a classified section of the newspaper flashes through my mind, a big red circle around one of the ads. "I think if you check it out, you'll find just what you're looking for."

Loretta is staring at me as if I've grown a second head. "That's what she used to tell me all the time." She takes off her sunglasses. Her expression is bleak, but in her eyes I see a spark of something else.

I see the ad so clearly I can almost read the telephone number at the bottom. "Yes," I say, with the assurance of an Old Testament prophet. "You really should. Especially if that's what Lila told you. She was always right about so much." And so dead wrong at least once. I glance over my shoulder. Lila's family is dispersing and I see Shirley heading toward me.

Loretta hesitates. "You know, Jack... they've threatened to fire us if we... if we say anything."

"About Lila?"

"Yeah." She glances over her shoulder, steps close enough for me to see the acne scars on her cheeks. "I guess I'm not telling you anything you can't figure out already, Jack, but that job.. that job you interviewed for? Well... it's been put permanently on hold. They... they aren't... they won't..."

"Loretta," I say gently, to stop the flow of her grief. "It's okay. I couldn't really see myself working there. Know what I mean?"

She sniffs. "Yeah, I do, Jack. I sure do."

"Don't forget now... today's paper. Help Wanted section, okay? I know it's in there."

"I'll buy you a drink sometime if you're right, Jack." She winks at me, then strides off with a straighter back.

"Wow," says Shirley at my elbow.

"Thanks for coming," I say. And thank God, it's Shirley, not Mrs. A, who overheard that last. She'd accuse me of hitting on the mourners. "Any word from Mel?"

Shirley shrugs. "Not since we talked. That's how this whole case has been, Jack. They take a step or two forward and then they run into a road block. I'm hoping the elections in the fall start putting pressure on the DA, but so far..." Her voice trails off, she shakes her head. "They keep running into walls."

"Like what?"

"I think the latest is that the powers that be in the police department don't agree Lila's one of the Jane Does."

"But..." I stare down at her. "I thought her profile fit... I thought you said..."

"Parts of it fit. Parts don't."

"Like what?"

"They won't tell me everything, Jack. Don't you see? There's pieces to this they're keeping under wraps because they hope it helps them catch whoever did it. And I guess the cabby's having second thoughts."

"About what?"

"About who left the Quaalude in the car."

"But I thought he positively id'd Savageux."

"He positively id'd Lila. See, I don't know if anyone's ever pointed this out to you, Jack. But you look a lot like Savageux. Mel noticed it right away. He showed the cabbie your picture, and he told Mel it was you."

"Shit. Is that why he wanted that photo of me and Lila?" I run my fingers through my hair. "Shirley, you don't mean to tell me he really thinks -?"

"Come on, now, Jack, we all know it's not you."

"I was fucking in jail while Lila was dying." I start to say it loudly, then lower my voice and drag Shirley even further away from the main group of mourners. "He's wasting his fucking time."

"I know how you feel, Jack." Shirley pats my arm. "Believe me, I know how you feel. But this is how they do things. And there's not a fucking thing you or I can do about it."

That night I sit at the kitchen table and try to stack the envelopes into a neat pile, but there're so many of them they insist on toppling over. I sit in her place, so I don't have to look at her empty chair, and build my little tower over and over. I think about the bottle of Jose I have stashed in my tenth of the closet, on top of the shoebox that holds the shoes Lila insisted I needed. I did need them, just not for any job. I needed them for today.

I remember how she tweaked and frowned and nodded when we bought the clothes. I'm glad I played along, I think. I'm glad we did that. It's the last time I remember we had anything close to fun together.

I run my fingers through my hair and think about the bottle of Jose. I think about the bills stacked and toppling over on the kitchen table. I'm going to have to start opening envelopes soon. I have to get a job, I think. Without Lila, without the grant, without the job, my prospects feel bleak. Maybe Shortman will take me back.

The message light is blinking on my answering machine, but I don't want to hear who's calling. I don't want to open the envelopes. I don't want to eat. If the door bell were to ring – which is does, in that exact moment – I don't want to answer it. I want to drink, but I can't seem to summon up the energy to get the bottle.

For a long moment I stare at my hands flat on the table, and think that nothing has to be better than this. Then the doorbell rings again, and I realize there really must be someone standing on the other side of it. It's not Shirley, I think, not Vinnie or Mrs. A. Not Loretta or Jody or any of Lila's friends. Not Dougless, either. She must've stayed in Jersey, I think, because I've not seen so much as a blink of her since Rosie's house.

The door bell rings a third time and I stumble out of my chair. "I'm coming!" I remember all the times I said that to Lila, and I sigh. I pull open the door and my jaw drops.

"Hi, Jack," says Jessie. She's got a backpack and a little suitcase, and she looks over her shoulder as if she's expecting someone to step out of the stairwell behind her. "Can I come in?"

Chapter 28

I can't believe she's standing there. My first thought is I can't imagine what Lila will say if she sees Jessie. My second thought is that Lila's never going to see anyone, ever again. My third thought is to wonder what Jessie's doing here in the first place and why she looks so scared. "Sure," I stammer. "C-come in."

"I hope I'm not catching you at a bad time," she says. She looks around. The place is trashed – the kitchen counters piled with dishes, the garbage can overflowing, the white-windowed envelopes all over the tiny table. "You... uh... your wife home?"

That's when I realize that Jessie doesn't know. The last time I talked to her was just after the last time I talked to Lila. I remember now. She never had my home number, and I haven't been to school. "My wife's dead."

"Excuse me?" She stumbles a little as I reach for the suitcase.

"Come on in," I say. "What d'you have in here? Bricks?"

"Books." She puts her backpack down by the door. Suddenly the apartment seems a quarter of the size that it did. She slumps onto the sagging chair beside the sofa, then straightens, as if she's afraid she might have to bolt. "Thanks, Jack... I really appreciate you letting me in. I- I just ..." She breaks off, runs a nervous hand through her hair. She looks like a nervous bird, perched on the edge of the seat. "I think...I think I know who took you from your mother, Jack, and why."

"You came all the way from Jersey to tell me?"

"I guess this is a bad time, huh? Would you like me to leave?"

I sink into the couch opposite and spread my hands. I can't stop staring at her. There's a glow around her that's unlike anything I've ever seen. I don't understand why she doesn't seem to realize it herself, why people aren't stopping her on the streets. Surely she's lighting up rooms wherever she goes. But I can see she's nervous, frightened, even, and I am very curious about what she has to say and why she has the air of a fugitive about her. "N-no, stay. I don't want you to go." At least, I think I don't. I don't know how to feel about Jessie. In New Jersey she felt like the other half of my soul. Now I look at her and want her to be Lila so bad my insides feel like they're bleeding.

"Um... mind if I ask what happened? To your wife?"

My shrug would do Shortman proud. "She was murdered. She left work to take some papers to a client last Monday, and disappeared. They found her body last Friday."

"They have any idea who?"

"Some of the marks on her... some of the stuff that they did was her... it's like the Jane Doe murders. But I guess now the police are thinking it could be someone trying to imitate that killer."

"Why?"

"Differences," I say with a huge shudder. I can't let myself think about this.

She looks stunned, but the glow doesn't dim a watt. The phone rings. "That's Shirley," we say in the same instant.

"Hi, Shirley," I say.

"You're amazing, Jack. Are you okay?"

"Jessie's here."

"Jessie from New Jersey? Jessie Woodwright?"

"Yeah."

"Oh, my God, I was about to call her."

"Yeah? How come?"

"Ask her where Rosie is. I've been trying to get a hold of Rosie for days now."

I turn to Jessie, whose overheard the question, because she says, "Rosie's dead."

It's my turn to nearly drop the receiver. "Are you serious?"

Jessie nods, and for the first time, the glow dims by the tiniest amount. Her lips are thin, her voice is flat. "A few nights ago the house caught on fire… by the time the firemen got there… and it's all volunteer down there… the place was completely engulfed. That's why I came here, Jack. I started to be afraid."

"You guys mind if I come over?" asks Shirley. "I'm in the neighborhood."

"You are?" I blurt.

"Yeah, Jack. I'm calling from the payphone outside your building."

Jessie looks alarmed when I explain that all the envelopes on the table are mostly bills, but she helps me clear a space so we can have coffee. "What are you afraid of?" I try to sound as casual as I can, while I make the coffee. That's when I notice that the last mug Lila used is still in the sink, still emblazoned with the outline of her lipstick. A wave of grief slams through my chest, a vise goes around my throat, and I have to hold onto the counter to steady myself.

"Ever since Rosie died…since Edith…Jack, it's like all the people around me are dying. I-I know you've just lost Lila, and Rosie and Aunt Edith were just…just friends, but…" She swipes at her eyes with the back of one hand.

"I understand," I say. Part of me wants to hug her, part of me can't stand the thought of touching any woman who isn't Lila. "It does seem like a lot of accidents, huh?" I manage to busy myself with the coffee mostly because I'm afraid that if I wrap my arms around her, I won't be able to let go.

"So last night I had this dream, about that red-haired woman – the one I saw at Rosie's. I've been seeing her around me, hovering out of the corner of my eye, like she was watching over me. In the dream we were walking on a beach, and she told me to come here, to come to you. So I took the dogs to Ginger's and she drove me to the train."

"Because of a dream?"

Her cheeks turn a soft shade of peach. She nods. Fortunately, Shirley knocks on the door. Before I have to try and figure out why Dougless has abandoned me for Jessie. Shirley gets right to the point. "What have you found?"

"The police let me into Aunt Edith's house," says Jessie. She gestures over her shoulder to the suitcase. "I-I brought some stuff... but –" She breaks off, shakes her head. "Maybe you guys should decide for yourselves... it's pretty.. pretty bizarre if you ask me."

"The police have decided her death was an accident," says Shirley. It surprises me she knows that. "What do you think?"

"I don't know what to think," Jessie answers. "Everyone else... everyone else even remotely connected to the clinic is dead. But at least I think I know why." She looks at me. "I think you're a lot more closely related to Nicholas Savageux than we realized. Because according to Aunt Edith's journals, the doctor in charge of the clinic – Edmund Sinclair – artificially inseminated at least a dozen women. Martha, your mother, was one of them."

"But my mother didn't have trouble getting pregnant," I say. "She had a bunch of kids before me. Weren't they with her husband?"

"Martha's husband – his name was Jesse – he died in April of 1970, Jack. You were born in March of 1971."

"Martha said you were made by an angel," Shirley says slowly. She looks at me, hesitates. "I-I never actually told you what made Luke so angry that day. He thought his mother had an affair. That's why..." she breaks off, shakes her head. "It got ugly."

"Why was this guy doing this," I ask Jessie. "I thought these were poor women.... Women with too many kids and not a lot of means – what was he doing getting them pregnant?"

"Breeding them," Jessie replies. "Aunt Edith didn't understand what was going on at first. But over time she realized... she realized there were instances where women had children ... many of them deformed...and..."

"But why?" I ask. "Was this guy nuts?"

"Obviously," says Shirley. "Maybe just a little?"

"He was a religious fanatic," Jessie replies. "According to Aunt Edith, Edmund Sinclair was a cross between a Doctor Frankenstein and an Old Testament prophet, a scientist who believed he was on a divine mission. He believed that his family was the one from which the Second Coming would appear. I found the place in her journal where she talks about finding him one night, in his office, drawing on these big sheets of newsprint spread out on the floor." She takes a deep breath and it's like we slide back in time even as Jessie's voice thins, into an old woman's quaver.

I didn't know what to do, though I think I should've known to do something other than what I did. Unlike the other sisters, I'd seen something of the world - I'd already finished a BA in Mathematics, and then nursing school, before I bowed to the Will of the " still, small Voice within" and joined the Order. So I'd seen something of the world; I was not so ready to accept all that men of authority might assure me with equanimity. It's why they sent me to serve at the clinic, as punishment for being right about the Monsignor's gout when his doctors were wrong. At the clinic, I was expected to learn humility under the tutelage of the greatest of the great – the esteemed Doctor Edmond Sinclair himself.

No hymn my sisters offered to the Almighty ever rang with more fervor than those sung in praise of Edmond Sinclair. He was wise, he was kind, he was rich. He used his money and his knowledge not for personal gain but in service to the poor. His name belonged in same annals as Carnegie and Rockefeller, Mellon and Vanderbilt. The only difference that separated Sinclair from the rest was his insanity.

I had stayed late on the ward that night. We had a few difficult cases – Mrs. Albion Sinclair had struggled mightily in the delivery of her twins, and I had stayed to comfort her when both were born dead, cords wrapped around cauliflower heads. The number of deformities among this population had been troubling me – environmental impact on pregnant women was an idea just beginning to take hold. But here in this rural, isolated community, there seemed clear evidence that something was to blame for the number of stillbirths and anatomical aberrations. So I knocked on Dr. Sinclair's door, because, despite the lateness of the hour, I could see a line of light beneath it.

I knocked again, then tried the door when I got no answer. It wasn't locked. I peered around the edge, expecting to see the Doctor sound asleep. Instead, I found him on his hands and knees, splayed like a huge incongruous child over huge pieces of newsprint, bright colored markers and rulers spread all around. He was still wearing his surgical scrubs, but he looked exactly like a child, in the middle of that dusty dark blue rug. "Dr. Sinclair? Are you -?"

I stopped when he looked at me over his shoulder. For a moment I thought he was going to leap at me. His eyes burned, his brow was furrowed. He looked like a man torn from a dream, and it occurred to me to wonder if Dr. Sinclair helped himself to his own prescriptions. "Sister."

"Are you all right, Dr. Sinclair?" *I pushed the door open, and I made my first mistake. I stepped over the threshold and into his madness.*

"I can tell you," *he said. He sank back on his heels, so that his hands rested on his thighs. He held a bright red marker in one hand, and a short, six inch ruler in the other.* "You're a sister, a nun, a holy, catholic person. You'll keep the secret, until it's time to tell."

"Tell what?" *I asked, bewildered by the charts spread out all over the floor, by the expression on his face.* "What is all this?"

"I'll tell you," *he said, with a wink.* "Anything I tell you... it has to stay between us, right? Otherwise you go to hell?."

He was confusing my religious habit with the sacrament of Confession, but it hardly seemed a good time to explain a point of doctrine. "Of course, Doctor." *I sat down in the one comfortable chair in the room when he pointed to it, trained by convention enforced by discipline to be obedient. That was my second mistake.* "Sure, I'll be happy to listen."

I was young, as I said. I thought I was going to hear some tale of marital woe, or maybe family distress... he was very close to his sister, Margaret. I was not prepared for what he said next.

"I have a secret," *he said.* "A secret in my blood." *He gestured to the swaths of newsprint.* "People would tell you I'm crazy, but it's all there... you just have to connect the dots. And I have... because I know." *He tapped one finger against the side of his head.* "I know."

I was confused. "Know what, Dr. Sinclair?"

"I know about our blood."

"What blood?" *For a second I thought he meant our supply of blood for transfusions, and then I thought maybe he meant blood type.*

"What blood?" *he answered, holding out his arms, undersides up, so I could see the pale blue veins marbling his alabaster skin.* "The blood — the holy blood that flows through these very veins."

"Holy blood?" *I was thoroughly bewildered.*

"It's in the blood, in the veins," he said, as if I hadn't spoken. "In the blood, in the holy blood. The blood from which the Son of God will spring." He scrambled closer, panting like a dog. "You believe, don't you, Sister? You believe in the Holy Blood of Christ, don't you? The day is coming, sister, coming soon." He swept his arms over his scribbled notations and equations, arcane as any alchemist's. "Rejoice with me, Sister, rejoice, the day of regeneration is at hand!"

He sounded like one of the patients on the psychiatric ward at Jefferson, from my student nursing days. "Doctor," I said, very slowly. "Let me have one of the janitors drive you home."

Again, he behaved as if he hadn't heard me. "Sister, the Bible talks about angels, about visions, right?"

"Yes," I answered, even more nervous.

"I've had many visions. This work we do, this work we share... the Lord has smiled upon us...and I have been rewarded... rewarded with visions and visitations... and knowledge, Sister, knowledge of things beyond the ken of men."

By now I was frightened. His face glowed, his eyes were fixed on some point over my head. "T-tell me," I said, and I made my third mistake. "Wh-what have you learned?"

"That God has come to Earth, Sister... that God has come to Earth!" He pressed his hands together, closed his eyes and shook I tried to calculate the distance between my chair and the door. He opened his eyes and fixed me with a stare worthy of prophet. "When you stand before your God, when you stand before him, naked and alone, do you feel him? Do you know him? Can you tell he's There?" His gaze held me in the chair, his eyes raked me bare.

"I...I...I..." I remember I heard myself babble some painfully schoolgirlish response. But this was the first time I'd met this particular demon and I didn't understand what I was dealing with.

"The Lord has come..." he whispered. "The Lord is come and lo, He shall return... awake and dance, oh daughter of Jerusalem! Awake and sing!" On and on he went, telling me a story of such fantastic bent I sat and gaped, held in the demon's grip. He talked about blood and family. He talked about names of people long dead, most of whom were named Sinclair. "We are the sons of light... the ones without blemish... the Sons of the Morningstar!"

I forbore to tell him that Son of the Morning Star was an appellation applied to Lucifer. But I knew that, I should've marked it, and I didn't. I was young, I was foolish. I should've marched out of the room and called the police then. But I didn't.

"After you were born, and taken away, Jack, Aunt Edith decided she'd had enough. She went to her superiors, told them that Sinclair was crazy... that he thought he was the carrier of some special blood, with some kind of special abilities, and that he was impregnating women. Shortly after that, the clinic was shut down. Aunt Edith left nursing and returned to teaching. She was still a nun when she died, I found out. She used her own name and didn't wear a habit, but she never gave up her vows."

"Did she know everyone connected with that clinic started to die?" asks Shirley.

"Yes," replies Jessie. "That's why when my father showed up at her teaching gig, recognized her, and showed her the notebook, she felt she had to warn him, for your sake, at least. Sinclair walked away with a fine and a slap on the wrists. Edith began to wonder if there was something more sinister than artificial insemination going on... something that could actually be causing all the deformities. But my father wasn't so much interested in the clinic – he was more interested in the connection between his family and the Sinclairs'. The clinic was a closed book, in his mind."

"But he was involved," Shirley says slowly. "Even if only peripherally, right?"

"Right."

Shirley lights a cigarette, the first she's had since she's sat down. "You don't mind, do you, Jack? I have to think. Everyone but Edith ... the other nun...Martha and your father were the only ones left. I think someone's just... finishing off the job." She looks from me to Jessie and back. "And that's how Winnie got in trouble. She was following a lead that led to Savageux. See, I don't think Savageux just thinks he can get away with pretending to play vampire. I think he thinks he can get away with murder."

Before either me or Jessie can respond, the phone rings.

I glance at the clock. It's 8 PM on the evening of my wife's memorial service and I can't think of a soul who might be calling me. I know who it isn't... it's not Vinnie, not Mrs. A, not Loretta. Not Shortman or anyone from school. So why am I thinking "work?"

"Hey, Jack," says the voice of Phinney McPherson. Cousin Phinney, I think, if any of this is true. There's an awkward pause. I can feel him struggling.

"Hi, Phinney," I say, to help him out.

"Jack, Muriel and I wanted to tell you how sorry we are... how badly we feel..." He stumbles and stutters through a long and tortured condolence. But there's something else, I can feel it. Phinny's not just calling me to tell me how bad he feels, which even he realizes is not anywhere near as bad as I do.

"I appreciate the call," I say. Poor Muriel is like a lamb in a lion's den. I hope she survives. "Tell Mrs. McPherson I hope... I really appreciate her thoughts."

"And her prayers, Jack," says Phinney, with all the earnest eagerness of an altar boy. "She's...she really just thinks you walk on water, you know. And um... we all do, really. That's.. uh... that's why..." He breaks off and I hear a big sigh. Poor Phinney. He's not usually expected to do difficult things.

So I decide to help him out some more. "You know, Phinney, I've been thinking, and I don't think I can work..."

"Jack, we don't want to make anything harder for you than this already is," he says, with relief.

"Of course not, and I appreciate that," I say. "Thanks again, Phinney and tell Muriel-"

"No, wait, Jack." He hesitates again, and I can practically hear the perspiration in his voice. What's so hard about this, I wonder. I hear a murmur of a woman's voice in the background, and I wonder if it's Muriel urging him on. "We... You know, we feel awful leaving you high-" He breaks off like he's been nudged. "Just because we can't have you here..." He tries again, takes a deep breath. "There's a client, Jack. A client who'd like you to work for him... he's in a position to offer you a job."

"Doing what?"

"Uh... well, I'm... to tell you the truth, I'm not really sure what the nature of the work is, Jack. It's just... well, you were the talk of the party, you know, and uh, well, after Muriel finished singing your praises..." His voice trails off.

The hair's going up on the back of my neck. "Well, who's the client?"

"He'd like to meet with you tomorrow afternoon, Jack – I know it's short notice and all, but he's about to leave on an extended vacation. Would you mind – would you like to – meet us for drinks? Say around four? There's a place in the Village – Chumley's – ever hear of it? He'd like to go there."

Everyone knows Chumley's, I think, a famous writer and actor haunt and a speakeasy in the 20's. Hidden behind an unmarked door, and only accessible through a tiny courtyard, Chumley's is hard to find unless you know what you're looking for. "Sure, I can find Chumley's. But who am I meeting? What's his name?"

"A long-time client of the firm, Jack – his family goes back generations with Armstrong, Henderson... they've been our clients – both personal and business for years and years." Phinney laughs, a nervous bray that even Shirley and Jessie hear through the receiver.

"What's his name?" I remember to ask.

"Jack, this is such an amazing opportunity for you. You want to be a writer – let me tell you, there're fewer more colorful characters. I mean, this guy is called the Boy Wonder of Wall Street, Jack, and he wants you to write his bio. I know you'll know his name... he's the one and only Nicholas "the Savage" Savageux."

The snakes in my stomach are blossoming into monsters the size of the one in Loch Ness. I hang up the phone with a strangled, "I'll think about it," before I begin to vomit into the sink.

Chapter 29

At some point, the women bundle me into bed. They cover me with blankets and bathrobes, and the top one is Lila's. I close my eyes with her smell filling my head, and open my eyes to a wide strip of golden white sand. There's a boardwalk on my left and an ocean on my right. Lila's leaning down over the boardwalk railing, yelling down at me. "Come on up, Jack, all the rides are free!"

The boardwalk boards are hot beneath my bare feet. Lila smiles and takes my hand and I forget this is a dream. For a while we're kids again. We ride and eat and slurp. On the merry-go-round it occurs to me that she's dead. "Lila," I say, tapping her on the shoulder to get her attention. "Lila, what are we doing here? Aren't you dead?"

"Not here," she replies. But the music stops abruptly, the merry-go-round grinds to a sudden halt. The smell of sun and salt water, burnt popcorn and cotton candy vanish and we're back on the strip of golden sand. Lila's standing beside me. She takes my hand, presses a kiss onto the back of palm. "You have to do it, Jack. I know you don't believe me, and I know you're not ready, but you're the only one who can."

"The only one who can do what?" I look around. "That ocean's not the Atlantic, is it?"

She shakes her head, and suddenly, we're surrounded by a jostling crowd of bodies, pressing forward. The girl with the maroon-spiked hair from the taxi, that I noticed going into the party with Savageux sticks her face into mine. "Figured it out yet, buddy?" she leers.

The sad-eyed girl in the white raincoat is next. "Thanks for taking me home." She reaches up and I feel a cool breeze on my skin instead of kiss. I sit up, gasping, out of my dream.

I remember the ghost of the man my father murdered.

I remember the look on the face of the girl with maroon-spiked hair.

I remember the flash of the body on the stretcher I "saw" being carried out of the church, a white rain-coat clad arm sticking out of the coroner's sheet.

I'm seeing the ghosts of the women Savageux killed, I think. And Dougless, too… even Dougless… somewhere back in time… was he responsible for her death, too? My thoughts spiral in all directions, my heart rate speeds up. I need a drink, I think. I notice that a line of light is burning underneath the door. I stagger out of bed, open the door. Lila'd be livid.

I'm surprised to see Jessie sitting at one end of the lumpy couch, curled up in a college sweatshirt that's mine. She smiles when she sees me. "Hey. How you feeling? Any better?"

"Shirley still here, too?" I ask.

"She went home around midnight – I don't think she could decide whether she wanted to stay and read more of Edith's journals, or leave and call the cops. She thinks that someone's taken up where Dr. Sinclair left off. She even thinks Rosie's death wasn't an accident either… because of her association with Dad. How do you feel?"

"I feel better than I did. It's – it's nice of you to stay…but… what're you doing up?" I glance at the clock. "It's three-thirty in the morning. Can't you sleep?" I sink down on the couch. "You… you want the bed the rest of the night? It's a lot more comfortable than this couch."

In the light of Lila's Salvation Army-salvaged lamp, her eyes are bright and she doesn't look tired at all. In fact, as I look at her, I see the glow, and I realize it seems to be coming from underneath her skin, as if she's shining with an inner incandescence. I blink, try to clear my eyes, but the more I try to convince myself it's just my imagination, the more obvious it grows. "No, I'm fine." She shrugs. "These last couple weeks... I just haven't needed much sleep. I don't know what I'm running on... but... I close my eyes and sleep for an hour or two at most, and then I'm wide awake the rest of the day."

To cover my confusion, I head into the kitchen, pour myself some orange juice. "Want some?"

"Sure."

As I hand it to her, she says, "Are you feeling any better?"

"I guess. For now."

"Maybe you better not go see Savageux." Her eyes are dark pools, her hair curls in delicate tendrils around her face. She closes her book and pulls her knees up to her chest.

"I think maybe I want to go meet him," I say, and in that moment I know I do. "I had this dream just now... this dream about Lila. It made me... really angry." In a couple sentences, I recount the dream.

"Are you sure that's a wise thing to do, Jack?"

I hesitate before answering. "No. No, it's probably not. But I know he killed her, I know he killed them all. I could tell the police, I guess... but the last time I mentioned I knew something they didn't think I should know, they decided I could be the killer. So maybe if I go, maybe I can find a way to help the police catch him." I nod at the book beside her. It's one of those old-fashioned composition books, speckled in black and white. Looking at it brings back bad memories of nuns with rulers. "What's that?"

"One of Aunt Edith's journals... she wrote it around the time she was getting to know my mother. There's a lot of stuff about me in here... it's... a little strange."

"To read stuff about yourself as a kid? Didn't she think you were cute?"

"She thought I was cute," Jessie reaches over and smacks my leg. "But mostly... mostly she was watching to see if there was... anything strange about me."

"Like what?"

"Like hearing things, seeing things. Knowing things."

"And did you?" There's a piece of me that's astounded to find myself sitting across from this woman, this odd woman at four o'clock in the morning in the apartment I shared with Lila. It's not just that she's here, it's that she feels like she fits... like she belongs. I don't understand why.

"Yeah – I'd forgotten about a lot of it. Reading these brings a lot back."

"You know, Jessie, I get the feeling there's a lot more here than we understand yet. I guess I buy the reason your aunt warned your father. But that doesn't explain her interest in you. That doesn't explain her friendship with your mother. I mean... here, on the one hand, you have this nun funneling information to this renegade crackpot academic, and on the other, she befriends his ex-wife?"

"Oh, they weren't divorced. According to this, my parents never got divorced. That's why Dad never married Rosie. He never divorced my mother. It's one of the things that really pissed Rosie off."

"But... I thought..."

"That my parents were divorced? Yeah, me, too. But then I didn't think Aunt Edith was a nun, either." Jessie taps the cover. "I get the impression from this that she was watching over us somehow. Now that I think of it, I do remember her helping my mother. But if she was a nun, who was giving her the money? Where'd she get the money to live in her house? I mean, it was old and all, but it was huge and impeccably kept. The woodwork alone... you'd walk inside and swear you were inside a church cause of all the wood... it smelled just like the pews."

"Maybe that's the answer," I say. "If she really was a nun, I guess she got money from the church. Maybe it was just part of, you know, nun stuff. Good works. Charity."

"Maybe." She looks up at me. "Aunt Edith kept in touch with your mother. Martha was a very devout Catholic... she developed epilepsy a few years ago.... Just started having seizures. That's when she started insisting you were alive. She also started insisting a lot of other stuff... stuff Aunt Edith passed on to my father."

"Like what? Stock market tips? Horse race winners?"

"Visions. She started drawing things and sending them to Edith. Martha apparently couldn't read or write very well, but along with the epilepsy came an ability to draw. And so she drew what she saw in her seizures, and sent at least some of the drawings to Edith."

"Why'd she send them your Dad?"

"Because they look just like the images in William Blake's engravings." Jessie fumbles in another composition book, hands me a creased piece of cheap lined paper. It's folded down the middle, and I gasp as I open it, and see what I recognize as a piece of a plate from Blake's poem, Milton.

"Jesus Christ," I breathe. "What the fuck…"

"I was hoping you could help me make sense of this. This is what you teach right?" She feels around inside her backpack and pulls out a thick manila envelope. "I got this from Rosie the morning after she was found dead. I don't have the background in literature to understand what she's talking about. But I bet you do."

"What is all this?" It feels like a ream of paper.

"This is more of Rosie's work. They weren't exactly happy little lovebirds. There was a lot of conflict in their relationship and a lot of it was around all this. Rosie was a tarot reader. Rosie was an artist. My father thought the answer lay in numbers, in Fibonacci sequences, and genetic codes. Rosie thought the answer lay in visions, in dreams, in the arcane and esoteric. And in poetry."

"I don't know what to think," I say.

Jessie leans forward. "You know, there is something different about us. We didn't make that stuff on the Weird List up. Edmond Sinclair was sure he had some special blood – maybe he was right. Just because he was crazy, doesn't mean he can't be right. Maybe that's what made him crazy. After all, isn't that we always wonder?"

It's bothering me the way she's saying We and Us like we're in some kind of relationship, like there's some kind of bond between us. Those words belong to me and Lila, and I squirm as Jessie uses them. It's not just Lila that's dead, I think. The final image from the dream flashes through my mind. It's not just that she's dead… it's how she died. I feel as if I'm perched on top of a very high mountain in the dark, which in all directions lies the precipice.

I think about the faces of the women in my dream. "In my dream just now with Lila… She told me I was the only one who can stop Savageux." I look at Jessie. "But that sounds so stupid, that sounds like something out of a comic book. This is real life, not some wild-assed movie."

Jessie makes a noise, and I see her face drain of all color. Her jaw drops, her eyes grow wide as she stares at a point over my shoulder. I turn and see the girl with maroon-spiked hair leaning against my bedroom door. She blows us a kiss, waves, and disappears.

The doorbell buzzes as I'm getting dressed. It's Shirley, with some disappointing news. "Mel wouldn't even consider letting you wear a wire…but here… I wanted to make sure I gave you this." From the bottom of her bag she withdraws a tiny black box. It turns out to be a tiny tape recorder. "Stick it in your jacket – and just make sure you press it on before the interview starts. It's pretty sensitive for such a little guy – he was a Hanukkah present from Winnie a year ago."

When I'm finally ready, this time it's the two of them who pat my jacket, smooth my tie, flick invisible lint off my sleeve. They both peck my check. Then Jessie says, "That's for luck. Go get him, tiger."

That's what Lila said. Another wave of grief, raw and new, explodes inside my chest. Jessie sees she's touched some nerve and she steps back, eyes troubled. It's not her fault Lila's dead, I think. It's mine. But there isn't time to beat myself up about it, because Shirley grabs my sleeve and tugs. "Come on," she says. "You don't want to be late."

When we get into her car, she says, "I'm not going to ask you how you're doing any more, until you stop feeling like shit, okay?"

I smile in spite of myself. "When do you suppose that will be?" I expect her to tell me when Savageux fries, but she doesn't.

Instead she shakes her head, and shrugs. "I don't know, Jack. I think it's different for everyone. It's different for you, now… at least you know what happened to Lila." She turns on the ignition and I take a closer look at Shirley.

For a second, she sounded jealous. I settle back in my seat. Her shoulders are squared, her eyes are tense. "How about you? Are you okay? You seem upset."

"Fucking cops," she says with a savage jerk into a left turn lane. "I've been busting my ass to do everything I fucking can to find Winnie... and now all they give me is beaurocratic bullshit. We have to follow the proper procedures... we have to follow department standards. Even Mel - you're about to sit down with the guy we all know is the killer...and he won't get you wired. Fucking morons is what they all are."

"They have procedures, right?"

"I'm about ready to tell them to take their procedures and shove them. Directly where the sun don't shine."

"Maybe you should take the tape recorder. I – uh – I don't want him to realize I have it."

"No." Shirley shakes her head. "I'm not going in. I'm afraid he'd recognize me. He's seen me at parties and opening nights and stuff... he might figure out something's going on. He's already about to book. Mel's trying to get an order preventing Savageux from leaving the country, but there's a problem with evidence. If nothing else, see if you can find out when he's planning to leave and where he's going to go, okay?"

I stare at the tunnel lights passing over our heads, ordered rows of bluish stars. I can't stop seeing the faces of the women in the dream. One by one they rise, mute and observant, as if watching, waiting, to see what I intend to do. I should call the counseling center, see if I can get some drugs, anything to make these faces go away. They're not nameless, they're not Jane Does. They were living, breathing women, with lives and hopes and dreams. And not one of them, I realize, is Winnie Chen.

That's when the lights start acting strangely. Each pair, as we approach, on either side of the tunnel blinks out. It flashes back on as soon as the car passes under it. I glance at Shirley to see if she's noticed anything, but her hands are wrapped around the steering wheel, her eyes glued to the fender of the car in front of us. As we ease out of the tunnel, I look at her and say, "You know it's a long shot he's going to say anything at all about anything illegal."

Shirley doesn't take her eyes off the street. "Then why does he need to have his lawyer sitting there?"

We get to Chumley's at 5:55. Shirley lets me off with a honk and a "Good luck." For a second, I'm disoriented, and don't remember the corner. I stumble around for a few minutes, as a light rain begins to fall. *Oh, come on,* I think. *Please not now. Don't get me soaked.*

The rain stops as instantly as if someone has turned off a faucet.

That's an interesting coincidence, I think. Just like the lights flashing on and off was a coincidence. Just like it's a coincidence I can see the faces of the dead women. I wonder if I can remember them all, if I made a list, if Melchior Gunn would follow up?

Fortunately I find Chumley's before I am consumed by such thoughts. I stagger inside, just as I see Savageux and Phinney coming in from the other entrance. I'd forgotten there was another way in.

Savageux is wearing sunglasses. We shake hands, and his is hot. I realize I've forgotten to turn on the tape recorder. If I'm expecting Dracula, I'm wrong. There's nothing cold and dead about Savageux. If anything, he exudes a kind of incipient energy. I can feel it snaking out from all around him, commanding the attention of every waitress in the room.

"Good to see you, Jack," says Phinney with undiminished enthusiasm. He pumps my arm with one hand while with the other, he summons a round of beers.

Savageux doesn't wait for Phinney to say anything more. He takes off his sunglasses. His eyes are dark brown, like mine. "I'm looking for an assistant," he says.

"What makes you think I'm right for the job?"

"Phineas told us... my wife and I.. about your unfortunate ... situation." He pauses. "We knew Lila. We both knew Lila."

A flicker of movement in the corner of the room catches my eye and I see a flash of white and maroon-spiked hair. "I'm not sure what I can do for you," I say, not sure whether I'm talking to Savageux or the ghosts. A group of giddy tourists slide into the seats the ghosts occupy and at once they disappear.

"Phineas tells me you're a writer," he says. "I'm looking for someone to tell my family's story. We've been influential Americans now for nearly three hundred years, but no one knows who we are. I think it's time to… to introduce us."

"Like the Rockefellers, you mean?"

"Like the Kennedys," pipes up Phinney. Savageux glances in his direction, and I wonder what Savageux has on Phinney that makes him visibly squirm.

"You have the idea," says Savageux.

"Why now?"

Savageux draws a slow breath, takes a sip of his beer. I can almost see him rehearsing what he's about to say. "After the … the unfortunate interruption, so to speak, at a party a few weeks ago, I feel a need to polish my image. I've been considering a political run."

He's lying through his teeth. He doesn't even sound plausible, and I look at Phinney to see if he's buying any of this crap. Phinny's unleashed his inner golden retriever. He's practically panting over his beer and I have the urge to scratch behind his ears. "I see," I say.

"What do you think, Jack? Great opportunity here, huh?"

I feel as if Phinny's licked my face. I shift uneasily in my seat, move the beer glass around in rings on the table. Accidentally, I topple the salt, and a few grains spill out on the table between us. "Sure, it's a great opportunity…" though I don't actually know to do what. If it were anyone else, I'd know exactly what was in it for me. Meet people, I guess, rub elbows with the rich and famous. Spend summers tagging after Savageux from yacht to golf course, winters from board room to ski slope to tropical paradise. But that's what would be in it for me if Savageux were…were what, I think?

Not a monster, Jack.

I remember what Jessie told me about how salt keeps evil things, negative energies away. I push a few grains towards Savageux's hand where it rests on the table top, and is it my imagination, or does he actually pull back a centimeter or two? I raise my eyes to his and as his gaze locks into mine, all I can think is *Tyger, Tyger, burning bright*.

No matter what my dream-girls might be egging me on to do, I mustn't forget that he is the hunter, and I am the prey. I can feel something like cold water trickling over my skin, or a thin tentacle, reaching out, testing my awareness, my tolerance.

Who overcomes his foe by force hath overcome but half his foe. His eyes are boring into mine. I sit back, shift in my seat, smile gently. "I just... just really don't know what to say."

Savageux leans forward, fingers knotted together. "I want you to take some time and think about it, if you need to, of course. I won't deny we ... well, my wife's tastes in entertainment...I guess some people would consider them a little extreme. But Clarissa adored Lila, and I just...just have such a feeling ... you're the man for the job. Do you think that sounds ridiculous?"

"I...uh... I've never written a biography," I say.

"I wasn't thinking biography - not right away. Maybe a series of profile articles, something modest, an op-ed piece in the Times, something like that. Maybe even something on our... alternative lifestyle. I have a lot of connections in publishing... "

"He even owns a newspaper or two," brays Phinney.

Savageux ignores him totally. "If you can string together the sentences, we can find the right venue." He glances at me, then down. "The job includes room and board... clothing allowance, too... at least for the first year. We'd want you to be close to us, so we'd let you stay in one of the guest cottages. They're small, but... cozy." He smiles. He thinks he has me.

"It's the least we can do," says Phinney.

Savageux leans back, places his arm along the top of the seat. He's looking at me like a morsel on a plate, a tempting tidbit he'd like to make disappear. That's exactly what he's planning to do with me, I think. Lila was just the appetizer. He senses the connection between us, he knows there's something there. He doesn't know what it is, of course. He just knows it's there.

We're cousins, I think. I wonder what he'd say if I told him that? He's watching me, waiting for me to say something. "I just don't know what to say." That's honest, at least. "It...it seems like so much, and I don't know..."

Savageux reaches across the salt and places his hand on my forearm. I notice he doesn't let his sleeve touch the table. "I know you've had a lot of struggle." He smiles, the way I imagine a tiger would if it could.

"It's the least we can do," says Phinney.

Savageux ignores Phinney, ignores the waitress who brings our beers. "I know about the money you owe. It really doesn't have to be as big a problem as you think." *Just sell me your soul.*

I don't really hear him say that part. I push a few grains of salt toward him and watch him pull back a full inch from the table. I feel as if I'm in two worlds at once, inside a strange place where space and time don't intersect quite as neatly as they usually do, where beings made of air and light are just as real, if not more so, than those made of flesh and blood.

"It's the least we can do," says Phinney. And he unwittingly saves the day, because the fact he says this now three times somehow breaks the spell Savageux's been weaving.

"Least you can do about what, Phinney?" I turn to him and meet his eyes directly without any sort of guile. But he won't look at me, not directly. His eyes slide to the left and to the right, and finally settle off into some point just above the top of my left ear.

"After all the unpleasantness, of course," he mumbles.

"Unpleasantness?" I don't take my eyes off Phinney, and I literally watch him start to sweat, big fat drops that collect around his hair line. "What are you talking about, Phinney?"

"Well, you know," he says. "Lila and all."

Savageux narrows his eyes and leans across the table, his sleeve still inches from the salt. "I thought you discussed this."

"Discussed what?" I ask.

Phinney actually cringes. He turns to me, his face flushed. He swallows visibly. "Well, Um, Jack, maybe you didn't realize...the whole reason Lila left work was to meet with Mrs. Savageux... her unfortunate accident..."

"You mean her murder?"

His face is turning white, the blood draining as I watch. "You...you'll have to excuse me – I think I'm going..." He breaks off, stumbles toward the men's room.

Savageux watches me. As the door clatters shut behind Phinney, he says, " My wife was very fond of Lila." He pauses, hesitates, and I can feel him assessing my reaction to her name. "We all thought Lila was very special." His voice is just a tone deeper, a tone richer. "She brought out things in Clarissa I never saw before." .

What's he suggesting? I wonder. That Lila had an affair with Clarissa... that she had an affair with the two of them? Nausea stirs in the pit of my stomach. He pulls out a business card, scribbles something on the back and hands it to me. "Come out to Greenwich this weekend. Meet Clarissa, meet our friends. We're having a party on Saturday night, a going away party, you could say. Everything gets going around ten. Why don't you come, Jack? Clarissa and I would love it if you did." He puts his sunglasses back on, though the gloomy afternoon has surely thickened into night by now. "Think about it, anyway. I'll send you something suitable to wear." He flashes another show of teeth, then strides through the door without any apparent thought of Phinney.

As if on cue, Phinney staggers out of the men's room, in time to see Savageux stride out the door. "Hey, Nick!...Oh, Jack... I'll get it the next two times, okay?" Then he bolts out the door.

I finger the card Savageux gave me, and for one deranged moment I imagine what it would be like to work for him.

He doesn't want to hire you; he wants to consume you. That's Lila's voice, tart, unmistakable.

I jerk upright, expecting to see her sitting beside me. But she's not of course, and in fact, all the tables in my immediate vicinity are empty. I place Savageux's card carefully in my pocket, and leave two of my last five twenties on the table. He's given me the ticket in, I think. I just have to figure out how to make it count for something other than a bid for my soul.

Chapter 30

Shirley's face is grim as I recount our conversation. "And you got none of it on tape?"

"I did get this." I pull Savageux's card out of my pocket.

"What's that?"

"He invited me to a party at his place this Saturday." I glance at the spidery scrawl on the back, then offer it to Shirley. "Here. Take it."

Her eyes widen and then she shakes her head, holds her hands up. "Oh, no. I've already tried that route."

"I don't think you should go, Jack," says Jessie. We're sitting in a coffee shop an hour after my interview. For the first time in a long time, I'm hungry.

"But this is such a great chance," Shirley says. "How can you not go?"

"He can't go alone," Jessie says.

"Maybe the police —" begins Shirley, but Jessie cuts her off.

"Shirley, I hate to say this, but I don't think the police —" She breaks off at Shirley's suddenly acid stare. "I don't think the police are taking you seriously anymore."

The glow around her is palpable to me now. What's odd is that it doesn't dim out under the bright fluorescent lights. I've never quite seen anything like it. But Shirley doesn't mention it, no one else seems to see it, and Jessie herself seems unaware of it. And now it hardly seems to matter.

Shirley takes a deep breath and for a second I think she's going to spit venom. But all she says is, "Yeah. You're right." Her face is sudden flat. She picks up her purse. "I have to go."

Instantly Jessie looks contrite. "Shirley, I'm sorry –"

"Shirley, wait," I say. "Maybe we can figure something out ourselves – "

But Shirley only thrusts a manila file into my hands. "Here. That's everything I know. You come up with any new ideas, let me know." She starts toward the door, but I reach out and grab her arm.

"Hey, wait. Listen. I have something to tell you." She's upset, so upset, I think. She's angry they haven't found Winnie and at the same time, she doesn't want her found.

Shirley's eyes are hard, her mouth a taut line.

"Winnie's alive. You're right. I don't know why, I don't know where. But I'm-" I glance over Shirley's head to Jessie. "I'm almost a hundred per cent certain she's alive."

That gets her attention. Her eyes flood with tears and she covers her mouth with one hand. "Wh-what makes you say that?"

I take a deep breath. I haven't exactly shared the contents of the Weird List with Shirley, but she herself says she's dreams of Winnie. "I-I've had dreams."

"Of Winnie?" Her eyes widen.

"No… of Savageux's victims – at least the ones he's killed. And…and Winnie isn't there."

Shirley turns away. "I-I… look, Jack, Jessie… I appreciate everything you've done, the two of you… but I just… I just have to go home now. Call me if you… if you think of anything."

She pushes past me and is gone. Jessie looks at me and sighs.

"I don't think Shirley believed me," I say as I turn the key in the lock of my apartment.

"It's not about what she believes," Jessie answers. "It's about what she doesn't want to believe… just like my father didn't want to believe that Rosie… that Rosie could be right." She looks at me. "Did you have a chance to look through the stuff I showed you?"

"Not yet."

"Well, why don't you read some of it, and I'll look at Shirley's stuff?" She nods at the table, where all the bills have been stacked in an empty shoebox and pushed to one side of the counter.

"You don't think I'm crazy, do you?" I say, as I pull the first sheaf of paper clipped notes out of the bulging envelope.

"Of course not, Jack," Jessie says. "I see them, too."

We don't say anything for quite awhile. I start to understand Rosie's ideas when it dawns on me that Rosie, like Blake, believed that the supernatural world and the beings that inhabit it are every bit as real as the physical world and all its creatures. Blake didn't see aliens, I think, scanning the notes and my mother's drawings, remembering Nathan and his ideas.

Blake saw angels and demons, gods and demigods. Blake saw a War in Heaven.

I see a guardian angel and a Greek Chorus of ghosts.

We are such stuff as dreams are made of... a line that to me implies that what we experience in dreams is just as real as what we experience in waking life. But that can't be true, I think. I can't let myself believe that. I think about Jessie and her sage and her salt. I think about the moon. I think about Dougless, about Savageux, about how it all seems to fit, somehow. It's like a Rubik's Cube, a cube with an extra dimension that not everyone can see.

"Jessie," I say. "I've been thinking about the red-haired woman we've both seen. She says her name is Woodwright, so I understand how she's connected to you. But I don't get how she's connected to me. Why'd she tell me to think of her as my guardian angel? Why does my life matter to her?"

"It's that Jamie McPherson connection. I think she identifies Jamie with you."

"So let's say I was Jamie, or I'm enough like Jamie I remember being Jamie. Was Dougless… in love with Jamie? Is that it, do you think?"

"Maybe." She leans forward, tucks a curl back around her ear, and I'm struck once more by the glow emanating from underneath her skin. "I found a book on legends and Scottish songs. The song tells about how Jamie was betrayed when someone set the clock ahead, so he was hanged before his pardon could arrive. But he was betrayed before that, according to the story. The reason he was captured in the first place is that a woman threw a blanket over his head, thereby preventing his escape. I think your Dougless could be that woman." She sits back. "What do you think of that?"

"The book doesn't tell the woman's name?"

"No." She shakes her head. "Women's names weren't considered important enough to write down."

"It does fit," I say slowly.

"Well tell me if this fits, too," she says as she hands me a calendar. "This is a calendar that goes as far back as the death of the first body. The red x's are the dates during which the women most likely died. I guess it's hard to say exactly when, because some of the bodies were already badly decomposed."

"So what do you want me to see?"

"Well, first of all, do you see the pattern?"

"Not really."

"Well, look. There's two... then a break of a month. Then there's three...all separated by about three weeks, give or take a few days. Then there's another break... this one two months. And the killings start up again... five in a row." She taps the calendar impatiently. "I think this is a Fibonacci sequence, Jack, and based on it, the killer is in the middle of a killing spree, and if Lila makes number six, which is what I suspect, then in the next six to eight weeks, two more are going to die."

"You really think so?"

"Yeah, I do. But that's not all I see here."

"Yeah? What else do you see?"

"Do you have any idea what this calendar would look like to most women? I think the killings are linked to a menstrual cycle. That's what it looks like to me."

"But... but why would Savageux....?"

"From the beginning, both you and Shirley have assumed that Savageux is the murderer. But what if he isn't? What if he just lets it happen? What if he just gets something out of watching? What if it's his wife?"

"You think a woman's capable of doing that stuff? Of killing other women that way?"

"Yeah, I do. If she were angry enough, maybe. If she thought she had a good reason." A strange look crosses her face.

"Like what?"

"Well, like maybe if she wanted a kid, and she couldn't have one. I read somewhere that all Savageux's kids are adopted."

"What even gave you that idea, though, Jessie? That sounds so far-fetched, so unbelievable…"

"You knew that all the women have some strange drug in their systems, right?"

"Yeah." I look at Jessie closely, but she won't look at me. "So?"

"Did you know they were all pregnant? Or had been, recently?"

Something cold slices through my chest, makes me pause and look her. "W-who told you that?"

"Shirley told me that," she answers, looking puzzled. "Didn't she tell you?"

When I calm down enough to think coherently, I call the police. To my surprise, and despite the lateness of the hour, Mel's at his desk. He heaves a long sigh and hems and haws and says since he doesn't have the autopsy report, he doesn't know.

"But it's true?" I press. "All the other women were pregnant?"

"Uh… well, not exactly. A lot of them…some of the older bodies, we couldn't tell… and it's not so much they were all pregnant when they were killed… what the lab results showed is that they'd all been pregnant.

"You mean most of them had given birth recently?"

"Or had abortions, or miscarriages. See, Jack, I didn't think this was a piece of the profile you needed to know… but these women… they don't have uteruses when they're found. And… um… neither did Lila. So we have to wait, for the results of the lab."

We're back to babies, aren't we, I think, and a piece of the puzzle snaps into place. Edmond Sinclair used the clinic in the Pine Barrens as a way to troll for wombs to breed. What if... what if someone's just picked up, I think, where Edmond left off? What if someone's just using the vampire thing to troll for wombs in just the same way?

I tell him about my interview with Savageux. He seems less than convinced than I am that Savageux's practically confessed to murder. "Jack." I can hear his chair creak. I can practically see his big soft eyes. "What about the lawsuit they're afraid you're going to file? You remember, don't you? Even the DA mentioned it." He draws a deep breath. "We don't know if that capsule the cabbie found in the back of the cab is the same thing as the one in the other girl's pocket. Seems there's a processing problem at the lab. It's going to take some time." He sighs. "Look, I know you and Shirley are good people, and I know you've both lost your partners. But you've got to stop running around playing Hardy Boys. Someone's going to get hurt. Or arrested." He pauses again, this time for emphasis. "You hear what I'm saying, Jack?"

"Yeah, Mel," I say, with a sick and heavy heart. "I hear you loud and clear."

"Tell him about the patterns," Jessie mouths. "Tell him about the cycles."

"Um, Mel – before you go, one more thing?"

"What is it, Jack?"

"Jessie – Jessie, this friend of mine – she thinks she's figured out a pattern – no, a series of patterns, I mean a double cycle of patterns..."

Mel sighs. "When she gets it all figured out, tell her to send it to me, okay, Jack?"

"Okay." I sounded lame and I know it.

"And, Jack, we really do care about what happened to your wife, okay? We're doing all we can. I promise."

I hang up, look at Jessie. "So now what?"

"Well," says Jessie. "I have an idea. What kind of party is this you've been invited to?"

"I guess it's one of his vampire shindigs. He mentioned his wife's...tastes in entertainment could be considered a little strange. He even offered to send me something to wear. So what's your idea?

"It seems to me someone needs to take a look around the Savageux estate. You've got an invitation.... But.... If there was a way to get in... disguised, then... maybe you could just look around... see what you could find, and then get out, even before Savageux knows you've been there...."

"And how do we do that?"

"We can drive the band bus."

"The band bus? You think the other girls would go for that?"

Jessie shrugs. "I guess we can call them, can't we? They said to call if I needed help. I mean, think about it, Jack... if someone, whether Savageux or his wife are conducting some kind of weird experiments or breeding babies, or whatever they're doing...they must have a lab or something to do it in. We can get a site plan of his property from the town, I bet... and then... it's just a question of getting in touch with the police." She folds her arms across her chest. "Think about it, okay, Jack? I really think it could work. What do you think Shirley would say?"

Shirley will drive the van, I think. Ever since Lila was found, she's needed to believe that there's a chance Winnie's still alive. Now that I've offered her the hope of confirmation, she'll jump at this chance to find Winnie.

I think about Lila, and wonder if it's possible there was a child she never even had a chance to tell me about herself. No matter how deep or inexplicable the bond I feel with Jessie – the one so deep I don't like thinking about – there's another I feel with Shirley.

She's not going to stop until she sees Savageux caught. And neither will I.

Chapter 31

Shirley's up for it. I knew she would be, so I'm not surprised when she offers to let us use her apartment in the Bronx as a base. What surprises me is that Jessie's band not only agrees, but arrives, early on Saturday morning, swallowing Shirley's renovated industrial loft in boxes of Joe, and the Goth chic they wore at the gig they've come directly from last night.

There's an immediate undercurrent of tension, however, and it's not until I overhear Kim ask Ginger, "Are you going to tell her?" that I realize that their assistance in this is about more than helping out a friend. They want to replace her, I realize, with the new singer they auditioned last Wednesday and who sang last night with a raw need and a husky growl that got the sparse crowd on their feet and cheering. I can see the smokey bar, hear the whistles and the claps, smell sour sweat and beer and leather. They've talked about it on the way here - and all three want Jessie out.

"Jack?" Jessie jiggles my elbow, and brings me back to peering into Shirley's opened refrigerator at an unopened carton of cream. "Are you going to get that milk, or are you waiting for it to leap into your hand by itself?"

I bang my head on the freezer handle. I turn and hand her the milk. It's nine thirty in the morning, and the sun is pouring in from the skylight high above, but Jessie is brighter than the sunlight, a red-haired sliver of pinkish incandescence that stands out against the sun. She takes the cream from my hand, cocks her head, and says, "Come on, Jack. You're missing the plan."

"What about our stuff?" Ginger's asking, as I follow Jessie into the room. I wonder if she's noticed that none of them will look her in the eye for long. "We can't pretend to be a band without stuff… I mean, my God, what if they expect us to play? We can't exactly say we lost our luggage."

"What kind of security is there going to be," asks Heather. "Are there going to be people with guns?"

"It's a party," says Jessie. "I really doubt there's going to be guns."

"I don't," says Shirley. "Don't kid yourselves… these parties are big, but…" She breaks off when she realizes that she might be talking us out of going. "The guards at the gates might have guns. But… you have to remember, they're going to assume that anyone who looks like you guys… driving a van that says Bitch Fest -"

"Bitch-FEAST," they all say at once, including Jessie.

"Sorry," says Shirley. "But you'll blend right in, and they're not primed to keep people in – their orders will be to keep the police and the press out."

"So you don't think we're going to have any trouble leaving? Even if we decide to leave a bit on the early side?"

"I've been to the Savageux estate – oh, yeah," she says when she sees the looks on our faces. "This is an estate, all right… complete with tennis courts and guest cottages – there's three of those – swimming pools – both in and out – stables, a converted barn – which is where I think they hold the parties… you name it, these people have it."

"How many times were you there?"

"The first time I was there was as a member of the press… they were holding a celebrity fundraiser and they let one reporter in from each paper. I took a garden tour a couple weeks ago – again it was for some benefit. I also did what Jessie suggested." She unfolds a piece of paper from her purse, and places it flat in the center of her glass-topped coffee table. "This is a rough sketch of the site plan Savageux filed with the town about three years ago when he had his barn enlarged." She pauses, looks around at the group. "Shortly after, the murders started."

The women ooh and ahh, and I peer at the sketch of the property. The barn and a couple other outbuildings sit diagonally to the rear and the side of the main house.

"Are these little squares all buildings?" Heather asks. "Does this guy have a house or a village?"

"Both," Shirley says. She taps the largest of the shapes. "This is the main house. The road leads up from the gate. It forks here, at the circle... you can go around to the barns and the back, or you go around the circle to the house."

I can smell Jessie's hair, right under my nose. She smells warm and soapy and sweet, a blend of shampoo and light sweat. "Is this an access road at the back?" Jessie asks. She points to the line that leads around the outbuildings and circles around the house.

"Yeah," says Shirley. "There's a pool over here, and I think, based on an aerial photograph they had in the office, there's enough trees and cover that you could pull the van around and not be noticed. This is going to be a big event... they had to file for a permit."

"So what're they going to do?" asks Kim. "Celebrate a black mass? Sacrifice a virgin?"

"To tell you the truth," answers Shirley. "I'm not sure what they do. Usually there's bands, and sometimes people selling stuff, sometimes people offering services... from blood-drinking to spanking. Sometimes, there're fortune-tellers. Think of a vampire version of Mardi Gras... and you'll get the idea." She pauses. "But that said... Savageux's parties are invitation only... no one gets in... right, Jack?"

"Did you say there're tarot card readers?" I ask.

"You want your fortune told, Jack?" Kim nudges my shoulder.

"Can you guys read cards later?" asks Heather. "We have to figure this out. If the van gets us in... we have to find a place to park it where it won't get noticed... and as close this exit as possible."

"What if that's blocked off?"

"Look – I don't know... we say we have to take some one to the hospital, or something, and drive through the gates or whatever it is."

"The back entrance isn't gated," says Shirley. "It's so far back from the house that you have to know it's there, in fact, to find the roads that lead to it. You'd drive past it if you did find your way back there. There's a low stone fence around most of the property, too... but it's not walled or anything... just big, and considering where it is, relatively remote.

"There's still the question of our stuff," says Ginger. "Do we bring it or not?"

"We can't bring it all, anyway," says Kim. "We have two more people to fit in. There's only room for four."

"Leave the two biggest amps," says Jessie. "Keep the guitar cases and the gig bags — the stuff someone would expect to see if they decided to look inside."

"So the plan is... we drive up... say we've come to play... drive to the back entrance, or somewhere near it, park the van someplace inconspicuous and let you two play Nancy Drew?" asks Heather. "How're you two going to blend in?"

"We brought extra leather," says Ginger. "We got your stuff, too, Jessie."

"Savageux sent me a – an outfit." I'm not quite sure how to describe the costume he sent me. Marquis de Sade meets the Sun King, I suppose. It consists of tight black silk knee breeches, a lacy black frock coat, billowy shirt, hose and high black heels, accessorized with a pair of silk padded wrist manacles, a leather riding crop, and a silken cat of nine tails, with tiny crystals imbedded at the ends of the tails. "I don't think I can wear it though."

"Why not?" asks Ginger. "Don't you think you should fit in?"

"I'm afraid I'll have a hard time running in high heels."

"High heels?"

"Three inches at least," says Jessie, snickering. "I've seen it. Tell them about the whip, Jack."

"I don't want to hear about the whip," says Ginger. "He can be the roadie." She reaches up and pinches my cheek hard. "So that's it, right? We drive in, pull around, you get out, look around, take pictures, we hang out, then we blow. Is that right?"

"Yeah," says Shirley. "You got it."

"What if you don't come back?" asks Jessie. "How long do we wait?"

"Half an hour," I say.

"No more than an hour," says Shirley. There's an odd note in her voice that makes me look at her, but her mask is clamped down tight across her face.

"Well, now that's settled," says Kim, "is there any place we can take a nap?"

At some point, I find Shirley alone. I ask her how she's doing, if she thinks she really wants to do this.

"This is the only thing we can do, Jack, don't you see that? The police aren't doing squat... Savageux told you himself he's planning to leave the country. He's going to slip away under their noses while they're all up to their eyes in procedures." She draws a deep shuddering breath. "I can't live like this any more, Jack. I just can't. I know this sounds cruel, but at least you know. You have a body to bury. You have a life to grieve. I don't even have that. All I have are dreams. And I can't go on, not like this."

I remember those three days between the time Lila disappeared and her body was found. It didn't take long, but I remember how every hour of those excruciating days dragged, every minute a slow crawl to the next. I remember how my skin felt too small for my bones, how I jumped at every noise, listened for every creak, every ring, glanced at every dark-haired woman's face. I can't imagine how Shirley's lived like that for what's now almost two months. "Tell me again about the dreams."

"I hear from Winnie. I get a phone call, I get a letter, sometimes I even see her, like far away, across a room, or a street. She tells me things, or she tries to... but I can never remember all of it, I can never hear all of it clearly. It's like I have cotton in my ears, or I'm wearing dark glasses, or she's in a big crowd and there's lots of noise. But everything I've managed to understand... it's all turned out to be true." She breaks off, bites her lip. "Maybe I should've told you before.. but the night.. the night after I met you.... I dreamed about Winnie, and she told me... she told me your wife was going to die. I'm sorry I didn't tell you, Jack. But I didn't want it to be true."

I look at her. I don't know what to say. Would a warning have changed anything? Would Lila have listened?

"It was just a dream, you know. I didn't know what to say, I didn't know how to tell you."

I shake my head. "I...I... Shirley, don't beat yourself up, okay? I don't know that Lila would've listened. She was pretty... concrete in a lot of ways, you know? Tell you the truth, I think she just would've laughed."

For the briefest of moments, I see her guard come down, her face relax. She's pretty, really pretty, or she used to be. I hope she is again, soon. "You look tired, Jack. Why don't you go lie down? This could be a long night."

"Okay." I am tired, I can't deny it. I feel like I've been tired for forever.

"There's a futon in my office and a quilt. Help yourself."

I walk down the hall, not sure what to think. Shirley dreamed that her missing partner told her Lila would die. And Lila did. The other things Winnie told Shirley have turned out to be true, too. *We are such stuff as dreams are made of.* But that's just a line from a play, I think... its meaning is metaphorical, allegorical, not literal. I find Jessie sitting in Shirley's office, peering at Rosie's notes.

"I still haven't made much headway with those," I say.

"It's okay." She smiles at me. "You come to rest?"

I nod, but don't sit down. "How come you didn't tell me you know about tarot cards?"

"I...I didn't realize it mattered."

"So... I guess they're not the Devil's instrument, like my mother used to say?"

"I guess it depends on how you think of the Devil," she replies. "Rosie was working with the images on the cards as a whole. Knowing how to read the cards doesn't mean I understand how Rosie felt they related to all this." She gathers up all the papers, gets to her feet. "Futon's yours. Get some sleep, okay?"

I lie down and stare at the maze of metal pipes far above my head, words and phrases flowing through my mind like a faucet I can't turn off, all myths and motifs and images that recur and repeat across time, across culture, from prophet to poet.

Wars in heaven... sacrificial lambs... in like a lion, out like a lamb... When the stars threw down their spears and watered Heaven with their tears... Jamie McPherson, hung before his time... betrayed before he was ready... Ready to do what?

I shift and sigh and turn on my side, tuck my arm under my head. Am I supposed to believe that I'm some cosmic warrior, sent by God to battle Evil? I open my eyes and see Dougless sitting on the floor beside me. "You!" I bolt upright.

She smiles. For the first time, she doesn't appear solid. Maybe it's the light, maybe it's the white wall of sound-proofing behind her. "I've come to say good-bye, Jack."

"Are you going somewhere?"

"I'm going home, I suppose, I don't know exactly, I've never made the crossing."

"What crossing?"

"The one from life to death, Jack." She takes my hand and her flesh has no weight, no substance. Her touch is no more substantial than a whisper. "I made a horrible mistake once, did a horrible wrong, and vowed I'd never leave this plane 'til I was able to make reparation. I've done all I can."

"What do you mean... done all you can... what've you done?"

"I held him off you as long as I could."

"Held who off?" I try to touch her, but my hand passes through her. "Hold who off?" I cry, as she fades completely away. "Who?" I scream, into the blank air before me. "What the fuck do I have to do?"

"Nothing, yet, Jack."

I open my eyes. Jessie's staring down at me. The room's dark, but for a slice of light that's coming from the open doorway and the blinking neon of a sign across the street. She's wearing black leather pants, a strategically ripped t-shirt and steel chains. In the otherwise dim room, she glows like a slim white flame. It's time to go. I was dreaming, I think. We are such stuff as dreams are made of. Is that what Dougless was trying to tell me? That dreams are just as real as... reality?

"Jack?" Jessie frowns. "I think you're dreaming."

"Yeah." I manage to sit up and swing my legs over the side of the couch. "Yeah, I was just – I was dreaming."

She spins on her heel and strides to the door. "Come on, it's time to go."

In the van I'm squeezed next to Shirley, who's directly behind Jessie. Her blonde curls are piled under a jaunty leather cap, she's wearing a spiked dog collar around her neck, and her own black leather pants, as well as a Bitch Feast t-shirt, just like mine. The rest of us are mostly silent as Shirley directs Jessie through the Bronx and out to the highways that lead to Connecticut.

We're creeping past Co-op City when Jessie turns to Shirley. "This'll be the story that gets you the Pulitzer, huh?"

Shirley goes rigid. "No Pulitzer for me." She grips the back of the driver's seat with white-knuckled fingers as we jounce over pot holes. "As of yesterday afternoon at five, I'm officially fired." She looks at me fiercely. "So this has to work. I don't have any other options. I had to turn in my press credentials."

She's desperate, I think. Desperate people do desperate things. Behind me, I hear Kim or Heather mutter, "What's press credentials go to do with anything?"

Shirley stares straight ahead as if she hasn't heard. Her shoulders are rigid. I can feel her willing Winnie to be there, willing Winnie to be alive.

Jessie's eyes meet mine in the rearview mirror. Yea, though I walk through the Valley of the Shadow of Death…my palms feel moist, and I can feel the low-grade buzz under my skull. The Grateful Dead's Friend of the Devil is a friend of mine peals through my head. Get a grip, Jack. I twine my fingers under the seat and grip so hard I feel the metal framework through the padding. I can't imagine what we'll find because I have no idea what we're looking for. .

Who overcomes his foe by force hath overcome but half his foe. Milton wrote that just shortly before Jamie McPherson was born. Whatever he thought he was doing… what if he was really writing about someone who was about to be born?

I think about Blake who believed that his writings... at least some of them... were not only divinely inspired but spiritually dictated by beings only he could comprehend. And there was the story of the Jersey Devil... associated with the same area as the clinic which did produce deformed children. The connections are tenuous, coincidental. If hindsight's 20/20, I think, and we can understand what we're seeing as we look back into the past, then we should be able to understand what's going to happen. Shouldn't we? My brain feels like it's starting to swell against the interior of my skull.

But what if we're not going back far enough? What if we don't fully understand what we're supposed to be seeing? For the first time, I feel myself a part of an enormous web, held by threads that twine through time and space, and in and out of dreams.

My skin's crawling. I don't believe in Satan. I don't believe in hell. I do believe in genetic mutations though. I do believe in crazy serial killers who torture people for fun, and in people who believe that the ends justifies the use of any means. And I believe that something very dark and sick and twisted resides in Nicholas Savageux - something he can't help, something he can't control, perhaps - but sick and twisted and terrible all the same.

Chapter 32

About a mile or so from the Savageux estate, Jessie suddenly swerves to the side of the road and comes to a stop. We've all fallen into a drowse. Ginger and Kim and Heather grumble softly, I hit my head on the roof. Only Shirley's in the exact same position I remember her being in before I fell asleep.

"What're you stopping for?" There's an imperious edge in her tone that makes me look harder at her, but she doesn't look at me.

Jessie rolls down her window. "There's a woman by the side of the road."

Dougless? The hair goes up on the back of my neck. I crane to try and see, when an unfamiliar voice says, "I'm really obliged to you folks for stopping."

"Are you all right, ma'am?" Jessie shifts, and I get a glimpse of a woman with broad cheekbones, sandy brows, and a very red nose.

"My car broke down," the woman says. "There's a big estate a mile or so up the road... I was wondering if I could hitch a ride up that way with you all?" She pauses, looks at the van, nods at Jessie's throat bandage. "You're going to the Savageux place, right?"

Shirley's head snaps around on her neck like a rubber band. "How'd you know that," she hisses.

"Your van, for one thing," the woman answers, her expression genial. "I don't mean to put you folks out... if you'd just tell someone at the house to call Lou's garage in Bethel, I'll be all set."

"We can squeeze you in," says Jessie. She cranes her neck around to look at me. "Can't we?"

"Sure," I say. "C'mon, Shirley. Scoot over. Let's not be shy."

Shirley actually flinches. She does move over, though, and the side door swings open. A stocky woman with light brown hair in a rain coat scrambles inside and perches next to me. She meets my eyes evenly. "I'm Eileen Fescue. Like the grass."

Fescue like the grass... I know that name, I know that voice. *If you ever come to Bethel, Connecticut, stop in and say hello.* Suddenly, for no reason I understand, I feel better. "I'm Jack ... these ladies are Bitch Fest."

Ginger interrupts with a hoot. "Bitch FEAST. Geesh."

Heather and Kim chortle.

"I'm new," I say.

"Right." Eileen winks. The night air pouring in through the window is heavy and wet. She twists around, nods to everyone, as Jessie pulls back onto the road. I remember the ride from the train station to Jessie's house, when I was crushed between two amps. This time I'm stuffed between Eileen on the one hand and the ramrod straight steel rod that is Shirley.

Shirley takes a deep gulp of air. "Turn here," she says to Jessie.

At the gatehouse, the guard looks at the card, looks at Jessie, looks at the van, and waves us through. We all breathe a sigh of relief. No one's stopped us, no one's searched us. We're in.

"Stay to the left," Shirley says.

We pass a sea of cars, catering vans and trucks. The music's already loud and crashy, there's people milling around the back already. I can hear splashing coming from the pool. The stone and shingle house reminds me of a scaled-down Norman fortress. It all seems so normal, so obvious... it's just a rich couple having a costume party. A costume party where all the guests dress as vampires. Just your typical rich kids, out having fun.

Jessie follows the road. The sketch of the map Shirley showed us wasn't to scale, and the distances are much greater than her rough drawing made them appear. And there's fog machines, electric lights set up and random people wandering, most looking like extras from some fifties B movie. There's more lace and fancy dress at this one, I see, less leather and chains. There's another kind of vampire represented here, more elegant, more refined. I wonder what the hell is wrong with Savageux that he needs to do this.

"That's because he's a vampire." The woman's voice doesn't sound like Dougless, but when I whip my head around there's no one there. We bump and jounce and weave, and at one point we're surrounded on all sides by a sea of writhing velvet clad flesh. Fanged faces press against the windows, dominatrix's clad in black silks and satins press full red lips against the windows and laugh.

"These people are crazy," Jessie mutters, with a tremor in her voice. She glances over her shoulder at me.

LEAVE. NOW. I hear the warning so clearly I look to see if anyone else has heard it too. The voice sounds like it could be Dougless's, and as we drive through the thickening crowd, I think I see her standing just beside the drive.

"Just keep driving," mutters Shirley. She leans closer to Jessie, the map clutched tight. "That way."

Eileen Fescue leans forward, peers around the seat, so she can look out the passenger side window. "Maybe you should head more in that direction."

Multi-colored fog billows all around us, borne by wind machines that carry the roar of bikes screaming up behind us, blocking our retreat, encircling the van, so that the crowd begins to press all around us. We're being guided, I think, propelled around the back of an enormous barn that is distinctly not at all drawn to scale on Shirley's map.

Behind me, Ginger leans forward and taps me on the shoulder. "Um… guys… where do you suppose they want us to go?"

I know what she's really thinking, what she's afraid to ask in front of the stranger. Outside, the bikers flash maces, chains and fangs. At last we are allowed to pull up.

Jessie's door is ripped open, even as the side door is. A courtier out of the court of Louis XIV bows courteously. "Welcome to the feast." He steps back and the fog billows into the van. In that moment, I feel a curious rushing sensation, almost as if a drug is entering my system, and my vision expands suddenly to encompass colors beyond the spectrum of normal sight. I glance around and see if anyone feels similarly affected, but no one else seems to have even noticed the fog. As if in a daze, I stumble out after Eileen, closely followed by Shirley.

She, in fact, knocks into me. "Come on, Jack," she says, her hands shoved deep in the pockets of her coat. She strides off, and is swallowed by the crowd.

"Hey, wait up, Shirley!" I cry, over the crash of the music from the speakers high above our heads. This place is like a carnival of the damned, I think, even more so than the one a few weeks ago in the East Village. It's private property, so there's more extremes here, if such is possible – more blatant nudity, more obvious bondage. "Wait for me!"

As I'm about to take off after her, Eileen Fescue taps me on the arm. "Here," she says. Our eyes meet and for a long moment, we seem to step outside of time. I remember how Rosie described David Woodwright's encounter with Balthazar Allende, and for a split second I understand exactly what it is he meant. She hands me a folded piece of white paper. "I think your friend dropped this."

I glance down. It's Shirley's rough – really rough – sketch of the property, the only map we have. "Thanks," I breathe.

"You sure you want to be here?"

At least that's what I think she says. She doesn't wait for an answer. She just turns on her heel and is immediately swallowed by the crowd that surges forward. I think I see Shirley entering one of the low buildings. I turn, to see if the band's okay, and somehow, I've gotten separated from the van. I'm not standing next to the van any more. The crowd's jostled me that far, I wonder. I'm pushed back against a tree.

"Jack?"

Suddenly Shirley's standing there. She tugs on my jacket. "Come on. I think I found the way."

"Wait, Shirley – I want to make sure the band's okay –" But she doesn't wait. She just shoves her hands in her pockets and strides off, so single-minded of purpose the crowd eddies around her, bouncing off her like so much living flotsam. I'm torn – if I don't go after her, I'm going to lose her in the crowd, and if I don't go back...

Swirls of color appear out of the fog, billowing around the heads of everyone I see. I stare. What kind of strange trip is this? I clutch the map, such as it is, and stumble after Shirley. I see her up ahead, a red swirling arrow of blues and jagged orange behind a muddy veil. I blink, trying to make sense of the colored lights I see dancing and swirling and twining like ribbons around all the people around me.

"Jack?"

It's Jessie this time, dragging at my sleeve. In the flashing, flowing lights and billowing fog, she stands out like a bright beacon. She doesn't shift, she doesn't flow. She just shines. I blink to clear my eyes. How could I have been in two places at once, I think, peering further up the hill. I think I see the tree I was standing under.

I pull the map out of my pocket. I unfold it, flatten it, try to make sense of it. I twist it and turn it and that's when I see it on the other side, a snake coiled around a sword, crowned with laurel leaves, and fine dark printing, tiny, really, just barely there, raised enough though, to brush against my thumb: *From the desk of Nicholas Savageux.*

That's when I hear my name called, over the whine of the wind, the roar of the crowd and the crash of the music coming out of the speakers in my head. "Jack!"

I feel a firm hand on my shoulder, I get spun around. It's Ginger. "We have to leave, I say."

"We have half the stuff unloaded," she sputters. "Come, you have to help us...this isn't exactly going the way any of us expected, you know? We thought we were going to be blending in with the crowd...not the fucking main attraction. But this..." She grabs my arm and tugs. "It's like they were fucking expecting us."

I hold out Shirley's map. "I think they were."

"What?" She glances down, tugs my wrist. "Come on, Jack. We're going to have to play."

A wolf howls over the wail of a saxophone, an eerie whine that twines through the music in magenta ribbons of sound. I can feel them running through my head, spiraling and twining into turquoise and a bright cerulean blue.

"Jack!" That's Jessie, suddenly in front of me. "Come on, Jack, you have to help us. We're the main act, apparently. This is not what we expected at all."

"We can't stay," I stumble after her, feeling drunk. "Jessie, wait, listen to me…" My mouth, like my mind, feels soft and loose. I have trouble forming the words. Vampire faces leer out of the night, and the same enormous bouncer from the church materializes out of the roiling fog, backlit by orange and crimson light.

"Come on," he says. "Aren't you the band?"

"Yeah, we're the band," replies Ginger with a snarl and a flash of silver fangs.

"No," I grab Jessie's arm. "No, we have to…."

"You're all expected," he laughs.

I shove the map under Jessie's nose. "Look at this, Jessie – Shirley… Shirley… I'm not sure what's going on here, but she… Shirley's in with Savageux somehow." *A friend of the devil is a friend of mine.* That's when my vision splits in half, and with one eye I see Jessie and with the other I see… something else.

It's swirling colors, luminous forms and far behind me, the sound of waves beating on a distant shore. I see shapes dancing and bobbing around Jessie, around all the others. Some have wings, some have horns. Some have long red tails. The ones around Jessie form an unbroken ring of luminous light, however, a blue-white glow so intense I have trouble focusing on it. It's the ghost of their glow I am somehow able to perceive in the real world.

I'm just not sure what's real any more. There's a twilight haze around everything, and out of the blare of the lights, I see Shirley's blond curls against a dark silhouette, which shakes itself into Nicholas Savageux. He's wearing a black brocaded coat and knee breeches and riding his back, I see a malevolent spider.

Fear not.

I don't know why I'm not supposed to be afraid, but suddenly I'm not. Whatever heavenly harmony surrounds Jessie extends itself to me, even though I don't feel or see any kind of gleam around myself. Reality has shifted and split into two separate halves.

It's the drug. There's a drug in the fog.

I don't know how I know this, but suddenly I'm very aware that whatever I've inhaled has somehow turned a kind of switch on in my … my being. I don't know if this is how the world is always going to be from now on, but it feels eerily familiar, like a trip I've tried before. It's the drug, I tell myself. It's just the drug. You breathed something funny, and now the world is split in half.

I think it's interesting that the weird lights remind me of Blake's descriptions of his angelic beings.

But I don't have time to wonder about anything any more, because suddenly Savageux is standing in front of me. I breathe in his musky cologne. It makes me dizzy on only one side of my head. "Hello, Jack," he says. "I'm glad you came. Did the suit not fit?"

"Just wasn't me," I try to say, but my words come out slurred, because my tongue suddenly feels too big for my mouth. On the other side of my head, I see what I can only describe as a vision out of Blake: a black mountain-top ringed with fire, the sound of a roaring furnace and the ring of a blacksmith's hammer. From somewhere far away, I hear someone say, "Let's get this party started."

I think Savageux actually picks me up.

His heart is beating under my cheek and my face slips against the slick satin covering his shoulder. I not only hear the blood rushing through the veins beneath his throat, I see it too, rivers of black and purple beneath the white skin, webbed over white bone. It's just the drug, I tell myself. Don't fight it… that only makes it worse.

Fear not.

I feel as if I'm being carried along by a wave of pulsing energy, and then I realize I'm not really being carried physically, I'm simply being swept along in the flood of human and other energy that snakes around and through the crowd. I don't understand why I hear music, I don't understand why I'm being dragged onto the stage. I don't know why the other women are suddenly gathered around me.

Ropes go around my wrists, my ankles, my chest, and suddenly, I'm hanging upside down. Jessie's face spins out of the haze, and coalesces before me. She's mouthing my name, and a disembodied hand reaches out of the mist, tries to brush my cheek, but I'm being lifted, up and onto an enormous cross. For a long moment, I hang suspended, staring down at Jessie, at the other women, at the vampires crowding at my feet. And then a voice rings out, high-pitched as a trumpet on Judgment Day : "He's not the one… she is." She is. They mean Jessie, but somehow no one else realizes that.

The band bursts into some discordant song and I am spun around and upside down.

I feel the blood rush to my head, I feel the pressure build behind my eyes. I close my eyes and my vision coalesces into a single scene. I'm standing on the beach and Lila's walking toward me.

She waves, and I see the Coney Island Ferris wheel rising in the distance behind her. The sand beneath my feet is warm and golden white. I can smell the salty air as the ocean rolls across the shore behind me. The seagulls screech from their perches on the jetties. I'm wearing Jessie's father's clothes.

"Am I dead, Lila?" It's the first thing that spills out of my mouth as she reaches up to kiss my cheek.

"Hang in there, Jack." She glances over my shoulder and I see that the sun is a bright red disk on the edge of the horizon.

"How's the Ferris wheel?"

She laughs a little, and her eyes meet mine. She looks great, I see, her cheeks all rosy, her eyes all bright. "It was fun but… well, you can't just go around and around forever, can you?"

"Lila, are you sure I'm not dead?"

She looks distracted, as if she's watching for something out at sea. "Jack, soon enough, okay?"

"Then why are you here? Why am I here? And where is here, anyway?" As far as I can see in both directions, the view is exactly the same... sky, sand, rocks. The Ferris wheel is gone.

"I'm here to say good-bye, Jack. I... I don't know why you're here." She stands on her tiptoes and kisses my cheek, squeezes my bicep, pats my chest. "See you somewhere." Then she walks into the water and dives beneath the surf.

I open my mouth to call her name, but a slim hand on my arm stops the air in my throat.

"Hello, Jack."

For a moment I think I might weep with relief. Finally, I think, finally, someone who can tell me what's going on. "Dougless... Dougless, am I dead?"

She shakes her head but I notice she looks worried. "Not yet. Try to hang in there, though. I don't think it'll be long now."

"Before I die?"

She gazes out across the sand. "He's coming, Jack." She reaches up, kisses the same cheek as Lila. "In all likelihood you will die, Jack. But if you can take him with you..."

"Take who?" I squint across the beach. It seems that the jetty has started to move, a dark line spreading out like a shadow rippling over the sand.

"Him." She points, and I see that one of the rocks has gotten very tall and very broad and is roughly the size and shape of a man. "He vanquished you when you were Jamie ... don't let your death be in vain this time, Jack... not this time, all right?" She stares up at me with me pleading eyes.

"I'm not Jamie, Dougless." I don't understand what's happening. There doesn't seem to be any other reality than this one, and wherever it is, things are turning into other things. The rough man-shape looks like the Incredible Hulk. Or Milton's fallen Angel.

"In a way, you are, Jack," she says. The wind whips her hair around her face. "You drive a cab the way he handled a sword, and you would've played the guitar the way he played the fiddle if it hadn't been scared out of you when you were young. But it's your way with words, Jack… your way with words that his… that sings across the centuries. They can't take that away from you." She presses a handkerchief in my hand, a scrap of lace and linen embroidered with a rose.

And then she disappears.

Nicholas Savageux stares down at me from a height of at least fifteen feet. He's wearing white leather, his flowing hair slicked back against his skull. When he smiles down at me, I see his fangs. He is a vampire, I think, a real vampire. I was right all along.

I stumble backwards as he bends down, hands outstretched, nails pointed as talons. He smiles as I fall backwards, into the surf. I scrabble backwards like a crab, just outside of his reach and I notice he doesn't dip his hand into the water, the foaming salt water that swirls around my feet. I feel the tug of the current and he straightens, hands on his hips, smiling a ghastly smile. In the reddish light of the setting sun, his face is like a skull's.

"The tide will take you out," he says.

I try to stand up, but the current is strong around my ankles and it coils around my knees like a python with far greater force than I expected.

"I don't have to go anywhere near you," he taunts. "The sea will do my work for me. All I have to do is watch."

The water is rising now, fast, above my hips. It's hard to kneel, hard to stand. The waves seem to crash in on me from all directions as if determined to drag me beneath. The Savageux-thing sits on a rock, folds his arms across his chest, crosses his legs and yawns. "Won't be long, I think. Won't be long at all. After all, we can afford to let you die. Clarissa says that it's Jessie who's the One, the One she's been looking for, all along."

That's the thing that breaks the spell. It galvanizes me into action, makes me realize I'm holding the scrap of handkerchief that was Dougless's. But it's bigger now, and stretching as it fills with water, and I remember the story of how Jamie McPherson died, betrayed by a woman who threw a blanket over his head. With a cry, I rush forward, out of the clutch of the ocean, straight up and on to the sand, holding my streaming white banner before me.

Before he can move, I'm on him. I wrap the wet fabric around his head, around his neck and we roll, over and over on the sand, while his flesh sizzles and burns and stinks. The thing that's really Nicholas writhes and squirms and morphs into a lizard so huge I can barely hold the handkerchief around its head. But I do, and it stretches, knotting around the creature's jaws, cutting off the creature's air, even as the roar of the ocean starts to get very, very loud.

From somewhere far away, I hear someone scream: "For Christ's sake, cut that poor man down!"

I open my eyes and I'm looking at a blank white ceiling. I hear the beep of machinery, the far-away tinkle of glass and the soft squeak of rubber wheels. An antiseptic odor fills my nostrils as a pair of clear blue eyes fills my line of sight.

"Hello, Mr. Chance." Eileen Fescue leans over me, her forehead creased. "Do you know who I am?"

Chapter 33

I try to answer, but all I do is choke. My tongue feels too big for the back of my mouth, my windpipe feels swollen from the inside. "Yeah," I manage finally. "You're Sergeant Eileen Fescue... like the grass. Can you tell me where I am?"

She smiles, pats my arm. I'm attached to an IV, I notice and a couple other things that beep. "You're in Greenwich Hospital. Doctors say you got real lucky. The rope around your neck apparently let just enough blood into your brain... no way you should've survived hanging upside down like that as long as you did."

"How'd you know to show up there?"

"I had a feeling that there was more going on at that house than fundraising." She shrugs. "There's a lot we might never know. Savageux's dead."

"He's dead?" That makes me try to sit up and my head starts to spin.

"Take it easy, Mr. Chance." Her mouth's grim. "He just toppled over when the police broke in. It's like the lights went out all at once. Massive aneurysm or maybe a heart attack. I suppose we'll have answers soon enough. They've called in a special forensics team from the FBI. No one's ever seen anything like Mrs. Savageux's lab."

"Mrs. Savageux? His wife? What about her?"

"She's a molecular biologist, and....I guess her father was a world famous geneticist? She – she was carrying on his work, I guess, or thought she was. She's under observation, now. No one's letting her out for a long time. I expect she'll end up a hospital for the criminally insane." Eileen gets to her feet. The rubber soles of her sensible shoes squeak as she walks to my window. I see trees, white clouds and blue sky. Wherever I am, I'm not in Brooklyn anymore. She peers outside. "Pretty day out there, Mr. Chance. You might want to see if they'll let you out in it. Sunshine would do you some good, I think."

I think of the brilliant setting sun Lila leaped into… in my dream… in my alternate reality experience… in whatever the fuck it was, because Savageux is really dead. How was that possible? "What about Winnie Chen? What about Shirley?"

Eileen hesitates just a beat before she answers. "Winnie was alive when they found her – the only one who survived… the uh… what the Savageuxs did to her. She was taken up to Yale, I think, and the other girl – Shirley? Is that her name? She's with her."

"So there's a chance Winnie will live?"

"And the baby, too."

"There's a baby?"

Eileen looks at me. "There were a lot of babies. Apparently Mrs. Savageux took up right where her father left off. So there were a lot of babies, and a lot of… other things."

I lie back on the pillow, turn away. I don't want to know any more. I don't want to know how Lila might've been made to suffer. I don't want to think about how all the other Jane Does died.

"We'll be in touch, Mr. Chance. I'm glad to see you're feeling better."

She's gone before I can ask her anything else.

My next visitors are the band. The women are quiet, subdued, their eyes shadowed and bruised. Whatever happened the other night, it seems to have cemented their bond, and from the way they talk, I can tell there's no more thoughts of Jessie leaving the band.

They kiss my cheek and press my hand, then file out, leaving me and Jessie alone. "What the fuck happened, Jessie?"

She looks uncomfortable. "I don't think any of us are sure, Jack. There was a... there was some kind of drug in the ventilation system, you know. It really... really fucked everybody's head up pretty bad. Apparently Savageux's wife...Clarissa? She had a thing for making up new drugs." She walks to the window, peers out. "But I... well, I was able to talk to Melchior Gunn... you remember him, right?"

"The cop who thinks I'm the killer? Sure... does he still remember me?"

She laughs. "Yeah, he remembers you. He doesn't think you're the killer any more. He knows it was Clarissa... Clarissa with Savageux's help."

"But why? What's wrong with her – what was wrong with him?"

Jessie hesitates. "It's... it's kind of sick. Remember how on Dad's charts you saw this tight corkscrew pattern? The two families – Sinclair and Savageux – twining tighter and tighter?"

"Yeah, like a couple of snakes," I say.

"Right. Well... apparently one of the women who visited the clinic was Edmond's own sister, Margaret. She was there on three occasions. All three times, she fainted for reasons unknown. All three times, she was alone with her brother in his office, passed out and unconscious. Approximately nine months later, she gave birth to Nicholas."

"Whoa." A snake writhes in my gut. "You're saying Edmond got his own sister pregnant?"

"Yeah." Jessie grimaces. "Nicholas's supposed father - Old King Cole Savageux – he was forty years Margaret Sinclair's senior. They'd been married for quite a few years before she had Nicholas."

"So...so what you're really saying is that I wasn't just related to Nicholas Savageux – he was my half-brother?"

"Assuming you're Edmond Sinclair's son, too, yes."

"And uh..." What occurs to me next is so disgusting, I actually feel sorry for Savageux. "So, that means... that if Clarissa Sinclair is also Sinclair's daughter... then... Savageux was married to his own half-sister?"

"Right."

"Wow. What about his wife? Who was she? Was she a Sinclair, too? Or wait... no, she must've been a Savageux. Right?"

"No," Jessie replies. "Edmond never married. He might've had Clarissa by one of the clinic women… or…" She breaks off, shudders visibly. "It's just… it's just bizarre, that's all. Mel Gunn sounded like he didn't believe a word of it – it's just…"

"Just what?"

"Impossible, that's what." Jessie shakes her head. "Mel says that Sinclair claims to have created Clarissa. In a test tube, using some weird combination of his own sperm and a de-nucleated egg."

"A what?"

"An egg that's had the genetic stuff in the middle taken out, the nucleus. That's what Mel says he claimed anyway. Who knows… I didn't read the stuff. But apparently… apparently she does have some kind of anomalies… physical deformities. I'm not sure she can ever have kids. They think that's got something to do with … with what she did."

"So the killings were connected to a menstrual cycle, after all?"

Jessie sighs. "I don't know. It's going to take a long time to sort it all out. At least… at least Mel Gunn doesn't think you're guilty any more." She gives me a lopsided smile and I realize she's come to say good-bye. She doesn't expect to see me again. She leans over the bed, kisses my cheek, but I turn my head, and our lips brush. I feel a stir of that uncanny familiarity. "Take care of yourself, okay, Jack?" She gives my hand a little squeeze. "Stay in touch."

She walks out the door, and as she passes in front of the blank white door, I see a glimmer and a sheen, and I wonder if I'll ever see her, or Shirley, again. It's hard to think about Shirley, but I know why she did what she did. She did it for Winnie, and I guess I can't blame her. Because if she hadn't, would I have been able to do anything at all about Savageux?

Maybe I don't have to stay in Brooklyn. There's insurance money… I could buy a car, drive across the country. I wonder if there'll be anything left after I pay off all the bills to buy a car any better than old Bessie. Hell, I think, maybe I'll buy old Bessie anyway, and fix her up, make her new. Maybe I'll stop in New Jersey on my way, try to catch Bitch Feast at a gig. I close my eyes and fall into a deep and dreamless sleep.

WHAT HAPPENS NEXT

I'm not expecting the knock on the door. Shirley and Winnie are still in New Haven, Eileen – who drove me home from the hospital in Greenwich - said she'd call if she had any questions. So far as I know, Lila's family has written me off like a bad line of poetry. I can't think of anyone else who'd be coming to visit.

I open the door and it's Jessie. She's wearing jeans and a green sweater, and her hair is long and loose. I notice how the curls tumble over her shoulders, and around her face, gleaming copper and gold in the sun streaming through the skylights. "Hi, Jack," she says. She's got that glow around her, and in the sun it's especially strong... almost as if she's simply a pencil thin wafer against a glowing ball of light. For a moment I am reminded of my experience at Savageux's party, when I saw those other beings, those things that reminded me of Blake. But that was the drug, I think. Those things weren't real.

I have to blink and stumble backwards. "Jessie...hey, come on in." I gesture to the apartment. "I-uh..I was just cleaning things up around here." There's a pile of laundry waiting to be folded on the couch, and one already folded waiting to be put away on the chair. Clean dishes are drying on the counter, the sink is full of suds.

"Wow." She looks around. "What happened to all the bills?"

For a moment grief wells up in my throat, grief and a deep gratitude to Lila, Lila who I will never forget. I'm writing a song about Lila, even though

I've never written a song before. But I can hear the words, the music in my head. "Lila took care of them," I say. "I got home to a letter from the firm. Lila had life insurance through them... something like five times her salary. Firm offered to double it, if I promised not to sue them. So I did."

"Really? From the way Shirley talked, it sounded like you could've gotten millions."

"Yeah, maybe. But is it worth the trouble?" I look around, shrug. "So now I've gotten all that cleaned up, I just have to figure out where I want to go."

"You're going to leave New York?"

"Why not? I don't really have anything holding me here. I got the garage to sell me one of their old cars...I got a little money, I got some space to figure out what's next." Then it occurs to me that it's a bit odd she's here at all. "But, Jessie, how come you're here?" For a split second, I'm afraid I'm back in a dream. "You're not dead, are you?"

She bursts out laughing. "Of course I'm not dead."

"Didn't you go back to Jersey with the other girls?"

"I did."

"Like a week ago, right?"

"More like two, now." She shifts unsteadily on her feet and I see a thin line of sweat beading across the top of her upper lip, moisture gathering on her forehead. "Can-can I sit down?"

"Sure, here, Jessie are you all right?" I help her to a kitchen chair and she bends over, puts her head between her knees. "Here." I dab a dampened paper towel against her neck, her forehead.

"Could I have some juice? A cracker?" She slumps back, looking a bit gray.

"Sure." I hand her the towel, grab a glass, pour juice, find the saltines. "All right?"

She swallows, chews, swallows some more, but nods.

I bend down over her. "Jessie, why'd you come?"

She blushes to the roots of her hair. "The girls convinced me to come. They said I should tell you, they said you should know."

"Know what?" I feel a force gathering in the space between our bodies, building into a solid mass with weight and invisible form.

"I'm pregnant, Jack."

Her words slam into me like a fist in my solar plexus and I stagger backwards, as my knees give way, and fall into the other chair. "Oh?" I manage. It can't be mine. How could it be mine? I never laid a finger on her.. except when I threw myself on top of her to save her life. But that wasn't... that wasn't sex.

But she's looking at me, looking at me in the way I've seen women do when they expect you to know something that appears obvious to them. "Sa..Jessie," I stammer. "You're not going to tell me you think it's mine."

She nods, all big eyes and pale cheeks. And curling, shining copper hair.

"Bu..but, Jessie, I never... we never... we only dreamed about it!"

She knits her fingers together. "Jack," she says, looking directly into my eyes. "I haven't had sex with anyone since I broke up with Jeremy and that was months and months ago. You're the only man who's been under my roof." Her voice gets progressively softer and softer as her face turns redder and redder.

"Bu...but... I didn't touch you." I stare at Jessie and I know she's remembering the dream we shared, under the willow.

We are such stuff as dreams are made of... Dreams, I think, dreams and imagination... who am I to say such stuff isn't real? *We are such stuff as dreams are made of...* The phrase rolls around in my head. Didn't I dream that I killed Savageux? And didn't Savageux die? I can see that she's telling the truth she believes, and who am I to doubt her?

"What would you like me to do?" I ask at last, mostly because I don't know what else to say.

"Angus and Lucy like you," she says.

"New Jersey's not that far," I say. "I was thinking of going further west."

"No one said we had to stay there," she replies, and with that, I know it's settled.

She finishes her orange juice. We wash and dry the dishes. I take my big black suitcase and fill it with my favorite jeans, my oldest sweats. I bring a box of poetry and the song I'm writing for Lila. I leave the bottle of tequila in the back of my closet, along with the suit and the jacket, the shirts and the ties.

It's dark by the time we leave. I unlock Old Bessie, hold the front door open for Jessie. We strap ourselves in. I push the key into the ignition. I want to touch her, hold her hand, kiss her cheek, but I know it's not time for that yet. It is, however, time to go. "Ready?" I ask.

"I'm ready," she answers.

I tap my foot on the old car's accelerator, and the street lamps twinkle like stars on the chrome of the cars that follow us over the bridge into Jersey.

The End

Born and raised at the South Jersey shore, Anne Kelleher wrote her first novel in high school. She now divides her time between the Big Island of Hawaii, and the northwest hills of Connecticut. An incurable optimist, Annie refuses to succumb to dystopic visions of a bleak future, and insists that the world we can create is only as limited as our imaginations.

Find more of Annie's work on Amazon, and connect with Annie on Facebook at www.facebook.com/annekelleherauthor, on Twitter at @annekelleherauthor, or at www.annekelleher.net.

Other Titles:

SF/Fantasy:
Daughter of Prophecy
Children of Enchantment
The Misbegotten King
The Knight, the Harp & the Maiden
Silver's Edge
Silver's Bane
Silver's Lure

Romance:
A Once & Future Love
The Ghost & Katie Coyle
Love's Labyrinth
The Highwayman
Wickham's Folly
Wickham's Fancy

High Interest/Low Level:
How David Met Sarah
When David was Surprised
Where David Went (coming 2016)

Tilton Chartwell Mysteries:
The House on Lake Jasper
The House on Lawton Road
The House on Hallowe'en Hill (coming 2015)

Short Stories:
Free to Good Home (collection)
After the Rapture
Enhanced

Celebrity Supernatural Series:
Conjuring Johnny Depp
Finding Southside Johnny
Raising Jerry Garcia
Walking with Elvis
Protecting Donald Trump

Made in the USA
Lexington, KY
22 March 2016